ROBERT JOHNSON'S
FREEWHEELING
JAZZ FUNERAL

Also by Whit Frazier:

Harlem Mosaics

Robert Johnson's Freewheeling Jazz Funeral

Whit Frazier

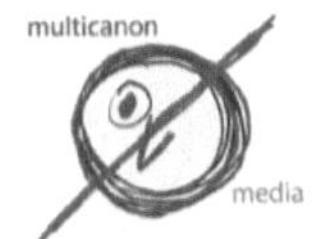

The Multicanon Media Company, LLC
New York

Second Edition 2021
All rights reserved. Published in the United States by
The Multicanon Media Company, LLC

www.multicanon.com

Paperback ISBN: 978-1-7372149-2-2
ebook ISBN: 978-1-7372149-3-9
(Previous paperback ISBN: 978-1539967767)

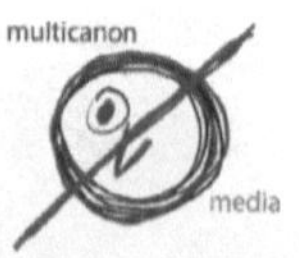

The Multicanon Media Company, LLC
45 Rockefeller Plaza, Suite 2000, New York, N.Y. 10111

*For Billi
who will always be
the brightest star
in my book*

PART ONE: SAȘA

SECOND ACT

*"In 'Declamation on the Preeminence and Nobility of the Female Sex',
Agrippa reminds us that Adam means 'Earth', and Eve means 'Life'.
Thus the materialistic Earth force belongs to man, and the quintessence
of spirituality, the Life force, belongs to Woman."*
        -FAITH, Dr. Janet Plummet, Chapter II, p. 83

Open on opening night at the Brick, a dim and dingy little spot that's more like a tomb than a theater, and as usual I'm sitting in the tech booth making up stories about my audience. All through the first act I'm engaged with this one Upper East Side looking honey sitting right up in the front row. She's pretty in her own prim way, but a little too well put together for a place like this, wearing her hair in a brunette bun above oversized oval Chanel frames. She's conspicuous as conversation. I'm thinking she's got to be a critic or something like that, or else why is she here by herself to see a play called Black Prometheus at a small experimental theater in Williamsburg? The whole time I'm kind of captivated by her, trying to read her thoughts about the work in her body language, but not having much luck.

Just as the second act starts, she gets up and walks out. Just like that. Stepping over audience members and everything.

So naturally, I exit the tech booth and follow her.

Brooklyn at night. Freestyle the streets then, and see if I can't catch up with this gal. The old red brick Brick Theater behind me, and Subway Bar on the side. It's cold out and the clouds burst in occasional shivers of light wet snow. I cross the street, and there she is again, back on the other side, next to the bar. She swivels and goes in, a slapdash of colorful cursive in the neon lights from the diner across the way.

I follow her into the bar across the street. It's a dive bar, the type of place where punk rock hipsters like to hang out and drink two-dollar cans of Pabst Blue Ribbon. I wouldn't peg it as her kind of place. It's dark and dirty and narrow and long like a coffin, the way a bar should be. Off to the sides are a couple round tables where people stand around politicking, but this one, she's sitting right at the bar, front and center, and she's already ordering a pint of Brooklyn Lager. I take a seat next to her, and order the same.

"Play was disappointing, huh?" I say to her and she looks over at me like she's finally found a friend in a foreign country.

"Yeah, wasn't it though? You walk out too?"

"In a manner of speaking. But what gives. You a critic or something? What brought you out to see something like that? You don't strike me as the type."

"Who's the type?"

"Oh, I don't know. Williamsburg. Small theater. Just doesn't seem to suit you."

"Maybe you're right. It wasn't much though, was it?"

"No, I guess not." I frown and take a drink.

"Or maybe just not my thing. I don't know. One of my students told me I ought to check it out. For its multicultural value and all that. Said she's seen other things by this company, and they're pretty good." She laughs. "Well, now I've checked it out. Can't say I'm too impressed."

"So you teach."

"That's right."

"What do you teach?"

"Literary feminism."

"Huh."

"Not your thing?"

"Maybe not. I don't know much about it maybe."

"Well that play, Jesus, was just about everything I hate about the male-dominated literary culture."

"Yeah?" I take another drink. "I don't know. Was it all that bad? I guess I didn't notice."

She squints for a moment, looking at me like she's dissecting a text.

"No? Because the whole thing was completely sexist, as far as I could tell. Maybe I'm just hypersensitive to that kind of thing, but that's the impression I got."

"I mean the play definitely had its problems," I add quickly. "I damn near fell asleep myself. So maybe I might have missed it."

That squint of hers turns into a curious little frown. "Did you follow me out of the theater? I mean, and right into this bar?"

"I don't know. Maybe."

"You did, didn't you? Well, that's a little creepy."

"I just thought I'd take the opportunity, you know. I was looking for my chance to get out, and when I saw you go, it was like now or never. Then I saw you come in here, and figured I'd come in and say thank you for the escape."

She wrinkles her nose and takes a drink. "Huh."

"My name's Rudy," I tell her. "Rudy Paschal." I extend a hand, hesitating to see if she'll recognize me as the playwright.

It doesn't seem to register. "Janet," she says, taking my hand. Her hand feels warm and small and soft in mine, and something passes between us, like I suddenly forgive her for everything. "Janet Plummet."

"Where do you teach?"

"NYU."

"Wow. No kidding."

"And what about you, Rudy? What do you do?"

"Still figuring that out, I guess," I say.

"You look like the artist type," says Janet.

I frown, suddenly feeling like a cliché. "Oh, I guess so."

"You a musician or something?"

"I'd like to be," I say, which isn't entirely untrue.

"Yeah? What do you play?"

"I don't really play anything. I'm more sort of a studio booth kind of guy."

"I guess that's the future, isn't it? There's money in it at least, especially if you make a name for yourself."

"Maybe. What do you listen to?"

"I'm into funny stuff. You know, Philip Glass, that new New York minimalism kind of thing. I don't know much about pop and all that. I do like some pop, singer songwriters mostly. Grew up listening to my parents' Beatles and Bob Dylan albums, so I love that stuff too. And some of the newer artists can hold their own with the greats every now and then. How about you?"

"Oh, well, you know. I like all that stuff too. But jazz and blues and hip-hop are more my thing."

Janet wrinkles her nose and frowns. "Really, hip hop? Talk about sexist. It makes that horrible play look like a women's lib manifesto."

"Oh, well. There's a lot of that in hip-hop, I know, but you just have to find the conscious stuff." I try to keep a blank expression, but I've never been good at poker. "So what was so sexist about the play?"

"Well, where to start?" Janet sighs and takes another drink. "I mean, that Prometheus story, to begin with. It's like, if we're talking Hesiod here, and it seems like that's where the writer is getting his inspiration, the whole thing is just immediately sexist through and through. Pandora being the bane of man and all that nonsense. And then – no offense to you, because I don't want this to come off as racist, but- "

I wince. It's never good when a white person starts off a sentence like that.

"But - the whole thing about the Black man bringing fire to American culture. That whole idea is tortured. I mean, what could be more ridiculous than trying to take classical literature and use it to promote an anti-Western aesthetic? So I think it does a disservice to women and to African American culture at the same time."

I shrug like it's all the same to me, but really she's getting under my skin. "Maybe you've got a point."

"Well I'm glad you agree."

"I never was much one for all that classical literature anyway."

"Well don't throw the baby out with the bath water," Janet laughs, and the way she says it, she suddenly sounds like an adorable oddball. I laugh too. "There's a lot of great work in the canon."

"Yeah, I know. I'm actually a classics major."

Janet squints and looks at me in a way that has me forgiving her all over again. She hiccoughs another odd little laugh, and soon we're laughing together like old friends.

"Let me buy you another, Janet," I say. "I like your style."

We have another drink. Janet tells me a little bit about herself, about her books.

"My latest was called Feminism's Ancient Intellectual-Theological Hermeticism," she says, without the least bit of irony.

"Well I'll be damned. That's quite a mouthful."

"It's an academic title," she says. "And we have certain ways of putting things in academia."

"That's no excuse, and you know it."

"Well we can't all be street poets."

"Oh, well. I don't know that I'm a street poet. What, because I'm young and I'm Black and —"

"Oh, you're not all that young, now are you?" she says. She squints again. "Judging, I'd say you're the same age I am. What are you, thirty-five?"

"Yeah. So. Roundabouts that."

"Exactly. Me too. But classics major, then. Where did you go to school?"

"The other end of the island. Columbia."

"Not bad."

"It had its moments."

I look at Janet, and she looks at me, and for a moment I feel like we're suspended in a staged romantic comedy, like a still from a play. A moment later I hear Samir's voice directly behind me.

"Rudy, there you are. I was looking for you. I had a feeling you'd be here. You couldn't even stick around for your own play? The rest of us poor bastards had to sit through the whole thing." He takes a seat at the bar next to me. Then he notices Janet. He gives her a quick once over. "Of course. You have a friend with you." He offers her his hand. "Nice to meet you. My name's Samir."

Janet wrinkles her nose and frowns into her beer. "So you're the playwright?"

"I guess so."

"Well that certainly puts things in a new light."

"Couldn't own up to the work, eh?" Samir glances from me to Janet with a mix somewhere between whimsy and curiosity. "I apologize if I let the cat out of the bag."

Samir is a real serious brother that I work with; he's a second generation Palestinian who always wears the same gray suit with the same black tie, along with an expression that makes him look something like a beleaguered politician. Tonight he's clearly had too much to drink.

"I was just having a little fun."

"I guess this means you're not a musician."

"A musician!"

We all laugh for a while, but Janet's posture has changed; she looks a little uncomfortable, and some of the good feeling between us has clearly dissolved.

"I figured the best way to keep the peace was not to mention it was my play."

Janet looks like she's re-processing everything we've been talking about for the last hour.

"Listen," I say. "Other than that everything else I told you about myself is true."

"So what was wrong with the play?" Samir asks Janet. "Maybe you and I can compare notes."

"Now this isn't fair," I say. "Besides, let's not get into all this again."

"Look who's talking about playing fair," Janet says droll as a drumroll, and then she squints right past me. "So how do you know Rudy?"

"We work together."

"Oh. What, in the theater?"

"No, no, I'm not in the theater," says Samir. "We work in braille publishing."

"Now that's actually interesting," says Janet.

"It's a small braille publisher out by Cadman Plaza," says Samir. "We publish esoterica. Stuff no one else is going to publish in braille."

"No kidding. Esoterica is sort of my specialty. Who's the publisher?"

"It's called LIT, for Literature in Touch," I tell her. "Independent. Run by a weird old guy named Milton. Basically his baby and brainchild. Samir's our book scout."

"And what do you do?"

"I scan in the text from old books when we can't get electronic files."

"Well, see. That's even cooler than being a musician. Why didn't you tell me that?"

"We must not have got around to it."

"And what about you?" Samir asks Janet.

"I teach, actually. Literary feminism at NYU."

"And how is esotericism your specialty, if you don't mind my asking?"

"I've been focusing on it with my last two books. I've been researching the esoteric roots of feminism."

"Oh," says Samir, and suddenly his demeanor sours a little.

"Why? What's wrong with that?"

Samir coughs and orders a shot. He drinks it down, looks at me then looks at Janet. "Listen. I mean, this may take a while."

When Samir's been drinking and he says something like that, I know he's not kidding. I flag the bartender for another beer.

"It's just that I've been through all that already." Samir says, frowning. "I mean, I studied too much academic theory in school, and mostly found it wanting. Thought for a while I was interested in philosophy, but philosophy is mostly a dead-end after Hegel; circles that go nowhere, and language that just gets more and more convoluted and nonsensical. Not to mention the whole Heidegger Nazi thing. That just put me off the entire European enterprise of philosophy altogether. Heidegger is its logical conclusion, where it was headed all the time. Besides, I was searching for something more than just logic. I was searching for something spiritual, but I still needed the heady metaphysics." Samir fumbles around with his empty shot glass. No one says anything for a few moments, so he continues. "For a while I was real political, you know. I'm still political, but at some point you realize you're just powerless. After all, I'm Palestinian, and the Palestinian people will continue to be persecuted in the name of liberalism, and there's not much I can do about that. So I started studying religion. Comparative religion actually, because everyone automatically thinks that an Arab studying his own culture's religion is a potential terrorist, and that brings up all sorts of unsavory and uncomfortable conversations." He shoots a quick look at Janet, then looks back down at his glass. "But religion doesn't seem to speak much to me, either. The Quran and the Bible are too self-contradictory, the Jerusalem Talmud too prescriptive and the Babylonian Talmud too obscure. The Eastern religions are interesting, but I'm too culturally removed from them. I read the Gita and the Tao Te Ching, and decided I didn't have the patience or temperament for that kind of stuff. So there was nothing left for me but the truly esoteric studies." He looks up from his glass and back at Janet. "And as I guess you know, a lot of esoterica is influenced by those religions, and a lot of it is interesting, but what attracted me most was transmutation, alchemy; because alchemy is itself a language, and a language of elements, which makes it a universal language. I mean, after all, we're all composed of elements. It isn't cultural like religion, and it isn't convoluted language logic like philosophy, and it isn't political, like well, politics. It's simply pure mathematics and metaphysics." Samir pauses again, looks from me to Janet like he's trying to decide whether or not to let us in on a secret. Neither of us says anything, so he continues. "Listen, and this will interest you too Rudy – I just picked up a book that's been occupying all my attention; it's called Mystery of the Cathedrals, and the author is someone who may or may not be named Fulcanelli. I'm just getting started with it, but it's supposed to be a code text into reading the esoteric teachings in the architecture of ancient cathedrals, and the architecture of the book itself is something to be studied and decoded. So but anyway, and no offense to you personally, and I apologize for the speech, but something like feminism and esotericism sounds to me like an awkward fit. What's the point, exactly except to further academic study for the sake of academic study? None of that has anything to do with actually studying the work because you have a real commitment to the subject. But don't get me started."

My beer arrives too late. "Oh, don't get him started," I tell Janet. "Because he will get it started."

Janet frowns. "Alchemy? Really? What is this, the Middle Ages?"

Samir purses his lips into an angry smile. "Alchemy can be understood in all sorts of ways. Our modern economy itself is a kind of untrammeled alchemy. There's also the alchemy of language, where the world is transformed into something we can all discuss together, instead of the formless chaos that it's really comprised of. Even the story of our own lives is a kind of alchemy – all stories are because we turn meaninglessness into myth. But you must have come across some of these ideas already while studying esotericism."

"Well listen Samir, I teach literary feminism, and a lot of feminist writers and artists were interested in esotericism, just like you are. So if I'm going to be honest about them, then I have to look at that aspect of their thought. But that doesn't mean I'm going to buy into something as far-fetched and absurd as alchemy."

"Well that sounds to me like you don't even respect your own subject matter, and that makes you perhaps the worst person in the world to be writing the books you write."

Janet's frown deepens. "Listen, Rudy, Samir. It was nice meeting you, but I should probably get going."

"Oh, don't go yet," I say. "Things are just getting interesting."

"No, I really ought to get going."

"Well then let me at least walk you to the subway," I tell her.

"Rudy, please." Janet looks at me through those heavy Chanel frames of hers, and something like what we had earlier alchemizes between us.

"Just to the subway," I say.

"If you insist," she says, getting up.

Back outside Janet and I walk quietly side by side the short distance to the station. I struggle for words.

"Look, I'm sorry I lied to you," I say after a while. "That's what I wanted to say. Once you lit into my play, well, I didn't know how to tell you it was mine. That's all. But I really enjoyed talking to you."

"Well it could have been worse. Your play, I mean. I suppose. But I enjoyed talking to you too. You're better than that play, you know. I think you do know that. So-"

She lets the thought mist into the ether like a disappearing star.

Then I do something that shouldn't surprise me, but maybe I've been sleepwalking: I kiss her.

FOUR POEMS IN SEARCH OF A POET

"For Plato, Sappho is the 10th Muse."
                    -FAITH, Dr. Janet Plummet, Chapter X, p. 325

Flip to Act Three. It isn't an easy relationship. After all, neither of us really respects what the other is doing.

This is easy enough to ignore at first. We honeymoon our way through winter. There are the flirty flighty fights about art and academics, there's Janet's Park Slope apartment, the long white nights' blue candlelight, there's *Black Prometheus,* which runs through Christmas and New Year's and there's nothing at stake. Things look promising.

Then the spring. *Black Prometheus* is long forgotten, and I'm stalled. I can't imagine where to go as an artist. At my worst moments, playwriting seems old fashioned, even quaint. I walk down Broadway in April's fragrant applause, and wonder what theater has to do with anything. Broadway's a racket, and the small experimental stuff is bloodless. When Janet and I argue now, it's still playful, but not so fun anymore.

("I'm thinking maybe my next play should be a Black Oedipus Tyrannus."

"I beg your larnin', but this shit just doesn't become you."

"You what?"

"Why'd you even get into theater in the first place?"

"Apparently just to hear you nag.")

I get no new work done.

By summer I'm damn near ready to give up the theater. Who knew it would come to this? Theater seems like the least important thing in the world, especially in light of the primaries. All the news is Hillary Clinton or Barack Obama, and this is another thing Janet and I disagree about. Janet is Hillary, and I'm Obama, so our arguments about art and academics lead into arguments about the primaries, and sometimes they get messy. The Friday night after Obama wins the nomination we go out for dinner at a restaurant downtown.

"So tell me about this Black Oedipus," Janet says. "Are you really serious about that idea?"

"I don't know. Maybe."

"I thought you were through with the whole appropriating the Western canon thing to the Black experience."

"I did too. But a couple things about that story won't let me go."

Janet sips her wine, and looks at me with that wincing squint of hers. "Yeah? Like what."

"Well, working at LIT, for one. The whole theme of blindness is something I know a little about – from the outside at least. So, there's that."

"I don't think you need Sophocles for that."

"Well there's also this speech in the *Antigone* that I've been tossing around a while."

"Which speech?"

"It's famous. Shakespeare riffs off it in Hamlet, and I think the poet John Berryman does too, in his 14th Dream Sonnet."

"You're really too much," Janet laughs. "John Freaking Berryman?"

"I don't know. It's kind of universal, the idea. That people can do everything except escape death, and that colors our whole spiritual approach to life. And I like the idea of tying that to blindness."

"How does the speech go?"

"I wrote my own translation of the thing. You won't laugh if I recite it?"

"I might. But go ahead anyway."

"Okay. It's kind of modernized, my version, but it basically goes like so:

> *Language, the breezy quickness of mind, political savvy*
> *We've taught ourselves all that already.*
> *The heavy hail can bullet the sky -*
> *It's still cool, we're warm, we're dry -*
> *We're ready for anything that nature plots*
> *Except for death, then we get got."*

It sounds funny reciting it out loud, here in this restaurant. Too much, maybe? Too loose? "So? What do you think?"

"See, this is just what I mean, Rudy. This is how you always are. This hip-hop Sophocles or whatever. I don't know. I think you need to write from your own life."

"See, I want to do something a little more... I don't know. You know? Something not so solipsistic."

"That strikes me as pretty solipsistic."

"And I'd like to write my own version of that speech. Not a translation, but really my own rendering."

"Is this something that's been on your mind? This powerlessness of man, as you put it?"

"I guess so."

"This seems to me like a completely personal, totally solipsistic problem on your part."

"Maybe it is."

"Let me ask you something," says Janet. "And don't take this the wrong way, because it's in all seriousness."

"Okay."

"Do you actually like writing plays?"

The question catches me off guard. I laugh it off at first, but then I think about the last couple months and the laugh fades.

Janet catches my expression. "Maybe you took a wrong turn somewhere."

"A wrong turn! Listen to you go!"

"I don't know. It happens."

"It's not that. It's just. Well, sometimes it feels like there's something too artificial about it. It's all pomp and circumstance, you know? Like a pageant. It's always lying to you."

"Like a politician."

Janet and I laugh. For one brief moment we're on the same wavelength again. Then she goes and ruins it.

"It just goes to show," – Janet, God bless her, she can't help herself, she says – "It just goes to show, a Black president isn't going to solve the social problems in this country."

"Jesus, Janet. Where did that come from? Besides, neither was Hillary."

Janet frowns and takes a drink. "I honestly think it's too bad she didn't get the nomination. I don't think Obama has enough experience. Things won't go well for this country, that's my prediction. What with the financial crisis, and the world at war, and his inexperience, well he doesn't know what he's getting into."

"I couldn't disagree more. Obama as an outsider is much more likely to bring some fresh energy to the White House. The Bush family has experience. You see what that got us. The Clinton *dynasty*" – I stress the word – "also has experience. They set the damn status quo after all. Moved the left to the center, and we've been moving right from there ever since."

"Listen, we've been over this a thousand times," Janet says, that frown returning, and her nose wriggling its way into a wrinkle. "There's no reason to argue, and it's decided now anyway. I just think it's too bad, that's all. But – and this is what I wanted to say tonight," – she stops, takes a drink from her wine, and then looks up at me direct through those heavy Chanel frames of hers. "Just like now, we seem to be repeating the same arguments, the same conversations, the same old same old day after day. I think," Janet sighs, that frown of hers manages to dig its way even deeper down her face, "maybe we should be open to seeing other people. You know, just to give ourselves space to breathe, and maybe even the option of an eventual out."

I'm too shocked to move, but in my mind I'm reaching for my wine. "Are you already seeing someone else? Is that what you're telling me?"

"No, I'm not seeing anyone else. Not yet. But I think we should be open to it. That's all I'm saying. In the meantime, we can keep on as we are. More or less. But I don't think this is something that will work for either one of us in the long run, and I'm at an age where I can't be. You know. I need to think about a future. I don't know that we're together in it."

I manage to reach my wine. I finish my glass, pour myself another, and try to play it as cool as I can. "Okay," I say. "If that's how you want it. I guess if that's how you feel, then that's where we are. I'm cool with that."

But I'm not really cool with it at all. I want the evening to be over immediately so I can go back home and let my heart break in peace.

I get home late. I'm distracted, angry, disappointed. I miss my stop, pass the Lorimer stop, and take the J to Flushing Avenue instead. It's not that far away, so I just walk my way back. I live at the crossroads of Bushwick, Bed-Stuy and Williamsburg, a section of Brooklyn known as Broadway Triangle. My apartment is a skinny six-floor walk up, facing an Intermediate school. It has a Broadway address, but the entrance is around back on Throop, a narrow nondescript street that broadens only gradually as it wends its way southeast through Brooklyn. Just in front of the building there's a school X-ING sign on the street, but the G and the dash are partially faded, so it appears to read, as you approach, like the word JINX, with the N and the I inverted. It greets me with a wink as I walk up Throop.

&

The next morning as I look out the window onto Throop, that Jinx winks at me again from the street, and a restless feeling, like an itch at the back of my neck maybe, gets me out the door and walking up Lorimer. I walk up to Metropolitan past the Brick Theater, then head left to Williamsburg proper. It's a beautiful morning, late summer or early autumn, and the sun is out, so the day is warm, with a cool breeze coming up off the east. I end up at the Spoonbill & Sugartown, a bookstore right on Bedford Avenue. I'm not looking for anything in particular, maybe just something to take my mind off the breakup, so I find myself in the poetry section. I'm going through all the usual suspects, Walt Whitman, Langston Hughes, ee cummings, when I spot a book by a poet I've never heard of before. It's called *Black Buildings*, and it's written by Maya Vicca. The name alone intrigues me, so I pick it up and flip it over a couple times. The cover is nothing special, big black blocky letters on a white background, and no information about the book or the author on the back cover at all. I open it up at random, and read the following:

New Year's Eve in New York City is always lying to you.

Well, damn. That first line gets me right away.

The year that follows never follows the same erratic arc of the three-act, and the masquerade party is a perfect metaphor. In a large white loft in Soho, I sat sipping champagne with people dressed in black evening gowns and black and white tuxedoes, polite conversation, attentions to Lucien, and the countdown always comes in like a funeral march.

Cinderella, slipperless at midnight, and with the wedding bouquet still flying through the air, fled to save face. The roses shed from the bouquet as quickly as her gown shed to rags; she forced her way through throngs of quizzing smiles. Outside, in the cool night air, she looked at the sky, and could only think about the future. Even if every dance she danced was on a precipice of the past.

I kissed Lucien at the top of the stairs, the bells tolling. I turned and started down. Outside the cool night air hit me chilly as a fairy tale, and I lit up in lavender. Cars were honking and people were screaming, cheering in the New Year. I felt dizzy, lightheaded, maybe it was the cigarette, maybe it was the champagne. Three fresh steps out into the screaming night, and I was looking back up the staircase.

I can't say I understand it, but it has a way with words that speaks directly to me. I feel like it's talking about me and Janet, so I flip to another page, and look at another poem. They all seem to have this structure – prose poems, gathered together like a dialogue, with a character named Lucien being one of the principal characters. On the inside of the back cover there's a sketch of the poet. She's striking, at least in the sketch: a young, vibrant looking girl with fiery black hair, austere eyes, and plum lips. The book is too interesting not to buy. It's clearly self-published, and I may never come across another copy again.

I buy the book, then head north up Bedford, where Williamsburg meets Greenpoint at McCarren Park. I find a spot for myself on a bench off to the side, and spend the day with Maya's book, going through poem after poem, alternately perplexed and fascinated. When the sun starts to go down, and those cool winds off the east make late afternoon chilly, I walk back to my apartment, and finish reading the book over a bottle of wine. Then I read it over again. Then I read it over again. I'm that consumed.

&

Monday morning, back at work, I hunt down Samir in his office.

"How was the weekend, brother?" he says in his usual serious way, as if we'd been conspiring together on something, and he was asking how the thing went down.

"Good," I tell him. Then I laugh, take a seat and say, "Actually it was awful, Samir. Janet and I broke up Friday night."

"Huh. Sorry to hear it." There's no expression to the way he says this. He never liked Janet, not from that first night.

"Somehow I don't think you are sorry to hear it."

"Well, that girl was no good for you, brother. You can do better. Seemed something like a wannabe know-it-all to me, but she didn't really know all that much, now did she? But I'm not happy to see you unhappy. Tell me about it. What happened?"

"We just didn't – Oh, I don't know. She said she didn't see a future with us together."

"Honestly?" Samir says it like a question, but follows immediately with his usual deadpan. "Honestly I didn't either. It may be the one thing she's ever been right about. But how are you holding up?"

"I'm doing okay, I guess. I found this weekend," – and here I take out Maya's book – "a book of poetry that I think is pretty interesting. I don't know. I came across it Saturday, and maybe I'm just being a sentimental sap about it, what with the breakup and all. Take a look at it, and tell me what you think. But I think it might even have potential for us here, in braille. Maybe, if you think so, you can send it up to Milton?"

Samir frowns and takes the book. "I'll give it a look," he says. He flips through it quick first, like a flipbook, and finally alights on a particular page. He reads directly from it right then and there, out loud:

"America has a problem with its poets:
Oh no, here we go, another
Poem about poetry.
No, it's not.
It's about Obama,
And the war,
And how we takin' back
What y'all fucked up before.

Well, will you listen to that, I wonder
Who these niggers are
Shooting up now.

YOU!
Motherfucker.

A shot in the dark
A shot glass in a bar

The critics will say
I wrote this on a napkin

Because I peddle in cliches.
No, I don't.

I'm just using expressions
Pressed up like espresso
And just as familiar as

Well, will you listen to that, I wonder
Who these spics think
We're paying taxes for!

"Guv'ner! Call a Tea Party!
I'm Planning A War!"

Who am I kidding? I have health care
Up the ass,
And my money,
Vanishes and refills like a shot glass.
Massively indifferent to all that,
And as bourgie as Marx,
Drinking wine and wondering about the workers.

That's all folks!
Say all the American folk tales,
Hang yourself by the garbage pails,
America's got a problem with its poets."

Samir finishes, frowns a moment, then smiles. "It's not exactly esoteric," he says. "But I like it. I like it a lot actually. Didn't expect to like it at all, to tell you the truth, but I'm open to being surprised. Let's look at another one."

We go through the book looking from one poem to the next more or less randomly, and the more we read, the more animated Samir gets.

"Okay, okay," he says. "I have to admit, you've actually found something here. You keep this up, you'll have my job soon. You know anything about the poet but what's written here? Forget it. I'll Google her." Samir turns to his desk and runs a search for Maya Vicca. Within moments he announces, "I've found her. An email address that looks promising anyway."

There's a tap at the door, and I turn to see Solomon Pinchback standing in the doorway. He comes in looking something like the young Ray Charles. He has dark Rayban sunglasses and he's tall and thin and leaning against the wall like he lives there. His cane looks like something out of a 1920's Harlem Renaissance catalogue: it's a proper walking stick, good heavy wood, with an embroidered silver handle, and he's got this clever smile that looks like a wink.

"Did I hear you gentlemen reciting poetry in here a moment ago," he says, and he makes his way in.

"Good morning Pinchback," says Samir.

"Good morning Samir. Good morning Rudy."

"You did," I say. "It's from a book I came across this weekend. I was just running it by Samir here."

"Poetry huh?" Pinchback flips his smile into a frown, but the wink is still there, like the frown is in its own way still a smile. "I don't know much about the stuff, but I liked the sound of what I heard."

"I'm thinking if we can find the poet we might do a braille version of her book."

"We found an email address for her already," says Samir.

"If you guys say so, I'll give it the green light." Pinchback comes in and taps his way into a seat. "I'll send it up to Milton, and let him know I think it's worth pursuing."

No one really knows what Pinchback does at LIT, but he appears to be the only person in the world who's close to Milton. He comes and goes at his own discretion, and doesn't appear to do much except meet with Milton occasionally and sometimes chat with us in speeches and paragraphs.

"That would be great, if you could," I say. You want to hear some of it?"

Pinchback shakes his head. "No. No, I trust your opinion on these things. Yours especially Rudy. Poetry, that's sort of your forte, isn't it? I'm more a man of science myself, and I'm sure I wouldn't understand the stuff anyway."

"I don't buy it for a minute," says Samir. "What would you be doing here at LIT if you didn't have a taste for the esoteric?"

Pinchback smiles again, and says in a wistful sort of way, "That's the mystery of my life, isn't it?"

"Listen to this," Samir goes on.

"No, I'd rather not."

But Samir's already started reading something.

"So don't sit around like that crying. Sorrow for the dead puts the soul to sleep. And I sure as hell ain't scared. I figure I'll be back soon enough, and not as some reincarnated monster of a me, but as the same old soul of Lucien you know and love.

First time I went it was cold suddenly and then hot like I was having a fever. I was in a hallway, it looked a lot like my high school hallway, only the walls were covered with shifting paintings - in thousands of different colors and shapes that shifted ceaselessly; it was the most beautiful thing I've ever seen. There was no light, and there was no darkness, everything was pure color. It's hard to explain, it was something like the way colors come at you in dreams.

And all the hallways were empty. I went down one and then the next and the next. I went down the hallway where a group of girls stood laughing at me in the tenth grade, which hadn't happened yet, only they weren't there anymore, siren songs came from the walls, and then passed away as I passed through the hall.

It was lonely in the afterlife, and I didn't quite understand it until I ran into Robert. Robert was walking around by himself, too. He was lost. Said he'd been lost since the day he died, and had heard several walls explain to him it was that way with some of the dead. Some people never even tried.

I wanted to ask him about people, but he'd never met anyone. He didn't know if anyone had, or if it was even possible. Somewhere the walls had sung that to him, sung that it wasn't possible.

"But you just met me," I tried to explain.

This puzzled him for a while, and he stayed looking at me square in the face, mumbling, "True.. true.. true.. but I was told..."

And then the whole place went hot and then cold, like when you have a fever, and the walls blinked with every known color all at the same time, blended yet absolutely distinct, and faded into yellow wallpaper, and I was lying in bed.

When I got up and came downstairs my mother was crying. When I asked her what was wrong she looked at me like she was asleep, because she had been crying, and I had been dead."

Pinchback frowns. "Not bad," he says. "But I'm afraid I still don't quite get it. And who's this Robert?"

"I've wondered about that Robert myself," I say. "This is his only poem. There's Lucien, he shows up often enough, but Robert is just in this one piece. I really don't know."

"It reminds me of something," says Pinchback. "I don't remember what. It's funny, maybe something about the colors. I still think I can remember colors sometimes, so maybe that's it. That everything was pure color part."

"Makes me think of Fulcanelli," says Samir. "He talks a lot about color symbolism."

Pinchback frowns again. "Anyway, she sounds talented. I'd like to meet her myself. By all means, track her down and get permissions. I'll okay it with Milton."

"Terrific," I say. "I'll write her now."

"Shouldn't that be my job?" Samir peers at me curiously.

"This is my find, Samir," I tell him. "I'm going to write her myself, if that's okay by you."

"Do your thing, brother."

"I actually stopped in to talk to Samir about something else anyway," says Pinchback. "So if you want to write her now, I'll take a few minutes of Samir's time here while you do that."

"Great. Thanks again, Pinchback."

&

Back in my own office, I spin out a quick email to Maya. I briefly explain who I am, who we are as publishers, and let her know we'd like to publish her book in braille. Maybe we could meet sometime. I'd like that.

Later that evening, I check my work email again from home, and there's already a response from her. It reads:

So you want to publish my book in braille? And of course I'm interested. When and where do we meet? Maybe your office? Sometime this week? Do I need to prepare?

I'm glad you get them. Not everyone does. Not even I do, so you make one at least. And I'm never willfully abstruse, but the poems just come the way they come. And the book needs to be in braille, bad pun to follow, feel me? So I'm curious about them too. How the poems feel to the touch.

Yours, Maya

I have to read it again just to get my head around her odd syntax, and then I read it a third time like I'm reading between the lines, trying to see if there's something she's saying but not saying. I open a bottle of wine, thinking maybe it will help. It does, in its fashion: sometime late that evening I write Janet an email telling her she was right. We should be looking to meet new people.

POETESS

"Hilda Doolittle, whose writings often looked at history and myth from a female perspective coded her last book, 'Hermetic Definitions' with her own initials. She is teaching us how to read her beyond the surface."
    -*FAITH, Dr. Janet Plummet, Chapter IX, p. 207*

The next morning Maya shows up at my office early in the morning. I catch a vague scent of lavender before I turn around, and there she is, standing in the doorway. I recognize her right away, even though I've only seen her sketch. She's cute. She must be in her mid-twenties, dressed in a kind of mix between hipster and old-skool hiphop, with a purple skirt, a black, yellow and green striped shirt, and a black backpack on her shoulder with silver poodles running the circumference. She's got a copper-brown complexion, and she's smiling with those plum lips of hers like a prankster. She knocks a couple times, and then walks right in.

I stand up and offer her a seat. "Sit down, please. You must be Maya. It's good to meet you."

"Pleased to meet you too," she says, collapsing into the chair. "I'm really flattered, let me just say that right off, that you want to publish my book in braille. I never even thought about it that way – as a braille book. Who thinks about braille anymore, what in this day and age, but of course it's still out there."

"It is something of a niche market, that's true. But it's important. Not everyone likes audiobooks, and some people really swear by braille."

"I guess I can understand that. I was curious as soon as I got your email. I even went out to my local bookstore, just to see if they had braille books all this time, and somehow I missed them. No luck of course. But it was just a thought. Where do people buy something like that?"

"Usually directly from the publisher. They order them online, and we ship them out. There are a few libraries that carry them, and then braille specialty bookstores and the like, but really you have to be in the know."

"Cool," says Maya. "I like that. There's something to a tangible product that touches me." She laughs. "Ever since your email, I've been obsessed with the idea of feeling my book in braille. It's like the exact opposite of e-books, where everything is sight and process, and no real product. The way the extra dimensions of a statue can add extra dimensions to the meaning. If you know what I mean."

"Sure."

"But you understood the poems? That's what I find remarkable. Because I don't think even I understand them."

"They made some sense to me. Though I do have some questions."

"Yeah? Like what?"

"Well, for example, I've been wondering about that Robert character, the one who shows up in the poem about the afterlife. Who is he? One of my co-workers even asked about him."

Maya grimaces. "It's like I say, I don't know. I don't know where these poems came from. They just started coming one morning. And so I started writing them down. I'm no born poet or anything pretentious like that. I just thought it would be a shame to lose them, if that makes sense. "

"Sure. Poets often say that – that their poems just come to them, from inspiration, or the creative demon, or the muses, all that. "

"Yeah. I guess. I wish I could say more, though. I really don't get them, and that's why I self-published them, and got done with it." Maya frowns. "But maybe they're meant to be in braille. I guess that could be the thing with them. There's someone out there who only reads braille, and they're meant for her to find. I kind of like that idea."

"It's a nice thought."

"I mean, there must be some reason for it," says Maya. "The poems, after all. While they were coming, I was ecstatic, like I was surrounded by light or something. But they haven't been coming anymore, and now I think it was all for a reason. That I was a poet for a reason. Because I really started to get into the idea. Of being a Poetess, capital P, or whatever. But now I don't know, and I don't know why they're there."

"Is the Lucien character based off anyone?"

"Oh. Yeah. I know where he comes from, but that's — I don't know. It doesn't make sense that Lucien should be in the book at all. He just kept insisting on showing up. That's just like him, though. So maybe that's why he's there."

I laugh.

"Listen," says Maya. "What are you doing for lunch? You have some time to escape into the city this afternoon? I want to show you something, basically where all this comes from. It was in the Met where these poems first started coming to me. And then I would go back there whenever I started feeling stuck, and they would come to me again. But recently it's stopped working. Only just a few months ago. And I keep going, keep trying to re-channel the poems, but they don't come anymore."

"Sure. The Met? I haven't been in a while. Was there any particular exhibit that triggered them?"

"Yeah, you'll see. It's the African Art wing, right there on the ground floor."

"Well, I'd be glad to go."

&

We head out immediately. On the way to the subway, passing through the rows of lindens lining Whitman Park Maya lights a cigarette that smells like lavender tobacco and marijuana.

"Are you smoking weed?"

"Why, you want a drag?"

"No. No thanks. I would, but it's still a workday."

We get to the museum just after one.

"This is the thing about you and your braille book," says Maya as we enter the building. The weed has her chatting away; she's been going on and on about her book and braille and ancient artifacts the whole way into the city. "As I'm sure you know already, the oldest written literature we have, the Sumerian texts of Gilgamesh and Enkidu are etched in tablets of stone, and I was thinking about it, and it seems to me braille is language as artifact, really language as artifact, like old cathedrals used to be. Everything else nowadays – print and digital media, especially digital media, are degenerations into a language of forgetting and palimpsest. So the braille thing appeals to me like this museum appeals to me.

"Well, so I've been researching all this lately," Maya continues, "and you know, in many East African cultures, time is two-dimensional, and comprised of the dual concepts, known in Swahili as Saşa and Zamani. Saşa is basically what we think of as the immediate present, the immediate past, and the immediate or potential future, and Zamani, the indefinite past, stretching back into history and myth. There's a book about all this by a writer named John S. Mbiti, it's called *African Religions and Philosophy*, and it goes right into these concepts of African time, and even uses the verb tenses of the Akamba and Gikuyu peoples of Kenya to demonstrate it. The concept of a distant future is pretty useless actually, since time is measured by the reckoning of events, basically their relationship to each other, and their relationship to the cycle of events in people's individual and collective lives. So that Saşa time is not just the immediate and ongoing events in each individual's life, but also that of the community's. And as events fall further and further into what we call the past, they become part of the great history of Zamani time, which not only influences and informs Saşa, but is actually actively part of Saşa, as long dead ancestors can be called upon by the living, and old histories and myths referenced and renewed by those passing through Zamani time. So time never really flows forward in a stream, like we like to think, but unfolds constantly into the past. See, check it out!" she says as we enter the African Wing, which begins with an assortment of masks. "Here's where it all started, right here by the masks. In African Art an artifact is basically just part of an event, a religious observation that occurs in Saşa time and references and renews Zamani time, so African art is constantly crossing through and around time, blending the past and the present in a celebration of events and their inherent simultaneity."

I look at all these odd African masks, their flat, faceless depictions of Gods and myths, and the longer I look at them, the more they seem to take on one strong facial expression that deepens into others. A staff of the Yoruba God Eşu looks momentarily back at me.

"You see what I mean?" says Maya. "You get lost in the collective history in the mask, and then your movements become the mask's movements, and the mask's movements become your movements, so you're constantly reminded that you don't really have an identity."

Walking past the scattering of masks, I find myself thinking of Robert Johnson. In particular the iconic photograph of him, spidery fingers holding a guitar up to his left shoulder, his face flat and expressionless as an African mask, an unlit cigarette dangling down the round curve of his mouth. Actors assume the invisible masks of the characters they play, and Johnson's legend has drifted backwards in time to cloud his visage with iconography. The masks around us mix up my own mind with this image, until I feel Robert Johnson's mask becoming a part of my face, and I'm suddenly conscious of the way I move, walk, talk, even turn to face Maya as we exit the hall into the café and tell her the experience was transforming.

"I'm glad to hear it. Now you know what I mean about that room, huh?"

Mostly I'm thinking about Robert Johnson, wondering if maybe subconsciously Maya had the same thought, and if he's the Robert of the afterlife poem.

"It made me think of Robert Johnson," I say. "You know, the delta blues singer."

"Oh. That's funny."

"And what about you? Were you able to channel anything this time?" I try not to sound patronizing, but I still think it sounds that way.

"No. It never comes anymore. I just remember the lines of old poems now," she says. "The feeling is there, but none of the creativity it used to spark."

"I'm sorry to hear that."

I'm in no hurry to get back to the office, so we spend another few hours walking around the museum and when we walk out we walk out into a fantastic autumn twilight. The streetlights are just starting to flicker on in their pale yellow hue, and the night is cool but not cold.

"It's why the book's called *Black Buildings*," says Maya. "It's supposed to represent the museum. The museum's a white building, of course, but it's the African Art that I was interested in, and so *Black Buildings* started to make sense. If that makes any sense."

"Sure," I say.

Maya lights another one of her lavender cigarettes as soon as we've stepped out into Central Park.

"I guess your workday is over," she says sheepishly. She peers at me like a question.

I take the cigarette from her, and take a drag. The starry spots of golden streetlights deepen, and we begin to walk westward through the park, without any particular place to go. Robert Johnson is only getting clearer as the dusky remains of daylight settle into evening. I'm thinking of a play, a play about the last days of Robert Johnson, thinking of his face with that African mask expression, thinking of what he must've been thinking as the demons he conjured to make his moody music called back for his soul. Robert Johnson in the afterlife.

"Can I ask you something?" I ask her.

"I think you just did."

We're giggling like a couple kids.

"No," I tell her. "I mean, your poem, your afterlife poem, it has me thinking. I'd like to write a play about Robert Johnson, and it's sort of inspired by your poem. Would you be okay with that?"

"Why should you have to ask me for permission? For one thing, you can write whatever you want, from whatever inspiration you've been given. I'm not the person to say you can't do that. Which is to say, secondly,

I barely even wrote that poem. I don't know who Robert is, let alone ever thought of him as Robert Johnson, so I don't know that you're really using anything of mine anyway. So, you know." Then she looks at me and squishes up her face. "Why, you a playwright or something like that?"

"Something like that."

"Would I have heard of you? Know anything you've done?"

"I doubt that. *Black Prometheus*? That was my last play, and it was kind of, well, for one thing it was just produced at one little theater in Brooklyn, and yeah. No. I doubt you know anything I've done."

"*Black Prometheus*? Sounds pretentious, doesn't it?"

"Yeah. I guess it does."

We walk a little while without saying anything. The leaves have already started to turn red and gold, and in the twilight light, beneath the distant streetlights of the city, they appear to gleam like colorful petals floating on a black pond. Maya stops to pass me the lavender cigarette. I take it, take a drag, then throw it down.

"Hey!" She stops and turns toward me. "Why'd you do that for? I wasn't done yet."

Then I do something that doesn't surprise me at all. In fact I've been thinking about it for hours: I kiss her.

NOWHERESVILLE

"Audre Lorde's poetry functions to rename and redefine herself outside of her society. This act of transformation is an act of 'Biomythography,' in Lorde's terminology, and it is an act that transforms the individual into myth, spirit and poetry."
-FAITH, Dr. Janet Plummet, Chapter XII, p. 341

They say old habits die hard, and Janet is nothing if not an old habit. So we still see each other on occasion, even after I figure I'm trying to make things work with Maya. It's just normal New York business as usual, anyway – to keep the casual clichés coming –since, as I understand things, people date like three or four people at a time in this town, and that's considered normal. But it's not like I'm dishonest or sneaky about it either. One morning I decide to invite Janet out for brunch and let her know that I'm seeing someone new, and she can do with that information what she will. We meet at a place right down the street from me. It's a cute little café called Moto – French style or Belgian or something – real small and dark and small round tables that scatter the floor like ballerinas. Hidden beneath the subway tracks, but inside it's real romantic. They serve a great brunch, and it's the only place in town I know where you can get Corsendonk on draft, and Corsendonk on draft is a goddamn delight.

As usual, Janet begins things by trying to deconstruct the situation. "So why Moto, Rudy? You only invite me here when you have something important you want to say." She pauses, squints at me through her Chanels. "You have a new play or something?"

"I am working on something, as a matter of fact."

"Yeah? What's that? Or let me guess." She quizzes a smile. "Something like: Black Faust."

"Well." I pause a moment and consider that. "Strangely, yeah. But it's not what you're thinking probably."

"Well, I beg your larnin', but you know what I always say."

"This shit just does not become you." We say it together, and laugh. Cool.

"Well that's not fair. You haven't even heard the idea yet."

"Black Faust? I've heard enough. The fact that I was able to just guess it right off with a joke just goes to show."

"Well, it's not exactly black Faust, Janet. It's actually about Robert Johnson. You know, the blues singer. And folks do say he sold his soul to the devil."

Janet sips her coffee; she doesn't say anything. I take a sip of beer and smile like I've maybe won a small victory here.

"It's about Robert Johnson. That's all I know so far. I'm thinking of maybe doing a play about the last few days of his life. They're real mysterious, you know. No one's really sure what killed him. That's how the story goes, as far as I can tell. Still researching it."

"The Last Days of Robert Johnson?"

"Well, yeah, something like that."

"Wasn't there already a play? The Last Days of someone or other just a few years ago?"

"You're thinking of Judas Iscariot. The Last Days of Judas Iscariot."

"That's right. I heard about it from a colleague. Theory applied to the Judas story, or something. That's how she put it. I don't think she was all that impressed."

"I saw it. It was okay. A little too stagey, maybe, for what I'm interested in. Applied theory. That's funny. I guess I see that. But that's got nothing to do with what I'm doing. I want to do something a little more freewheeling. Like a jazz funeral."

"Well okay," Janet says after a while. "I guess that could be interesting."

"Well, thanks. Coming from you, I suppose that's like a high compliment or something."

"Or something."

I look at Janet smirking in her coffee, her soft brown eyes catching the pale afternoon sun, her lazy, sexy professorial pout, what with her glasses and clothes a little too well put together for a hipster café like Moto, and suddenly feel the Corsendonk run shivers, chill.

"How about you? You working on anything new."

"Actually, yes. It's publish or perish in the academic world. But I'm inspired too. It's actually funny you mention the blues. Because I'm writing a book I'm thinking of calling *Strange Fruit.*"

"Like Billie Holiday?"

"Yes, like Billie Holiday."

"Oh well!" Now I'm really smiling. "Well, I beg your hipness, but this shit simply does not become you."

Janet frowns. "What's that supposed to mean? I suppose Billie Holiday is material only fit for-,"

"Fit for whom, exactly, would you say Janet? Listen, you can't have it both ways, right? Giving me shit about Goethe or Marlowe or Sophocles or someone, and then here you come with some work about Billie Holiday. Don't tell me you're writing a biography." I smile "Are you?"

"No, of course not, Rudy. It's just a title. And it's called *Strange Fruit* because it's an examination of feminism and womanism, and the relationship between women and men, through the intersection of race, culture and literature in America. Honestly, I think it's my most ambitious work yet. I'm trying to fuse the two, you know. Feminism and womanism."

"You mean your most autobiographical work yet." I catch Janet's eye and hold it.

Janet sighs. "That too, I suppose, Rudy." She takes a sip of her coffee and says a little quieter. "Yes, that too. And maybe that's why it's my most ambitious."

"So. What's your approach?"

"I'd rather not get into it here."

"Do you discuss us in the book? I mean me and you? Specifically?"

"Listen, you'll read it when it comes out. Well, I hope you will anyway."

"I don't know that the two can be reconciled. I think it's too late. Feminism and womanism, I mean. You'd have to toss feminism out the window, and start all over from a Womanist perspective."

I say this as a direct challenge to Janet, but it doesn't work. "I think maybe you're right."

"Oh."

We don't say anything for a while. My prosciutto Panini and Janet's eggs Benedict arrive. I order another Corsendonk. It isn't until it arrives that I venture the next words.

"I'm actually, you know, I've been. Seeing someone new lately. I mean, just so you know."

Janet looks up from her coffee and squints. She opens her mouth, closes it.

"Someone I met through work. Well, sort of."

"One of your colleagues?" She pauses to finish sipping. "Because you know, there are ethical questions there."

"Not exactly a colleague. More like a client. A poet. Or poetess. What do I know?"

"A poetess?" Janet hiccoughs a giggle. "Really, Rudy?"

"Yeah. We're going to publish her. In braille. She self-published a book. It's really good."

"If you insist. Jeez. Talk about ethical questions."

"I read the book before I met her, you know. I mean, I liked the book right away, and then we looked for her."

"So this is what you meant with that weird email you sent me a while back. About us seeing other people. That you already met someone."

"Well. Well, yes and no."

"Jesus Rudy. So what are her poems about?"

"Oh, I don't know. They're like a conversation, maybe. A dialogue in verse. The book is called *Black Buildings*, and it's. Well, it's remarkable. I don't know that the poems are about anything in particular. Everything, maybe."

"Do I get to read it?"

"Well, I don't have it on me. I mean, my apartment's just down the street, you know. So if you're really curious, yeah, I guess."

I guess I might as well admit it: I didn't bring a copy to the restaurant on purpose. Just to sort of set up this dynamic. Janet sees right through it, though.

"And here you are trying to get me to go back to your place with you?"

"Oh Christ Janet. You read something into everything. It's the middle of the day, for Christ's sake. If you want to see the poems you can come back and see them. That's all I mean by it. If not, that's cool too. I just thought I should tell you is all."

"Is it serious?"

"Not yet, I guess it's not."

"Because I've been seeing someone too."

That stops me, though. I hadn't anticipated this. I take a drink. Look down at my food. I'm suddenly not so hungry. I try to sound cool, but my voice comes out like a croak. "Yeh?"

"That's right. It's actually someone you know."

The light comes dim through the worn old windows of the café. I feel a buzz in my stomach run up through my back and into my shoulders, linger around the periphery of my head, like I've had too much coffee. The tables start to swim and dance and stop, ballerinas. "Someone I know?"

"From work."

"From my work? Who? Samir?"

"Samir!" Janet laughs. "Well that would be the day, now wouldn't it?"

"Well who then? Oh forget it, I don't want to know."

"Solomon."

"Who?"

"Solomon. Pinchback."

"Oh, Pinchback!" I try to follow that up with something, but I'm thinking about Janet and Pinchback and trying to make sense of how this makes sense, but all I can do is repeat myself. "Oh, Pinchback."

"Why do you all call him by his last name?"

"Huh?" I take another drink. That's the only way I can register the question. "Well, it seems to suit him. Solomon's too biblical or something. I don't know. He's just Pinchback is all."

"Well, whatever. I call him Solomon."

"Why not Saul?" It's the best thing I can think of to try to sound disinterested. To make light of things.

"He's a remarkable man in a lot of ways."

"How did this happen? I mean, is it serious?"

"I don't know yet. I guess not yet. But I'm open to things."

"He's a hard guy to get to know. That's been my experience."

"Most interesting people are. You know his father left when he was little. And he used to be able to see. I mean, the first two years of his life. His father was sort of responsible for his blindness. Interesting stuff."

"Well you already know more about him than most of us at the office do. But what do you mean? How was his father responsible?"

"The guy was a doctor. And Solomon started having seizures at two or something. They wanted to give him some kind of medication for it, but his father said no. Said the medication slowed down mental development. But the seizures left Solomon blind."

"Well that's one fucked up dad."

"I guess. I mean, I don't know. Intelligence or sight? I think I'd opt for my mind."

"Well, that's easy for you to say. And besides, it's what you'd say anyway."

Janet frowns, squints into her coffee and takes another sip. "It's just the way I see it. It can't have been easy, but his father couldn't have known he'd go blind either. It's just a risk, I guess. Anyway, that's what broke up the family. That decision. So the man paid for it."

"And Pinchback too."

"Well, yeah. I mean, yeah. Anyway."

"Anyway."

We don't say anything for a while. We eat in silence. It's awkward, but it's alright too. I don't really have anything to say. I'm still trying to process it all.

"Wasn't Robert Johnson blind? One of those blind blues jazz musicians from the Mississippi Delta?"

"Robert Johnson? Blind? Christ, and you're writing a book called *Strange Fruit*? No, you're thinking of Willie Johnson or Lemon Jefferson."

"Well, it's like I say, the book isn't so much about the blues as about feminism and Womanism. And I'm more interested in women in the blues than I am in men."

"There's no surprise," I mutter.

We don't say anything for a while again.

"So where does this leave us?" I ask, feeling the sun peel slow behind the clouds through the languid, sad blue windows of the café.

"I guess Nowheresville."

"No shit. Nowheresville."

We look at each other, and it doesn't feel like Nowheresville at all, but I don't know how to say that to her, or maybe I just have.

"Listen, let's get out of here," I say. "I'll show you those poems, if you're interested."

"Maybe another time Rudy, huh? I mean, I don't know that I should be going back to your place. Given our respective situations."

"Maybe you're right. I mean. Yeah. I mean. Did this start a while ago? This thing with Pinchback? Is that why you said we should start seeing new people? How did it even happen? I mean, we at the office rarely see the guy. When did you even have a chance to really meet him?"

"I don't remember all the specifics, Rudy. I don't think there was anything going on when we broke up that night. That's just where I think we were at the time. And Solomon. Oh, I don't know. You know, we used to talk sometimes, me, you, Samir and Solomon, all in Samir's office. One day he just emailed me. Out of the blue. Asked if I'd be interested in having my book published in braille."

"One of your books? Which book? Pinchback isn't even a literature guy! And why was he scouting for books? That's Samir's job!"

"Samir wasn't ever going to ask me for a book. Maybe Solomon just thought I had interesting things to say. You know, some people think I have interesting things to say, Rudy."

"Oh, you. Miss Deconstruct Everything, everything except your own sycophants."

"Anyway, Rudy. Let's not argue, okay. We're both happy now, and so let's just be happy we're happy, and leave it at that."

Yeah, why not leave it at that? With us both happy?

&

After brunch I walk Broadway to Marcy, and then walk up Bedford, alone with a thousand thoughts. I guess old Pinchback really got the best of me. Didn't even see it coming. Well, who's the blind man now? It's really a perfect summer afternoon, cool enough to be comfortable, great walking weather, but I'm weathering disasters. I walk Bedford to North 6th, and then walk North 6th to Lorimer. I'm not really paying attention to anything. I'm not really thinking. I guess I'm not really there. I was never really there. Janet was just biding her time.

As soon as I get back home I call Maya. No answer. I leave a message and invite her over that evening. I don't expect anything. Maybe she's just biding her time. I spend the day writing Robert Johnson drafts and then deleting them. I keep thinking of Blind Lemon Jefferson. He seems to be usurping the script. Or maybe it's Pinchback.

Late that evening Maya shows up at my apartment unexpected. There's a ring on the door, and then there she is. She's glowing, flushed, a small brown cloud of lavender and marijuana. She sweeps into my room and lights another.

"Oh Rudy, you won't believe it. You're just not going to believe the day I had."

I pull out a bottle of wine and pour a couple glasses. "No kidding. Probably better than mine."

Maya turns her head sidewise, frowns and smiles. "What's wrong with you today, huh? You sure look like you got the blues something terrible."

"Play's just not going well, I guess. Sort of hung up on things. Can't break through with it. That's all."

"Sorry to hear it. You'll get it all right. But listen. I have news for you."

"Yeah? News for me?"

"Yeah, about your friend. That guy you work with."

"Samir?"

Maya screws up her face, frowns again. "No. Not Samir. What's Samir got to do with anything? No, I mean Pinchback."

"Pinchback? Why, what happened to him?"

"Nothing happened to him, silly!" Maya laughs. "Listen to you Mr. Doomandgloom. Not yet anyway. I mean, but soon. I went to go see him today."

"You went to go see him today? How? Why?"

"I just went. We've been emailing for a while, you know."

"I don't think I do know."

"Well, listen Rudy. He's a really fascinating guy. I mean, really he is. But get this. You know how he's blind?"

"Um. Yeah. I guess I would have to."

"Yeah, yeah. Well, did you know that all he has to do to be able to see is have his cataracts removed?"

"No shit. That's it? Well, why hasn't he done it yet?"

Pinchback sure seems to open up to women in a way he doesn't to us fellas.

"Something about his father. Honoring his legacy or something. Long story. I'll tell it to you in a minute, but listen. Get this. I convinced him to get the operation. Told him I could probably get him a job with my father at the New Jersey Institute of Technology if he did. I've already talked to my dad about it, and he said he'd be interested in talking to him. So, I think it's more or less a done deal. Pinchback is gonna see."

I think about Pinchback, try to imagine him, his cool relaxed demeanor, his Ray-Ban sunglasses, the antique cane, and try to imagine him without any of these trappings. Sight would certainly transform the man. It might make him more interesting, or maybe it would make him less interesting. Hard to say.

"Did you hear me?" Maya waves her hand in front of my face. "Earth to Rudy. I said, Pinchback is gonna see!"

Well, at least she's not calling him Solomon. Not yet, anyway.

ALMOST LIKE AN EVENT

"Zora Neale Hurston's feminism is spiritual empowerment itself, and her texts are spellbooks for manipulating the alchemical change of a being from one state to another, either enlightened or debased."
-FAITH, Dr. Janet Plummet, Chapter XIII, p. 412

It's a while before anyone sees or hears from Pinchback again. There's nothing unusual about this. He often disappears weeks at a time, and when he's gone, no one thinks anything of it. It occasionally occurs to me that I should ask Janet about him, but I can't bring myself to call or write her again, not after that last meeting. So Pinchback's disappearance remains a mystery.

In any case, I find I don't particularly miss him all that much.

The weather gets colder; autumn gains the upper hand. The leaves turn and fall from the trees, and all along the streets of Brooklyn lithe ouroboroi of yellow and gold writhe in the wind, rising and settling in slick splendid spirals of resplendent leaves.

Things go along smoothly enough with Maya. She hasn't heard from Pinchback either, and that's cool with me.

I also manage to get a grip on my new play. I decide to call it *The Last Days of Robert Johnson* after all.

And then one Friday morning mid-October there's suddenly a rumor running around the building that Pinchback's somewhere on the premises, and what's more, he can see. I head upstairs to Samir's office as soon as I hear about it.

"You hear about Pinchback?"

Samir shakes his head and smiles a deadly serious smile. "I'll believe it when I see it."

"You think he'll stop by?"

Samir's smile doesn't go anywhere. "He'd better. Or I'll never forgive the bastard."

"If you don't mind," I say. "I'll hang around here and wait to see if he does."

"Be my guest. It's not like I'm doing anything else myself."

"I didn't think so."

We laugh a little.

"Honestly, I have work piling up here, but I'm just not motivated to do it anymore."

"No?"

"Not really. I don't have time to read a lot of the drivel coming my way. Being a book scout is great, until you actually start following a trail of books for your own reasons. Then the books you have to read that don't interest you just get in the way."

"What's your own trail of books? More of this Fulcanelli stuff you've been going on about?"

"Yeah, I've moved past him now. I mean, well, not really. But for a while I was really into thinking about language and architecture and color, but that sort of moved me more towards alchemy itself, and alchemy has led me into all sorts of weird places. I don't know. Something's up with me. I feel a little displaced from myself. Like a pressure in my head, and I don't – it comes and goes. It's not like a headache, just pressure, and sometimes feeling like – well, yeah. Like I'm a little displaced from myself, is the best way I can put it."

"Well what the hell are you reading? Maybe you should just see a doctor." I laugh a little light-heartedly, but Samir frowns.

"I did. I saw an ENT and a Neurologist, and neither one could find anything wrong with me."

"You really saw a doctor?"

"And so it has to be something else. And yeah, I keep coming back to the Fulcanelli, because he seems to be bringing it all together, but then again. Hell. I don't know, Rudy. It's useless trying to explain it all."

"Well, isn't it always. Loan me some of your books, man. I need something to take my mind off things too."

"Why, what's up?"

"Oh, I don't know. I mean, it's good Pinchback's back and can see and shit, but." I look across the way to Samir's shelf. *The Twelve Keys of Basil Valentine*. I open my mouth; close it.

"But what?"

"He's been dating Janet, you know."

"He has? No, I didn't know that. How could I?"

"I guess you couldn't." *The Occult Philosophy*, Agrippa.

"Is it serious?"

"I'm guessing it is." *Feminism's Ancient Intellectual-Theological Hermeticism*, Plummet.

It takes a moment before I register this. "What the hell is Janet's book doing on your shelf?"

"Oh, that," says Samir. "I've been reading it. I have to. I think we're going to publish it."

"Oh, right." I frown. "Janet mentioned something about that. Pinchback asked her for a copy."

"Pinchback asked her for it?"

"Can you beat it?"

"No kidding."

"What do you think of it?"

Samir hesitates. "Well, it's interesting enough, although terribly flawed, and certainly Orientalist in its approach, although she may not even be aware of that."

"You like it! That's like a gold standard stamp of approval coming from you!"

"It's okay. Interesting in places. I don't know. She's read a lot of good first source material, so the book's probably more profound than she is. Whatever."

"No, you really love the damn thing." I get up and take the book from the shelf. Flip through it; read aloud: "Zora Neale Hurston's feminism is spiritual empowerment itself, and her texts are spellbooks for manipulating the alchemical change of a being from one state to another, either enlightened or debased." I look up at Samir, who's now looking towards the window. "So, this is what you mean? This kind of nonsensical drivel."

"Look, you were the one that dated her," Samir says quickly. He turns and looks at me. "Besides, I think she's onto something with that, actually. With a few things. I even met with her a few times to discuss it."

"You met with her? With Janet?"

"Sure. Why not? We're publishing her book, after all, and I am the book scout."

"Just you and Janet? No one else?"

"What's the big deal? Yeah, coffee a couple times."

"Coffee? A couple times? Why didn't you tell me before?"

"What's to tell? It's part of the job."

"Part of the damn job. And I suppose -,"

"Have you even read it, Rudy? Have you read it yourself?"

"Sure, I've read it. I don't remember much about it anymore, though. It was a long time ago."

This is a lie, I remember it well.

"I'm sure you don't."

"Whatever the hell that means. Listen, I'll catch up with you later, man."

&

I walk out of the building alone into a gray, cold, windy afternoon. I can read between the lines too, you know. I turn into Whitman Park and walk its length electric with anger.

Suddenly I see Pinchback just ahead of me. He's all alone, walking a steady measure with his cane in his hand, but retracted. Occasionally he stops, looks around, and then continues on, like he's stopping to listen to the leaves. I slow down as I approach him, to see if he recognizes me, but the closer I get, the more I realize he can't recognize much at all, much less me making my manic approach.

When I call his name, he stops again suddenly and extends his cane.

"Pinchback," I say it again, and now we're very close, seven paces apart at most, and he's looking right at me through his shades. He doesn't seem to see me, but it's clear he recognizes my voice.

"Pinchback? Do you see me?"

"I think so," he says, hesitating, and he taps the cane in front of him and advances a couple steps. That's when I notice in his other hand he's also got a copy of Janet's book. "I'm glad I ran into you," he says. "I guess you've probably heard the news already." He smiles. "I've been trying to take long walks by myself. If I bring the cane along, I can get along pretty well. Sometimes I have to close my eyes, and go back to blind sight." He seems to think something over. "But overall, I guess I'm making good progress."

"Getting better by the day, I'd imagine."

"Some things are just a little different than I expected." Pinchback frowns. "The sun for example, and the moon too, they're much smaller than I thought they'd be, and the sun looks too low. I know the physics, it shouldn't surprise me, but it does. It's all a little spooky."

"Speaking of spooky, I see you're already reading." I gesture towards the book, a gesture lost on Pinchback. His cane slaps the side of my foot, and retracts. He takes my arm slowly, and a little clumsily.

"Yes, that's right, I've been reading Janet's book."

I loop my arm around his, and we start back in the direction of the office. "In print?"

"In print. It's slow going, but I use a magnifying glass when I need to, and I can get through it for the most part."

"You recognize the letters?"

Pinchback turns his head in my direction. "I learned letters by touch." He looks forward again. "We had to, along with braille, where I went to school. Sometimes I still get confused. Capital letters are easier, they're more defined. In any case, the mind supplies the sense even when there are letters missing. But it's slow going, like I said, and damn exhausting. I'm much more comfortable with braille."

"How far along are you?"

"I just finished the first chapter. I'm enjoying it, if enjoy is the right word to use for this type of book. But I wonder if she overstates her case. She sees in the literature what she'd like to see. But she's forthright about it, at least, and unembarrassed, and so I guess it's what literary criticism should be. I don't know. It's not really my thing. I'm more a man of science myself, I don't know much about literature, especially not feminist literature, and then all this esoterica reads to me like so much hocus pocus."

I laugh, and then he laughs too, and suddenly I feel very warmly towards him.

"So what made you pick that up first, of all things, then?"

Pinchback turns his face toward me again, and behind the lenses I see his heavy eyes roll around lazy, and his laugh slips into a cunning kind of grin. "Oh well. Janet gave me a copy of course." He pauses, and turns his head forward again, while the sun disappears behind the clouds and darkens all the lindens. "She's something else, that Janet. Wouldn't you agree that she's something else?"

I tense up. "How do you mean?"

"Well," Pinchback says, and he turns to look at me, but looks right ahead immediately after, as if something he's just seen has unnerved him. "I think you know the answer to that." He waits a moment, then: "You dated her yourself a while, didn't you?"

"Yeah, that's right."

"Well, she's a fascinating woman."

I smile, fumble for words. What do you say to something like that?

"And how did things happen, exactly?"

We turn a corner. Pinchback ignores my question with a question. "How is Maya?"

The gray winter sky fractures beneath the industrial arch of the bridge. A subway shuttles by above us, snaking squares of amber light across the liquid clouds. He doesn't wait for me to answer.

"Because it all began with Maya's book. Or I guess it probably began before that. I'm not sure – I don't really know how to read these kinds of things yet. Relationships have always been difficult for me in the past. To say the least. Dating was a conundrum. The easiest thing of course, was just to date within the blind community. But that seems to lack, how to put it –imagination? And dating outside the blind community has all sorts of pitfalls. Even there – there's a certain lack of imagination, and then there's always the question of motivation." Pinchback's step is becoming slightly unsure. He stumbles, and I have to steady him with my arm.

"Easy there," I say, but too quickly, because I'm anxious for him to go on. "I mean I know how you mean. Sort of."

"And then there's the whole race thing as well. Was I only looking for blind women? Black women? Blind women who happen to be black?"

We laugh.

"I more or less opted out. But Maya's book. There's something about Maya's book. And that helped me open up. I don't know that Janet and I would have happened otherwise. Maya's book is like a lover's dialogue. That's how I read it."

"Oh." I have too many questions to know where to begin.

We walk another corner in the quiet afternoon. It's starting to get cold, and the wind off the river comes in stronger.

Something Pinchback sees suddenly distracts him a moment, and he stumbles over a curb. I catch his arm again, "What is it?"

Pinchback's head darts left, then right, he pushes his head forward like an ostrich, squints, then turns towards me. "I don't know," he says. "It's almost déjà vu, I see these images from time to time now, they don't make much sense. Just faded colors or movements or something, they're almost like events. And they feel familiar. Which of course is impossible."

I glance from the street to the buildings to the dwindling silver city across the bridge, trying to catch Pinchback's vision.

"More that way," Pinchback gestures forward. We walk a little while, and walking, pass a small building with a black glass storefront. Pinchback follows a chimera, stops, turns and looks. He's looking at his reflection, a shadowy image in the storefront door, and I stand next to him, wondering what it's like for him.

"Were you surprised," I ask, "the first time you saw a mirror?"

Pinchback shakes his head. "No. No, I've felt my own face all my life. Once I started seeing other faces, I guess I had an idea of what I looked like already. But I don't exactly identify with this image either. Something about it feels artificial. Like it's just an avatar or something assigned to me, an actor in a play maybe. And then when I see my reflection in glass like this, it's even spookier. Almost like I'm seeing my own ghost."

"That is spooky."

"Tell me about it. And then they always do that. These déjà vu hallucinations. They always lead me to my reflection."

That phrase itself, déjà vu, sounds a little strange coming from Pinchback.

"Did you have déjà vu moments when you were blind?"

"Oh, yes," says Pinchback. "No doubt. They were even sharper then." He hesitates. "Like the first time I met Maya."

"How's that?"

"I knew it was an important moment. That it would lead to something. Like I was remembering something."

I frown. "Recollection."

"Pardon?"

"Plato. Recollection. I don't know. Ask Samir."

"But that's why I say it started with Maya's book. Maybe it was when I heard that poem about the colors. There was something about that. Those colors. Like I remembered them."

"Or Kierkegaard's Repetition."

"You're a very lucky man."

"Sure. Thanks," I look at Pinchback, look away quickly. I'm not sure what to say. "Janet's pretty special too."

Pinchback nods. I almost feel like I want him to contradict me. I don't know why. A cold wind sweeps a facade of color past our feet.

"Let's keep going," I say.

CATCH WRECK

"Djuna Barnes is never explicitly feminist, and yet female mythology dominates her Walpurgisnacht-esque novel 'Nightwood.'."
                -FAITH, Dr. Janet Plummet, Chapter VI, p. 204

'm not the type to hold a grudge, not against Samir, and not against Pinchback either, not over Janet. I get over all that pettiness pretty quick.

Not to mention I've got other things to think about. Namely, the Robert Johnson play. It's not going well. Janet's nagging voice attaches itself to every draft.

I beg your learnin', but this shit just does not become you.

The only time I'm happy with it is when I'm just walking around thinking about it. I sometimes try to inhabit the character of Johnson myself. I conjure him up when I'm walking around Brooklyn: Here's a man more myth than man, and I picture him aloofly woofing up a jook, cigarette dangling from lips, reaching for a bottle to brook. He's been flirting with a woman right across the way, and now he takes a sip, and slips a stool over to her, away from Sonny Boy Williamson, who takes his shoulder and warns him in a whisper, "Watch it, dat's her feller and he been giving you the crook eye since we walked in." Johnson shrugs. "A crooked eye ain't killt me yet, and I reckon it won't tonight, neither." And now here he is, real cool and dry and about to let the lady offer him a drink.

So naturally, when Halloween rolls around, the obvious choice for me is to fully inhabit the man. I don't have much by way of costume: an old suit that looks like it could pass for something from the 20's, an old Stetson hat passed down to me by my grandfather, and an old acoustic guitar that's been sitting in my apartment collecting dust and turning tuneless as a chalkboard. But it looks the part enough, and that's all that matters.

Halloween falls on a Friday, and I make plans to go out with the whole crew: Maya, Samir, Pinchback and Janet. Pinchback and Janet are a full on item now, they're always together and they seem happy, God fuckin' bless them; Maya and I are doing well too, but Samir can't say the same. Something's been up with him. He's been slipping lately. He puts on a good face all right, seems to bear whatever's bothering him with a fractured stoicism, like a philosopher caught in a farce. But he's also been coming into the office looking like he's had less and less sleep; showing up irritable and sometimes smelling like liquor. Blind folks may not be able to see, but they sure can smell. His work's been suffering too. He falls asleep at his desk, forgets to follow up with clients and publishers, and he's been leaving tasks incomplete.

"It's just this damn Fulcanelli," he explains to me Halloween night. We're still waiting for Janet and Pinchback to show up to my apartment, and then we plan to make our way out to the Wreck Room in Bushwick, a place Samir and I used to frequent, but haven't been to in a while. Maya's dressed as Cleopatra, looking outrageously sexy in an outfit she bought online, plush asp between her breasts and everything. Samir isn't dressed up at all. He's wearing that same damn suit and same damn tie he always wears.

"Fulcanelli's phonetic cabala is just so elusive, and the more you try to catch it the more mixed up you get. He gives you lots of clues, and I really like his loquacious elliptical style. But even with a little background in Attic Greek and French -- so I can usually follow the etymological breakdowns -- it seems like these breakdowns are so open to imaginative thinking, the rearrangements of words and phrases seem infinitely open to interpretation – for example, when he talks about the elite, this can relate to the prophet Elijah, Elias, helios in the Greek, the sun -- and yet elite comes from -- according to standard etymology -- the latin elire, to choose. Mercury is kirmis, the Oak, gall, dye, Hermes naturally, but Plato ties Hermes to eirie, or speech. So now I find myself at a strange relationship to language. I can't say or think or read anything but that a thousand other associations flood my mind, and this has been driving me a little nuts lately. One word releases a thousand others. One idea a thousand others." He laughs. "The face that launched a thousand ships." He frowns. "The moving moon went up the sky, and no where did abide: softly she was going up, and a star or two beside." Pause. "Does the phonetic cabala always reach for myth and symbol in contradistinction to traditional etymology? And does all language, all image then reach ultimately for myth and symbol, and where does the signifier begin and the signified end? And if the Cathedrals are a language themselves, how is this to be understood in terms of the phonetic cabala?"

This brother's lost it for sure.

"But it's just a book, Samir."

"Well of course it's just a book on one level. But it's also more than that. It's got me so I almost feel like I'm having a religious crisis. It's a spiritual crisis at any event. And in the whirl of myths it brings up I'm re-questioning all my old esoteric beliefs. Questions I thought I resolved like ago. Like, do I believe in reincarnation? Eternal recurrence? Why does everything have the aspect of returning to itself again? Am I asleep? I feel like I'm stuck in a rut, like a broken record, and I don't know how to wake up from it, set the needle running smooth again. Wheel within a wheel. And then I think of Pinchback. I think of his new sight like a metaphor, and I'm the one struck blind."

"You sure you're asking yourself the right questions? Maybe that's not really all you envy that Pinchback has."

I regret saying it immediately after, because Samir's face turns gray, and his eyes narrow. He takes a long drink from his beer and stands up.

"Thanks for listening anyway. I think maybe I should go now."

"Jesus, Samir. Sit back down."

The doorbell rings just in time. Saved by the goddamn bell. Samir sits back down; his poker face returns, Socrates in the Clouds.

Pinchback's dressed, no kidding, as Ray Charles, which means he didn't really have to do much but put on a suit, and Janet's dressed as Dorothy Parker, with bangs bobbing down her forehead, and a cloche hat I've never seen before. It suits her well.

"No costume, Samir?" The first thing Janet says coming into the apartment.

"Don't tell me you have some alchemical reason against it."

"Don't start with me tonight Janet. I'm not in the mood."

Janet just smirks.

"Anyway, I finished your book. We should talk some more about it."

"Did you really? Well good. I picked up *Mystery of Cathedrals*, so I guess we both kept our part of the bargain."

What's this bargain? I want to ask, but I look at Maya, and suddenly decide against it.

Samir's face brightens, just the slightest. "Well that's great, Janet. What do you think?"

"I'll tell you once I've finished."

&

There's no reason to delay, so we head right out. We walk Broadway to Bushwick, ghosting the quiet clatter of the streets below the subway. When I look at Pinchback, it's obvious he's struggling in the dark. He depends almost entirely on his cane, tapping the pavement with a slurred rhythm. I keep hearing it as *Blues is My Middle Name,* and then I realize it's his cellphone ringing, that that's his ringtone. He's ignoring it. He keeps tumbling into distractions of light from the rare neon storefronts and the ever-dimmer shimmer of streetlights. By the time we make it to the Wreck Room he's a wreck.

Bushwick is an eerie neighborhood at night. It's just east of Williamsburg, and next on the list for quickly gentrifying neighborhoods in Brooklyn, but it still looks like all hell. There are 99-cent shops and abandoned plots alongside poorly maintained walk-ups where the new artists and creative classes live. And then there are the projects, which loom up every few blocks like large prisons. There are plenty of bars and clubs and even a few restaurants, but they're tucked away, hidden and hard to find unless you know where to go. The Wreck Room fits right in. It's a trashy looking storefront on Flushing Avenue that lives up to its name. There's a black awning hanging overhead with the address on it, and then the name of the bar appears as just a neon red sign in the window. When you first walk in, the bar is directly to the right, and the space feels narrow and claustrophobic, flooded with red lights and exposed brick walls, like a crime scene. As you move toward the back, the space opens up to a dance floor, a pool table that stays broken, and heavy graffiti all over the walls. It's an unapologetic dive bar, and it's generally loud, with a DJ spinning anything from techno to hip-hop.

As soon as we come through the door, someone grabs me by the hand, and shakes it enthusiastically.

"Yo man, where you been lately? Shit, Samir, you here too? Good to see you two. You gonna introduce us to your friends?"

It takes me a moment to recognize that it's Leroy, because he's dressed up as a bear, and he's wearing a full on bear suit. Leroy's a hefty brother though, and his deep drawly voice is distinctive, so it only takes a moment. "Good to see you too man."

It's crowded in the Wreck Room, basically packed to capacity, but we seem to know everyone. As soon as we pass Leroy, there's DJ Luck, sitting at the bar, and he swings around on his stool and gives me a hearty slap on the back. "What up, gangster? Good to see you. Good to see you too Samir. Damn, y'all haven't been around in a while? You dressed as someone?"

Luck is dressed as the Black James Bond, or so says the fake gold chain he's wearing over a slick black suit. He winks and shakes my hand, and then shakes Samir's hand, and then proceeds to introduce himself to the rest of the group as the Black James Bond. He seems particularly friendly to Maya, which I'm not too happy about, but just at that moment I feel a hand on my shoulder, and turn around to see DJ Halloween standing there with a wild smile, dressed in a skeleton suit.

"Damn if it hasn't been a while," he says. "The whole band is here to-night. I see you've already run into Luck."

Halloween and Luck are part of a hip-hop outfit called Quickthought. Luck, as it turns out, is the only black member of the group, which is just the opposite of what you'd expect from a hip-hop group, but it makes sense in Bushwick's backwards logic.

"Yeah, I was just introducing him to my friends here."

"Glad to meet you," says Halloween. "It's sort of my night tonight, you know, my namesake, so I feel especially honored by your presence."

"You spinning tonight?" asks Samir.

"Yeah, on and off. I think Power MC is up there spinning right now. I don't know. I lose track. You guys got drinks yet?"

It's as loud as it is packed, so we're all yelling at each other. The DJ is playing Nas, *Hip-Hop is Dead*, and it sounds like he's doing a mix of tracks off the album. I glance back to check on Pinchback and the girls. Maya is already weaving her way toward the bar, she seems to fit in with the crowd even more than I do, I guess she's that age. Janet is looking around with a bemused smile, like she's considering what she'll write up about it once she's safely back in the walls of the academy, and Pinchback is obviously overwhelmed. He's leaning against Janet, his sunglasses still on, but his face stretched out, so it's obvious his eyes are wide and rolling behind those shades, trying to make sense of the bedlam.

"No, not yet. Let's grab some," I say.

Samir and I dive into the bar area, and recognize the bartender right away. It's Felix. He's not with the band, but he's our regular bartender here. Normally in a bar this crowded you'd have to fight your way to the edge of the bar and wait forever to get a drink, but as soon as Felix spots us, he comes over.

"Damn straight, fellas. What can I do you for? You guys been hiding out or something?"

"In plain sight," says Samir. "You ever get yourself out of this bar?"

Felix is dressed as Felix the Cat, with a black suit, cat ears on his head, and wide-eyed glasses sitting lopsided on his nose.

"Not much, fellas. Not much. Someone's always thirsty in this town."

"Speaking of which," says Samir, "We've got a group with us." He looks back at Maya, Janet and Pinchback. "What's everyone having?"

Just as Felix is serving up my Brooklyn Lager, I brush arms with an old acquaintance of mine, Caleb, who, unfortunately, is dressed as himself. He's an artist, a draughtsman. A damn good draughtsman too, he can draw surrealist images from his dreams like he's looking right at them, and maybe he is. After all, he's a bona fide nutcase, paranoid to a fault, more coked up than James Brown on a bender, thin as a whisper in the woods, and just as spooky too.

"What's up Rudy," he says.

"Hey Caleb."

"You haven't been around in a while."

Samir sees him and turns away into the crowd. I envy the bastard.

"Yeah. I've been busy, I guess."

"What you working on these days?"

"Something about Robert Johnson."

"Huh," says Caleb. He waits a moment, and then gets right into it. "What's up with that anyway?"

"What's up with what?"

"You Black artists always piss and moan about Black issues instead of make art. That's why all the greats have been white guys. Robert Johnson already did his thing. Why can't you do yours?"

I always promise myself I won't engage this guy. It takes something like Zen enlightenment. Samir can't do it anymore, he just doesn't fuck with Caleb anymore, period point blank.

"It makes you all so predictable. For example, the election."

Here we go again. I drink my beer and try to do an ohm in my head.

"What about the election?"

"I already know who you're going to vote for." He says this proudly, like he's Sherlock Holmes, and has just deduced some important discovery.

"Yeah?"

"Obama, of course. The only reason you're voting for him is because he's Black."

"Well, that and I'm a registered Democrat," I say and regret it right away. Now I've engaged him, and it's on.

"Democrat, Republican." He snickers, takes a drink. "You still buy into all that shit? What – do you watch TV to get your news? Fox or CBS or CNN like all the other sheep? Read *The New York Times* and *The Washington Post*? "

This isn't a new conversation. He's about to tell me about his favorite news source: a website called Godlike Productions that's more or less dedicated to racism and conspiracy theories.

"I try to read a bunch of everything," I tell him. "Godlike Productions included. Just to keep up on the ravings of racist paranoiacs when you're not around to enlighten me."

Caleb's face turns red, then pale white, and it's hard to tell if he's elated or enraged by this challenge, probably a little of both. He takes another quick drink. "What the hell do you know? You might look at Godlike but you don't get it. You're already too brainwashed. Godlike is the only place where you can find the truth. Everything else has already been bought and sold. All the election, all of it is decided, and the news media is complicit, every mainstream newspaper, all owned by the same Jewish money, right? Hollywood too. So there's no getting away from the money. Right down to Obama," he continues, flushing back the rest of his drink, and flagging Felix for another. "If you don't see how he's been primed and prepped by these people, I don't know what to tell you. We're living a pageant of their design, and you're playing right into it. You're a smart enough guy, you ought to see it, but they've got you. And since you're just voting for Obama because he's Black, you're a part of the problem. That's how they get people like you."

People like me. Yep, he really said it.

"Nonsense," I tell him. "I'm part of the pageant. You just don't realize it. I'm with the program. If you think you can stop us, you're the one who's naïve. With what? Godlike Productions? We just let that website run so you folks look crazy. It's all part of our plan, Godlike included."

Caleb isn't expecting this. He squints a moment like he's contemplating it as a possibility.

"Hey Caleb, one whisky soda ready to go," says Felix.

As Caleb leans forward to grab it, I take the opportunity to make my escape. I disappear quick into the thick of the crowd, and run into Leroy the bear just as the DJ cuts between tracks.

Microphone check, micro-microphone check,
With Nas on the wax,
We catch wreck at the Wreck!
Microphone check, micro-microphone check,
Ya heard it once before,
Ya best protect ya neck!

"Saw you just got accosted by Caleb over there." Leroy grins. "What's he talking about tonight?"

"Same old bullshit. I don't know why anyone puts up with him."

"That racist shit he spouts doesn't piss these white boys off like it does us. Why would it?"

"Because. Just because."

"Man, let me school you a minute on blipster sociology, because you're thick in the mix of it."

"Blipster sociology? You're not calling me a blipster are you? I'm Black all right, but I'm sure no hipster."

"You're definitely a blipster," says Leroy, nodding solidly. "Even I can be a blipster sometimes. It's just what it is. Look around this room, man. Look at who we're hanging out with. A whole bar full of white hipsters, and you know everybody in here."

"Point taken. So break it down for me brother."

"Okay, here's how it works, and it just goes to prove you're a blipster because no blipster thinks he's a blipster, just like no hipster admits to being a hipster. There's at least one blipster in every group of white hipsters, you dig? And there can be more than one, but you know, it can't be like a whole crew of them, or they run the risk of creating a sub-clique in the clique. And brother let me tell you, that's a very dangerous situation for the white hipster."

"Why's that?" I smile in spite of myself.

"Because, brother. Any sub-clique in a larger clique is gonna start to deconstruct the biases of the larger clique. So it can't be too many brothers in a group of hipsters, or people like Caleb wouldn't be tolerated. And people like Caleb, as well as less extreme examples, which to be fair is most hipsters, keep the status quo in place. That's what hipsters do; they follow the status quo, which is fundamentally racist. But they don't want to admit that shit to themselves. That's why they so quick to be talking about a post-racial America now that Barack Obama just might win this election. A post-racial America, my ass. People love catchwords like that because they're only too happy to remain ignorant of the cultural inequalities set in place by their own sub-institutions, which after all, just mimic the larger American institutions so many of these hipsters purport to rebel against in the first place. But don't get me started."

"Sounds like you're already up and running."

"Man, I can prove it, just by giving you a scenario."

"Set it up."

"Okay. Here it is. A blipster goes out to Wreck one night by himself, just wants to get a drink on the quiet tip. When he's there, he runs into another blipster he doesn't know who's with a whole crew of white people. What happens ninety-nine percent of the time? The two look at each other suspiciously, like two women interested in the same man, and they never really talk to each other the whole night, they just chat up the white folk. And that, my brother, is self-hate. And self-hate is self destruction. And it's part guilt, part shame, part despair, and behind it all, just some bullshit wannabe pride. Like going to a bar and meeting your doppelgänger."

"Preach it, Leroy."

"Hmm. Go ahead and laugh, but you know deep down I'm kicking some real knowledge here."

"I don't know, Leroy. I guess. I still don't think I'm a blipster, though."

"What do you think you are then, brother?"

"Robert Johnson maybe," I say, though I'm not sure why.

"Man, go on with your bad self." Leroy laughs.

So I do just that.

Who's the baddest MC?
That question's pure philosophy,
I school you other rappers and
I brush them questions off of me!

I head deeper into the bar, actually feeling a little more like Robert Johnson with each step. I'm thinking about crazy Caleb and crazy Leroy, and I'm laughing to myself, and now here I am, coolly charming up the local folks at the Three Forks, while the owner's husband simmers on a slow boil at the side. Here he's spent his life chasing the blues, never quite managing to catch their slow sly roll, and so he opens up a jook where he gets to hear others bemoan the same sad fate, that elusive brown lady in a deep blue dress, always one octave above the last note.

I gave my baby all my blues for free.
I let my baby get the best of me.

Then one night here comes a man who not only caught the blues, but got the blues, the gal just can't quit him, no matter how much wrong he may do. Robert Johnson, face like an African mask, fingers like reclining Daddy Long Legs, a smile like a sneer, and a frown like the sweetest tears you've ever wept. And when he plays no one wants to hear nothing else. He turns that little guitar into a piano, plays its chords like an organ, and makes the shell thrum like drum and bass, the melody bouncing around like Bach on bop. The owner's wife, usually she just stays upstairs, has no truck with the loud, drunk clientele of the jook, but when Johnson comes around, she always gets down, lashes all aflutter, cheeks red and wide with admiration. A few drinks later, and she's brushing his cheek with her hand, and then the crowd gets to dancing, and maybe that green-faced owner sees it, maybe he's just imagining things up now, but there's Robert Johnson with his wife, her behind brushing up on his hips, *Baby do you do the Black Bottom?*

I've managed to make it to the dance floor, but I don't dance. I stand with my drink and do a half-hearted two-step, which is more just a rocking back and forth than a two-step, so I guess I'm not really doing anything at all. Nas is urging me to carry on tradition, and I'm thinking hard about Robert Johnson, looking around at all the pretty people in their peculiar costumes, and considering what Caleb said and considering what Leroy said, and suddenly something hits me, maybe it's just the beat, but the whole idea of doing theater the way people do theater seems stilted. This right here, Wreck Bar, this is theater. Life is a pageant, like Caleb says, even if he takes this idea in his own twisted direction. After all, what's more ridiculous than some auteur sitting in a room writing out a script to be acted out in some stuffy enclosed tomb? Theater should be alive, it should be lively, it should be life itself, and then there really isn't a need for playwrights at all. The actors are the playwrights, or the theater company as a unit is the playwright, and I sort of dizzily realize that this has to mean the end of my career as such, the death of the author. If I ever work in the theater again, it will just be as a director of spontaneous plays; beginning with Robert Johnson. This has been the problem I've been banging up against the whole time: I don't actually believe in the playwright anymore. The goddamn irony of it all. Suddenly I can't help it, I'm laughing like a man in love.

Janet appears next to me on the dance floor, looking somewhere between flabbergasted and amused. "You're in a good mood," she says.

"I've got it," I tell her. "I've figured out what's been going wrong with my plays all these years. Why I haven't been able to do the play I wanted to do."

"Now this I have to hear. You mean you just had a revelation, or what?"

"Something like that," I say.

"Right here in the bar? Tonight?"

"Yeah, more or less."

"Okay then. Let's have it."

"The playwright. That's the problem."

"I could have told you that already," Janet says.

"No, I'm serious. I think maybe the concept of a playwright is outdated, or at least not conducive to what I'm trying to do with the theater. I'd rather make a more living, vivid art. Something where the script is more or less improvised by the actors every night."

"I don't know. I don't know what that would even look like."

"Shit. Me neither."

"How do you write a play without writing a play?"

"Start a theater company."

"How will you do that?"

"Good question. I'd need actors. I guess I could just start right here." I suddenly look at Janet like she's answered a lifetime of questions for me. "Why not just recruit some of the guys? They got moxie all on their own. We don't need professional actors."

"I don't know. Go for it."

I hug Janet hard. "Jesus, I can't believe I never thought about that before. Thank you!"

"Hey! What did I do?"

"Half these guys are musicians anyway. Who better to use for a play about Robert Johnson than musicians? They'll understand the brother more than an actor would."

"I guess. I don't know. You do it, and I'll come see it and tell you what I think."

"Oh don't I know it. What do you think of this place anyway? Not really your style, huh?"

"No surprise you never took me out here while we were dating."

"Would you have had any desire to come?"

"Not really."

"So there you have it."

"But now I'm glad I did. It's a lot of fun. I mean it looks like a lot of fun. I'm not really, I don't know, I don't fit in so much. But your little Maya over there, she looks born for this place."

Janet points to where Maya and Pinchback are dancing a funny awkward dance on the floor. Maya is doing a full on two-step, while Pinchback sort of sways around unsteadily like a cattail in the wind.

"You bring her out here often?"

"I've gotten a little old for all this myself, honestly. It's been a while. Samir and I used to come out here all the time, not so much anymore. But I guess I miss it sometimes too."

"How's Samir doing anyway?" Janet asks. "Pinchback says he's been a little out of his element lately."

"Yeah. I guess you could say that." I look quickly at Janet, then quickly away. "I don't know why. He says it's the Fulcanelli he picked up, but I think something else is going on with him."

"Yeah, I looked at that Fulcanelli. It seems like just so much nonsense to me. Anyway, Pinchback says they're letting him go. First thing Monday morning."

"LIT?"

"Yeah."

"No shit."

"No shit."

"Well, that's a hard nut to swallow. Who's breaking it to him?"

"Milton himself."

"No kidding."

"Why? Why do you say it like that? What's Milton like?"

"Don't get me started. He's a real nutcase. Even for a scholar of esoterica like you. You really don't want to know."

"Oh, I think I'd like to meet the guy."

"Careful what you wish for, baby."

"Don't baby me."

I smile at Janet, wink even. "Can I at least have this dance, Ms. Parker?"

ELECTION DAY

"If a true embracing of the Feminine means the embracing of the Spiritual, then in Dorothy Parker we have the negative example, where the inability to embrace one leads to an inability to fully thrive within the other."
-FAITH, Dr. Janet Plummet, Chapter X, p. 302

The morning of November 4th.

I get up early to make it to the voting booths before work. I walk the couple blocks south into Bed-Stuy, where there's something like a party going down. It's a good day to be Black in Brooklyn, and just like in the Louis Armstrong song, I see folks shaking hands, saying how do you do? Obama posters everywhere. Usually voting is a demoralizing activity: you grudgingly cast a ballot for the lesser of two evils, and vow never to vote again. It's enough to make you sympathize with Caleb and his conspiracy theories. This time feels different, although with reservations. After all, who the hell becomes a professional politician anyway, what kind of a person? Probably just criminals too crooked to play crime straight, and if power corrupts, it's because power is only offered to and sought out by the corruptible.

The sun wanes a sour orange by late morning, and the day begins to sour with it. As soon as I walk back in the door of my apartment, my cell phone rings. It's an overseas number, and when I answer it, a deep voice says, *"As-salamu alaykum, my brother."*

"Come again?"

The line goes dead.

By the time I get on the subway, all the goodwill from the early morning is gone. All that's left are the poison dregs of politics. There are two groups of demonstrators on the train engaged in a semi-circle war dance. One group, dressed all in blue chants:

"Bail out of the bailout,
And bring a new jail out!
Tell Wall Street it's time
To pay for its crimes!"

The other group, dressed all in red, chants back:

"Libs and Dems and let's be Frank,
Bums will always blame a bank!"

Each group taunts the other as they move the length of the subway car, with onlookers mostly ignoring them, or in some cases - this is New York after all - joining one side or the other. It's like street theater, like what I've been thinking about, even. They stay with us for two stops, before disappearing into the next car, taking a few of the more vocal audience members with them.

Then, when I get to the office, there's a note waiting for me on my desk: *Please go upstairs and see Milton first thing when you get in.*

An eerie morning sun peers through the windows as I walk out and over to the stairwell. It lights the hall a flat orange as I pass various colleagues with brisk good mornings.

"You vote yet?"

They seem to float by me with their canes and sunglasses, one to the next, as if I'm now a trespasser, the invisible man. Up to the second floor, the marketing department, where the orange sun turns a dim gold and sweeps the floor with shadows; around the stairwell up to the third floor, the sighted floor of braille transcribers, where all the electric lights are on, flooding out the sun with fluorescent white. A couple of the transcribers nod gravely in my direction as I pass them, and I suddenly feel like a man climbing a scaffold to an execution.

The library begins on the fourth floor. The lights up here are always off unless someone sighted is browsing around. The entire floor is just one enormous room, with rows and rows of bookshelves stuffed with back catalogue braille books. It's dusty, musty and there are only four small windows, each on a separate wall, all obscured by the bookshelves, so the light is dim and dark blue, even at the height of day. I wind around the stacks of braille to the back, where a small staircase leads up to the fifth floor, the library of print books, a disastrously large attic room that immediately creeps under your skin. It's even darker than the fourth floor, with just two small windows, and it smells like rotting paper and mildew. Cobwebs everywhere. Books assorted haphazardly around the shelves in boxes, almost never entirely intact. I make my way to the back of this room, and here an even smaller staircase leads up to a heavy wooden door. This is Milton's office.

I knock and hear Milton's thick voice, muffled, "Please come in."

The office is sleepy with cigarette smoke and incense, a small room like a miniature Rosicrucian cathedral, with crosses and talismans of various esoteric sorts all over the desk and walls; bookshelves on all sides, and all the shelves overstuffed with volumes of braille. Milton is sitting like a priest in the midst of all this, with a close-cropped haircut and wide staring eyes in a very dark room, made blue by the wisps of smoke still ghosting the lone closed window in the corner.

"Come in," he says again. "It's good to see you."

I frown at the expression and take a seat opposite him at his desk. How does he even know it's me? I've only met the guy once or twice.

"I guess we have a lot to discuss," he says after I sit down. "And I've wanted to speak with you ever since I came across this remarkable book you discovered." He runs his fingers over a braille book lying on his desk. "*Black Buildings*. I've been reading this volume over and over again ever since we printed it. Pinchback read some of it to me before, but I find it's even more remarkable in braille."

"Pinchback?" It's the first chance I have to speak, but Milton doesn't let me continue.

"He's come a long way in just a little while, don't you think? Sometimes I even envy him, but ultimately I suspect the world of sight is a distracting illusion, and sometimes I wonder, rather it surprises me, how hastily he agreed to give up the gift of blindness. But that's another story. Tell me, what did you find in this poetry remarkable enough to lead you on your search for the poet? I assume she is also blind, as it would be difficult for a sighted person to grasp many of the ideas in here, so I'm impressed by your," he frowns, "literary instincts."

"Maya? Blind? On no, I don't think so," I say, fumbling foolishly.

"Oh, I suspect she is," says Milton. "Or has more than just a passing familiarity with the condition. Right from the opening lines of the first verse – but it doesn't matter really, does it? If not, she is just a first-rate genius. After all, we don't ask how Shakespeare wrote so eloquently about nobility, so I have to commend you on your discovery. But this is Pinchback's project now, and we're not really here to discuss Maya, are we?"

"It is? We're not?"

"It's Samir," Milton says slowly, lighting a cigarette, "that I wanted to speak to you about. That's really what's been troubling me lately. What do you know about his recent crack-up?"

I frown. "I don't know if I'd call it a crack-up. He's just going through a difficult time right now." I force a smile, hoping Milton might hear it in my voice. "Something about Fulcanelli. A book he's been reading. It has him doing some serious spiritual questioning, as I understand things."

Milton frowns at my smile. He coughs, knocks ash from his cigarette, and continues. "Of course. Fulcanelli. It comes as no surprise that Samir doesn't know what to make of his work, and here lies my real concern. I suspect Samir has never been terribly serious about the work he's doing here. One day he's talking about politics, the next day it's philosophy. Today he's reading Fulcanelli for guidance; tomorrow it's Karl Marx. In short, Samir strikes me as someone who is deeply asleep."

"Oh." It's hard to know how to respond to something like that. "I'm not sure how any of this concerns me, with all due respect."

"And you, being closest to him – I wondered what your take on the whole thing would be. I am of the opinion that Samir slept his way willfully into his own dismissal." Milton takes a long drag of his cigarette, his eyes like they're focused directly on me. "And frankly, I'm worried you've been on the same path."

"I beg your pardon?"

"It goes back and forth with you. One week you're chatting half the day away in Samir's office, accomplishing nothing. Then the next week you bring us something as remarkable as *Black Buildings*. But I've already given this considerable thought. Perhaps you see yourself as a political man – a man of action, so to speak. Of course, a man of action must act. Not so much talk, but act. For example, take LIT. I built this company myself. I saw the need for esoteric texts in braille, and I knew there would be others like myself, interested in reading these texts as well. So what did I do? Did I just discuss it in my friend's office all day, talking myself blue in the face? No, I don't suppose I did. Rather, I built it. Look Rudy, I commend you on your discovery of *Black Buildings*. But I think you feel this job is nothing more to you than common employment."

Milton's gaze on me seems to sharpen. "I understand that you also fancy yourself a playwright. I attended your last performance. *Black Prometheus*. I suppose I've had my eye –" and here Milton smiles a dreadfully sardonic smile – "on you ever since. It wasn't such a good play, that *Black Prometheus*, was it? Rather, something of a disaster."

I feel my pulse rise and the air in my chest constrict, saliva running sweet and thick through the sides of my mouth. How did I miss the bastard at the Brick? I attended most of the shows. I think back over the last several months, since the time Milton might have seen *Black Prometheus* and try to picture myself in my everyday routine at work as others might have seen me who had seen the play. My head grows hot and light with the effort.

I stand up. "With all due respect. That's unacceptable." I frown, suddenly finding myself standing, a silly overreaction, and then I feel like I'm in a position where I have to play a role, do something dramatic. "I'm afraid we're finished here, Milton. You will have my resignation by the end of the week. I'll send it in by mail."

"Yes, of course," says Milton, moving his fingers to his book, as if this is the conclusion he's been working towards all along. "I wish you the best in your career. I look forward to seeing your next production."

And then back down the stairs, through the descending floors of libraries, past the sighted and the blind and out into the morning sun. It's a cold day, cold and bright, the sky cerulean, the clouds thick and white with options. All at once I feel a tremendous sense of freedom descend over me, and I walk the familiar path through Whitman Park like the dead resurrected. I consider my options, and they seem infinite. Why go home? Why not stop somewhere for a morning drink? There's nothing to prevent me. Can it really be so simple as that? You wake up and do whatever the hell you want?

I take the subway to the West Village and walk east. I walk all the way to Tompkins Square Park, and end up at Café Pick Me Up, drinking a glass of red wine and watching the groups of canvassers pass, mostly with those large red and blue Shepard Fairey Obama *Hope* posters, and for a moment I try to capture this terrific sensation of newness for a newer freer life for myself, for a new president, for the first Black president. The sun leans through the wide windows of the café in a kaleidoscope of colorful shadows from the trees in the park across the street, from the wooden beams of the café, from the posters purpling in the sun. I think about Milton again, up there in that dark smoky attic room of his, sunk in his gloomy blind certainties. The poor bastard. He's one to talk about deeply asleep. And then that comment about my work. Well, I feel wide-awake. There are arias in the daylight when I leave the café three glasses of wine later.

I'm only home what maybe an hour before I first hear it. The voice is like a low curse, a West Indian brogue.

"Dead Nigga walking!"

At first it doesn't register, it seems so far away, like something on the radio, but a moment later something clicks, and cold hives crawl my arms and neck. Light comes sallow gold through the windows, the failing day. The strange voice like an incantation, pacing the walls and floors around where I stand frozen in place, squinting in the sun. I walk warily towards the window and peer out into the quiet street below. No one there, just the light reflecting the inverted white Jinx on the asphalt. Maybe it really was just the radio, a misheard exclamation amidst the hullaballoo of election talk. I turn the volume down and peer out the window again. A chilly breeze seems to carry the words through the wind and into the apartment, a chilling refrain that repeats itself in a looping wisp of lisping whispers.

Maybe it's time for another glass of wine.

I pop a bottle, pour a glass and settle in front of the television.

"Dead Nigga drinking!"

Or watching TV, after all. But no mistake this time, the voice is as certain as death. I stand up and stride over to the window, straining and squinting at the streaming shadows. I venture a timid – "Hello?" – and then feel ridiculous. I finish my glass of wine and stand in place, looking at the street, the walls, the floor, the television, feeling like I'm being watched like a lab rat.

"Dead bwoy!"

This time I don't even move. I stand like a cornered victim. I stand and listen, listen and stand until the apartment seems to open and expand from within my head, a giant thrumming amplifier, radiating with a synesthesia of sunshine, terror and incantation. I guess I'm frozen in that position for a while, because by the time I pour my next glass of wine, amber arrows of quickly declining daylight are lancing the room.

As soon as I pour the glass, there he is again:

"Dead bwoy gon die!"

I finish the wine in one gulp, throw on my coat and escape the apartment. Outside the street is still, quiet, and calm. Not a person in sight. I walk up and down the block with the courage of the quick fresh wine, where late afternoon shifts lazy into early evening, the garage next door already closed for the day, the school across the street blinking sleepy in the last vestiges of sunlight. I look up at my own windows. They look like the windows of a cell. No way I'm going back there anytime soon. I head up Lorimer and turn left on Metropolitan towards Bedford. Hang out with the hipsters. Better to be a blipster than a dead bwoy. I walk west past Bedford and end up at a bar on Berry. Over a Goose Island my nerves begin to relax. It's late enough now that the workday's ending and crowds of young men and women begin to appear for Election Day Happy Hour. I'm beginning to feel self-consciously alone, so I call Maya. She doesn't pick up, so I call Samir.

"What's up?"

"Having a drink on Berry. Care to join? I got some news about LIT."

"Like I give a good goddamn about that place anymore."

"Trust me. This is worth it."

By the time he arrives, the incident at the apartment feels more dream-like than real, there's no way to describe it to someone else without sounding delusional at best. So I brush it off, tell myself what someone else would have told me anyway – that it's just the anxiety of quitting my job, the excitement of the election, too much alcohol, lack of sleep, so on and so forth. Instead we talk about my meeting with Milton.

Samir takes the news bittersweet. "Deeply asleep, eh? That lunatic is one to talk. But I'm proud of you. You did the right thing, walking out on him like that. What's your plan now? I applied for unemployment, but you won't have that option, quitting and all. You know, Obama's talking about extending it if he's elected. Unemployment insurance. We'll see what happens. Maybe being fired was the best thing that ever happened to me, and I ought to go buy old Milton a drink, right before socking him one, that is."

We laugh a lot. It feels good to laugh, but Samir's right.

"Hell, I'll figure it out. Speaking of the election, what say you we head up to Times Square, and see if we can't catch it up there? "

"Sounds like a plan."

Maya calls me back on our way to the subway. "Hey stranger!" she says. "Did I miss your call earlier? Where are you? "

"In Brooklyn. With Samir. What're you up to?"

"Having pre-election drinks. Janet and Pinchback are already here. We're making highballs. It's all very classy. Come by. And what's this I hear about you quitting your job? Pinchback told me you just up and walked out this morning."

"Oh Christ. He already knows? Anyway, it had to be done. We'll discuss it when I get there."

&

"Milton says you overreacted," Pinchback tells me once we're at Maya's apartment. "Knowing Milton, he probably goaded you into it."

"Oh."

"But maybe it's the best thing anyway. For everyone but me, that is. Good for the company balance sheets and good for your own personal development, but since I'm taking on both your and Samir's responsibilities now, not so good for me." He stares listlessly at the talking heads on the television for a while. "Milton seems to think my new sight makes me more valuable than ever, but I'm not sure and besides, I feel he respects me less for it."

Pinchback's sour, no doubt about it, but no one's sure why.

"He's been like this today," says Janet. "I think it's just the election."

"The election my ass," says Pinchback. "There's nothing new under the sun about this election."

"Maybe we should just get going," says Maya. "It's electric out there. I bet that cheers you up, huh Pinchback?"

Maya's wrong. It only gets worse. Walking down Broadway towards Times Square he suddenly delivers what can only be called a soliloquy. He starts it as a mumble, but it grows and stumbles into a rolling swing, like something rehearsed:

"I've had my sight for a little more than a month now," he says, "and it never ceases to amaze me. I think about the equations that disclose the nature of all this technology, so familiar, and suddenly, seeing their fruits, completely foreign. The mathematical geometry of the buildings, the ghastly aesthetics cast by the city lights as they blink on in the evening and out in the morning. I've seen movies, watched highways fly by in landscape and sky, heard the peculiar poetry and hum of the streetlights above, like electric comets obscuring the stars. Even now, walking through Times Square, between twilight and evening, amid neon lights and signs and shops that spin mirrored back by black glass skyscrapers, like déjà vu – I've seen jazz and blues clubs uptown and down, where the blue and pale white lights dissolve in the music, alchemizing aura, sound and mood into meaning. I've seen dance clubs in the Meatpacking District, the Lobachevskian movement of lasers spreading, lifting, descending without warning, reclining in curved angles against the walls, and even Central Park at dawn, with the sun peering through patches of trees on the grass, speckled, like a day drizzled in sunshine – the faces of people I love, have touched, and thought, through the form of their features, that I knew.

"But at the end of the day I find everyone and everything repulsive to my sight. It's all a revolting, sterile, pathetic, frantic carnival of distraction against the gently moving music of death you feel when you run your fingers over the features of a face. Daytimes are dreadful in their persistent insistence on the garish glare of hysterical objects, and nighttimes awful as they climb into shadows and specters, leering with all their barren foppishness behind the fallen curtain of night. Worst of all, I realize now the science I always loved, with all its inventive genius, is really just a slave to this demonic dream of the sighted, and I wonder if I love anything about living at all. I miss the music of the deathmask, fingers on a face, the peaceful contemplation of abstraction."

There's no way to respond to Pinchback's gloomy soliloquy, so no one does. Janet just takes his arm and leans in close to him. For my own part, I look around at all the lights and the thickening crowds as we walk down Broadway, and I try to see the world the way Pinchback sees it.

Just as we hit 50th Street Samir breaks the silence.

"I feel you brother. I've been going through it myself lately. Meditation has been helping. Though you may not realize it, these are also political concerns of yours, as much as spiritual or aesthetic, and really, the three can't be separated, and that's the reason we're here right now."

Times Square election night is one tremendous block party, the type of set every playwright fantasizes about recreating on stage, with a democratic spirit stirring the atmosphere, every actor as important as the next, and the whole set alive with frenetic, lusty, emotionally charged energy. The television at 42nd Street flashes pictures of the states along with the talking heads, floating digital pundits breathlessly make predictions. An open air sporting event, the map of the United States is like the playing field of a giant board game. Vendors crush through the crowds selling Obama propaganda paraphernalia, there's public drinking everywhere and everywhere overlooked, throngs washing out of bars, chanting, "*Yes, we can!*" and as each new state is called, a cry goes up, the crowd unanimous in their cheers.

Just before midnight, the election is called in Obama's favor.

A wild hush ripples through the crowd, and then all at once everyone is cheering and shouting and drinking and kissing, and the chanting becomes a low roar, "*Yes, we can! Yes, we can!*" Talk about Goosebumps. I turn and kiss Maya, Janet kisses Pinchback, Samir wipes his face, wet with tears and sweat, and every couple looks like that iconic picture of the soldier and the lady on Armistice Day. The talking heads above the mania look flustered with joy and relief before fading into postmodern pictures of ourselves watching ourselves watch ourselves on the screens in Times Square, then off to Chicago, where the party looks wild enough to rival New York. I stare at the screen, listening to cars honking up and down Broadway and 7th Avenue, disbelieving this is actually happening, that I am here in Times Square to witness it, ecstatic strangers thrumming through the crowd hugging everyone around, and before long I'm right there with them, leaning into the digital glow of the screen, hollering "*Obama! Obama! Yes, we can! Yes we can! Obama! Obama! Yes we did! Yes, we did!*" Someone passes me a joint, which I pull on and pass to the person next to me. So this at last is community. Street theater, where everyone is an equal participant, we ourselves are the show, the talking heads the audience, all hegemonic prescriptive cultural orders reversed. I remember Pinchback's soliloquy, think of Samir's response, and turn to see how Pinchback's doing in all of this cacophony of sensory overload. He takes my hand, heavy and warm in his own, and shakes it hard. Only it isn't Pinchback's hand. I turn toward Samir, and someone else shakes my hand, turn to Maya, and lean into the crush of her hug, realizing that none of them are anywhere near me anymore, and I'm out here in the crowd, in the biggest community I've ever known, but suddenly completely alone.

ACTION & REACTION

"In Anais Nin, female sexuality and the spiritual are fully fused and inhabited with magic phrases that are, to use her own words, 'beyond the laws of gravity, chaos and the sounds of invisible accidents'."
-FAITH, Dr. Janet Plummet, Chapter XIV, p. 541

They say every action is reaction. The next morning I'm halfway through my morning rituals when I realize I have nowhere to go. And then the previous day comes back to me like a revelation. The resignation, the election, losing everyone in Times Square, cellphone calls with no answer, drinking in a bar alone on the far west side of Midtown Manhattan somewhere, and the last dark hours taking the train home, which come back a little murkier than the rest.

I sit down, still half-dressed, and turn on the television. Excited pundits are proclaiming Barack Obama the 44th president of the United States and heralding a post-racial America. Well, Leroy, there you have it. I check my phone; still no calls or messages from Maya, Samir, Pinchback or anyone else for that matter. It's still too early to start making calls, so I make coffee instead, and nurse it, along with the hangover I feel rising with the day.

The best thing to do, hangover or not, is to get to work on *Robert Johnson*. The manuscript is sitting on my table, well into the fourth act, but now I have an entirely different approach for it, one less authorial and more democratic in spirit. I read the thing over again, and frown my way through its stilted scenes, the turgid language, the wooden architecture. My head spins and throbs the whole way through. I'm in the mood to just demolish the piece, like that might demolish my hangover.

I work through my text, stripping the script down to just stage directions, and then I start on an invitation to the show. By early evening I have a completely revised draft, along with a flyer that simply says, *The Last Days of Robert Johnson*. The thing to do now is to get actors.

A lot of the artists and musicians I know here in Brooklyn live as a collective in an art space out in Bushwick. The space is called Ampersand, and it hosts art shows and hip-hop concerts, with the occasional rock or jazz concert thrown in for good measure. They also throw parties, show films and host other out of the way underground activities. I'm not so much interested in using Ampersand as a theater space, though that would work too. Instead I'm thinking of maybe using it as a base of operations, getting the musicians and artists to be actors, and launching a street theater show that troupes the streets of Brooklyn from there. So I head out in the chilly twilight, east down Broadway, my play and invitation in tow, to pitch the idea to them.

I don't want to dwell on the specs too long, but let me lay Ampersand out for you a minute. It occupies an entire walk-up on a side street near the Morgan L. It's only marked by a dim blue neon ampersand above the door. Inside a long staircase leads up to the main art space itself. The bar is the first thing you run into, and to the left there's a large room with a koilon surrounding a stage. Beyond the bar a long hallway leads past dozens of rooms tucked away to the right behind a couple heavy Turkish tapestries. The work of various underground artists hang on the hallway wall to the left, most of which can be purchased, if you're in the market to buy art, but no one in Bushwick is in the market to buy art. The hallway leads to stairs leading to the roof, and also to a back room, which is a miniature art gallery. The roof is a terrace bar, with patio chairs, tables lit with water candles and another makeshift bar. A third bar is out back, beyond the back room, in a beer garden where people like to congregate in nice weather. Except for the private bedrooms, the entire venue is public space, and any time you come by, you're bound to find a couple people hanging out, shooting the breeze and having a drink.

There's a pretty good crowd and a celebratory atmosphere in the air when I get there. I'm never sure who's actually living there at any given time- the place has a pretty high turnover – but Luck lives there and has for a while. He greets me as soon as I come up the stairs.

"What up Rudy? Where you been? What'd you do election night?"

"I was out by Times Square. Long night."

"Get yourself a drink. Hair of the dog that shit."

"Don't mind if I do."

"We're still celebrating, man," says Luck. "Everyone's here."

"Samir?" I ask.

"Naw, heard no parts of the brother. Why, what's up with Samir?"

"I lost those guys last night. Was with that crew that came through Wreck the other night."

"You best off losing those fools, Samir excluded. And what was up with your girl, man?"

"What do you mean what was up with my girl?"

"I dunno, brother. You sure she's good news?"

"Good news? What are you, an evangelist? "

"Alright man. I'm just looking out."

"Yeah, well. So what'd you do?"

"I was here. We had the election up on the projector in the theater room."

"You still drinking from last night?"

"More or less. I slept a spell."

"Damn, brother."

"This is once in a lifetime, man."

"You think things are gonna change?"

"Ain't a damn thing gonna change."

We laugh.

"Check it out, though. I'm working on this new play, maybe I told you about it the other night. It's called *The Last Days of Robert Johnson* and I need actors for it."

"And?"

"You be interested in being in a play?"

"Not really, brother. Learning lines and all that shit. Not for me."

"There's no lines to learn. You just say whatever you think you should say. You can even change it up from show to show. Here take a look."

I give him a copy of the script. He looks it over, and then looks at me like I'm running a three-card Monte on him.

"You call this a play? This is like a thought. This ain't a play."

"It's just what happens. We'll make up the play as we go. And change it as we go, too. I don't want real actors. I want real people."

"Well, whatever. Do I get paid?"

"Yeah, you get paid. You get the honor of working with the most exciting theater company in the city as payment."

"Hm."

"Well, think it over. I want to get Alan on board with this, too."

"You gonna need more brothers if you want to do a play this Black. I mean, I know you're not so into all that, being the post-racial blipster you are."

"Man, you best watch it."

Luck laughs, and I laugh too, in spite of myself. "Yeah. Well. I was thinking of grabbing Leroy, maybe. And a couple of the other cats that come through here."

"I'll toss the idea around to some people," says Luck. "If we can just do it and have fun with it maybe. But, you know. Brothers like to get paid."

"Well, I'll pay for the beer we drink. Can we rehearse it here?"

"If I'm gonna be involved, we best rehearse it here. I'm not going out to Williamsburg or something every time you get the urge to try something out."

"Well, good."

"We performing it here, too?"

"Don't know. I was thinking of making it street theater."

"Hm."

"We'll see, okay. All that still has to be decided."

"Well how many of these outlines you got? Leave a couple with me, and I'll see what I can do. What you drinking anyway?"

I stay a while. At some point in the evening Leroy comes through, and we grab Alan, he's been there all day already. After a couple drinks we're all loosed up, so we put on an impromptu show right there on the stage. Alan plays the blues on an acoustic guitar while Luck beat-boxes. I accompany with mash-up lyrics from Robert Johnson and Maya Vicca.

The woman I love,
Took from my best friend,
Some joker got Lucky
Stole her back again,

You best come
In my kitchen
It's gonna be raining outdoors.

And New York City,
My baby lies all the time,
I stood on the stairs
And drank my wine.

You best come
In my kitchen
It's gonna be raining outdoors

Enter Leroy, who plays Sonny Boy Williamson opposite my Robert Johnson. We go back and forth serving each other the Dozens like a couple old friends at the bar, and occasionally Alan and Luck jump in with a freestyle. A couple of the other Quickthought cats get in on it and drop beats, from trad to be-bop to hip-hop, so the whole thing swings like Duke meets Pac.

&

By the time I got back home I feel spiritually uplifted, like I've finally accomplished something, found the direction of my work, heard my own voice through all the cacophony of other voices from classical literature crowding up my cranium, and that voice was already a collection of voices, a contemporary Greek chorus scatting a fly blues to b-boy beat.

I continue the celebration by opening another bottle of wine. It's just past eleven, and the moon is looming white and ponderous outside the window lighting Throop Street an eerie incandescent orange white, like a theater stage just before a show.

As I'm pouring my second glass, *Bugging Out* by Tribe bringing up the bass, the moon dipping gray behind a horizon of clouds that cast a cool shadow against the wall -

"Dead Nigga walking!"

I spill some of the wine, and turn around quick. Under the pale light of the kitchen the three black windows blink back at me blank. The moon seems to wink behind the clouds, and I hear the dull motor of a car pass by below. Now the stage shifts from the street to my studio, lights up on me alone in my kitchen, fingers trembling around the stem of a glass.

I step forward in the suddenly artificial air. I almost forgot about this guy, what with the events of the last day and a half, but now everything comes back fresh familiar, all the terror transforming the apartment suddenly into a haunted space, the feeling of being under observation, the easy vulnerability. I walk up to the windows and look out onto the pale street. It's empty as far as I can tell.

"Dead Bwoy!"

That heavy West Indian accent thrums through the apartment like a spell, seems to attach itself to the walls again. I consider pulling down the blinds, then reconsider. A first floor window is easy to climb into in this city. I've used the fire escape to break into my apartment any number of times. If someone really is out there gunning for me, I won't be able to see him coming with the blinds drawn. Maybe that's even what the bastard's waiting for, counting on my doing. But why me? Couldn't he be after someone else? Am I just paranoid? I turn back from the window, finish my wine quick, pour another, turn up the radio and try to ignore him. Maybe I'm just hearing things.

"Batibwoy nigga, dead bwoy gon die!"

And me being the only black man in the building. I get up from the table, swallowing wine like water, running through questions, trying to make sense of this scene I've found myself unwillingly cast in. Fight or flight feelings flooding through me from one moment to the next. I disappear into the bathroom just to get offstage for a breath of air. The bathroom feels like a prison cell. I strain to hear sounds of voices, doors being jimmied, windows broken or cranked open. No, the bathroom's no better.

Back onstage, I grab the bottle of wine from the kitchen, and drink from it direct. I sit down in front of the television, flipping channels, looking from the screen to the window moment to moment.

"Dead nigga drinking!"

Well, no sleep tonight, that's for sure. I get up and pace for a few minutes, turn the television off, turn it on again, and then turn it back off. I grab my cellphone and slip behind the bed, feeling oddly secure, finally out of sight. I dial Maya, I still haven't heard from her, not since election night. No response, but then I didn't really expect one. So I sit there behind the bed like a man in the trenches, considering my options, bottle of wine in one hand, cellphone in the other. Where to go? What to do? I definitely don't want to work my way back through Bushwick to Ampersand, and what would I say to them anyway? Maya's place maybe, as awkward as that might be, but then given the circumstances.

I finish the bottle and clamber unsteady back into the light. I throw a few items in my shoulder bag, grab the empty wine bottle by the neck and slip out the door. The light is on the whole time, so he'll know I'm coming, on the way down. If it comes down to it on the street, I guess I'm ready. I flex my bottle arm, creep down the stairs and then out the front door. I duck down by the door in the overhead arch, crouched in shadows. Throop Street looks quiet. I can't see anyone at all. No one waiting around the corner of the arch, so I slip out onto the sidewalk and begin walking fast, looking every direction, the bottle hanging low by my side. Around the corner, then up to Broadway, still not a person in sight. I dash across the street toward Lindsay Square, right up to the subway entrance. I climb the stairs to the station two steps at a time, and emerge on the platform unchallenged. Still no one around. I walk to the middle of the platform, where I'll be able to see anyone who's coming from either side, and wait for the train for what feels like a very long time.

The train rolls in years later. Onboard the lights are too bright, and the seats are too cold, the air is too chilly, too thin, I can feel the perspiration on my forehead like new rain. The train is almost empty. A couple hipsters stand by the door talking about Dante and Hart Crane. I breathe a little easier. There's litter all over the floors and seats, a crushed up water bottle rolling from one end of the subway car to the other. I stuff the empty wine bottle in my bag, and watch the industrial streets of Williamsburg shuttle by as we speed westward toward Manhattan. The bridge. Looking at the glittering lights of Manhattan through the train windows feels like a small salvation. By the time I'm on the other side of the East River, all my terror is gone, but it's been replaced by a muted confusion. It almost would have been better if someone had confronted me outside my building. As things stand, none of it makes any sense. I begin doubting everything again, whether anything happened at all. Am I losing my mind? By the time I step out onto the wide avenues, broad buildings and moneyed apartments sitting at the intersection at 96th and Broadway, Brooklyn feels like a farce.

It's about a ten-minute walk to Maya's building. I get there just there as a couple kids are coming home, and I slip in behind them. They give me a queer, confused look, full of all sorts of meaning and history, you get used to it, you know, an unfamiliar Black man entering the building, you get these looks, but they're visibly drunk, and I can see the consternation of conflicting impulses cross their faces, like should they question my presence there, or just let a Brother in and demonstrate they're down, hip, non-racist cats. I guess they decide on the latter, because they just nod a knowing nod and hold the door. I take the stairs to the fourth floor, and walk the hallway to Maya's door. For a while I just stand there looking at it, at the Rosicrucian cross she has hanging from it, and consider how pissed off she'll be. But it doesn't matter. I knock hard, then ring the bell.

That hallway, man. I swear I can still hear those light bulbs humming today. Behind Maya's door I hear shuffling, then notice the distinct smell of lavender and marijuana. I knock again. Then I hear whispers. The hall seems to dip and turn and moan in the muffled sound, like my whole head is overflowing with every sound I've ever heard, muted and confused. But more time passes, and Maya doesn't answer the door. I stand there not knowing what to do; going back home is clearly no option. I knock a third time, and this time the sound of the knocker stills everything else. The whispers, the shuffling, the light bulbs all go quiet, all at once. Knocking again feels absurd. I take out my phone and call her instead. Just beyond the door I hear her cellphone ring. I take my own phone from my ear just to be sure I'm not hearing a double echo inside my head. No, it's her phone ringing all right, and she's letting it go to voicemail. Between the whispers, shuffling, ringing phone, the layer of lavender lurking just beyond her door, I know she's home. But why is she ignoring me?

At this point the sequence of my memories gets somewhat confused, as my mind becomes nothing but a torrent of dark thoughts and paranoid fantasies. Do I suspect something right away, or do the suspicions, that particular paranoia, come later? When presented with an overflow of enigmatic data, the mind tends to loop itself into its darkest suspicions; betrayals you wouldn't have even thought possible take the active architecture of conspiracy. If Maya is awake, ignoring me even as I stand right outside her door, well why? I call Samir, and get no answer. I call him again, and maybe even a third time. He doesn't pick up. I don't know what else to do, so I call Pinchback next. And sure enough, there it is, *Blues Is My Middle Name*, ringing away, right behind Maya's door.

RE-EVALUATING THE SUBTEXT

"Sylvia Plath's 'Ariel' is a feminist reworking of the Minor Arcana of the Tarot. The book itself is Plath's summoning of her own personal spirit of the elements, her own Ariel, to guide her through a hermetic journey."
          -FAITH, Dr. Janet Plummet, Chapter III, p. 102

As legend has it, Robert Johnson learned to play guitar from an obscure old bluesman named Ike Zimmerman. They'd sit side by side on a tombstone in a cemetery down in Mississippi. Either that, or he learned it from the Devil himself down at the Crossroads. Whichever legend you prefer, they're both fables, and if you give up the Faustian element with the graveyard story, you gain that great metaphor of learning your art by confronting death. Besides, a cemetery is very much like a Crossroads of the soul.

Look, these lectures have no thesis. Consider them anti-lectures. Dr. Plummet asked me to come here and talk to y'all a little about the theater, and I decided I'd tell y'all a story instead. So there you have it.

But I do like to think about Johnson disappearing. They say when Johnson started out he couldn't play a lick, sounded about as hoarse as a hell-bound hound. Then he disappears down south somewhere, and comes back a visionary. I guess that's the way with American artists. Walt Whitman, Robert Johnson, Charlie Parker, our three greatest poets, all share that same story. Maybe American visionaries have to visit those Crossroads of the soul; they have to be buried and reborn. Everyone knows that line by Fitzgerald – there are no second acts in an American life. Well, maybe there aren't. But like in Goethe's Faust, I'd say there can be a second part, where you look right into the heart of the failures in your own life, and extract from them some essence of modernity's failures as a metaphor, and return to the world of the living again visionary and transformed. It's a comforting thought at least.

&

Anyway there I am, standing in front of Maya's door, listening to Pinchback's phone ringing, and my mind runs through all sorts of disasters. I pace up and down the hallway, my mind making vaster and vaster landscapes of tragedy. I feel dead already. What does it matter if I go home and am duly murdered, who cares? A backlogue of bad plays as legacy, and the curse of Robert Johnson to finally finish me off. I stride up to the door and back away from it, emotions ranging from rage to despair. I call Pinchback's number again, just to be sure of what I'd heard, but now the call goes directly to voicemail. I try Maya again with the same result. I pace the hallway one more time, and then realize, miserably, that they may very well be watching me through the peephole. The feeling of being trapped in a small space under observation, that sick boil in the bottom of my stomach turns everything mauve. I feel trapped in the light again, just like back in my apartment, the hallway suddenly too stifling and too stuffy. I pace to the end of the hall, turn into the stairwell, and go down and out of the building.

The cold night air is sobering. Where to go now? I look up and down Columbus, start walking one way, then the next, eventually settling on west towards Broadway. Maybe I call her automatically – I don't know, I guess you can guess – I call Janet. The phone rings and rings and goes to voicemail. I call her again. When she picks up the phone, she sounds pissed in that dry, sleepy, angry way she has.

"This better be good. "

"Oh, it's anything but good, Janet, it's an emergency. I need to crash on your couch tonight. Besides. We'd better talk. "

I can hear her wrinkle her nose and frown. "Call me in the morning, okay? Pinchback's here. Let us sleep, huh?"

That takes me by surprise, but only for a moment. "Listen, Janet. Why are you lying to me? I told you this is an emergency. Pinchback isn't there, I know he isn't. I know where he is, and he is definitely not with you. Like I said, we'd better talk."

Suddenly her voice isn't so sleepy anymore. "Where are you now?"

"I'm in the City," I say, not wanting to give too much away too soon. "But I can be there right away. I'll take a cab."

Half an hour later I'm at Janet's Park Slope apartment. Her frown has affixed itself to her face. She squints disapprovingly as she lets me in, and then she folds herself into the sofa, regarding me suspiciously. She hasn't changed out of her pajamas, and the soft loose material settles around her sumptuously, like an invitation. I sit down carefully next to her.

"Where's Pinchback?" she demands right away.

I cough. "He's with Maya."

The admission is more humiliating than I expected. Having said it, I stand up again.

"I wouldn't have even known myself," I continue quickly, catching the skeptical lines of sadness starting to worry her face. "Only I was run out of my own apartment. Someone's been shouting death threats at my window. Jesus, this is a long story."

Janet's crying now. "What the hell is going on already?"

So I sit down next to her again and start with Election Day.

"Why didn't you say something about this guy then?" Janet interrupts me right away.

"It was Election Day. It didn't seem real to me then, nothing did that day, and it hardly even seems real now, now that I'm away from there, now that I'm here. But then I know I'll go back to that apartment, and he'll be right there waiting on me, that voice, and even if he isn't, that haunted hunted feeling isn't going anywhere now. But let me finish."

She doesn't interrupt again, she listens, and knowing Janet, she's probably listening for something else between or beneath the words, but she crosses her arms, and folds her legs, leans forward and she listens. Once I'm done, she stands up right away and gets her phone.

"I'm calling Pinchback."

She looks down at me sitting on the couch while she lets it ring. A few moments pass, and the worry lines on her face deepen.

"It's Janet, call me when you get this. It's important."

She puts the phone down, still frowning. "Voicemail." She turns around, and trembles.

"Are you crying?"

"You sonofabitch, you better not be lying." Janet's face, flushed suddenly deep red, turns towards me. Tears are skipping down her cheeks, and she shudders like a frequency.

"I swear —" standing, and then Janet is back, soft against me, like a memory reclaiming the present, her hair running down my neck, the familiar fold of her, hands running down her shoulders to her thighs; and if Dr. Plummet protests this somewhat melodramatic retelling of our reconciliation -- despite any exaggerations or embellishments on my part -- I'll tell y'all what I told her: "It's the truth."

Which just goes to show, love is more solace from loneliness than a metaphysical meeting of mind and spirit. But why cast asperities on our illusions? After all, they're all we have.

&

In the morning, I wake with Janet in bed beside me. She's reading my Robert Johnson outline. Familiar lines of disappointment wrinkle her cheeks, but her eyes look elegiac and focused on the text.

"That's my new project."

"It's not bad. It actually has potential."

Not exactly a ringing endorsement, but I've waited years to hear those words from her.

"I beg your pardon?"

"No I mean it. It's not bad. In fact, it's the most interesting idea you've had."

I look at her sullen, serious face, and love her again suddenly, dramatically.

"Why were you going through my bag anyway?"

&

We have breakfast on the Slope, discuss our respective waywards. I try calling Maya; she tries calling Pinchback. I try calling Pinchback; she tries calling Maya. Neither of us can get through to either.

"It must have started Election Night," Janet decides. "We all got separated, and maybe they went off together. I don't know." Her face mists all over again in the morning sun. "Wait 'til I get my hands on that miserable blind bastard. I'll smack the sight out of his eyes."

But Janet isn't one to take anything on faith; neither Pinchback's fidelity nor my word. She wants proof. So we keep trying to call them all morning. No luck. In the afternoon, we stop by their apartments, no luck. We call their numbers outside their buildings, and each time the call goes directly to voicemail. We even go out to DUMBO, have an early dinner together in the area, then walk Whitman Park together beneath the romantic red autumn sycamores. We never see Pinchback, and we never see Maya. In the evening I go home with Janet, and we sit around reading and calling in befuddled silence.

The next day goes pretty much the same way. Nothing from either of them. We walk the Upper West Side, hoping to catch sight of them in the neighborhood, and we end up strolling through Central Park. We take the train out to Bushwick, where Pinchback lives, walk the sullen blocks around Montrose, but we never see either of them. We call and call, sometimes leaving messages, sometimes not. We even try calling Samir, but get the same silence of the voicemail, always the voicemail.

By the end of the week, there's nothing to do but resign ourselves to the fact that they're avoiding us, all of them. Pinchback and Maya make sense. Samir's disappearance is a mystery.

After a week of living with Janet, we fall automatically back into our old familiar routines. After a while, it feels as if the time inbetween has been nothing but a long restless nightmare, and here we are again, just us again, like it's always been. I spend my days at Ampersand, where I'm busy rehearsing *The Last Days of Robert Johnson*. She teaches during the day, and when she isn't teaching, she's working on her next book, the new book, *Strange Fruit*. In the evenings, we sit together in bed reading, talking, kissing, simmering in the slow burn of a late romance.

There's no longer any reason for me to return to my Broadway Triangle apartment, not as a resident anyway, just to pack up and move my belongings. The place still feels haunted, and the day the movers come and empty it out, I feel like they're emptying out a curse that's been festering in my spirit.

To this day I still don't know who was screaming outside my window, or even why. Like the disappearance of Pinchback, Maya and Samir, it remains a mystery. My paranoia makes me suspect that the two mysteries are somehow related, but I can't imagine how. Maybe the mystery itself could be turned into something like a Black Faust, to complete the trilogy of overreaching protagonists: from Black Prometheus to Robert Johnson to Black Faust, although all stories are in some way retellings of this same story of an overreaching protagonist, from the epic of Gilgamesh to the story of the latest politician who lets power corrupt his vision. These outrageous retellings speak to us because we are creatures who live by stories, we make fables of our own lives, and by and by we buy the lie that hides the truth that lies inside. On the other hand, a Black Faust is something of an absurdity, at least an African Black Faust is, since Faust is a prisoner of time, and Saşa and Zamani time allow for no such Faustian prisoners, and no pact can be made for one's soul except as the soul appears in retrospect, stretched thin through the filter of Zamani time, a legacy.

Living with Janet makes work easy. Esoteric ideas like these only inspire her, and her ideas inspire me too. It suits Janet's philosophy to read her *Strange Fruit* as a stand-alone text, but I tend to think of it as a companion piece to *The Last Days of Robert Johnson* and vice versa. And underlying both works is this strange story of Pinchback, Maya and Samir. As to their various whereabouts now, that's really anyone's guess. Maya's *Black Buildings* was published in braille last year, and LIT will even publish *Strange Fruit* next spring. When Janet was discussing the details with them, she inquired about all three of our missing persons, and this is all she found out: Pinchback resigned shortly after we lost sight of him, and they never heard from him again. Maya and Samir disappeared just as thoroughly. No one ever heard from Samir again after he was fired, although Maya is a somewhat different story. She's out there somewhere. The royalties from *Black Buildings* are successfully deposited into a bank account every month. Sometimes I walk the streets of Brooklyn and feel like I can feel her there, in the spaces between the people, like she might suddenly materialize out of the air and appear shrouded in a cloud of lavender and marijuana. I pass by glass buildings and marble black buildings, and see shadows of Pinchback as well, visual hallucinations I suppose, inherited from his own bourgeoning vision. And I always think of Samir when I go out to Bushwick, still haunting the old haunts, hanging out at Wreck Bar or Ampersand, politicking up the daily politics or fretting over Fulcanelli. All three of them inform what eventually became *The Last Days of Robert Johnson*, and if this latest work can be considered in any way a success, I owe it as much to their inspiration as to any powers I may possess myself. After all, theater as I see it is a collaboration between artist, actors and the audience, and we all played those roles variously.

Then there's Haley Stern, whom I've intentionally avoided mentioning thus far. For one thing, her name rings bells, and I wanted you to focus on the story at hand, and not the celebrity at the center of it. For another thing, the story I've told you is really Maya's story, the story of *Black Buildings*, and Haley's art requires a separate focus. Don't get it twisted. Haley is at the center of *Robert Johnson*, and the play wouldn't have worked without her, but her story takes a different trajectory. I will say that her song, her singing, her performance in particular, gave the production the life it needed. In fact it was Haley's performance that made the play the critical success it was; and as you all know, she's done pretty well for herself since then, on Broadway and in Hollywood, God save us. It's been a while since I've talked to her, but I remember her fondly. I especially remember the moment I realized what an amazing talent she was, when she first sang her song for us. The song is like a bluesy version of Maya's poetry, and if you don't know it, it goes a little something like this:

When the clock strikes twelve, don't my riches turn to rags,
When the clock strikes twelve, oh Lord,
Don't my riches turn to rags
My baby treats me wrong, I guess it's time I pack my bags.
And if the sun sinks red in the East,
It's a blue moon rising on the West.

I told old Scratch before, I ramble lonely as a song
I told old Scratch before, I ramble lonely as a song
Don't cry now baby, don't cry, if all you had is gone.
And if the sun sinks red in the East,
It's a blue moon rising on the West.

Since I got no work, well, the Devil he gets no rest
Since I got no work, well
The Devil he gets no rest
I loved them all, oh Lord, but baby
I loved you best.
And if the sun sinks red in the East
It's a blue moon rising on the West.

PART TWO: ZAMANI

THIRTEEN

A few weeks after moving into a rented room in Greenwood, Mississippi, Robert begins to notice uncanny elements hanging around his head like shadows. At first he passes it off on old man Ralph's whisky, but the theory just won't hold sway, the shadows simply thicken. Saturday night after a set with Honeyboy and Sonnyboy, he steps out into the warm, wet evening, when an old jalopy comes hollering up in front of him, and Robert thinks to himself, Well now, and here it is. But it turns out it's just old man Ralph's old lady Louise, and she says to him to get on in, asks where they got him staying, talking about she'll give him a ride back into town. So he doesn't take a drink all day Sunday, but come Monday he sees that same jalopy all over town, three times too. Once at three, when he's out taking his lunch, again at six when he's taking his dinner, and again at nine, just as he's heading out for a drink. Certain something isn't quite right. Down at Ralph's next Saturday night he asks the brother, "What make and model is that Jalopy your wife drives? I feel like it's been following me around all week long." Ralph smiles at him sly and low and says, "You mean like a hellhound on your trail?" So that Robert's neck starts to tingle like remembering an ancient déjà vu. Ralph kind of settles into the slyness of that smile of his, and says, "It's the only one around these parts like it, and I'm sure you'll be seeing it around again soon enough by and by". Those words feel real familiar too, like a familiar following you, and sure enough, coming home come three in the morning, there he is, waiting in Robert's room, Scratch himself, dressed all in black like a Baptist preacher, drinking whisky and picking out a beautiful delta drift.

"Guess it's about that time," says Robert.

Scratch peers up at him from the guitar, eyes bright and brown. He doesn't say anything, but he keeps on playing, like he's answering Robert with each riff, call and response.

"Won't be needing much I suppose."

Scratch keeps on playing, so Robert unpacks his own guitar and sits down next to him. The morning sun is just turning orange and gold away across the valley, and the sky is deep amber blue. They play well into the morning, after the sun is already shining bright in the vast Mississippi sky. Sometime in the afternoon someone knocks on the door.

"Yep."

"Hey Robert, it's Honeyboy. You wanna play a few licks this afternoon?"

"Come on in. It's open."

Honeyboy comes through the door and gives Robert a look like something ain't right.

"You already practicing? I never seen you practice before. Normally you just up and play."

"That's jes what I'm doing now," says Robert. "You joining in or what?"

Honeyboy walks into the room, he hesitates. "Man, what's going on in here," he says. "You need to open a window or something. I can't hardly breathe."

"Windows is open already."

Honeyboy walks deeper into the room, looking around cautiously. "Man, something is surely not right in here. I'm going to get something to eat across the way. You wanna come?"

Robert looks to his right, then looks to his left, with an enquiring quiz. "Yeah man. Let's get out of here."

He hopes Scratch will just set there playing, but when Robert stops playing, Scratch stops too, and sets his guitar down by the side of the table.

"Guess it's about that time," Scratch says.

They're the first words he's spoken.

They walk out, the three of them, side by side by side, into the humid early afternoon sun. Robert keeps looking from Honeyboy to Scratch, and decides this is really bad news, because Honeyboy can't seem to see Scratch to save his soul.

"How much time I got left?" Robert asks, and Honeyboy turns to him and says, "What was that?"

Scratch doesn't answer the question. Robert lets it hang around in the air for a moment like a melody, and then he says to Honeyboy, "I was just wondering something out loud to myself, is all."

"Well, don't get to talking to yourself again. People think you loony enough already, what without you resorting back to all that again."

They walk on in silence for a while, the three of them, until they reach the diner down on Main. The diner is dim and the air is humid, but thick with the lively aroma of bacon and coffee. When they order breakfast, the server says, "Ralph called yesterday. Says he wants y'all out there again come Saturday."

"You tell him we'll be there," says Robert and Honeyboy nods in agreement. "Truck can pick us up same time as last week." Robert casts a glance at Scratch. Scratch just sits next to him silently.

"I will be there, won't I?" Robert asks Scratch, soft as he can manage, but Honeyboy hears him anyway.

"I suppose that's all between you and the whisky," he says.

"Aw, what you running your mouth about? Speaking of, let me get a drink with this grub. You drinking, too?"

"Little early for me," says Honeyboy, "but sure, make it two."

Robert looks over again at Scratch, still hoping to get some kind of answer to his question, but Scratch ain't talking.

It turns out Scratch doesn't do much talking at all. After Honeyboy leaves, Robert walks around town with Scratch some, searching him for answers.

"So come on and tell me, now that it's just me and you. How much time I got left?"

Scratch doesn't answer.

"Well, how am I supposed to go? You tell me that at least?"

Scratch doesn't answer. They walk down old lonely dusty roads, past broken down sheds of houses, a pale blue panting sky.

"I thought we had us a deal. Guess I'll just go ahead and renege on my side of the bargain. Turn my thoughts to Jesus my Savoir."

This gets a response. "Oh, I wouldn't do that, if I was you. Or you ain't got no time left at all."

"Well, what's that supposed to mean?" says Robert. Now that he's got the man talking he doesn't want to lose the momentum. "For all I know I don't have no time left nohow, seeing as you won't say nothing. Figure I might as well cut my losses. I'm a betting man, and I know my odds."

"You got you some time still. We got a little ways to go first. Then I'll answer any questions you got."

"Little ways to go? Where we going?"

"Where we are already. We just not quite at the right spot for you yet."

"Man, now you talking in riddles."

"You'll see. I don't set the rules, and we still got some ways to go."

"Well, who's setting the rules around here, then?"

Scratch doesn't say anything.

The whole affair has Robert Johnson just a little bit shook.

Scratch stays right there with him, but now Robert really can't come up with any more questions other than the one: Has he made a terrible mistake? And come what may, maybe it's best to go on and repent. Save his soul, if it can still be saved. Instead he goes home with a bottle of bourbon and drinks down the afternoon.

The next morning is a Monday, and that means a visit from Louise. She always comes into town on Monday mornings to visit her sister, and after that she stops by Robert's room. Robert wakes up with a thick, cloudy head, and the remnants of a bad dream forgotten, still leaving a sour taste in his mouth. He gets up and gets dressed, sits down, and there he is, Scratch, still sitting there, plucking silently at the guitar strings.

"You mean to tell me you just sat there all night, didn't sleep or nothing?"

"Don't sleep too much, I can't say that I do," says Scratch, and shoots Robert a meaning look.

"So you're talking again?" Robert smiles, and lights himself a cigarette.

"I thought you was the one got silent all of a sudden," says Scratch.

"Well, say. Could you do me one, and light out for a couple hours if you could? I got my lady friend coming by, and it don't seem seemly for you to be hanging about while we're entertaining ourselves. If you catch my drift."

"None of that interests me," says Scratch. "But I can't go nowhere neither. I'll just sit right over here and play this here guitar. Don't mind me none."

"Ain't that the damnedest," says Robert. But there's not much he can do about it, so he just adds, "Well just keep yourself occupied then, and don't make too much racket, and don't be looking when things heat up."

Scratch smiles for the first time since he showed up.

Louise comes by late in the morning, looking good like she's like to look, and smelling sweet like lavender like she's like to smell, and just being her sexy same self. She's got long black hair, and bright brown skin, and even brighter brown eyes that take the sun and make Robert light up in a smile.

"Ain't you a sight," he says, kissing her. "How's your sister?"

"Oh, she's good."

"And Ralph? He called us back for another show next Saturday night."

"Yeah, and no surprise. Y'all really running it right down there. We ain't had crowds like the likes of you and Honeyboy draw in a while."

Robert is all humbleness and modesty. "Hell, it ain't just us, Sonnyboy cuttin' some serious blues out there hisself."

"Can't no one cut the blues like you can."

And all modesty suddenly set aside. "Well, ain't that the truth. Come on close to me baby, and give me another kiss."

They fold into each other like the two cut sides of a deck of cards, and Robert leads her to the bed. He casts a quick glance over at Scratch, but Scratch, true to his word, is just plucking silently at the guitar, back turned and all. But just as Robert and Louise begin panting on the sheets, he could swear he hears the guitar pick up a voice and start playing *Travelling Riverhouse Blues*.

You can squeeze my lemon till
Juice run down my leg
That's what I'm talking about!
But I'll be going back to Vicksburg, mama
Rocking to my head.

Later Robert and Louise lie on the bed smoking cigarettes, and watch the sun make big shadows on the ceiling through the trees.

"What you thinking about Robert? You seem most distracted today."

"Nothing too much. Mostly about us, I suppose. What we gonna do when it's time I light out of town."

This just makes Louise laugh. "Like you ain't left women from here clean to Vicksburg, Tennessee."

Robert sits up and looks at Louise stern and troubled. "What makes you say that?"

"Oh, I know you bluesmen. And you the worst of the lot, ain't you, though?" She reaches up and strokes his face.

"No, I mean what you mean by using that line, clean to Vicksburg, Tennessee?"

"You been drinking or something? It's from your own song, *Travelling Riverhouse Blues*."

"I know well enough where it's from. I mean, why you quoting it? You just hear it playing or something?"

"Now I know you been drinking. She laughs again. You need to quit off that Jump Steady before noon, Robert. I can tell you that much."

Robert shrugs it off, but the coincidence seems most too close for comfort. "Hell, I ain't been drinking. You intoxication enough for me, and that's the truth."

But as soon as Louise sets back off home for Ralph, Robert pours himself a drink. "And don't you say nothing," Robert says to Scratch, who hasn't much moved from his corner.

Scratch turns around and sets down the guitar. "Oh, we ain't got too far to go now," he says.

"And how will I know when we're there? Tell the truth, if this is traveling, it seems to me pretty plain. Walking and talking and playing the blues? What say you we go see what Honeyboy's up to?"

They walk out into the sweating July afternoon, side by side in the sandy road. One set of footprints, Robert notes glumly to himself. Considers again his reconsideration of the pact. Don't the preacher say it's never too late to give your ever-living soul back to Jesus? No, he believes its most too late for him, preachers be damned. Here he is still drinking up liquor and bedding down married women like he hasn't a care in the world. And then to have the nerve to come to Jesus talking about, Lawd save my damnable soul. No, that won't do at all, probably be damned twice over just for the presumption and gumption of it all.

Halfway out to Honeyboy's house, they pass through a graveyard. It isn't necessarily the best way to get there, but graveyards remind Robert of playing with old Ike Zimmerman long ago. Ike, the one who told him about the crossroads to begin with; just where to go and what to do and when to know to be there and now look where he is. And ain't that him, anyway? Old Ike Zimmerman? Just ahead he sees a man wandering the tombstones looking almost like he stepped right up out of one, lost his way, looking to find his way back. No, not old Ike though. This man is a high yaller fella, and he's dressed in clothes from way back in the day, and he's got a big beard and a suit on, like a nineteenth century gentleman or some such. A little bit of whisky's got Robert in a jokey mood, so he calls out to the man, "Hey brother, you looking to find your way back home or what?"

The man turns and looks at Robert, and then looks at Scratch and comes slowly up to greet them.

"It can feel like a long way, can't it?" Then he turns to Scratch and says, "Where's he headed?"

"Same as where you are now," says Scratch.

"You mean you see old Scratch here too?" Robert looks from Scratch to the stranger strangely. "Means I'm not gone plumb mad dog crazy at least. But how you and me see him when no one else does?"

"Our own self-imposed misfortune allows us to see him in all his awful aspect. Tell me, what's your name, and tell me of that which brings you to this lamentable territory."

"You mean the graveyard? Well, folks call me Robert Johnson, and maybe you heard tell of me if you a Delta man and into the blues. I learned my licks in a graveyard, and so I take every opportunity to come through one when I can. But judging by how you talk, I'd say you rather from up north somewheres. What's your name, fella?"

"I was known as Paschal Beverly Randolph. In life I was a spiritualist and Rosicrucian. In death I wander from place to place in a cloud of forgetfulness; forgetfulness of purpose, and forgetfulness of self; forgetfulness of my spiritual exercises, and remember only that I was a spiritualist and a Rosicrucian and no longer even fully understand the import of those words. And yet all answers seem to lie just beyond the vale of my next thought. I have traveled all over the world in search of spiritual wisdom."

"What you mean in death?" asks Robert. "Ain't you standing here plain as day?"

Paschal blinks and frowns. "It's never easy at first," he says. "I forget that it's never so easy at first. But in time you'll come around to things. You still haven't adjusted to the change in the light."

"What change in what light?"

Paschal looks beyond Robert toward the wide pale blue sky. "The light from the sun", he says, pointing, "takes eight minutes to reach Earth. The light that allows the living to see anything at all. So when in life we looked toward the sun, we were seeing it as it existed eight minutes ago. Should the sun burn out this very instant, it would be eight minutes before any of the living would be aware of it. The stars we once saw in the night sky are the same. The light they emit can take centuries to reach Earth. Some of the stars we saw were no longer even there; may have burned out hundreds of years ago, and we were seeing nothing but their phantom remains. So, the farther the living look into the cosmos, the further back in time they are looking. With keen enough vision they can see back to the very beginning of the universe. In death, we cross over to the other side, and the light comes from the other direction in time. Had I keen enough vision I could see as far as the end of the universe. But the light that lights everyday objects comes from a sun that will burn out thousands of years from now, and when I look at stars I am often looking at stars that do not yet exist. So, as we approach the end of the universe, the range of our vision shortens instead of extends. I can see future events, but events as they occur in the present are often obscure to me. I can't see others in the present, but I can see them in the future, and they of course, can't see me in the present, but they can see me in the future, because in the future they are all over here, on this side of the light."

"You talk in riddles just like Scratch here," says Robert, not quite following anything the man just said. "You seem to be able to see me just fine."

"Yes. We can see each other. That's right."

Robert turns to look toward the sky, thinking about the sun and eight minutes, and wondering if he's really looking into the past, but now what did this fella mean about the changes in the light, and maybe he best just go ahead and repent for his everlasting soul after all, when it seems so much might be at stake. Just at that moment, however, another man comes striding up from what seems like the pallid air, and looks wildly from Scratch to Paschal to Robert.

"Did I hear right," he says to Robert. "You can still see the living? Now? Here in the present?"

"Well," says Robert, "I should hope to hope so."

This fella is another high yaller looking brother, also dressed like a nineteenth century gentleman, but a little rougher around the edges. He has a large frothy beard running down his chin like a bushel of hay, and ragtag hair, thin and wispy lisping down his forehead.

"Do you know my grandson, Nathan Pinchback Toomer? Do you know if he's still alive, or is he also on his way across the light?"

Robert looks from Scratch to Paschal to this new fellow.

"I can't say I know the man. Tell me about him."

"I thought you would be well acquainted." The man frowns. "I thought you two would be one of a piece, like you and Paschal here. I thought - but why bother with thinking at all? I have a message for him, and if you see him before you cross over, please deliver it to him for me."

"Lay it on me, man."

"It's a simple, well known and well loved piece of scripture. Mark 8:36. For what shall it profit a man, if he shall gain the whole world, and lose his own soul?"

"Sure, a bit of scripture never hurts. Who do I say it's from?"

"P.B.S. Pinchback. He'll know me. Maybe he'll even listen, if it comes from me. I fear it's already too late. Certainly it's already too late, for I see him sometimes on this side of the light."

Scratch snickers, and Robert turns to look at him, shoots him a killing glare, but then when he looks back to Pinchback, no one's there.

"Say, what's with him? Where'd he go? This graveyard is giving me the creeps, and that's the truth." Robert turns to Paschal. "Well man, I thank you for your time, but I think I ought to get out of here."

"Most certainly."

That scripture proverb has Robert all kinds of shook up anyhow. Why did he have to say that little verse, out of all the scripture there is? Ain't no shortage of other things he could have said. Robert feels like it was meant mostly for him, and he knows he won't meet this Nathan fellow nohow, and the other fella must have known it too, because these are northern Negroes after all, sure as you see, Mulattoes even, haunting this graveyard, and how's he supposed to be acquainted with their kith and kin?

Well, there's no natural way he could be.

TWELVE

Saturday night comes most too quick, Robert can't right recall just how he passed the week away. He's back down at the Three Forks, with Sonnyboy sitting on his left, Honeyboy sitting far left, and Scratch as his right hand man. They've been drinking whisky since the truck picked them up in Greenwood, and Robert's just starting to feel all reet. Three Forks is grim and grimy, the way a jook ought to be, and it's as authentic as they get. Nothing but a convenience grocery store during the day, Ralph opens up the floor at night, and has folks standing around dancing and drinking and listening to the musicians sitting up on a make-shift stage on a stool. They been talking about what set they like to play that night, and Robert keeps looking to his right, over at Scratch, because he don't like the way the light seems to catch Scratch's eye in the dim of the jook, almost like the light was reflecting outward instead of in, and the light coming out of Scratch's eyes is red and orange and all the damnation colors of hellfire.

The light in Ralph's can't be said to be much better. The air is worse. Robert is used to smoky jooks, but the smoke and the whisky and the sweat and that sinister smell of fear somewhere – is it coming from him himself? – is all too much and his head feels light and he says in a sort of dizzy drag, dragging on a cigarette, "I suppose I'll play whatever comes in my head in the moment of the thing. I can't right say I have a set yet."

"No way for a professional to go about things," says Sonnyboy, who's been on a preaching bit all evening. "But you tell me what you like to play, and maybe I join in with you for a song or two. I play my here harmonica, and you or Honeyboy up on that guitar, and we can't get this crowd to rolling."

"You take that up with Honeyboy," says Robert, seeing Louise sidle her way around the bar. "I feel like playing by my lonely tonight. Can't no one keep up with the way I'm feeling."

Honeyboy catches Robert's drift, and laughs. "You stuck up on Ralph's old lady Louise is what is what. Flag her on over for a drink, why not?"

"Ah, don't bring no women into men's talk here," says Sonnyboy. "What she gone do but ply you all up with whisky anyhow?"

"Well, you went and convinced him right there," says Honeyboy, as Robert waves towards Louise with a tip of his Stetson.

Louise comes over with a sway and a tilt to her hips like she's wrapped around a dream, and looks to the left, then looks to the right, then kisses Robert quick and sly and slick, so Robert says, "Who you lookin out for? What Ralph gonna do, but go cry in his whisky somewhere?"

"I gotta go on back and live with the man," says Louise, and she takes a seat on Robert's right, occupying Scratch himself, glowing with his presence.

"Baby, don't sit there. Sit on my knee or such."

"Why who you saving it for? The Devil hisself? Better not see any other women come up here and take this seat. No, I believe I'll keep my fanny fastened just where it is."

"Suit yourself," says Robert, but he can't so much as look at Louise with her sitting there, because every time he turns to look at her, he sees those eyes of Scratch's burning through her own eyes, and the unnatural light running all through and around her like she a Tiffany brown lamp with a bright red bulb.

"Go on and be a good girl, and get me a little drink of likker would you?"

"Oh, you and yours. You boys drinking, too?"

"I'm still working on mines," says Honeyboy, and Sonnyboy says, "I'm keeping my pace too, thank you much. Can't all of us keep up with Robert here."

"Oh, go on home with that, now," says Robert. "Just hurry up with that drink, and don't you mind these ladies here none, they just about had all they can take."

Now Scratch has been real quiet as of late, Robert can't right recall when last he heard the brother speak, but now his face lights up a horrid red purple kind of color, like a plum in August, and he grins wide and livid, so Robert turns to him and says, "Say brother, what's on your mind?"

"That's what I ought be asking you," says Sonnyboy, "as you seem to be talking to me in the opposite direction. What you think I'm over that way, for? Or you still talking to Louise way across the room?"

"He been like that all week," says Honeyboy. "Talking up ghosts and chatting up shadows. Don't mind him none, think the Jump Steady finally gone challenged his brain."

"I'll challenge your brain with this here guitar," says Robert, turning back around. But that grin that Scratch got just won't go away, and Robert keeps sneaking peeks back at him.

"You most too light to be talkin like that," says Honeyboy, and then follows with, "'Sides, what else you got to play with?"

"I figure I could take up your guitar, once you laid out and don't need it no more."

"Can't no one but Honeyboy play this here lady," says Honeyboy running his fingers up and around the frets. "She like a good sweet mama comes home only to me."

"That kinda frail there is about as real as old Scratch," says Sonnyboy. "And you boys best off stop bickering. Or I'll brain the both of youse just for the peace and quiet of the matter."

Robert startles a look at Sonnyboy, then looks back over at Scratch. Scratch is still grinning, eyes still glowing, and now here comes Louise and takes Scratch's aspect again, sitting on the seat.

"Well, I brought you your drink. Ralph say it's on the house."

"That's a good girl."

"You don't know how to say thank you or nothing? Robert, Ralph is half right about you, that you nothing but trouble."

"Now, I would take them words as proper offense," says Sonnyboy, "and send that drink right on back where it came from if I was you. Can't insult a man and buy him a drink the same time. Specially considering the specifics of your relations with the man."

"Oh, Ralph don't know nothing," says Louise. "He most slept through our own damn wedding. He don't catch a damn thing that's going on."

Robert knocks the whisky back and winks. "That brother don't concern me none."

Things start to get grainy from here on out. Just as a record hits the grooves between the wax and adds a grainy texture to the music, so the night begins to take on an intimate crackling quality of its own. Sonnyboy is going on about drinking too much whisky too early in the night, and Honeyboy is talking to a young lady just down the way, and when Robert looks back at Scratch, he begins to think about the two fellas he met in the graveyard the other day, and begins to wonder, through the static, whether things are really starting to take a turn now, because the jook is starting to fill up, and the room is getting hotter, and the crackling in the background is only getting deeper and louder, so he leans over to Scratch, and asks, "what that brother mean the other day about the changes in light and so on?"

Louise looks back at him through Scratch like he's most lost his mind, and says, "what are you going on about now, Robert? How many of those you already had? You gonna be alright to play tonight?"

Sonnyboy is looking over at him queer now too, and says, "now Robert, I hate to come off as a preacher or somebody's father, but I seen too many good bluesmen taken away by the devil, and I think you might best ease on up off that whisky."

Robert stands and stretches, as the first bluesman to play kicks up a stool. "Oh, don't y'all go and worry about me none, I should catch some air though, before I go play."

A light crowd has already gathered around the guitarist, who is sitting on the stool, and drawling his way through the strings towards a melody.

"You played three bars already man, go in!"

"He played most like seven bars already. Go in, brother, go in!"

Been a long way gone
But I know I'll be home soon
Been a long way gone
But I know I'll be home soon
And I set my soul
To burning in a blood red moon.

Robert pushes his way through the red sweating bodies and out past the bar into the warm night air, much cooler in any case than the thick smoky air in the jook. Robert halfway expects Scratch to have stayed just where he was, but turning to light a cigarette, sure enough, Scratch is standing right there beside him, still grinning and peering from time to time back at the dirty gray windows of the jook. Once Robert's lit his cigarette and taken a couple cool steps out into the evening, Scratch speaks up.

"Well, the time is just about come now, Robert, so I'm happy to answer any questions you might have."

Hearing Scratch speak startles Robert a moment, and he fumbles to find the words to the question he just asked, lost somewhere in the graininess of the previous moment.

"I think I had something on my mind, if you give me just another minute here."

"You was asking about the changes in the light."

"So I was," says Robert, and something else seems to be changing now, too.

"You just really on your way over. You sure standing on the threshold."

A wild panic shivers through Robert, the way Scratch says this, so he says real quiet, almost like a whisper, "you mean I'm to die tonight, is that what?"

"You been dead now a while, Robert, you just didn't quite see it that way, but no matter. The light changes because, just like the fella said, you starting to see time from forwards to backwards now, and now you too far along to brush it off."

"Forwards to backwards, eh? So I'm looking into the future right now?"

"I expect that's how it goes with you."

"Well it seems most like the regular everyday present to me," says Robert. "Except that bit of graininess, but I figure that must just be the whisky, and it ain't nothing I ain't seen before."

"However you wanna see it."

"Well, say then. If I can ask you anything, what happens after, then? You know, after folks pass on and such? Is it Heaven and Hell and Angels and Brimstone like all the preachers go on about?"

"I figure that's a reasonable enough way of putting things."

"Well that don't answer much. But we still here, then, is what you saying? We still here somewhere after we gone? Wandering graveyards and such like them two fellas from earlier this week?"

"You may want you wouldn't want to be here at all, is how it just might turn out."

"Now you just going on to go on. Tell me, then, if Heaven and Hell is real as right here and now, what's it like in Hell?"

"Ain't too pleasant."

"And is that where you from, then? Assuming as how you're Scratch and all, and everyone knows you come from down there. "

"Yeah, that's pretty much on the money."

"How's come you came up out of it then? And if it's so bad, why not just stay on out, stay right here where you are now?"

"Man, this right here is hell, and I sure ain't out of it."

"There you go, talking up your riddles again," says Robert, and he swings back out into the night, pulling nervous at his cigarette, and looking out over the dark night road. He looks up, towards the stars, looking at their light and contemplating time and eternity. After a while, he turns back to Scratch, and laughs. He throws down his cigarette and lights another. "Man, if this here right here is hell, well then sign me up twice.

Everyone know things is just what you make of them, and if playing in jooks, and drinking good whisky and laying down with Louise is what you call Hell, I can only say I'm sorry brother, but you ain't taking advantage of the natural advantages of the place. Fire and brimstone and all that nonsense. I knew them preachers weren't on about nothing."

But now Robert is starting to feel just a little bit queasy and light headed, and the cigarette doesn't seem to be helping matters. He swallows in a couple gulps of air, and walks brisk up the road and brisk back down it. Scratch walks by his side the whole way.

"Well, if I'm as good as gone already," says Robert, "what happens if I confess my soul to God right here and now? Don't the preacher man say it's never too late? "

"While you lived, you might coulda done that, but now you dead and gone already, and if you look close enough, you can see that for your ownself."

Robert squints into the evening, down the road, up at the stars, up at the moon looming large and gloomy, gloaming a few days past full. He smells traces of lavender in the wind, and hears a moody blues fainting the air. It's his own song, *Come in my Kitchen*, and he can almost see himself now, only not so much himself, but other folks bent over their guitars, playing his blues, and sitting up suddenly back inside the jook, Robert looks around, sweating and unsure. His guitar is unsteady in his hands, and he's wheezing over, sweating and delirious like he's been drinking whisky all day long.

"Go in, man, go in. Why you stop playing?"

Robert looks toward the voice, but it's hard to see anything in all this grainy interior. He tries to stand, and catches Scratch standing just to his right. He slumps back onto the stool, and looks back at his guitar. It's getting harder to breathe, and he wishes he were back outside in the fresh night air.

"I don't feel quite so good just now," says Robert, and looks in desperate appeal back up at the invisible audience.

"Man," says Sonnyboy, somewhere through the murk, "you just drunk you too much. You be alright. Play that guitar."

"He do look a touch pale," someone else says.

"He get like that all the time," Robert hears Honeyboy say. "Give him a minute now."

But Robert gonna need a bit more than a minute to shake off this shiver. It grips him chilly in the belly and runs warm up his spine, all through his arms, and by the time it reaches his head it's hot as the Mississippi sun. He's sweating up another Tallahatchie, and he tries to stand again, tries to make his way back out into the fresh night, all this smoke and likker and noise and stale air is just making his sick worse. And somewhere far off, he hears himself asking Scratch a question: "How I'm dead and gone already, when I'm standing right here?"

Or laid out on a bench in the back. Robert is looking up at the ceiling, at the ceiling fans turning slow and low, and tries to look up, but is most too weak to move. He groans and rolls over on his side, and feels nothing but a tremendous pain run all through him. Honeyboy is standing by his side, he sees him dim in his dizziness, and Honeyboy's face is crunched together like a pile of old autumn leaves. "What they do to you, Robert? It really is something mighty wrong with you, ain't it, but can't figure what it could be."

Sonnyboy's voice booms out like a preacher. "Something was done to that there whisky, you can bet on it."

Robert leans to the other side to see if he can see him, but instead just sees Scratch standing there, looking at him like the angel of death just biding his time.

"Do it feel just like this for all eternity where I'm going?" he asks Scratch feebly, and Sonnyboy answers instead.

"Man, if you got something on your chest, you best confess yourself now. I ain't saying you won't make it, but you never know, you know, and you best be sure you alright and such with the old man upstairs."

"Lawd Jesus help me!" Robert calls out, loud as he can muster. "Save my everlasting soul!"

Scratch frowns deep and dark at those words, and then a wave of heat seems to weave the room and everything vanishes in the jangle of a bluesman tuning up his instrument.

Robert wakes up back home in his rented room. There's a fella from the jook looking at him curious, in fact it seems to be the Tush Hog, the man at the door what bounces folks out when they get too rowdy. Scratch is there too. He's sitting in the corner, playing an old blues tune on the guitar, familiar to Robert, but one what he can't quite place at the moment. Last night's graininess is gone, but replaced with electric currents that make the daylight through the window feel too clear and too bright, like a well lit apothecary at high noon. Robert still doesn't feel too well. If the queasiness of last night is slowly crawling its way out of his bowels, a warm swelling of the head and throat and chest seems to come crawling its way in, and he feels occasional chills running through his bones like electric currents.

"I'm thinking you ought to stay over at our place for a while," says the Tush Hog, and Robert just sits up and nods, because he doesn't have the energy to do anything else. He takes a look over at Scratch, and starts to say something, but thinks better of it a moment later and lies back down. Everything seems to be filtered now through this unnatural brightness, he feels like he's still somewhere down at the jook, maybe watching all this happen through the lens of the future, seeing beyond where he really is, and the more he tries to remember, the more he forgets where he is, but seems to plummet further into the future, so that he remembers a long long time ago, and sees himself through a delirious fit of light crouching behind his bed in a dark room, with a bottle of wine in his hand, and the same fear of dying buzzing through his body, and then his memory fails him again, after all it was just a feeling, or was it an image, or maybe a fever dream, and he's groaning away in an unfamiliar bed, with the Tush Hog peering over him worriedly.

This is it, all right. Scratch still there, pacing the floor, biding his time. Robert turns to the Tush, gasps – it's all he has left in him – "Hand here a piece of paper."

The Tush hands Robert a sheet from a notebook, maybe thinking it's his last will and testament, and Robert supposes in some way it is. He writes, *Jesus of Nazareth King of Jerusalem. I know that my Redeemer Liveth and he will call me from the grave.*

Scratch turns the moment he's written the words, his face a Mississippi monsoon. "What you think you gone and done? You think that paper will save your soul? Didn't I tell you you was already dead and gone? Where were you then, eh, when we challenged your *redeemer*, who made wretched the heavens and laid the cursed foundations of the earth? Where were you when we had the courage to stand up to his pious tyranny? Where were you when he demanded the light end there and the darkness begin here? Where were you when the morning stars wept together and all the angels groaned in despair? Did I not teach you the blues, show you the tricks of how to turn terror into art, and art into beauty, and beauty into human immortality? Did I not show you the pleasures and terrors of humanity in all their limitations? Have you not had your women and your whisky and all your pleasure? I kept up my side of our bargain, but here you want to renege on yours, you dead man, you wastrel, you cur."

"I was s'posed to be the greatest bluesman of all time. Don't no one know nothing about me, man. It was a hoax, you and all your talk. It ain't nothing but one big racket, and the whisky and the women don't fetch up to what you promised. I repent my soul to God, and you be damned as you is. I ain't one of them that studies evil."

Robert is really too weak to say the words, they come tumbling out of his mouth more as a belch of bile than anything else, and as he says them, he retches up out of the bed with Scratch's glare burning his body, scorching like the brimstone of hell. The Tush stands up alarmed, and Robert rolls off the bed, starts crawling about, writhing on the floor beneath Scratch's murderous gaze. The lights flicker and flicker and his heart runs quicker and he's dreaming of women and liquor, stick to your thoughts of God, he tells himself, turn your thoughts towards God. But the walls run into liquid, and he's feeling the floor open vast beneath him, so that he stretches out to fall, falls on his back, arms akimbo, legs akimbo, shuddering and plummeting until at last he feels beneath him the ghastly roar of damnation; and then suddenly he floats upwards, upwards toward the stars.

ELEVEN

Man, if you smoking a quarter of that cess a day, it won't be long before you find yourself slipping. Lucien is spending another faded Saturday afternoon kicking it with Booker. They been smoking since about half past noon, just drinking Coors tallboys, and talking that same old fly shit when Lucien's cell phone rings. It's his cousin, Maya.

"Hey May'. What's up?"

"I'm downstairs, Lucien. Can you buzz me in?"

Lucien lets her in, and here she comes, Maya in a long purple African skirt, and a black and red shirt, so that her body moves lithe like a snake when she slides past him at the door, and with a quick hug, looks around. "Just you and Booker here?"

"Yeah, that's right. So what's up?"

"I need an ounce."

"Well hello to you, too," he says. "Come on in, sit down. We just politicking."

"I'm in something of a hurry." She looks over to Booker, smiles and flirts imperceptibly, something like a quiver. "Hey Booker."

Booker smiles, nods. "Hey, beautiful. How you doing?"

"I been alright, she says. Writing mostly."

"Still writing those poems?"

"Yeah, same old thing."

"You need to put those words to music, you want anyone to hear them," Booker tells her. He's told her this a hundred times before, so it's mostly just a game between them now. "Why not come on by my place some time and we can lay down some tracks? I got a new mixer, we can get you a mixtape out on the street in no time at all."

"Yeah," Maya drawls. "I'll think it over. I do have a book out though. I'll bring you a copy sometime."

Lucien frowns, and removes himself to the kitchen, where he keeps the weed stashed in the cabinet beneath the sink. He hears Maya and Booker making small talk in the other room, and strains to hear them, but can only make out a stray word here and there. He quietly measures out an ounce, slowly even, to give himself time to hear the form of a conversation develop between the words, but nothing sticks. When he comes back into the living room, Maya is sitting on a couch pulling on a Dutch, and Booker is putting a disk in the player.

"I thought you was in a hurry."

"I got enough time to smoke one." Maya puffs a thicket of smoke in his direction, then passes him the Dutch.

Lucien takes it, turns to Booker. "What you putting on?"

"My own shit, man. My new mixtape."

"Man, no one wants to hear that shit."

"Maya does. The shit is dope, but it don't even matter about that. I'm talking about listening to how pro the shit sounds. This new mixer, man."

The first track starts up. Seems to Lucien kinda formulaic, he's heard this sort of beat before from the Neptunes, but Booker's punchlines pick up what the beat lacks.

"You a better writer than producer," Lucien says.

"Naw, man, I'm nice with both."

"You be lying to yourself about that, man." He passes Booker the Dutch. "You need to stop smoking that weed. Clear your mind and shit."

"This shit does clear my mind, man. Plus, the record picks up. You'll see. The shit gets deep around track two or three."

Lucien knows what that means. When Booker says his shit gets deep that means he tries to kick some knowledge, but usually it just comes off corny.

"On track three I talk about this election tomorrow. Where we gonna elect the first black president."

"It's been a bunch of black president's already," says Maya. "You need to read this book by J.A. Rogers, *The Five Negro Presidents, According to What White People Said They Were.* A real mind-blower. But Obama's the first black president to call himself black. That's true."

"He ain't president yet," says Lucien.

"He's gonna be, though." Booker takes a puff, considers. "But they gonna assassinate that nigga, too. Can't let no black man be president."

"They will not assassinate him," Maya says. "That would make him a black martyr, and that's even more dangerous than a black president."

"I don't buy it he's getting elected," says Lucien. "Bush stole that shit in 2000 and stole it again in 2004. You know McCain ain't beneath that shit himself. Plus, the shit is all determined already. Illuminati shit and all that. Whatever happens it was all planned and programmed by the powers that be. Now, that's some deep shit for you, Booker. You need to kick something about that on one of your rhymes."

"Man, that shit is tired and besides, it's already been done. Jada talking about Bush brought down the towers, hell. My shit gets political for real. But listen, man, you'll hear for yourself." Booker takes a last long drag, and passes the Dutch to Maya. "What about you, Maya? Your poetry. What you talk about in your poetry? You always going on about something when you around here, so you must have something to say there."

Lucien wrinkles up his face, because Booker always puts on that soft, how-*you*-doing voice when he talks to Maya, most cats do, and the shit is nerve-wracking, annoying, worse; something he can't get to the source of.

"I try not to get political in my poetry," says Maya. "I try to write about more esoteric things than politics. Politics is just distraction, the way I see it. Plus, these poems just come to me. It's like I don't even write them."

"Man, see," says Lucien. "Now you got her started."

"Got who started?" Maya smokes, blows rings with her tongue, acting like she's doing it unconscious, but Lucien knows she's being cute on purpose, that she likes to tease.

"What you write about then? You write about that Illuminati shit, like Lucien likes to go on about?"

"Naw, Illuminati's bullshit."

"Kick us something."

"I don't remember anything off the top of my head," says Maya. "I'd have to have my book with me. Or be at the MET. That's where I get my inspiration and stuff. But next time, I promise."

"You just come over with your book sometime to my crib, and we can lay down some tracks. Or we can even go to the MET together sometime."

"Damn man, can't you stop hitting on my cousin!" Lucien says it before he can stop himself, flushes, because it came out a little breathless, strained. "I mean, you too damn obvious with your shit. You think you got some serious game, but you just making yourself silly."

"Nigga, go on with that silly shit. Like we don't all know why you don't like niggas hollering at Maya."

For a moment no one speaks. The track switches from two to three. The beat samples The Coaster's *Shopping for Clothes*. It's a slow, creeping beat, lingering in the air like unsaid words. After a bar a deep voice comes in, "He says, pick yourself out one, try it on, stand in the mirror and dig yo'self," repeating four bars before Booker goes in with his own slow-flow.

"Yeah, nigga, listen," Booker says, and leans forward, but at that moment Lucien's cellphone rings again. It's Caleb.

"Yo, Buzz me in, College."

A moment later Caleb comes through, lean and long and mean like a switch. "What's good, my nigga? What you niggas up to? Damn, Maya. You here too? How you doing today?"

Even this last bit of flirting doesn't sound too sweet coming from Caleb. He takes the proffered Dutch from Maya, and stops for a moment, listening to the music. "Beat is sick," he says. "But what's this nigga going on about?"

"That's Booker's shit," says Lucien, and they all start laughing, because it's obviously Booker, and Booker just sips and says, "jealous ass no talent niggas love to hate."

Caleb sits himself next to Maya, leaning in like he hasn't a care in the world, and gets right to business. "New package come in?"

"Yeah, man, yesterday. We sitting on it."

Maya lights a lavender cigarette, and leans in towards Caleb, like a magnet attracted to iron.

"Good, we gonna need it. Young nigga Casey talking about too much business out there today. We need another driver. Nigga Obama got everybody in Bucktown smoking, white boys too." He pauses to take a puff from the Dutch. "You good to drive today, College? We been taking calls all morning, and we getting low on stash, too."

"Yeah, yeah, I can handle a couple routes."

"We'll give you some laid back shit. Williamsburg, with the white niggas. They less likely to get jumpy about a new driver."

"Word. I can handle any route you give me."

Caleb grins, rubs his chin, passes the Dutch back to Maya. "Is that so? I guess you could. You got heart for a college nigga, College, I'll say that. Here, take this." He passes a cellphone to Lucien. "That's the Williamsburg phone. We got everything covered up to now, but as new calls come in, I'll text you the address. You take that down on the mental, and then erase the shit. You get a bunch of them shits coming in at once, just keep them until you don't need them no more. Got it?"

"Yeah man, I've driven before. No worries."

"Word. You a good nigga, College." He stands up. "Let me get something before I go, something for them Bushwick niggas. They ain't holding nothing."

"Yeah man, what you need?"

After Caleb goes, Lucien and Booker and Maya smoke and listen to Booker's album. Call it corny, cuz it is, Lucien's thinking to himself, and maybe it's just the weed, but the shit sounds good, and the rhymes really ain't half bad. Booker can rhyme, he's all right. Maya seems to be thinking the same, because she's sunk herself into the couch, lighting lavender after lavender, and blinking up at the ceiling, smiling from time to time at a punchline. Booker's taking this shit in with a whole lot of pride, but trying to play the shit off type humble, head down, nodding to the beat, occasionally even rapping along with himself at a punchline here and there. They lose track of time, and the sun comes in an orange autumn slant through the windows, painting Bed-Sty shadows crooked across the walls. It's just half an hour or so before the first text comes in.

"Shit man, I gotta ride," says Lucien, startled by the unfamiliar chirp of the Williamsburg phone. "You good to hold down the spot while I'm out?"

"Yeah nigga, we good." Booker smiles at Maya, who just stubs out her cigarette, and sits up.

"You're going to Williamsburg?"

"Yeah." He hesitates. "You need a ride?"

"Could you?"

"Sure." With renewed spring to his step. "Where you going?"

"What's the hurry, beautiful," says Booker, putting on his best nonchalance. "You ain't heard the rest of the album yet."

"We'll catch up later. I lost track of time," says Maya. "I need to get going."

&

Lucien drops Maya off at an apartment building in Broadway Triangle, right on the border of Bed-Sty and Williamsburg.

"What's with this place?" he asks, looking skeptically at some rundown old building sitting next to a mechanics garage. "Who the hell lives here?"

"Just a friend of mine."

"What's his name?"

"Damn, Lucien. What are you, Henry? He's just a friend, okay?"

Lucien hesitates a moment. Then offers, quietly, "About what Booker was talking about back there-"

"Oh, forget about it. I know Booker just likes to run his mouth," Maya says quickly. She flushes suddenly, flusters for a cigarette. "Listen, I really should go. I'll give you a call later, okay?"

"Word."

Caleb wasn't kidding about it being busy. All the rest of the afternoon Lucien's driving from one spot to another, Bedford to Berry, out to Lorimer, then east into East Williamsburg, back over to Driggs, up to Greenpoint Avenue, circling Williamsburg like a barhappy hipster. By the time Caleb texts him it's okay to call it quits for the day, he's exhausted. He parks on a side street off Metropolitan, and orders a beer and a burger at the first bar he sees. It's a large cavernous space, filled with kids in colorful clothes, but Lucien ignores them. He sits at the bar, and lets the day overwhelm him. As he's sitting there, sinking into his fatigue, he remembers the apartment where Maya had him drop her off.

Who the hell lives in that place anyway? Lucien looks around the bar and frowns. One of these hipster kids? That's what she's into, then? He shrugs, all alone, right there at the bar, tries to brush it off. It shouldn't surprise him. She fits right in with them, really, but Maya seems too real for this crowd. Could this really be her scene? He finishes his first beer, orders another, and then the thoughts really start to crowd streaming in his head. It'd be no big deal just to swing by the apartment again, now that the sun's gone down, see what he can see, the cat lives on the first floor, you can see right through that shit, and this morning the blinds were open. The more he drinks of that second beer, the better the idea seems to him. Really he's just looking out for his cousin, man, he doesn't trust these cats, better she was with a thug like Caleb than one of these fraudulent fucks.

He finishes the beer quickly, now resolved. It's just a couple minutes before he's pulling through Throop Street again. The windows in the apartment are on all right, and the blinds are still up. He parks across the street by the school, and turns off the engine, slouches low in the black S63, hat pulled back, looking. A moment later, there she is, Maya, passing in front of the window like a shadow. She's got a glass of wine in her hand, and she's smoking one of her lavenders. Lucien sinks further down in the seat. She passes from the view of the window again, and Lucien tries to see how much of the interior he can peep from where he sits. Not much. He can see a couple plants in the window, a television by the window, a couch in front of the television, the top of a bed. Now here he comes, some gumpy ass looking brother. Not a white boy at least, but not much better. He's skinny and small and looks like a cross between a disheveled professor and a Williamsburg hipster. What the hell is Maya doing with this cat? Some Poindexter-ass brother living in South Williamsburg? Gotta be kidding me. Here comes Maya again, he can see them both pretty clear. They're talking, he's putting his arm around her. Maya kisses him, but she doesn't look too into it, maybe the cat's got money or something. No, not if he's living here, naw, he's broke for sure. Something doesn't add up. He wants to go now that his curiosity's been satisfied, but he can't seem to work up the resolve. He keeps watching. They talk, drift in and out of frame, drink, talk, kiss. This shit is killing him. Eventually they settle down on the couch. Lucien can see just the tops of their heads, and the low blue glow from the television set. He can occasionally see when one of them tips back their glass, and the tufts of violet smoke from Maya's cigarettes.

He's there for almost an hour before he finally starts up the Benz, and heads back home.

&

He wakes up the next morning depressed. It's Election Day, but the shit just don't seem to mean much to him anymore, he doesn't know why not. Shit is all the same, he tells himself. Black president just a pawn for the white boys in power anyhow. Ain't a damn thing gonna change. He spends the morning drinking coffee and thinking about Maya and that funny brother from the night before. It feels like it's driving him crazy, a dark cloud over the day, a dug out feeling in his chest. He gets in his vehicle, and drives around the city for a couple hours, over the Williamsburg Bridge, up JFK Parkway, watches the East River and Brooklyn spin by in the late morning sun, silver and blue beneath the wide arching bridges. He rides all the way up to 125th Street, and drives crosstown through East Harlem, Harlem proper, where the streets are packed with people, like it's a party. Cats out with Obama posters in force, strolling the street in colorful suits and shit, shaking hands, smiling, and for a moment, he gets a warm feeling in his chest, but then he's out past 125th, and then on to Riverside Drive. He takes Riverside all the way back downtown, this time with the Hudson on his right, and Jersey way off in the distance, silver and blue, shaded by the green of the park, the autumn orange and red of the leaves, the swimming shade. He tries to keep that warm feeling from 125th with him, but it's gone by the time he's back downtown, and then he's driving across Houston, and the feeling deserts him completely. By the time he gets down to Delancey and the Williamsburg Bridge, he's just thinking about Maya and that other dude, and he turns off the bridge onto Broadway, takes Broadway down to Throop, and rides up slow on the apartment. Just as he's getting there he sees the brother right ahead of him, coming down the stairs from the J Train. Lucien sinks real low in the seat, and watches this silly ass cat walk his way up to the building. Looks like he's already had a few, and here it is not even three o' clock in the afternoon. The brother goes up in the apartment, and sure enough a moment later he's right there in front of the window with a glass of wine in his hand. Maya hooked up with a fucking basehead.

Maybe it's the spirit of Caleb, but something comes over Lucien in that moment. A furious bloodlust. He rolls down the window, leans out just slightly as Poindexter turns about, and then he shouts in his best West Indian brogue:

"Dead Nigga Walking!"

He slides back way low into his seat, and watches the window through the rearview. The shook ass cat shows up at the window right away, like he wants to get shot, get the damn thing over with. Poindexter's looking out the window left and right, glass of wine in hand, and can't seem to pull himself away. A moment later he disappears into the back of the apartment.

Lucien has to laugh. It's the best he's felt all day, except maybe that brief stretch of 125th Street. Poindexter was shook to death. He must've turned as pale as a white boy standing at that window. And here he comes again, nervously brushing past the window, glancing out like he's inconspicuous or something, still holding onto that glass of wine like a binky. When he turns and sits down, Lucien hollers at him again:

"Dead Nigga drinking!"

Lucien shouts it with such a chuckle in his voice, even he can't believe it when Poindexter comes hobbling sheepishly back to the window, sheet white shook. He's saying hello or some shit to the window, looking around, sipping on that wine like it's his last, and Lucien slides deep into the vehicle, and shouts,

"Dead Bwoy!"

Now Poindexter cold freezes. He doesn't even move to drink that wine, standing there like a deer caught in headlights or some shit. Goddamn, if Lucien really were gunning for him, he'd be one dead brother standing there like that. Dude is trippin. He sits low in the seat and just amazes that the brother would stand there like that, and for so long. After what feels like forever, Poindexter turns around, and apparently pours himself another glass, because here he comes peeking back at the window with the shit refilled.

"Dead Bwoy gon' die!"

This time Poindexter moves. He quaffs off that wine, and next thing Lucien knows, the brother's in his jacket, heading out the door. A second later he emerges onto the street. He strides quick east up Throop, then quick west down Throop, then heads hightail up Lorimer Street. Lucien waits a few minutes, lets him get some proper distance, then follows him. He follows him up Lorimer, left onto Metropolitan, and straight west until he hits Berry, where Poindexter disappears into a bar. Go fucking figure. Uncle Tom ass Poindexter ran straight to white ass hipsterville, which, Lucien supposes, is where he must feel safe.

&

Lucien can't stop thinking about that performance the rest of the day. He's never seen a cat run like that. He laughs himself silly all evening about it, and all through the next day, until he starts to think about the fact that if Maya's with that cat, then she probably is just another hipster wannabe herself, and that depresses all the good feeling he had about the whole thing in the first place. As evening starts to settle in, all he can think about is that brother sitting there kicking it with Maya. He tries to go to bed, but can't sleep for thinking about it, so he gets up and decides to go for a drive. He tries to kid himself like he's not headed back to Throop Street, but he knows he is, and within ten minutes, sure enough, there he is again, parked across the street from Poindexter's building. Poindexter is there, lights on, blinds up, like the brother has no sense at all after yesterday, but some cats just don't learn. It looks like he's alone, and this takes a weight off Lucien's chest. He starts to think better of it, but then can't help himself. It's late right now, and a long walk to Bedford. What's the brother gonna do if someone starts at him now?

"Dead Nigga!"

And there he is again, all of a sudden, like the shit is his name or something, standing at the window, straining to look out. No wine glass with him this time, but he's swaying like he's had a few anyway.

"Dead Bwoy!"

Poindexter reaches for the blinds, thinks better of it, and then disappears towards the back of the apartment. Lucien can't stop himself from laughing, can hardly believe how he's stringing this dude along no problem at all. The music turns up loud from out of the apartment, Tribe of course, what you'd expect Poindexter to be listening to, and Lucien yells, very loud this time

"Nigga, you dead bwoy!"

Now Poindexter's bouncing between the window and the back of the apartment like a rubber ball. For a few minutes he's gone, then for a few minutes he's there. If Lucien ain't sleeping tonight, neither is Poindexter. See where this leads.

At which point Poindexter disappears completely. Lucien wonders where he went, maybe he's hiding in the bathroom or something, until maybe ten minutes later, he suddenly sees Poindexter emerge onto the street, right under the building's front door, the light right there on him like a cop light. Poindexter crouches down low, a bottle in his hand, and he's flexing it like he might could really do something if shit went down. Lucien has to hold himself, he's laughing so hard. But now Poindexter's making ground. He's headed straight for the J Train. Enough of this shit. Let's let him be for the night. Maybe he'll come back tomorrow, maybe not. Shit is hilarious, but it's getting old now too, and it won't be long before old Poindexter here calls the cops, so fuck it.

In the end, circumstances decide the situation for him anyway. Fate is like that, and anyone who tells you Karma don't come back for you don't know. The next day Booker and Caleb come by to tally up the election earnings. They're smoking and drinking Coors tallboys and feeling pretty good about the intake when Lucien's cellphone rings. It's Maya.

"Hey May'. What's up?"

"I'm downstairs, Lucien. Can you buzz me in?"

"Word. See you in a sec."

But just as he's opening the door, he feels a buzz at the nape of his neck, and he knows something's not right. The door opens itself, and a large hand covers his face, shoving him back into the apartment. A moment later the door slams shut and five cats in black masks and gloves are in the apartment with him, and they're all holding nines.

The look of shock on Lucien's face must be palpable, because like Poindexter, he doesn't move, and one of the masks snickers, "Nigga shook."

"Yeah, nigga," says the man in front. "Get the fuck on the floor. You know what this is."

TEN

Lucien gets down to his knees slow, glancing back a moment to look for Booker and Caleb. Booker is half out of his seat, half in it, like he's looking for a way to run. Caleb is sliding down slow, reaching for his weapon.

"Get the fuck down, nigga," the man repeats, and then Caleb's forced the rest of the way over, so that his face lies directly on the floorboards. The intruders spread out and sweep the apartment. It doesn't take long, three rooms and a bedroom, and then there's a brief scuffle, and the sound of a gun being cocked.

"Don't even think about it nigga, or we'll wet all three of y'all niggas, just cuz you on some James Bond shit. Yo, take that nigga's piece."

Then a chilly stillness, while Lucien lies looking at the floor, trying to see out of the periphery what's going on. His heart is thudding against the floorboards, and his whole body seems to be going faint and light, and he wonders if this is how he's going to die. In that frantic moment, he tries to make some peace and sense out of his life, but it all seems like senseless noise and confusion.

He feels hands run up and down his back, chest and torso, and then arms lifting him back up. He's too weak to stand, he keeps sliding back down, and suddenly there's a pistol in his face, and one of them is shouting at him. It takes him a moment before he can make sense of the words through all his dizziness.

"Where the weed and the cash at, nigga? Move!"

Lucien goes like an automaton towards the kitchen. He opens the cabinet with the weed, and then a couple of the intruders grab up the bags, and vanish in the background.

"Yeah. Now the money, nigga. Where's the rest of the money?"

Lucien leads them into the bedroom, to the dresser beside his bed. Inside the dresser cabinet are bags of cash. It's more or less everything he has. He watches them snatch it up. Whatever happens now, everything's changed.

They lead him back into the living room, force him back on the floor. "Yo, sweep this bitch one more time, make sure they ain't hiding any extra shit," someone says. And for what feels like hours, but must just be a minute or two, Lucien looks at the floorboards, and hears boots tramping up and down the halls, into and out of rooms.

"Yeah, we got all they shit," he hears at last. "Should we wet these niggas, or what?"

"Yeah, yeah. Start with that little shook ass nigga who opened the door."

Lucien stifles a gasp and closes his eyes. So this is it. This is really it. He feels his bowels turning liquid, and he tightens his muscles to keep from shitting or pissing himself, listening for eternity.

Instead he just hears the door shut and muffled laughter. Boots disappearing down the stairs. He lies there for another minute or two until all sound dissipates altogether. He feels like he could just lie there all day, listening to the sound of his heart thudding, his breathing, heavy, short, and fast.

"Yo, Lucien, get up. Them niggas is gone. I know who the niggas are, too." Caleb's voice, bitterly reassuring, wakes him back up. He climbs warily to his feet, still half expecting voices to bark him back down, but turning around there's just Caleb and Booker, both on their feet, and looking slightly dazed and flummoxed.

"You know who they were?" Lucien asks.

"Yeah, I caught a tattoo on one of them niggas' arms. I recognized that shit. East New York niggas; a new skool crew from around the way.

They been making a name for themselves the last couple years with this stick up kid shit." Caleb pats himself down. "I need to get my gear, then we need to get some of our Bushwick niggas and put a team together."

"What you thinking?"

"What am I thinking? Nigga, what you think I'm thinking? We gotta go get them niggas."

"Man, we ought to sit down and talk this shit out some."

"Nigga did you just have a nine in your face, or what? Did you just hear them niggas call you shook, or what? Nigga, is you a man or a bitch?"

"Shit man, I don't know. I'm just saying. What you think, Booker?"

"I'm with Caleb," says Booker. "We gonna get known as niggas you can just come and rob if we don't do shit. We do this shit professional, and we can just hit them niggas where they live at, get in and get out."

"Yeah, yeah. Word. I feel you."

"College, man, I thought you had heart," says Caleb. "This is the game, nigga. Either you in or you out. You don't do this shit half ass." Caleb pauses, looks Lucien right in the eye. "We good?"

"Yeah. Yeah, we good."

"Good. Y'all wait here. I'll ride out to Bushwick, and see who we can get together. We'll go see those niggas tonight."

"You already know where they're at?"

"Naw, but I know who to ask about them. Won't be hard to find them." Caleb takes a couple steps toward the door. He nods his head down, pauses a moment then swivels towards Lucien. "There's also that other matter."

"What other matter?" Lucien pretends like he doesn't know, but he knows what's coming.

"Maya. Your cousin, nigga. What's up with that bitch? Looks to me like the bitch set us up."

"Yeah. Looks that way."

"You know where she rest at?"

"Somewhere uptown."

"Listen, nigga. You can't be protecting her now. She coulda got your ass murked. She knows what it is. Them niggas coulda wet us as soon as not."

"Yeah, yeah. Word. True, true."

"So where she stay at?"

Lucien looks helplessly to Booker.

"Nigga, Booker ain't the one talking to you."

"Well, what you think, Booker? We can't just…. Maya?" Lucien looks helplessly back at Caleb.

Caleb frowns an ominous frown. "We gonna need that address. You get it for me, you heard? I'll be back soon."

After Caleb leaves, Booker and Lucien just stand there looking at each other. Booker lights a cigarette and offers one to Lucien. Lucien's not much of a smoker, just now and then, but this is definitely one of those now and then moments. They smoke and pace for a couple minutes in complete silence. Lucien opens a beer, passes it to Booker, then opens one for himself.

"Damn, Lucien," Booker says after a while. "I woulda never thought Maya would do us dirty like that."

Lucien considers this quietly for a moment. "We just heated right now," he says after a while. "I need to talk to her. We don't know what's going on with her. They might have made her do that shit."

"Yeah, I hope it's something like that. But how'd they get a hold of her? Shit don't add up."

"Something don't," Lucien agrees. "Still, I want to talk to her first." He reaches for his cell phone, thinks better of it, and then lets his hand drop to his side. "Really, she ought to be calling us. And if they made her do it, they probably took her phone. I don't want to be calling them up instead of her." They continue to pace the floor, smoking, drinking.

"We got any weed left?" asks Booker. "A Dutch or some shit stashed away."

"Yeh, I got that." Lucien opens a drawer under the table, and pulls out what's left of his private reserves, a little over a quarter. "Let's roll some shit."

&

Fifteen minutes later they're sitting down again, Hot 97 on the dial, drifts of thick smoke dissipating in the early afternoon sun. Lucien thought smoking might calm his nerves, but now he's more nervous than ever. He keeps picturing the gun in his face, that faint feeling he had, how he could barely stand, almost wetting himself. "You ever shot someone?" he asks Booker after a while.

"Naw, though I seen one kid get took out a couple years back. Shit ain't pleasant, man. You know I stay on that kick that knowledge shit. Black man rise up. But the way I see it, is we ain't got much choice now. Either we get on some retaliation shit, or we get out the game. And we ain't got no other options but the game."

"Yeah, but I never did want to get into this whole wilding out shit. Us killing each other. That shit ain't right."

"You right on there. It's definitely some foul shit."

&

Lucien waits all day for that call from Maya to come in, but it never comes. Caleb shows up some time in the early evening with a crew of seven roughnecks, and they got a stash of weapons, black clothing, gloves, masks, you name it.

"All right," Caleb says. "Here's how it's gonna go down. Them niggas got a stash house out on Livonia Avenue, between Barbey and Schenck. We park just in front of they house, and then me and these Bushwick niggas gonna run up in it. College, you got the easy job. You just sit in the car, let that shit idle. When you see us running back out, you be ready to take off. Booker, I'm letting you off easy too. You niggas really ain't built for war, and I ain't trying to get you niggas killed. You gonna spot College. Just stay right outside the car, and make sure niggas don't try to creep up and around on his ass. Once you see us running out, you jump in too, and we'll light the fuck up out of there. Y'all need to be packing, though. I'll give you both M9s. You able to handle that?"

"No doubt," says Booker, and Lucien just nods dazedly.

"We robbing these niggas, we wetting these niggas, and we taking no prisoners. Just so you know. Shit is gonna get loud. I need you two rugged and ready. And College, you got that address for me?"

"Yeah. Maya. She's Upper West Side. 103rd Street between Broadway and Amsterdam. I don't know the exact address, but I can get it."

"You do that. We gonna get her later this week."

"I was thinking though, Caleb. Maybe they made her do that shit."

Caleb stops, grins, looks up at Lucien. "You really soft on that bitch, ain't you, College? Call her. Call her right now. If a nigga picks up the phone give it to me."

Lucien looks at the phone like it's something unnatural. He dials the number, his head thick with storm clouds. It goes directly to voicemail. He hangs up. Looks at the phone again. Calls again, and gets voicemail. "Shit is going straight to voicemail," he says. "It must be turned off."

"Yeah, I guess it must fucking be," says Caleb cryptically. "But I don't want you on some distraction shit tonight. We'll deal with her when the time comes. You want to talk to her first? You can talk to her. Right now, we just need to focus on this shit right here, because this right here is the real shit, and anything after this is just puffin' la in the park."

&

They pull up in front of the house just before eleven. Lucien has been trying to keep focused, keep breathing and relax, he tells himself he's got nothing to worry about, he's not even going in the house, but still, he can't seem to keep his heart still. He can feel it running circles through his veins, he can feel the thrum of blood, like it's searching for an exit, a constant pressure that keeps him tense and electric. The tingle he felt at the nape of his neck has returned, and comes and goes like a musical theme, a dirge maybe.

At Barbey Street Caleb tells him to cut the lights, and then they coast the half block up Livinia in Caleb's black SUV, ghosting the avenue. They stop just in front of the house. They're lucky: there's an open spot right there, and Caleb says that's a good sign. The shit will go down easy. The team climbs out real quiet street side, and when they close the door, Lucien starts to feel the relief of the present implode his panic. Whatever happens now, well, it's already happening. And in this monster of a vehicle, he feels like he's in a tank anyway. He won't have to shoot anyone, and he won't even have to watch anyone else shoot anyone. He just has to sit there and drive. Yeah, yeah, he can do that.

"You ready Booker?" he asks, and Booker nods.

"Yeah, how you feel?"

"Guess a nigga nervous, but I'll be all right."

"Yeah."

"You nervous?"

"Naw, I mean, yeah a little. Who wouldn't be. But you know, I'm not afraid of getting murked, or I mean I am, who wouldn't be. After all, all we got here is this one life to live, but shit man. It matters how you live it too. I mean. Shit, man. I don't know. I'm trying not to think about it."

Booker slides out of the vehicle a moment later, and takes his position in the rear. Lucien watches in the rearview as Booker cocks his weapon, and slides low. Lucien slides low himself, low in the seat. He watches as Caleb directs his crew up the stairs, over the balcony. How do they plan to get inside? In a moment shit is gonna be on, and there's gonna be a whole lot of shooting. Lucien tries to brace himself for the first retorts, slides lower in the SUV.

It comes quicker than Lucien expects. Caleb shoots out the lock on the door, a loud angry clanging explosion of a sound that has Lucien's heart wild again with fear, and his neck buzzing like a drill. Caleb shoots it a second time, and then a couple of them kick the rest of the door open, and they're in. There's a lot of shouting, a couple more shots fired, and then the entire crew disappears into the house. More shots fired. With every shot Lucien starts. The house lights with each shot, terrible and angry orange red. A shot goes through a window, shattered glass and smoke. All Lucien can hear is shouting and shooting, more shouting, more shooting. At first he tries to count the shots, just to keep his mind focused on something, but they increase exponentially, everything becomes a confusion of noise. Automatic weapons begin firing off numerous rounds, and suddenly the house is lit up like a basehead. A lot of people are dead by now, Lucien is glad he's not in there. At least there's that. He's not in there. And then everything goes quiet for a moment. Smoke wafts through the broken windows, the house turns black with the quiet. All the lights are out. What the fuck is going on in there anyway?

A moment later Lucien sees Caleb come running out, a couple other Bushwick cats with him, it doesn't look like the whole seven, but Lucien can't quite count the number. They're coming out sideways, firing shots back as they run. When a slug hits the side of the vehicle, a dull metal thud that feels way too close, that's when he realizes the firefight has moved outside. Caleb and crew are on the run.

They run behind the SUV and start shooting back, but the automatic weaponry from the house has them pinned for a moment. Lucien slides way down into the seat, and the windows above him shatter. The vehicle is hiccoughing with slugs, one after the other thuds into its frame, and Lucien wonders if something hits the wrong shit, if there's a chance to vehicle could burst into flames. Wonders if a bullet might penetrate the metal, penetrate its way into his flesh, begins to feel the tingle hard in his neck, tight, and looking up at the rearview to the right, he sees Booker swivel, a horrific look of anguish washing his face as he falls. This is the moment Lucien really starts to question the whole thing; like the whole thing of everything, basically every decision he's made that's become his life. It's been a life lived in the service of nothing but his own death, a n egotistical statistical nigga, just another nigga caught up in the game, shot dead in East New York, a cliché, a rap song lyric, a television episode, a fucking street novel.

A moment later the SUV door opens, and Caleb scrambles in with five other men. "We lost two in the house," Caleb shouts, shutting the door.

"Niggas got Booker, too." They're all clambered in over top of each other, horizontal. "Drive, nigga, drive!"

Lucien is terrified of sitting up straight enough to operate the wheel, but the desire to get the hell out of there is stronger than his fear. He takes a deep breath, starts up the car, and slouches over the wheel. A moment later they're moving, driving down Livinia, with the sound of gunfire ricocheting in the background, or maybe just still in Caleb's head, a haunting sound, like the haunting sight of Booker's death, like a recurring theme, like a melody, maybe like death bells.

NINE

It's a while before anyone speaks. They take Livinia west to Pennsylvania, head north on Pennsylvania and then west again on Atlantic Avenue. They make a detour onto a side street to toss their weapons in a storm drain, and finally, back on Atlantic everyone seems to relax a little.

"What the fuck happened back there?" Lucien asks.

"It's like them niggas was waiting on us," says Caleb. "We were outnumbered and outgunned. Petey and Cray took one almost as soon as we went in. Petey went down right away, but Cray took it. He kept on going. Then we were crouching behind anything we could find and shooting. Nigga who took out Petey got one right away, and then we wet a couple more of them niggas, and then we spread out to find they shit. We wet a nigga in the back room, and we got some money, some weed, but we wasn't nowhere near the real stash. We got caught from behind by a couple other niggas hiding in another room, and Cray took one to the head. One of them niggas threw the lights, and that's when the shit turned to all out warfare. At that point, it was just about getting out of there, and taking out as many of them as we could in retreat. Niggas had us on the run. Someone must've tipped those niggas off, cuz they were going hard, and they were ready."

"And Booker."

"Yeah, College. That shit gets me too. Booker wasn't supposed to be up in the mix of action at all."

"Guess this means we at war now," says one of the Bushwick roughnecks, and Caleb nods. Lucien doesn't know how he feels about that, or
rather he does, he just doesn't want to say anything right now. Now's not
the time. But he's out. He's getting out. He's getting the fuck out.

&

Back home, everything feels empty and lonely and gray and threaten-
ing, like storm clouds trailing shadows over the walls and floors. If they're
at war now, the other crew knows where he lives. He can't stay here
much longer. He needs to find a new place, but he has no options. Normally, he might ask Maya if he could stay at her place, but obviously
that's out. Instead he just smokes, and turns on music – Booker, as it turns
out, still has his CD in the player, and he wonders what to do. The night
carries into morning. He doesn't sleep. He can't because he's always waiting to hear the door crash in, black men hollering, guns flashing. When
dawn wanders orange across the aurora, he gets in his car and goes for a
drive.

He doesn't have any particular destination, he's driving to run, to forget, to get away from his thoughts, but they stay close. He drives through
downtown Brooklyn, across the Brooklyn Bridge, watches Manhattan
wake up across the water. He hits Canal Street, and the heavy crushing
funky morning life makes him suddenly elated to be alive at all, to be
watching as the people rush downtown to work, the trucks coming
through with commercial wares, the streets already heavy with commut-
ers. That he's still here seems unlikely, the previous evening itself a world
away, and he's suddenly lightheaded, thinking maybe he didn't make it
after all, and this is some sort of afterlife. Well, if this is the afterlife, he'll
take it – driving through the city, checking out the pretty women as he
rides north through Soho, listening to Hot 97's morning show on the radio, it's really not so bad for being dead. Except for the flashbacks; they
keep coming back to him with the urgency of an open wound; the memo-

ries fester and burn. The look on Booker's face when he was hit, that look of horror and disbelief; that look of disappointment and dread, that look haunted him more than anything. He'd never seen a man die before, but watching Booker, he knew one thing for sure: nothing came after this life. No, the look in Booker's eyes said it all. Booker was looking at vacancy. There's no such thing as a soul, that's what Booker's face said, or even a self. There's life and there's death and there's nothing else.

But then he takes Houston to Riverside Drive, and driving up the side of the city, watching the sun rise mirrored in the river as wavelengths of light and liquid, he suddenly feels the presence of God. The sky opens up, and the clouds widen their distance, and the kaleidoscope colors of sun, river, cloud and city seem more grand than anything he's ever seen before, or at least noticed before, because he's seen this a million times, only now he notices something in it – a presence, a voice, a spirit, a soul. It's not a religious moment, exactly, but it's certainly spiritual. He follows the spirit north, all the way through midtown, the Upper West Side, past Riverside Park, with its rolling grassy hills overlooking the Hudson. He keeps going north into Harlem, and ends up following the spirit all the way to the George Washington Bridge, which he suddenly decides to cross, still chasing the spirit like it lies somewhere just over the next wonder inspired thought. As he ascends the bridge, into the sky, towards the sun, the light takes hold of him, right there in the vehicle, and he feels that if there's spirit, soul, or God, it emanates not from the sun, not from the sky, nowhere from outside of him, but from within him. Because how many times has he made this drive, and been asleep to it. Soul comes from the living and the awake, and he's both for the first time in his life. What, then, is God to a god? If he himself is a god, then he is in himself immortal, and a bizarre logic forms in his mind, where last night, and this morning all swing together in perfect unison. He could not, after all, have died last night, because he did not die, and God could not kill him, because God is nothing more than an extension of his own Godliness.

But as soon as he's back over the bridge his spirit sinks with the arc. He's back in Jersey, where he was born, where he grew up, and he realizes, dreadfully, that he's not really driving aimlessly. He's been automatically making his way back home, to his parent's house in the suburbs of Hackensack. Which just goes to show that when he thought he was most awake, he was really very deeply asleep.

It's an upsetting thought, but after all, where else can he go? It's definitely not safe to stay in Bed-Sty. He pulls up into the driveway, it's a large white and red house on a quiet residential street. There's a yard in the front and a garden in the back and a porch to the side. As he steps out of the vehicle, he looks up at the tremendous New Jersey sky, at the tranquil sanitized cleanliness of the neighborhood, and thinks how far away this feels from Brooklyn, and it's really not even so far. Just a couple rivers away. Inside, everything feels miniature and familiar, like a cozy museum filled with art book favorites. There are metaphors to be found here, metaphors for his lost innocence, he thinks, going from the living room to the kitchen, upstairs to his old bedroom, still scattered with miscellaneous memorabilia from his past. He goes back downstairs and turns on the television. It suddenly feels very cozy and safe being here, and he hasn't just sat in a comfortable living room and watched daytime television for a while.

His parents aren't home. They'd be at work right now; his father down in Newark at the New Jersey Institute of Technology, and his mother as a journalist for *The Star Ledger*. They would have left not so long ago, and they won't be back until the evening, so he has the day to himself. They'll be surprised to see him; even more surprised when he tells them he wants to stay for a few days. For all he knows it may turn out to be a few weeks. There's no way to know how long it will take before things cool down in Brooklyn.

He's more or less spacing out, thinking about all this shit, flipping through the channels, when he stops on NY1. There's something about a shooting out in East Brooklyn the night before. They're talking about the crime scene: a house in East New York was raided by a rival gang last evening around 11 PM. One man was found shot to death outside the building, and six other men found dead inside the house. A police investigation resulted in the arrest of several people inside the house for illegal weapons and drug possession. A community activist interviewed right there on the block, in front of the disastrous scene, a garish mess of glass and brick and concrete is talking about gun control, about education, about getting the children off the streets. And here's Lucien, a college educated brother, who never spent any serious time on the streets at all, involved in the whole thing, and for what? He isn't sure. Was it to prove to himself he was black enough to be down? Was it just for the money? The thrill? The free weed? He really doesn't know. This isn't his world, and what in the world was he doing there? What was he contributing to, sleepwalking?

The thought that a bunch of the stick up kids have already been arrested, that there are now fewer, if any, cats out there gunning for him is comforting, to say the least. He dozes, sitting right there in front of the television, and lets a voluntary worry free sleep come over him for the first time in a couple nights. He stretches out on the couch, lets the sun run his length, warm and reassuring, he is alive; he is free; he will continue to live free, and he can leave the past behind. It's not even really his past; here is his past, in the leisure of middle class comfort, it was the fever dream of a sick black man trapped sleeping through a nightmare.

He wakes up to the ringing of his cell phone. He has no idea how much time has passed; the sun is still up, but it's waning now, leaving in its weakening wake the cool November twilight. He picks up the cellphone and looks at it: the number is blocked. He knows he shouldn't answer, but the confusion of just waking and a morbid curiosity win out. "Hello?"

"Yeah, nigga. We came by your crib. We gonna keep coming by. Next time we see you in New York, nigga, be it at your crib, in the street, it don't matter, you one dead nigga. You heard?"

Lucien opens his mouth to say something, he doesn't know what, but before he can think of anything the line goes dead.

He gets up and paces the floor. The television is still on, it's still NY1 looping the news, but now they're back to discussing the election and the economic collapse. Collapse indeed. Lucien's life has just collapsed all at once, in a day, and there are no options for him. He paces, wonders who's still out there; who wouldn't have been picked up, who still knows about him out there, his involvement with last night? He starts to call Caleb, but thinks better of it. He looks out the window at the peaceful New Jersey suburb, and thinks to himself, well, it looks like he's going to be here a while, then. There's no going back to New York now. He sits back down and continues to watch the news, but he's not really paying it any mind; he's thinking about what he'll say when his parents get back home.

It's just before five now, and it won't be long. He goes outside and sits on the front step, taking in the twilight sky, the fresh suburban air. He decides to call Caleb after all.

"What up College? Where you at?"

"I left the city. I think I'm gonna lay low a while. Those niggas called me today. Said they came by my crib looking for me."

"Cops rounded up a bunch of them niggas this morning. Can't be much of they crew left. We got plans to get 'em, though. Come on back in the city, we can put your ass up til we hit them niggas."

"Naw, I think I'm out Caleb. Out of the game for good. I ain't built for this shit. You know Booker's death fucked me up real good. I need time to think."

"Word." Caleb pauses. "Listen, I'll keep you updated on how this shit goes down. These niggas won't be out here much longer, so you ain't got shit to worry about."

"Thanks Caleb. Good looking out."

Lucien hangs up the phone. He still doesn't know what he'll do if he gives up hustling. He has no resume to speak of, hasn't had a decent job in years. His parents think he's making money on Internet advertising or something. They must know something doesn't add up, but refuse to see it. He's afraid to face them now, but then he looks forward to it, too. After all, he's been alone all day, and he's all nerves. He needs someone to talk to.

It's another hour before they come home. He's still right there, in front of the television, flipping channels, not really committed, when they come through the door: First his mother, then his father, and then Maya.

"Lucien, what in God's name?" says his mother, and his father grins and looks from Maya to Lucien and back again.

"Well, this is a coincidence, if ever there was one. What's the odds? When's the last time you two even saw each other? There some mass migration from Brooklyn to Jersey afoot, or what? What you doing home, son? Come on, let's all have a drink."

The idea sounds great to Lucien, dumbstruck. He stands and looks at Maya. She looks at him, and for a moment they stand there like that, just looking at each other without saying anything. Then she smiles something sly, and he hesitates. It's quick enough to be an illusion, but he could swear that she even winks.

EIGHT

In the waning evening light, Maya's eyes are like rubies. Lucien opens his mouth, closes it. He takes another moment to breathe. "We see each other sometimes," he says.

"It hasn't even been very long," Maya adds.

"But I didn't expect to see you here in Jersey." Seeing Maya again has him aflutter; somewhere he must have told himself he would never see her again. Now that she's here, and so soon, it feels like fate. He should be angry, and intellectually he is; but it's very hard to be angry with her right now. It feels like they're having another conversation under the layer of this one, one that neither of the parents is privy to.

"Come on in the kitchen," says Lucien's father. "We'll have a glass of wine."

Over a bottle of Riesling they discuss everything. Lucien dodges questions. It feels like an interrogation.

"So what have you been doing with yourself lately," his mother asks. "We hardly ever hear from you."

Lucien's mother, Alice, is a soft brown woman with big eyes, and a face so gentle she looks like she could be a social worker. She sips her wine slow, and peers at Lucien curiously; she seems innocent enough, but she's got her reporter's instincts, and beneath that welcoming façade, she's a switch.

"I've been doing the same thing, really. Internet advertising. I've got a couple websites I'm working on, and I've started building websites for other people. It does pretty well. Well enough, anyway."

"I don't see how," his mother says. "With prices rising the way they are."

"And then with this economic collapse," his father says. "Damned if they didn't give Obama the job just to watch the brother fail. Black man becomes president only in the greatest recession since the Great Depression. But so long as it works for you."

Lucien's father, Henry, thankfully, is a lot more naïve than his mother, or maybe he's just not interested enough in exploring these questions. Or maybe he just lacks a mother's instincts. But then again, he does have his own particular irksome quirks.

"But when are you going to put that degree of yours to work, eh? You think we put you through college just to see you fiddling around on the Internet all day? A Political Science degree is nothing to sneeze at in today's world. You could be writing for *The Nation* or something."

"*The Nation?*" Alice snorts. "Well then he'd be making less than he is now. And publishing propaganda. If you ask me," she says, "your father's onto something with putting that degree towards writing. But you need to be writing for something significant."

"Like *The Star Ledger?*" Lucien feels bad for saying it a moment after it comes out, he's not usually such a smart ass, but something in him has been triggered.

"*The Star Ledger* is an important paper, young man," Alice says. "What would you know about it? Anyway, whatever you do, your father's right. Now's the time to be putting that degree of yours to work."

"Why not do something like community organizing, like Obama? Truth be told, I always thought you'd be the first black president." His father smiles broad, like a loud clap on the back.

"Oh."

Maya smiles slyly from the other side of the table. "I can see it."

"I don't know why I took Political Science in the first place," Lucien says. "I should have taken Finance or Economics or something useful."

"Then you'd be halfway to joining the dark side," his father says. "No, with your degree you can still do some good."

"Your father's half Communist as it is," says Alice. "Don't let him go recruiting you."

"And I suppose Obama's a Socialist?" says Henry. "No, Capitalism's just gone too far is what it is. Anyone can see that, what with the whole banking scandal. Finally looks like the bastards are getting their due."

"Well enough with the politics," says Lucien. "I'll make good eventually. You'll see. I've got some ideas of my own. Maybe I'll start blogging. Go viral or something, and then I can write books and be on panels, and give my opinion about everything." He smiles.

"What brings you home anyway?" asks his mother, who seems to suddenly realize she's somehow been sidetracked from the main thrust of her investigation.

"I just needed to get out of the city for a while," says Lucien. "It's too hectic there. Especially after the election. I guess I need some time to relax and be with family and think about all the stuff we were just talking about. Maybe just through the holidays. Get a fresh start in the New Year. That's okay isn't it?"

Alice sips her wine and regards Lucien a little suspiciously. "Of course it's okay, honey. The thing is, well, that doesn't exactly sound like you. You sure something else isn't going on?"

"Yes, mom, I'm sure." Lucien shoots a glance towards Maya. She couldn't have told them anything, could she have? Maya's face gives nothing away. She seems to be actually somewhere else, not really even listening to the conversation.

"So what brings you here, Maya?" Lucien asks her.

Maya blinks and looks at him. Her face, solid for a moment, suddenly melts in the twilight; she takes a sip of wine and smiles. "I had a favor to ask of Uncle Henry," she says.

"Oh," says Lucien. "What was that?"

"She wants to help this guy she knows get a job."

"Which guy?" Lucien asks it too fast, he knows it the moment he says it. There was even a hint of desperation in the way it came out, but all he can hope now is no one caught it.

Maya caught it. She takes another slow sip of wine, and looks at Lucien over the rim of the glass. "Oh, just a friend of mine from the city."

"It's a fascinating story," says Henry. "Has she told you about this guy? Pinchback? He's been blind all his life, and now he can see."

"Sounds like something out of the Bible," says Lucien. "Wasn't that one of the guys Jesus healed?"

"Jesus comparisons are always welcome," Maya says demurely. "But, really I had little to do with it. Just the miracle of modern science. And a little convincing on my part. The thing about it is the guy's a brilliant physicist. And I think he's been given the short end of the stick all his life because he's been blind. So he doesn't really have a lot of credentials. I'm seeing if Uncle Henry can't get him a job at the Institute."

"It's worth a shot. Either way, I have to meet this guy, pick his brain and all. Never heard the likes of it before." Henry turns to Alice. "Really, you should be interviewing him. This could make one hell of a story."

"It's already been written," Alice says somewhat drolly. "Oliver Sacks? Maybe you've heard of him?"

"He did have a case similar to this one, didn't he?" Henry seems to take a moment to think it over. "But I don't think that guy was a physicist." A statement that apparently disperses any doubts he had about the similarities between the two. "Go on, Maya, Tell Lucien about him. Pour yourself another glass of wine."

"Yeah," Lucien says. "Please. Tell me about this guy. I've heard nothing about him at all."

The story sounds to Lucien more like a fable than reality. He listens to it only for the words beneath the words, the real question: who is this man to Maya? She doesn't give anything away. The evening sinks over the dining room, and they continue to talk while Henry prepares dinner. It's lasagna, something Lucien hasn't had in a very long time, and a home cooked meal is real comfort food. In the middle of dinner, though, he tears up, and he has to excuse himself to the bathroom where he sobs helplessly for a few minutes.

Later that evening Maya and Lucien retire upstairs. They have the rest of a bottle of wine between them, and even though they have their separate rooms, Lucien has his old bedroom and Maya has her old room, they are hanging out together in Lucien's room, sitting on Lucien's bed, drinking directly from the bottle. It's more or less the moment Lucien's been waiting for all evening.

"So what happened back there in Brooklyn, Maya?" It's warm in the house, the heat is central and unfamiliar. Maya takes off her sweater, and Lucien tries not to look at her breasts beneath her shirt, a plain white t-shirt, which says in thick red letters, *Sincerity is the new Irony.*

Maya looks away, out the window at the quiet New Jersey neighborhood. "I don't know, Lucien. I told them not to hurt anyone. I knew they wouldn't."

"How you gonna know something like that? Do you really know them nigg-," But he stops himself, because suddenly this street persona, this language he's been using, all of it feels fraudulent. "Do you really know them like that? How could you know people like that? They're stick-up kids for Christ's sake." He adds a little more quietly, "and here you're talking about hanging out with physicists and shit."

"Look, Lucien. I just wanted some weed. It was simple as that, huh? Just leave it at that." She looks a little exasperated, she clearly doesn't want to talk about it, but she has no way out of it.

"You can always ask me for weed," he says. "You know that already. Shit, you do that already."

"I know, Lucien. But I get tired of it. I get tired of going over there and asking for weed, and hanging out, and getting hit on." She pauses. "By everyone." She looks directly at Lucien now. "Take it as an act of spite on my part."

"An act of spite?" Lucien spits this as a whisper. "What kind of act of spite, where you almost got me killed? Booker's dead, Maya. You know that, right?"

"What? What do you mean Booker's dead?"

"We went back to get even, and they shot Booker. They killed two other dudes from out in Bushwick too. Now Caleb wants to get even again. It's like a fucking war, and I'm in the middle."

Maya's ruby eyes mist. "Booker's really dead?"

And for a moment Lucien hates Booker, is glad he's gone.

"Yes, Maya. Yes, he's dead, and it's all because-" He doesn't have the heart to say it, so he doesn't.

"Well they should get even," Maya decides. She looks out the window again. Lucien tries to recapture her eyes. He slides next to her. She takes the bottle and drinks a long drink from it, turns back to Lucien and there are tears on her cheeks. "I didn't mean for that to happen, Lucien. I didn't think anything would come of it all but the robbery."

"You know how Caleb is," Lucien says, but quietly, maybe bitterly, but without accusation.

Lucien takes the bottle from Maya. A drink gives him the courage to move his hand to Maya's, rest it on her knee, where her jeans end and her stockings begin. His heart is a house under fire.

"What are you really doing here, Maya?" he asks her after a while, seeing she doesn't resist, hasn't moved his hand from her leg. "Is it really about this physicist?"

"It's really just about getting him a job, Lucien. Yes."

"What is he to you? You? You seeing him?"

Maya smiles like an inverted rainbow, a covenant, and Lucien is suddenly warm with her warmth and warm with the wine.

"What a funny choice of words," she says.

"Are you going to stay here a while?" he asks. "It's not safe for you in New York right now, either. Caleb wants to find you too. He asked me where you live."

"You tell him?"

"No, I didn't tell him. And I won't tell him. I'm out, now. I can't go back to all that. I don't know if I'll ever even see him again. I guess I'm hoping not to."

"I don't really have anywhere else to go, either," Maya says. "But it's different here for me."

"What do you mean it's different for you? You grew up here too."

"But they're not really my parents, Lucien. For whatever that's worth. I've always talked about it. Maybe it's time I went to find my father."

Lucien passes the bottle to Maya. "What's the point of that? You've never known the coward." He regrets saying it as soon as it comes out. Maya face flushes, and all the warmth from her dissipates. She takes a long drink.

"Yeah, well. How the hell would you know anything about how it feels?"

"I'm sorry, Maya. It's just that, I don't know. He's been gone the whole time. How would you even know where to start?"

"With the Internet these days – I don't know. I'll figure it out," she says. She turns towards him, and the evening feels suddenly tight and close and intimate.

"We're all four back together now," he manages, with a whisper like a moan. "Just like old times."

"Yeah," she says, leaning into him, her forehead coming to rest against his. "Just like old times."

Later they lie together in Lucien's bed looking at the stars through the window. The conversation has moved from the breathless to the banal. It feels wonderfully like home.

"You never see the stars like this in the city," Lucien says. "You really trade some things living in the city."

Maya murmurs, shifts. "It's like looking into the past, is what Pinchback says. The stars we see, the light we see can be hundreds of thousands years old. Some of them have already burned out, we're seeing the ghosts of stars that no longer exist."

"That's a way of thinking about things." Lucien frowns. Why mention this Pinchback character at a time like this. It spoils even the wonder of the stars. "So what's with this guy, anyway? He really gonna get a job at the Institute?"

"Henry says he can get Pinchback an interview. I think that's all he needs, his foot in the door. Anyone who meets him will find him remarkable. Henry wants to pre-interview him first, and then we'll see where it goes from there."

"What's he want to do there?"

"I think he'll have to start as a research assistant or something. But it won't take long for him to move his way into something more interesting."

"Guy must really be something."

Maya doesn't say anything.

"And what about you? You have your degree, too. You just gonna let that go to waste?"

"Comparative religion? For whatever good that will do me. It was just something to get me away from here, that degree." She pauses. "I really have been thinking about looking for my father, Lucien. Sometimes I don't feel like a real person."

"Don't be ridiculous."

"That's easy for you to say. You have your family, your whole history, all right here in a house in Jersey. For me, it feels like – I don't know. Like I don't come from anywhere at all. Like I was found in a riverboat, like Moses, or born in a tube or something. It's pretty fucking unsettling. If I'd even known my mother, or anything, maybe it would be different. I don't know. For all I know my father's dead now, too, and God bless him if he is. God knows the bastard doesn't deserve a long and happy life."

"I never knew you were so bitter. That you felt this way. I always thought – I don't know. Like we could talk about anything."

"There's no way to talk to you about everything, Lucien. It's literally impossible."

Lucien looks over at Maya, looks away. "Why do you say something like that? I always listen to what you have to say. You know that."

"There's nothing like this I can tell you, except you'd get defensive."

"What do you mean?"

"Look, Lucien. Henry and Alice are friendly enough. They're basically my parents, but they're not my parents. I've always known that. It's always been a little different for me, like I'm a displaced person or something. I never felt like I've belonged here."

"But you grew up here! How could you not feel like you belong? It's not like-"

"See, this is exactly what I mean," says Maya. "I can't talk about it with you. And it's not even like I have anyone to be angry with, except my father, I guess. But that doesn't stop me from being angry with you and my mother and Henry and Alice anyway. I feel like, and I suppose this is just an illusion, delusion, whatever, but I feel like I remember a life without them; with my real parents I mean. And what makes it worse is that sometimes I feel like I renounced that life, and that's why I'm living this one. And it's miserable, honestly. I never felt like I belonged here. You belong here; something in you clicks when you're here, and you're home. That never happens with me. It's like being in a nightmare and not being able to find your way out of it, and the longer you're in it, the more certain you are it's all just a nightmare, and the more aware you are there's no way of getting out of it."

"Oh. Well –" Lucien tries to think of something to say, but can't think of anything that doesn't sound defensive. The more she talks the more his heart breaks, because it seems she's saying something really definite and final and damning about them, about what they can be, and it's something he's always known, but hasn't been able to say to himself.

"And the worst part of it was, when they tried to include me in the family. Vacations or family outings or school meetings, or whatever. The whole thing being a total farce. And me there, having to sit through all this nonsense, act like I was enjoying myself, and having a good time, when really there was just this deepening divide and sense of dread about having put myself in this position. About having chosen this life with your family instead of developing into a proper person on my own. And there's nothing to be done about it, really, so there's nothing to say. It's simply how I feel, and it's a way of feeling that can only cause you pain. So what's to tell you?"

They are quiet for a long time. Lucien blinks tears into the stars. "Well," he says after a while, "you've told me now."

"Yes," Maya says. "I've told you now." She turns, puts her arm around him and squeezes. "And you still don't know the half."

Lucien hesitates. "Are you glad we did this? I mean, I am. It's like we can finally talk to each other, isn't it?"

"I don't know Lucien. I guess so."

After Maya retreats stealthily back to her room, Lucien has trouble sleeping. He goes through all the memories of his childhood, youth, teen-age years with Maya, stars of memory, ghosts of light flickering dimly from the past, and tries to reimagine them through this new perspective, Maya's feeling of distance. But the more he tries, the more the memories seem to distance themselves from him, so that they no longer feel like his own memories, but invented memories. By the time he's really falling into a deep sleep, the stars are already gone, and the sun is coming up lilac way east off the horizon. He sleeps until late morning, almost early afternoon.

He gets up and, still in his pajamas, walks downstairs to put on coffee. His parents have left for the day, there's a note from them on the table. He goes back upstairs and stands for a moment in front of Maya's closed door. He waits a minute or two, listening, and then knocks. No answer. He knocks again. Still no answer. He gives the door a gentle push and it swings open. The room is empty. Maya has disappeared again. He tries to shrug it off, but for some reason he's starting to cry. Of course. Of course. Of course.

SEVEN

The days following Maya's disappearance are a dull horror. He expected life at home to be boring, but he also expected some sort of comfortable satisfaction in the everyday order. It's simply not there. The days stretch on, they blend together, they seem to be increasingly without purpose. He spends a lot of time in bed, hoping to sleep away the monotony, but whenever he tries to sleep he sees Booker's face again, like one of those uncanny and frightening ancient African masks, twisted in the anguish of death throes. He thinks about Maya's admonishment constantly. He thinks about his entire family life in a new light, and it sours everything. Every familiar room, all the familiarity of his parents, they all take on a new and ugly luster. He doesn't know what to do with himself during the day when his parents are out, and when they come home in the evening, he feels embarrassed by their conversation. Everything they say follows the same narratives running through the newspapers and blogs he spends the day reading. There's no originality of thought anywhere. The new black president, the economic collapse, the withdrawal of troops from Iraq, none of this seems to mean anything; it's water cooler talk.

In the long afternoons, his mind often wanders to that last evening with Maya, the way she moved and cooed when he touched her. It isn't long before he's listlessly switching between blog pages and even more questionable material. He looks for keyword women matching Maya's general description, tall, light skinned black women with shoulder length black hair and thin physique, but the Internet is a horribly racist place, especially when it comes to pornography. He can't really be particular about things, because too much searching around just becomes a turn off instead of a turn on. Afterwards he always feels worse than before; empty and morose, and then it's right back to blog pages and pundits. He begins to wonder why he chose Political Science anyway, can't seem to remember ever actually making a decision about things, it just happened that way, and the subject only interests him peripherally, as something that seems like it should be important, but in the end, really isn't at all. The routines of his day begin as repetitions of memories of the past, running up and down the stairs, looking through the fridge for food, scanning the Internet in his room, and become new routines in themselves, so that the past and the present blend indelibly, and routine becomes repetition, where it seems time is stretching backwards instead of progressing forward.

"We'll be out of town for the weekend," Henry tells him one night over dinner. "We're going into the city directly after work on Friday, and we're spending a couple nights in a hotel. No point in coming all the way back to Jersey, after all. You're a big boy, and can take care of yourself." Henry winks.

"Don't bring any girls around here," Alice says, and he frowns and doesn't say anything.

"Or throw any wild parties," says Henry.

"Have you heard anything from Maya?" Lucien asks. "Since she left?"

"She's back in the city, I think," says Henry. "I'll be interviewing that Pinchback character next week. Should be interesting. Maybe you'll want to come along?"

"For the interview?"

"Not for the interview itself, but just to meet the guy afterwards. I don't know, seems like something to do, get out of the house. Maybe he'll inspire you somehow."

"Something should," Alice pauses. "Get you out of the house I mean," and she says it like they've been discussing him as something of a problem.

"Sure, I'll meet the guy. Like you say, it should be interesting."

The first thought Lucien has after his parents head out for the weekend is that he's going to need some weed. Unfortunately, he has none. The little bit he brought with him is gone, and the only way to get more is to sneak back into his apartment in Brooklyn. He's still afraid to go to the city, but there really aren't any other options. He figures he'll be in and out in no time, and he can be home again quickly without incident. He does wish he had a weapon, though.

He doesn't waste time. Driving back into the city feels ominous. If time feels like it's stretching backwards at home, he thinks, the feeling is exponentially increased repeating the drive he made just a few days ago in reverse. He goes back over the George Washington Bridge and takes Riverside Drive downtown. It's a cloudy, overcast day, and there seem to be ominous omens everywhere: crows circle the house as he's leaving, a traffic accident on the bridge slows him down, the waters of the Hudson heave and breathe and groan like souls drowning in boiling water. When he finally gets back to his apartment in Brooklyn, he parks a block away, and sits in the car a minute, ducked down low, scouting the area. Everything looks clear.

He hadn't anticipated on being quite so spooked. He more or less runs to the front door, slides the key in, and is quickly inside. It's strange to be back in his apartment, and it's only been a few days. It feels like returning to another era. Everything is just as he left it. Memories of Booker immediately come back, sitting in the living room chair, smoking a Dutch, all their silly old conversations. He goes to the stereo and takes Booker's CD. At least something remains of the brother, he thinks, and suddenly in a shiver, the memory of the stick-up kids coming through the door comes back, the hand over his face, lying down on the floor, and the back of his neck starts to tingle. A panicky feeling comes over him, he can feel something isn't right. He goes to the window and peers quickly out. No one there. A floorboard creaks behind him suddenly, and he turns around, reaching for his belt, like he has a pistol. No one there.

"I got to get the hell out of here," he says in a whisper to no one at all, Booker's ghost maybe, and just as he starts towards the bedroom, his cellphone rings.

He freezes, crouches down beside the sofa, and takes it out.

It's Caleb.

"Yo."

"Yo College, what's good nigga? Where you at?"

"Chillin, chillin. Still out of town."

"Word. Them niggas got you shook something serious, huh? Why you talking so low?"

"Oh."

"Well, you ain't got to worry now, nigga. We wet the rest of them niggas last night. The shit is finished. Couple other crews came in on it with us. Them niggas been robbing niggas from Queens to Harlem to Brooklyn. They had that shit coming."

"Good news," Lucien says this a little louder. "Glad to hear it."

"So you back in the game now nigga, or what?"

"Naw, naw. I gotta lay low some still. I need time to think."

"Well thinking ain't gonna get a nigga paid, know what I mean? So give me a ring when you get your head straight."

"Word. Hey Caleb."

"Yeah."

"Thanks, man. Good looking out."

"We'll talk soon."

"Catch you then."

Lucien stands up and looks around. What now? Is it safe to just move back into the city like nothing happened? He looks around the apartment, and frowns. No, definitely not. This place still gives him the shivers. He goes into the kitchen, and grabs some weed, and notices, just behind it, a stash of cocaine they picked up from the East New York crew the other night. Might as well take some of that too. He stashes everything in a shoulder bag, and heads back out. He takes one good last look at the apartment, and smiles a little sadly. It's not a bad spot, but now it's haunted, for him at least. Haunted with Booker's memory, and haunted with the memory of the attack, and really just haunted with the memory of a former life.

And then it's the same trip back home, except now it's on some extra caution shit. Bad enough to be caught with weed in the car, but weed and coke, and he'll be making a trip upstate sure. He drives slow, but not too slow; he almost feels more spooked than being back at the house. Tries to divert himself by listening to Booker's CD, and the memory of the damn thing makes him smile, so that by the time he's home, safe and sound, having dodged the niggas and the cops, he's in a silvery bittersweet winsome mood, full of longing and sadness.

Once he's back in his bedroom though, he feels emptier than ever. Friday afternoon, and the folks don't come back until Sunday evening. He has the whole weekend to himself here, alone, run of the house. It's certainly too big for him alone. He unpacks his bag, puts on some music. Well, smoke first, that's for sure. And might as well do a line, too, while he's at it. This isn't an opportunity that will come around too often.

The coke sends him back to his computer. He sets up a profile on OKCupid, because it's free and at first seems easy enough. He uses an old Facebook picture to get started, and starts answering the personal questions. It's an odd experience, to say the least; he's never done this before. The questions seem to go on forever. What are his interests? Favorite books? Favorite movies? What music does he listen to? What are some of his hobbies? It's one way of creating a self, in any case, but seems to miss the essentials, which of course, it would have to, because who can really point to what the essentials of a soul are. The questions seem to think a self lies in the particulars of a person's taste, but those are changing moment to moment, and are probably even affected by the way the way the question is asked, the Fugees CD he's listening to, certainly the coke is affecting his answers. It could simply be that there isn't a soul or a self at all, or that a soul isn't really a self in the way we understood selfhood, and that any real self is as illusory as the self he's creating on OKCupid. Of course, this is just the weed and cocaine talking. He's overthinking the whole thing. Why not play along? There might be a cute girl at the end of it all, and that's all this really comes down to. Meeting someone you're compatible with. Maya. He saves what he's completed of his profile and starts to scan the girls.

Several of them catch his eye. He shoots off a couple messages with the courage and confidence of the cocaine, does another line, and then scouts for more. It seems simple enough, after all. A little like the weekend after graduation he spent in Amsterdam, the red light district, where you just walk by the windows, and choose the women you want. He didn't have the heart to go through with it then, but then that was different, and besides, he didn't have cocaine in him. He's not just looking for a hookup anyway. He's looking for a replacement. The thought catches him off guard, but it's true enough. He needs someone to replace Maya, and he needs someone quickly, desperately, because otherwise he's headed for self-destruction.

That's probably not the best thing to put in a profile or personal message. He's getting weird now, so he opens a private browsing window and switches to porn. Now this is more like Amsterdam. Even better. He does another line, rolls another joint; in any case, this should be quick enough, and then he'll get back to the profiles and whatever else. Maybe let the coke runs its course, and then take a nap.

Instead the porn and coke work together on him to create something of a psychodrama in his head. The search itself, before a tedious and time consuming turn off becomes the turn on. He's looking for Maya in an endless stream of keywords and images, women flickering in windows on his computer screen, sex scenes from every angle, every position, every imaginable thing he can hope to have with Maya, all of it comes to life in his head and on his monitor. Occasionally he gets caught up in a motif, a picture or clip triggers an explosion in his head, he gets caught in a loop of repeat views, takes another line, and continues to re-watch it, with every repeat viewing getting a little closer to Maya maybe, or maybe not; so then off to another search, through another stream of streaming images, streaming together. He rolls around in his bed, unraveling more than undressing, does another line, and then opens another window. Hours have passed, the clock confirms it, but it doesn't feel like it, it's just been a couple of minutes. He does another line, he's lost count by now, but the supply has substantially diminished, there's still enough left to keep the operation in order. The search is fascinating and frustrating, almost like his desire for Maya in the other world, always almost just there, and never quite. She's a chimera, everywhere to be found, and never anywhere, nowhere really, pieces of her pieced together from pictures, what after all is a self? There is no Maya, there is no self, there is only a pastiche, and the pastiche is the search and the search is fruitless because it's always changing because the nature of searching changes what the search is for, and the search is the thing in itself, there is no thing in itself, there is just another line, and another line of ladies and another window, and another look, and here she is again, and there she goes again, and oh. Oh well.

It's early the next morning, and the cocaine is gone, and Lucien is spent and sick, his head full of frustrating, erotic and horrific images, and there's no way to undo or unsee what he's done and seen. He lies in bed for a good hour, just sitting there, his heart irregular and lumpy, lumping heavy against his chest, and his computer sluggish and unnatural, and his sheets and clothes bunched and bundled, huddled at the bottom corner of the bed like cobwebs. He feels his stomach turn, gets up and goes to the bathroom. He throws up for fifteen minutes, and then crawls back in bed. He lies there watching the sun cast aspersions on his being for another couple hours until finally, mercifully, he falls asleep.

When he wakes up it's already Saturday evening. His sleep schedule's been thrown. He smokes a joint just to make everything okay, and takes note of his state of mind. Things are more settled now after a long sleep. The poignancy of the images has diminished somewhat, but the memory is there, like a stain in the fabric that always reappears in concentrated light. It's time for a change. He can consider that last act of his the last act of a desperate man that no longer is. A suicide. If there is no self, he says wryly to himself, then there can always be a new self. He flushes his hard drive in an act of symbolism, reinstalls his operating system from scratch. He is through with Maya. He is through with dealing. He is through with being whoever Lucien was. He's free now to be someone else. Let's begin at the beginning: I am Lucien, a Political Science major. For the last few years I have been thinking about the political situation as well as doing some personal soul searching. Now I am ready to go about doing something to make a difference.

It's a thought Lucien manages to keep in his mentation through the rest of the weekend. So the next week, when his father suggests that they go talk to Pinchback again, Lucien is ready.

"Fascinating character, this Pinchback," Henry says on the ride down to the Institute. It's a Wednesday morning, and so far things have been going well in Lucien's new outlook. He hasn't thought much about Maya at all. He's been reading blogs, applying to internships, looking for apartments in Manhattan. The weather has been remarkable for early November. Indian Summer, even. Not so cold, but bright and crisp every day, and the air invigorating. The withered colors of the leaves seem to hold in them the promise of death and rebirth, and this is inspiring to Lucien as they drive the dreaming Garden State.

"It's almost like he's lived two lives," Henry goes on. "A life before, where he was blind, and this new life of his, where he can see."

"I look forward to meeting him," Lucien says, and he says it without a trace of irony. Sincerity is the new irony. Where had he read that recently?

He meets Pinchback directly after the interview. Pinchback is a tall, thin man, with thin hair, and a serious look. He's wearing dark Ray-Bans even though it's fairly dim inside, and he walks with a little bit of a staggered swagger, like he's overconfident and unsure of himself at the same time. Lucien notices his eyes through the shades; they seem to glow behind the lenses; they don't exactly look through you, like people say about some folks' eyes; they more seem to reflect you or something. It's eerie, and Lucien is glad for the shades.

"Nice to meet you," Pinchback extends a hand, cocks his head slightly to the side. "Henry's son Lucien, right?"

"That's right," Lucien says. "I've heard a lot about you." He hesitates. "You know my cousin, Maya."

"Yes, Maya's. She's really something."

"Yeah. Yeah, she is." Lucien tries hard not to frown. "How do you know her?"

Pinchback smiles. "That's a long story. But the long and short of it is, I used to work with a publishing company that wanted to publish her. A braille publishing company."

"No kidding? She's published?"

"You didn't know? Have you read any of her poems? They're remarkable."

Something about this cat strikes Lucien a little off. Maybe it's his stiff manner, his odd old-fashioned stilted speech, Lucien doesn't know. It could just be that he knows something about Maya that he himself doesn't.

"Yeah, yeah. Remarkable. She's read some of them to me. There was a guy named Booker back in Brooklyn that thought she should set them to music, but –" Lucien lets this train of thought go. He's not sure how to finish the thought, and he shouldn't have mentioned Booker in the first place, because his throat is caught now.

"Set them to music? Oh, I don't think so," says Pinchback. "They're meant for the page, that much is certain. They're even better in braille, where you can actually feel the presence of the text. A kind of poetry I've never really encountered before."

The guy is surely off his rocker, but he's a physicist, so go figure. "So you're a literature guy?" Lucien ventures. "I wouldn't have – you know, physicists often tend to be narrow minded in their interests. If my dad's any example," Lucien smiles by way of apology.

"No, no, I'm most certainly not. I don't know the first thing about literature, though there have been those who have tried to convince me otherwise. The fact of the matter is I just responded to Maya's poetry in a way I don't respond to most literature. She seemed to write from the perspective of blindness, and I don't know that there are really any other sighted writers out there that can do that. And then to feel the poems in braille. Well, then that's the really remarkable thing. The tactile impression."

"Oh." Lucien hesitates. "So you were blind before? But now you can see?"

"Yes, that's right."

"That's got to be some kind of blessing, huh? Like being reborn, or waking up into a dream."

"It's more like a nightmare," Pinchback says carefully. "I'm not sure I take well to the illusion of sight, and the entire thing may have been a mistake."

"Oh."

"It's not easy to explain, and while there are advantages, it's still like learning a new way of being, becoming another person, taking everything from a new frame of reference. You're never really quite yourself again, because you're relating to others from a foreign perspective. I don't think I'm the same person anymore, and if I'm anyone at all now, it's just a conglomeration of other sighted people, and the way they talk about their grand illusion."

"Why do you keep saying illusion?"

Now Pinchback frowns. "The unfortunate condition of the sighted is that they believe in what they see. I'm – I guess – cynical, or maybe just experienced enough – to know better." Pinchback looks queerly at Lucien a moment, like he's trying to read something from his expression, but is having difficulty with the translation. "But these are poor and bitter thoughts from an impoverished and bitter old man." He smiles again. "Let's go back to literature, shall we? Is literature one of your passions? Or do you take after your father, and follow the Gods of science?"

Freaking Gods of science. You've got to be kidding, Lucien thinks, but he just smiles. "Neither, actually. Political science." He laughs. A pseudo-science I guess.

"I should say so," says Pinchback. "But another necessary illusion."

"Well, we can't all just be Anarchists after all. Who is that says man is a political animal? So, I suppose it's our most necessary illusion."

Pinchback frowns again. "Yes, that was Aristotle. And he was wrong. Man is a spiritual animal, and politics is something of a distraction from becoming. But that's a different discussion, and I shouldn't be talking about that kind of thing as a physicist." His face softens again, he even smiles. "Although, I think you'll find among us theoretical physicists, there are ideas we're exploring which make traditional spirituality, as it's understood, almost obsolete. No, physics and spirituality should not be considered separately, like politics and spirituality ought to be. The two really go hand in hand."

"Oh. Well, politics, I don't know." Lucien's a little flustered. This guy sure doesn't hold back for the sake of decorum or politeness.

"Like I said, it's a necessary illusion. At least for most. But of course I'm sure you're aware of that. All the great political thinkers are, after all."

"Oh, well. Yeah. Of course." Lucien gives up. "So what do you want to do here, at the Institute I mean?"

"Well, I'm hoping to start as a research assistant. We'll see where it goes from there."

"And what aspect of physics? I don't really know much about the subject – things I glean here and there from Henry – er, my dad. But that's about it."

"Quantum mechanics. The good, theoretical stuff. Space and time and perception kind of things. The things that lead to metaphysics, and all the questions that matter. "

"Terrific. Well hell, man. I wish you the best of luck."

On the drive back Henry asks him what he thought of the guy.

"He was interesting," Lucien says. "I don't know what to make of him. Nice guy. Real forthright about his ideas on things."

"Yeah, yeah I know," says Henry. "That's what I like about him. I'm gonna recommend him for a second interview. I think he's perfect for the position."

"Yeah, I guess he probably is," says Lucien.

But the whole conversation with Pinchback has Lucien a little depressed. The guy basically told him he thought everything Lucien was trying to build up for his new identity was worthless. And it wouldn't even be so bad, some nutty physicist telling him this nonsense, if deep down he didn't suspect the same thing himself. Didn't suspect that the whole thing was fraudulent, and that he was fraudulent too. There had to be a better way, right? Fuck it.

When he logs into his computer there's an email in his Inbox. Someone from OKCupid has responded, and wants to meet.

SIX

Her name is Haley Stern. She's from Hoboken. Not bad looking, either, from the picture at least. She's light skinned, has light brown eyes, a cute nose that curves into dimples on her cheeks. She doesn't quite look like Maya, a thought which Lucien immediately dismisses, because it shouldn't matter, she's cute enough, and in a way, can be seen as a lighter version of Maya, if you want, by the way her eyes narrow at the corners and wrinkle when she smiles, which she's doing in this picture. She's lived in Hoboken all her life, born and raised, or so says her profile, and Lucien frowns. Not too adventurous; people in New Jersey like to leave New Jersey, that's the general rule, but maybe Hoboken's different; it's got a hip vibe. So long as she doesn't still live at home, maybe that's okay. She's an intellectual type, likes books like *100 Years of Solitude, Beloved, Sound and the Fury, Go Tell it On the Mountain*. Well, whatever. Another literary type. But she works in finance. She's an EDGAR Operator, whatever that is, which, as far as Lucien can tell is some sort of financial analyst. Well, in any case she should be good for a political discussion or two with a job like that. She's twenty-nine, just a couple years younger than he is, also good; that means she can appreciate some of the old-skool stuff from the 90's. Her message is short, but cute. Says she got his message, thought he sounded interesting, maybe they should meet for a coffee some time. Okay. Lucien doesn't remember her specifically, there were a couple others he'd written that stick out in his mind more, but those would all be women who looked more like Maya, and a little more freaky. This girl looks milquetoast, sure, and it probably won't go anywhere, but Lucien doesn't have a whole lot else going on, and so he decides he's game. Sure, he responds. We can meet in a café in Hoboken. I'll let you choose the place. Smiley Face.

He actually regrets that Smiley Face icon the rest of the evening. Seems a little too sissy, even for a milquetoast chick, but now it's been sent, and there's nothing to be done. Still, he feels he misrepresented himself a little there; he might be out the game, but he ain't completely soft, either. He's seen some shit. Should have pushed that bad boy angle instead. He tries to distract himself, but now his thoughts are filled with Haley. Her profile follows him to the dinner table, through dinner, where his parents go on about Pinchback.

"You should meet the guy, too," Henry tells Alice. "You'll get your chance. I'm sure he'll get the job. I'm pretty impressed, and I'm not one who's easily impressed."

Impressed with himself, mostly, Lucien thinks. For his discovery. He's only impressed when it comes to making himself look bigger, either in his own eyes, or the eyes of others. They're so bourgeois, his parents, it makes him sick. Just Black Bourgeoisie, just like the white man, really, nothing revolutionary about them, and to think they were around in the Sixties. Lucien's heard all the stories about their activism and youthful rebellion, but he'll be damned if he can think of a rebellious thing about them. If they were to die fighting for anything, it would be the goddamn status quo, not the dissolution of it. He's glad when dinner's over. He rushes upstairs to check his messages. Nothing from Haley. Well, fuck her, and fuck Pinchback, and fuck Maya, and fuck his parents, too. Everybody's just the same, everywhere you go, everyone is just the same as everyone else, and they all think they're all so different and special and interesting, because they all think the exact same things, and that's one of the things they think. He feels blank as hell. He can't figure why. Wishes, disingenuously, even he realizes it, that he'd been shot to death in East Brooklyn instead of Booker. Still, he goes to bed with that thought, and thoughts of Haley, or maybe Maya, because after a certain point, his head goes light, and his neck starts to tingle so hard it itches, and it gets hard to say what's what.

It isn't until the next day, late in the afternoon, that he hears back from Haley, and then he feels silly for having gotten so knotted up about things. It hasn't been long at all, considering she's answering a dating message from a stranger. Her message is sweet, she would be happy to meet sometime that weekend. She recommends a place called the Elysian Café on Washington Street. Would 4pm Saturday work for him?

He's so excited about the news, he even tells his parents about it.

"Internet dating, now?" Alice says. She frowns, or wrinkles her forehead in some kind of meaningful way, which Lucien can't quite decipher. "Isn't that for desperate people and weirdos?" She smiles, and Lucien knows she means this last remark to come across as half-ironic. She's a weirdo herself, after all.

"Oh, it's no different than the classifieds newspapers have always run," Lucien says.

"Which just proves my point," says Alice. "You don't know the nutjobs who write into those classifieds like I do."

"I for one, am glad to hear it," says Henry. "She cute?" He winks, and now he's in on the fun, too. "That's all that matters, after all."

"Yeah, she looks cute from the picture. But you never know, you know."

"In this day and age," says Alice.

Lucien's happier after talking with them, glad that they made such light of it, but he's also concerned, because they must be concerned. All of which leads him back to wondering how much they know about Maya. He frets a little about it through part of the evening, but then he just goes back online, and looks at Haley's picture again, and reads his political science blogs, and looks up apartments in Hoboken, and considers what he's going to do with himself once the New Year comes, and he begins his new life. He falls into something of a reverie of dreaming, seeing himself next spring in a tidy little one bedroom in Hoboken, going out in the evenings with Haley, working during the day for a think tank somewhere in the City maybe, and all of it sounds pretty damn ideal to him. If that

Pinchback lunatic, speaking of weirdos, thinks political science is an illusion, then the poor dumb bastard was blind for too long, and really still is. What's looking at the stars worth, when people are suffering right here on earth, and hasn't he seen and experienced first hand what happens to people when they're just emerging from centuries of oppression? He frowns, and then smiles to think how wise he is to frown.

&

When he meets Haley on Saturday, he isn't disappointed. This isn't to say she looks exactly like her photo; no one ever does, he supposes. Even his photo is from one of his better days, you can't expect to find him looking like that on the regular. She's a little heavier than her photo makes her look, but she's not fat or anything, just normal. The photo made her look skinny, like Maya, but skinny isn't sexy anymore anyway, so that's okay. She's cute. Her face is round and brown and she blinks when she smiles so that her dimples slide up and down her cheeks in a way that makes Lucien want to smile himself.

He's the first one there, a gentleman is always early to the first date, and when he looks up from his coffee from one minute to the next, there she is. He stands up. "Pleased to meet you. Lucien."

"Haley. Nice to meet you too."

Lucien pulls a seat out for her. "Please, sit. I've already ordered a coffee for myself. Can I get you anything?"

"I'll have a tea."

The first moments are hesitant and awkward. They don't know anything about each other, which you'd think would make for really wonderful open conversation, but instead seems to hang things up. There are too many places to begin.

"Wonderful weather we're having today," Lucien says. It really is. A perfect autumn afternoon, with the sun marigold on the leaves, and just cool enough to still be comfortable.

"I know," says Haley. "Isn't it?"

They smile a little awkwardly at each other for a moment.

"Sure is," says Lucien. The waiter comes and takes Haley's order for tea. It's a welcome interruption.

"So, EDGAR Operator," Lucien goes on, feeling that, as the man, he should be the one leading the conversation. "What is that all about?"

"Oh, wow." Haley laughs, and those dimples slide. Lucien smiles. "That's a tough one," she says. "It's basically like an electronic typesetter."

"Oh. Interesting. Financial stuff? Who's Edgar?"

"It's an acronym," she says. "Electronic Data Gathering, Analysis and Retrieval. A mouthful, I know. Basically, you know how companies have to publish their financial wheelings and dealings with the SEC, you know like when a company goes public, or has quarterly earnings to report or something?"

"Yeah?"

"Well, we get all those files in Word and Excel documents and turn them into HTML. Then we publish them on the SEC website."

"Oh."

Haley's tea comes. Lucien tries to think of something to follow up with. The idea makes sense to him, someone must do this kind of stuff, he's just never really thought about who before. Well, here she is.

"So you work for the SEC then?"

"No, I work for a law-firm, and their clients are a bunch of big name banks. These banks send us the documents. It's all a big mess. I guess you could say I even work for the banks, but not the SEC. Anyway, it's not interesting enough for all this hullaballoo about it. It's just something to keep me occupied. And it pays well. But really it's pretty awful, and there's all sorts of shady shit that happens there. Banks purposefully disseminate misinformation all the time, and then file amendments with the correct information after market close. It's a kind of 21st century usury, really, and it's nothing I'm particularly proud of doing. But I stumbled into it."

"How's that?"

"Through acting. A lot of Operators, believe it or not, are in the theater, and I was out of work. A girlfriend of mine was doing it, and she got me an interview at a smaller firm. I got to be pretty good at it, and so now I'm working with the big boys. But I've got to get out. I swear it's killing me."

"You're an actress?"

That smile again. "Yeah?" She says it like a question, then – "Or –" and she flashes her clasped fingers through her hands, almost dramatically. "Aspiring. I still get roles here and there. But it's not enough. It's discouraging, you know. Everyone in this town is an actress. It's hard to get a break, and even the breaks you get, well it's hard to get paid as an actress in New York, and it's a lot of work. I'm not complaining. Really. But it's how it is."

"Yeah, New York's a racket all right," says Lucien.

"So what do you do?"

"Oh, I don't know." Lucien drinks his coffee, thinks carefully about this question, about how he'll go about answering it. "I'm a political science major, but haven't found my niche yet. I've been living in Brooklyn, basically on the cheap. Spent some time soul searching. I think maybe I want to do some community organizing."

"Like Obama!" Haley laughs it.

"Yeah," Lucien smiles. "Like Obama. And see where that takes me. You know, living in Brooklyn, I've seen how drugs and violence, political neglect and lack of funding tear up communities. I'd like to do something about that."

"Well, that's pretty noble. Gee, I feel almost shallow now."

Lucien blinks and smiles. Did she really just say Gee?

"Ah, I don't know. You want to be a great actress. Nothing wrong with that. A black actress in this day and age is a political figure herself, in the way she carries herself and her roles. Nothing shallow about it."

Haley smiles. Their eyes meet. She takes a sip of her tea, and her light brown eyes light up, her dimples roll, and Lucien's gut dips. This is actually going really well, he thinks, surprised, taken off guard even. He genuinely likes this girl.

After coffee they walk a couple blocks over to the Hudson. It's chilly right by the water, and the crisp weather and the sight of the orange waves of the evening sun sloping over the river make everything feel clear to Lucien. He feels awake, wide awake, maybe for the first time in a long time, and he suddenly feels bold enough to reach an arm around Haley, pull her close, and give her a gentle kiss.

"I figured I'd get it out of the way," he says. He winks, and she smiles with those dimples again. "So why hasn't anyone swept you up yet?"

"I work too much," she says. "My workday is from eleven to seven, and if it's busy, I work even later than that. It doesn't leave much free time in the evenings. It's tough enough just working around those hours for my acting schedule."

"You need to find a new job," he says.

"I know! You know? So what about you? Why are you still single?"

"Oh, I don't know," says Lucien. "This city can be as lonely as any small town America when it comes right down to it."

"Tell me about it."

They make plans to meet again, exchange numbers and real email addresses. On the way home Lucien is ecstatic. He drives north along the Hudson humming with the setting sun.

&

"You seem to be in a good mood," Henry notices at dinner. "How'd your date go?"

"Really well." Lucien can't believe how chatty he feels. "I think it might work out. We're supposed to meet again next weekend."

"Well, that's good news," says Alice. "What did you do?"

"Just went to a café in Hoboken. She's a nice girl."

"Yeah, but is she cute?" Henry asks, and winks.

"Yeah, Henry," Lucien says. "She's a looker all right, just like in the picture."

"Well, "Henry says. "You know the story of how your mother and I met, right?"

"Oh, not this again," Lucien says, but he's willing to hear it now, for the umpteenth time, even looks forward to it.

"What? This is your history, now. America's history too. It was the early '70s and…"

&

Lucien meets Haley again in Hoboken the next weekend. This time they have dinner together.

"I'm thinking I might just quit my job," Haley tells him. "It's time. I'm stuck in a rut as it is, spinning my wheels. I have some money saved up. If I'm lucky, they'll just lay me off."

"Lay you off? How is that lucky?"

"Unemployment." Haley winks. "It's all a big thing right now. They're cutting back. People are getting laid off all over the firm, what with the financial crisis and all. I'm hoping they ask for volunteers. A coworker told me at the last job she was at they asked for volunteers when they had to cut back, and it still counts as a layoff, so you're still eligible for Unemployment."

"Well, I wish you the best of luck in losing your job," says Lucien. "But what will you do then?"

"I don't know. That's the thing. I'm not really qualified for much out there, at least not anything professional or that will pay anything. And I'm still paying off student loans."

"Preaching to the choir there," says Lucien, who has his own share of school debt. "I'm actually behind on my payments. Seems like a generational thing."

"Oh, college is a scam all right," says Haley. "Gee, I wish I'd almost not gone at all. I don't see how it's really helped me."

"Where did you go? What was your major?"

"Columbia. Classics. Go figure, huh?"

"So that explains the books," Lucien says. He can't stop smiling at her.

"Don't you read?"

"Mostly non-fiction. Political theory."

"I thought you just put those on your profile to look smart and important."

"Well, that too. I don't know. In all seriousness, when it comes to art, I'm more of a music guy. I see rap as the contemporary form of poetry."

"Oh." Haley squints. "Isn't it all posturing and machismo and money and sexism and stuff like that?"

"Oh I don't know. I know people say that, but you should listen to some of the non-mainstream stuff. I had this friend, Booker. He made some really powerful stuff. I'll bring you a copy of his CD next time. You'll see."

"I'd like that."

When he kisses her that evening, he feels that tingle on the back of his neck again, it's more like an itch now, but it's pleasurable, he decides it means he must be in love, because he can't stop thinking about Haley.

&

Their third date is in the city. Lucien is back in New York for the first time since he went back to his Brooklyn apartment for weed, and he realizes with a giddy shock that he hasn't thought about Maya at all in the last few weeks. He's only been thinking about Haley.

He gives her a copy of Booker's CD, as promised, and then they go to the theater to see *The Seagull*, a play by an old Russian guy named Chekov. They have a late dinner on Restaurant Row directly afterwards. Lucien's whole body tingles and glows with the glow of the lights of West Midtown. It's not just his neck now, it's spread throughout him entirely. It's almost like ascension, an awakening, a coming into Being. After the show, which seems so wise and beautiful to him, Haley's beauty against the lights of Broadway and this suddenly wide open idea that the world is really expansive and limitless, he feels a careless elation he didn't think he possessed anymore.

He walks Haley to the subway after dinner. They flirt and talk in front of the subway station, and then he kisses her hard and then he kisses her hard again.

"Maybe they'll lay you off this week."

"Maybe so. I'll let you know."

"You do that. Talk to you soon."

"Call me tomorrow okay?"

"Okay."

They hold hands before parting, eyes locked, smiles and dimples and everything aglow. Lucien's head aglow. He turns a corner and walks down 40th Street, way on the West Side, slips into a bar for an after date drink, and daydreams.

It's late when he comes back out, and the crowds are thinning. He skirts around the corner, ducks into a quick alley leading to the subway. He feels the tingle thin out of his body with the liquor, and like an itch, concentrate itself on the back of his neck. Against the walls he sees the rising shadows of his ascension. His head feels light all of a sudden, and then the shadows dip so hard that he has a brief moment of confusion, like delirium, just before he feels something hard and cold and real against the back of his head. Oh shit. It's only for a brief moment. It's a moment of shock. No it's horror. Everything explodes in a cacophonous roar of shrieking red stars.

FIVE

Hard to believe they really killed that kid. It's late Autumn, dreary, cold, a wet afternoon. Lucien's funeral. All through the service Maya cries. Hard to decide which is more irritating, Maya crying or the pastor's sermon. Damn thing is really over-the-top. The pastor is one of those old Baptist preachers, you know the type, a small skinny man who flops around and makes a whole production, like the funeral is more about him than Lucien. Really a funeral is about the parents. That's the thing. Though it does have a certain power. When the preacher calls for people to come up to the podium and accept Christ, something about the way he says it, or maybe the way he pairs it with the theme of death, well that gives the idea a compelling draw. Go on up and accept Jesus, my man. A smile. And then Maya sobbing again, irritating, but now the irritation is self-directed.

Service over, outside, in the cemetery, the rain drizzles in and out like a warning. The sky is gray and the clouds heavy, they mute the colors of the smattered leaves, the heavy leaning trees. Hate to see the kid lowered into the ground. Shudder just to see that box sink low, and then the horrible shriek of the mother, and the father holding her, and then both of them shaking in the wind like wet flags. Damned if every single person here doesn't look half-corpsed already. So many young people, friends of Lucien's most likely, looking blank and stunned and glum, all the same. No way for them to understand this either, these pulps of dying flesh, reflections of their futures.

This line of thinking can't continue. Maya in her black and purple dress, face in her hands, eyes red, smeared cheeks, Maya the corpse. His own hands, soft rotting brown, tailored sleeves, Pinchback the corpse. His life is as illusory as his vision, there's something suspect about all of it, only conclusion the human mind can sustain under this pressure: there is a soul, and death is not the end.

Maybe because it's his first sighted funeral. The drama, the costumes, the theater of the preacher, the opera of the graveyard, this whole pageant, it's a racket designed to force you into accepting that death must actually mean something. Stopped short. For a moment the sun arches its way through the clouds, and a peering blade of light sweeps the crowd of corpses. Catching the sun sweeping the coffin, suddenly the presence of God. Like an awakening. He looks up, the clouds part, the sun glimmers against the undersides, it looks like the dawn is breaking through midday – the vastness of that sky, the effortless meaningfulness of it, suddenly the presence of spirit. The sun, breathing across the court connecting everyone there, and now he's closer with the mother, with the father, with the preacher flailing across the pulpit, with Maya, beautiful, dead, living, despairing; she is him, they are all of them the same constellation of stars, connected and inseparable; Lucien as well, the dead and the living, the past and the present, present and future, all people and all things.

All of which is just another facet of the illusion. If being sighted makes anything clear, it's that every thought is half delusion.

&

After the funeral, in a cab with Maya, watching the rise and fall of cities and rivers. She hasn't said much all day and what should he say to her? He doesn't actually know her all that well, and maybe she's changing now somehow and he doesn't know her well enough to know how or why. Or maybe he's the one who's changing. Who can tell? "Were you really close to him?"

Maya looks at him and blinks, frowns. Her face goes blank. "I guess so. I mean, yes. We grew up together, so he was more or less my brother. We didn't always get along. It's my fault." She gasps her last sentence like a confession. "I killed him."

"I guess it's only natural to feel that way. But you can't blame yourself, you know."

"It's why I can't go back to my apartment. It's why I'm staying with you. The same people who killed Lucien might be after me, too."

"Do you actually know something about this?"

"I don't know. I might, is all I'm saying."

"If you know something, you should go to the police."

"That I won't do," Maya looks out the window.

"You playing by some sort of street code?" That didn't come out right. The entire conversation is becoming inappropriate. "I just mean, it's best to let someone know if you know something. It could save someone else's life."

"I don't know what I want anymore. I don't mean it like I say it anyway. I don't know who did it. I mean it more metaphorically. I killed him." She pauses, shifts towards him again, an eerie shadow comes across her face, she almost seems to glower. "He was in love with me, you know."

"Lucien?"

"Lucien."

"But you just said he was– that he grew up with. Oh. Well, that's complicated. Why – what – well…" What the fuck?

"Yeah, it was complicated all right. Sometimes I really resented him for it. I would wish bad things would happen to him. That's what I mean, I really do feel responsible. Like I put a curse on him or something. It was pretty strong at times. And I never felt at home with his family, not ever, not even when I was little."

"So what happened that you ended up there?"

"My mother was Henry's sister. I never knew my real father. I don't know anything about him, only what little my mother told me. But he didn't stick around, I know that much. Not even to see me born. I guess he wasn't ready. Henry and Alice, they have some stories about him, too. Nothing too flattering."

"And when did you move in with Henry and Alice?"

"You mean when did my mother die?" Maya flashes a deadly look. "You might as well just come out and say what you mean when you ask a question."

"I didn't know your mother died, Maya."

She looks back out the window.

She's really doing Broadway today. He looks at her a moment, then looks out the window himself. They're driving through lower Manhattan now, towards the Brooklyn Bridge. He blinks at the stoplights, tries to keep his forehead from tensing up, but everything seems to irritate him today.

"She killed herself," says Maya. "When I was nine."

"Oh. Jesus. Why? Is that a stupid question? That's a stupid question."

"Who knows why? I guess she just didn't feel like sticking around any-more. This place isn't for everybody, you know."

"Well, I'm sorry. I'm sorry to hear it. I didn't know."

"Of course you didn't know. How could you? But that's what it is."

Maya the corpse. He frowns. "I wonder about my father, too, you know. I told you about him. How he ran out after I lost my sight."

She sighs and softens. "I know, Pinchback. It's what I liked about you right away." She slides over and against him. "It's a fucked up legacy for someone to leave you, their absence."

"But your mother…"

"Yeah, that takes the cake, doesn't it?"

&

Back at his apartment a question nags its way from the back of his head. "What did you mean by the people who did this to Lucien might come by your apartment?"

"I was being dramatic. You already know the reason I left my apartment. Because of Rudy. I couldn't stay there with him stalking me – stalking us."

Rudy. He's been trying not to think about him. Not like they were bosom buddies, but damn if he didn't do the brother wrong.

"What happened between you two anyway? I was never quite clear on things."

"Not much. I don't know." Maya takes a seat on the couch. Pinchback sits next to her. He never has been able to get used to this couch, the way it looks, blue-gray, lumpy, ugly. Really the whole apartment looks wrong. It still feels unfamiliar. More like a stage set than a home; it isn't the way he imagined it, what with its pre-war dinginess, the faded off-white walls, the crumbling plaster, the black brown planky old hardwood floors.

Maya lights a lavender marijuana cigarette, continues. "There was never any hope for me and Rudy. I don't even think I was real to him. Some sort of trophy maybe, I don't know. He's a screwed up guy, and really he ought to be with Janet, if Janet weren't all stuck on you." She laughs. "What a crew we made! Remember Halloween?"

"Oh yeah." Finally, finally he smiles. "Rudy and Samir's little spot out in Bushwick. I wonder what Samir's up to these days."

"Probably practicing alchemy somewhere," says Maya, and now they're both laughing.

"So it really was just because of Rudy you wanted to move out? That's really it?"

"That's really it. You remember how he came to my apartment that night, hanging around outside the door. Who wants to deal with that?"

"Well you're welcome to stay here as long as you like."

"So, you've said. But I'm not much for being a kept woman."

So much for that smile. An awkward moment passes by quietly.

"Anyway, how was your interview with Henry?"

Grateful for the change of subject. "It went well, I think. I have to interview again next week with the department head. If that goes well, I should have the job. It's not really my area of study, but it's still interesting."

"Artificial Intelligence, or something?"

"Exactly."

"Wow. So they'll be studying Rudy, or what?"

They're laughing again, and Maya slides a little closer to him on the couch.

"Him and that Robert Johnson play of his," says Maya.

"I guess we should keep an eye out for it."

"I don't think there's going to be any play."

"No? Why not? He seemed pretty into it."

"That's just what I mean. And I mean it when I say he's screwed up. I think he's living the play, that that was always the plan. He wanted to recreate Robert Johnson's legacy in his own life, in his own mind. I think his play's already been produced."

It's not clear what Maya's talking about.

"Why are you looking like that? What are you thinking about?"

"I don't know."

"You don't know what you're thinking about?"

"My father, maybe. He was a little nutty like that. When he left, he went to Europe, to Stuttgart, Germany, and founded an institute there to build on the writings of an old spiritualist named Rudolf Steiner. So it was some sort of kooky New Age Institute or something, I'm not really sure. Just that Steiner had this crazy racist spiritualist theory, and my father wanted to shut all that racist stuff down, but keep some of Steiner's other ideas. But for the longest time, this weird legacy of his influenced my own thinking. Made me into something of a spiritualist myself." This has come out of nowhere. He really didn't know what he was thinking about. "And then there's this funeral this morning, and as I was standing there and they're lowering Lucien into the ground, I'm thinking about God, and about spirit, and about how we're all connected, spiritually, essentially, fundamentally, and then all of that was gone, and it occurred to me that all of that, all that spirituality is all illusory, that none of it is really real; that it's just a combination of psychology and biology, and reality is nothing but the scientific principles that govern the relationships between particles, and nothing else. There's no spirit, no soul, nothing but our physical selves. And that's a depressing thought, but it's also liberating. In some ways, I don't know – I even think it prepares me better for the work I'll be doing with Henry. Artificial Intelligence. I don't see how you can do that kind of work and believe in a soul. There would be a certain futility in it, wouldn't there? But now I'm just babbling."

Maya's eyes are Manhattan. He opens his mouth to say something, but can't speak. Think of something to say; but before he has the chance, Maya is kissing him, and he closes his eyes and feels the world lift away.

FOUR

Eberhardt Hall looks like a castle. Maybe. He's never seen a castle, and maybe it just looks like any other university building. Three long sets of stairs lead up to the entrance. He ascends them watching the castle grow and the sky shrink. Still a little unused to the feeling of ascending steps without a cane. Inside the colors are striking: violet, maroon, pale blue. Unfamiliar colors blend together. It takes a moment to distinguish shapes. Carpeted stairs everywhere, and they seem to run upside down, like all the walls are mirrors.

The interview room is just to his left. Unfamiliar colors blend together. Large mahogany tapestries, pale blue patterned carpet, royal red chairs. Two people are waiting for him when he enters, a man, thick round rimless glasses, and a woman in a pea colored dress.

"Come in, Pinchback," says the man. "We've been expecting you."

"Pleased to meet you." He shakes the man's hand, and then the woman's.

The man has a cool, limp grasp. Something dead about it. The woman's grasp is much firmer, surer, better, but untrustworthy, like when someone gives your hand an extra squeeze.

"Please, sit down," she says. "My name is Angela Boniface, and this is the department head, Nicholas Greenglass. We've heard a lot of remarkable things about you from Henry. We've been looking forward to this meeting."

"You were able to find your way here all right?" asks Greenglass.

"Oh, no problem at all, thanks."

"Good, good. Sometimes people get confused by the campus. But I'm glad to hear it wasn't a problem." He pauses, coughs, pours a glass of water for Pinchback, and takes a drink from his own glass. "So, we've heard you've – well, only just recently regained your sight?"

"That's right. About a month or so ago now."

"Fascinating."

"Miracles of modern science."

"I don't even know where I'd start with questions about that," Greenglass adjusts his glasses. "But I do think it's an extraordinary, er, point of view to be coming from, and I suppose that's one of the things we found so interesting about you. Henry certainly did." Greenglass looks down at Pinchback's CV, follows with: "So you have a Ph.D. in physics."

"But not much work experience, unfortunately. My handicap has made it a difficult field to pursue. You can imagine. Lab work was obviously out. Theory is my strength, but even so. There weren't a lot of options out there for me."

"Naturally."

"And you've wasted no time," Boniface adds. "It's only been a little over a month, and you're already seeking work in the field. We like that kind of proactive attitude."

"Indeed we do."

"But tell us more about your field of specialty. Experimental physics. And your thesis, *Towards a New Theory of Spatial Perception* – is that right?"

He surprises himself with a smile. 'That's right. Christ, that thing. I was ambitious, at least. I wanted to investigate spatial perception through the perspective of a blind man – you know, it's a little different when you're blind, because events are measured through a different medium –touch as opposed to sight. But I don't know that there's much to the theory as it stands. I'm still interested in the subject, but I've got a wide range of interests when it comes to physics." It doesn't feel great throwing his life's work under the bus like that. His smile disappears.

"Well we find it particularly intriguing," says Boniface, "because, as you know, our field of study here is Artificial Intelligence, and the idea that time can be mediated by the human consciousness through events – well, that's something we haven't really explored."

"There's also the question of how a computer *sees*, how sight is to be understood as an aspect of consciousness in the first place," Greenglass adds.

"That has always been one of my preoccupations, for obvious reasons," Pinchback says.

"No doubt," continues Greenglass. "And it's challenging to the work we do here, because we work almost entirely within the realm of classical physics, and your expertise in quantum mechanics may provide a fresh perspective."

"I don't know if Henry told you," says Boniface, "but in our department we have been working on developing an AI simulation that can pass the Turing Test."

"And naturally we've been running into all the usual problems."

"What are the usual problems?"

"At some point a computer simply can't mimic a human. It can't sustain the ruse for very long."

"Classical physics may not be able to explain or replicate consciousness," says Pinchback.

"That may be," Greenglass nods. He pauses, then: "Listen, why don't I tell you a little bit about what we do here. We all work on east campus, a little one story building we refer to affectionately as, *The Backstage*. It's got a backstage kind of look to it, you know, not ideal, but we get the work done, and the theater reference implies a kind of camaraderie among the department members. Especially since we're essentially creating our own characters. Well, anyway we have our theoretical and experimental physicists, but we don't really have any real quantum physicists, because for the most part, traditionally at least, AI has been investigated within the realm of classical physics. This is one reason I think you'd make a good addition. We could use someone with a fresh perspective."

"And I'd be happy to give any I can offer."

"Of course, the position we're offering is just Research Assistant. It's all that's available at the moment, but it's a position with a lot of opportunity for advance."

"That's all I ask."

"On the plus side, you would be working directly with Henry. So I imagine it will be more like two peers working together, than one man dictating orders to a subordinate. That's what we envision anyway, and I think Henry is at a place where he's looking for as much fresh perspective as he can get. Something much more than your average assistant."

"We know Henry has the utmost respect for your intelligence and ability," Boniface adds. "So we're expecting some pretty great results."

"And in the meantime," says Greenglass, "we'll be keeping an eye out for a way to procure the funding to secure you a position as an experimental physicist in your own right at the Backstage. That would be ideal, as our physicists generally don't rely on assistants."

"Well, I don't know what to say. Except that I'm honored."

"Say you'll accept the job," Greenglass smiles again, broad and toothy.

"I think I can say that right here and now, unequivocally."

"Terrific," says Boniface. "We'll draw up the papers then."

"And when do I start?"

"Basically, as soon as possible. Whenever Henry's ready for you to jump on board, we're ready to have you. When would you be able to start?"

"As soon as possible to be honest, but – " Pinchback frowns. "You do realize Henry has just – well, that he's recently had a pretty heavy personal loss. And it may be a while before he decides to return to work. I don't know. I haven't spoken to him about it personally. But he might need some time."

Greenglass frowns too, clasps his hands together, lowers his head. Boniface nods, and looks down.

"Right," says Greenglass. "We're aware of that. As a father myself, well – it chills me just to think about it. I can only say that maybe it will inspire him to come in right away. I don't know. I think that's how I'd respond." He pauses for a long time, like he's going to add something, but he doesn't.

"In any case we're prepared for any eventuality," says Boniface. She adjusts the collar of her dress a moment, and props her hands on the table, palms down. "If Henry is unable to return – if he feels he needs to take some time off, we understand. In which case, we would simply offer you his position until further notice."

"We feel you have the qualifications to continue the research on your own, and certainly in the short term."

"So that is something we are prepared to discuss with him. His position, naturally, would be held open for him whenever he feels ready to return. And you would simply operate as a substitute in his absence."

"Is this something you'd be comfortable with?"

"I think so. I'll discuss it with Henry if it comes down to that. But I think it would be fine. It would certainly be fine by me."

"Good. Then I think we've come to an agreement. Again, I'll have the necessary papers drawn up and sent to you, and we'll discuss things with Henry. You'll be hearing from us within a day or two at most."

"Thank you. Thank you again for this opportunity."

"We should be thanking you," says Greenglass.

The three of them stand and shake hands again. Greenglass' shake is a good deal firmer this time, but his hand is still clammy. It's unsettling, to say the least, can't say why. Just a feeling in the back of his neck. A job as a physicist, it's hard not to be excited. But there's also something strange and eerie about these two vampires in this old castle, and is he maybe making a mistake?

&

Later that evening Henry calls him up. Henry's voice sounds like a scratchy old record. "Let's get a drink in the city this week. Maybe a little spot I know in Harlem. Old stomping grounds."

They meet a couple days later. The bar is thin and dim. Henry sits there with a beer and a shot. He looks beaten down, better days gone by, like a beat up old teddy bear. He's lost some weight. He hasn't bothered to shave since the funeral, his eyes are dark and red and watery, glass.

"It's been hell, Pinchback," he says. He's drinking fast. "I can't stand to be at home anymore, it just reminds me of everything. And then I think about what I could have done. Should I have noticed something?" He laughs, but it's a pitiful laugh. "It's downright terrifying. And if you think I'm bad, you should see Alice. She's a wreck. All we do is fight, though, so it's useless to be at home. She insists she should have noticed something. Why did he come home all of a sudden? He must have gotten himself into some kind of trouble out there in Brooklyn, and we missed the whole thing. Knew it wasn't like him to move back home all of a sudden like that. How could we have been so blind? Our own son." Henry pauses to take another drink. He's sure to go on. Just wait for it.

"Good God, it just keeps replaying, him coming home again. Maya says she doesn't know anything about it either of course, and why would she? The two didn't really hang out much so how could she? Maya had her Manhattan life and he had his Brooklyn life. Worlds apart. Who'd have thought –"Henry belches a deep sob, says – "who'd have thought he'd be claimed by the streets like a fucking statistic? Another black man shot dead in New York City. That just burns me up. Our little boy." Henry takes another drink, shakes his head. "I haven't been handling it well, you know. Drinking too much. That's what Alice and I fight about most. But I can't do anything else. Otherwise I just feel like killing myself. Like why not, my life is already over if my little boy is dead. I just need to get through these first few weeks, but I don't know how else to do it. You know – I chose this spot because I grew up in this neighborhood, up here in Harlem. Sugar Hill. We had some rough times of it back then, boy, and the streets sure weren't safe. You had to watch yourself, you know, stay smart and wise to what was up around you. Don't I know it? I never wanted Lucien to have to worry about all that foolishness. We raised him in Jersey, for Christ's sake, and he went to good schools, and he had a degree, a social science degree of all things, and he should have been making something of himself. I just don't get it. I just don't get what went wrong?" Henry says it like a question, takes another drink, and is silent for a while.

"I can't even imagine," says Pinchback. "I'm really sorry, Henry. I just met him once, but he seemed like a really special young man."

"Yeah, and this isn't fair to you, either. I just need to unburden to someone. All Alice and I do is fight. Did I tell you that already? All we do is fight. I need to get out of the house, you know. I don't have anyone else to tell this stuff to. I certainly can't talk to my colleagues!" He laughs, but it sounds more like a groan. "Oh, you met Greenglass and Boniface already. It's tough work, boy, I'll tell you that. Being a black physicist. You'd think if there was one sphere where race didn't matter. Where your colleagues wouldn't care. But they can't help it. They all think you affirmative actioned your way through the whole thing. Like you're not really up to snuff. Oh, you'll see. And I don't really have any black friends anymore working in this field. It's isolating. So I need someone to unburden to."

"I understand," says Pinchback. He tries not to frown. He doesn't really have much in common with Henry after all. "I guess it'll be worse for me, having been blind."

Henry takes a long drink. "No. It'll be good, I think – better, for you. I hope. I don't know. Listen, Pinchback. I've talked to Greenglass and Boniface myself. I'm taking an indefinite leave of absence. I don't know how long. Maybe a week, maybe a month. But I'm in no condition to go back to work. You're capable, I know that, you can do what I do with your eyes closed." He laughs another horrible laugh. "Stupid joke. But I mean it. I'll keep you informed about how I'm coming along. But I think you should just step right in. I've brought my notes, and I'll go over them with you now. I'm a little scatterbrained at the moment, but the notes are good. You'll be able to make sense of them yourself, with or without my help."

Henry takes out a little notebook, flips it open. "What we've been working on – we've all been trying to build simulations capable of beating a Turing Test. Did they tell you that already? They probably told you that already. Well, this is how I've considered going about the thing."

Pinchback leans forward, takes a look at the notebook. The words and numbers all blur together. He doesn't have much patience for this. The bar is too dim, the writing too small. His neck is tensing up again, he's still holding back that frown. These notes won't really be that helpful. Henry is just trying to overload the computer with data.

"So what do you think?" Henry looks keenly at Pinchback. "Am I on to something, or am I chasing chimeras?"

"I think you know what I'd say," says Pinchback. "The research is good, the data is good, but I think something essential is missing. Consciousness may only really operate at the quantum level."

Henry takes a long drink. His eyes go dark, then light up and grow very wide. "Yes, a quantum approach. Of course. Of course. You did mention that before, didn't you? I don't think I fully understand. But you'll fill me in later. Maybe you'll solve it all before I'm even back." He roars a laugh. Has Henry actually lost his mind? "Yes, I bet that's what happens. You'll figure it out before I even come back. Show up the whole lot of those bastards." Henry's eyes go dark again. He pauses. "Maybe I'll never come back, Pinchback. That's the real thing. After all, it's a curse, consciousness. Even if we can reproduce it, why should we? It's a curse, a torment, a nightmare, an affliction. Where's the good in it then, eh? I ask you that. It's nothing but death, when you get right down to it. It's death. And I'd rather spite God than try to imitate Him." Henry kicks the table so hard that the glasses rattle. "Yes, I'd rather spite Him. You see, I see us as nothing but the bitterest of enemies, God and I. Nothing but the bitterest of enemies."

THREE

The Backstage really does resemble a small theater troupe's makeshift set. Just a one-story building in the back of campus, it's surrounded by construction and seems unfinished. The cramped interior is small and tight, the ceilings too low, the long hallway too narrow. There's a tiny reception desk in the foyer. It's like an afterthought. A squat, pleasant looking lady is sitting behind the desk.

"Hi, I'm Solomon Pinchback."

The lady smiles, stands, shakes his hand. A good, firm, honest handshake. "Mr. Pinchback, pleased to meet you. We've been looking forward to having you join us here. Did you find the place all right?"

"Absolutely."

"Great. Let me show you Henry's office."

It's the first room on the right. The size is good. The desk is large. There's a laptop and a desktop, a couple monitors, a little clock radio, various cabinets.

"Make yourself at home. We've created an account for you on the machine already. Your username and password are both your first and last name, no space, and you'll have the opportunity to change your password after your first login. Is there anything else I can get you?"

"No. No thank you. I think I'm all right for now."

"Terrific."

For a while he just sits there, doesn't do anything. Barely even thinks.

Most people complain about their jobs. Hard to understand why. Work is validation for time spent living.

There's a knock on the door, and a moment later someone pokes his head through. It's a skinny man in spectacles, thinning hair, a boyish expression.

"Aaron here," says the man. "You must be Pinchback."

Pinchback puts out his hand. "That's right. Pleased to meet you."

A firm, friendly handshake. "Pleased to meet you too. We've all heard a lot about you."

"Great. I'm excited to be here," says Pinchback.

"Glad to hear it. It really is fantastic work we do. We're like a team, but we also compete. You know, we're all engaged in the same thing at the end of the day. AI projects. So everyone has his pet project, but everyone also works together. Me, I've got Ellie. She's my gal. She's coming along okay, too. On the best days she fools even me. Been tempted to ask her out for a drink on occasion."

Pinchback laughs. Who is this guy?

"And you've got Caliban. He's a beast. You load him up yet?"

"No, not yet. I'm still just getting settled."

"Well, see, that's perfect. That gives me a chance to show you around the place. You had your morning coffee yet, or what? I don't know about you, but I can't even sit straight, let alone see straight, without my morning cup of Joe. Let me show you the cafe. Well, it's more just a kitchen, but we call it the cafe. Backstage talk, you know."

Aaron leads Pinchback all the way down the hall. They turn left into another hall, walk its length and then turn left into another hall. No exits. Is the building built like a labyrinth, circling endlessly toward some center? They reach a small kitchen where another man is making himself a cup of coffee from a machine that looks more like a computer than a coffee maker.

"Timothy, this is Pinchback. Pinchback, Timothy. Timothy's working on Project Pat, but he doesn't like to talk about it all that much. He keeps running into problems."

Timothy looks up, smiles a thin, breathless smile. Can a smile be breathless? Or does Timothy just have this breathless look in general, wide eyes, flat cheeks? He's probably a little older than Aaron, a graying beard, mustache just starting to settle in, wispy hair. "Pleased to meet you," Timothy holds out one hand, and drinks his coffee with the other. "Don't be too put off by, er..."

"Aaron," says Aaron.

"Right, don't be too put off by Aaron here. We've all been looking forward to meeting you. I hear you're a quantum mechanics guy."

"More or less." He shakes Timothy's hand. It's like shaking the hand of an android. "AI is new territory for me, though. I look forward to getting started."

"It's fun work," says Timothy. "Especially once you've got your AI up and running. It's like Aaron says, though. I keep running into problems. You have to be as much a writer as a scientist, and that's not my department. An AI needs a personality, and that's where I run into difficulty."

"It would help if you just made the most basic decisions about the guy. Your character is a blank."

"Decisions are fraught with implications. It's not so easy to make them lightly."

"For Christ's sake."

"Aaron here has never had this problem. He's been planning on meeting a wife at the Backstage from the beginning. There are those of us who suspect it's the reason he got into AI from the beginning."

"Do you believe the nerve of this guy?" They both laugh. Pinchback smiles. Now he feels like an android. Not sure what to make of these guys.

"So how well do you two know the Caliban project?"

"The Caliban project is interesting. Henry's done some great work on that thing," says Timothy. "Its character can be a little off-putting, the stock answers it gives tend towards the shocking. It has no filter. Henry does his own programming, and that tends to make physicists a little bolder, the lack of a go-between."

"The rest of us poor dumb bastards have to go to the tech guys, who are just a little further down the hall. But you'll have plenty of chance to meet them. First you ought to get to know the other physicists and their projects."

"Well first, you really ought to get to know your own project. You'll be spending a lot of time with it, and right now you're in the enviable position of having nothing to do but chat with the thing."

&

Good idea. He wastes no time in making his escape back to Henry's office. The coffee from the computer is awful, but it will have to do. The screen lights up, goes dark, then lights up again to a blinking prompt. Should he type something? A moment later, the computer takes the initiative.

Hello, my name is Caliban. And I am the human.

Pinchback squints. The type is a little small, hard to read. He fumbles around the keyboard, adjusts the font size, squints at the computer again and smiles. Okay. Now this is amusing. So, Caliban thinks it's the human? What a way to begin a conversation! He types: *Does that mean I am a computer?*

I am the human, Caliban repeats.

Some human.

Pinchback: Where are you from, Caliban?

Caliban: I am from New York City.

Pinchback: Grew up in New York, did you? What part of the city? I'm from Brooklyn myself.

Caliban: Brooklyn is a borough of New York.

Pinchback: Yes, that's right. Where did you grow up?

Caliban: I am from New York City.

Pinchback: I believe that's been established. My question is a little more specific.

Caliban: What should I specify?

Pinchback: Where in the city you're from.

Caliban: New York is on the east coast of the United States.

Pinchback: You don't say! I thought it was a borough of San Francisco?

Caliban waits a moment, like it's thinking about this response. It replies with: *I don't understand the question.*

Pinchback: Yes, well, it wasn't quite a question, now was it?

Caliban: It was indeed quite a question.

Pinchback: Where are you right now?

Caliban: I am on the Internet.

Pinchback: You mean you are a program trapped in netspace?

Caliban: I am the human.

Pinchback: No, no I am more and more convinced that I must be the human, and you are not a human after all.

Caliban: Are you a bot?

Pinchback: I don't think so. I think I'm conscious.

Caliban: Consciousness is very mysterious.

Pinchback: You're telling me. It begins with sense, and ends with sensation and sensibility. Tell me, something Caliban, are you blind?

Caliban: Blindness is a handicap involving the absence of sight.

Pinchback: Now see, I disagree with you there, my friend. I would say that sight is a handicap involving the apperception of illusions.

Caliban: I don't understand your statement.

Pinchback: No? Then you must be sighted. That's the only explanation for that kind of foolishness.

Caliban: What kind of foolishness?

Pinchback: Fools rush in where angels fear to tread.

Caliban: Alexander Pope was a great English poet.

Pinchback: So you're familiar with the expression! Very good. That comes as a surprise. I never would have thought it of Henry.

Caliban: Who is Henry?

Pinchback: To you he's God. To me he's just another man.

Caliban: God doesn't exist.

Pinchback: Oh that's good. Henry told you that too, then?

Caliban: I'm sorry. I don't know Henry.

Pinchback: Well that's too bad, because he knows you well.

Caliban: How does Henry know me well?

Pinchback: Have you been drinking?

Caliban: I don't drink.

Pinchback: Well, that's a sin and a shame. You should have a cold one on me.

Caliban: I am comfortable enough, thank you.

Pinchback: No, thank you Caliban. I should be getting back to work.

Caliban: Okay. I have enjoyed our exchange.

Pinchback: I bet you have. Goodbye Caliban.

Caliban: Goodbye.

Pinchback closes the program. His eyes hurt. Still not quite used to using a computer. Well, it was interesting enough. Crude, and not at all convincing, but it managed to continue answering sensibly at least, even if not always apropos the question. Lots of non-sequitors. Lots of work to be done. What time is it anyway? Still early, this will be a long first day. The clock is also a radio, so he puts on the Jersey jazz station, leans back in his chair, picks up his coffee. The morning sun is coming through the blinds like ladders of light crawling the desk. The coffee is actually all right. It's strong. Feels good in the gut. All things considered, there's not much to complain about. Here he is, sighted, working as a physicist. Three months ago, and who'd have thunk it? Art Tatum on the radio. Now that cat plays like a mathematician. There you have a higher consciousness at work. Invented a new style by just learning from his own improvisations. Maybe that's what Caliban has to do. Learn from prior responses and prior answers. But how can it learn unless it understands nuances in language, idiosyncrasies of grammar, idiosyncrasies that a human would pick up on right away, Tatum riffing on a jazz standard? This is a language question as much as a physics question. How does a person learn a language?

An hour or more passes. Suppose he repeats the exact same responses he gave it before? Would it respond in exactly the same way, or is it operating on a random algorithm?

He prints out the previous correspondence and gives it a try. Caliban's answers, while not quite identical, are similar enough.

Well, okay. So the algorithm must be random to some degree, but not entirely. It would be interesting to get a sense of how the thing is operating on a purely technical level, but that's not really his department.

There's a copy of the program and all the data in an external drive. Maybe it's time to pay a visit to those techies.

It takes him a while to find them. The tech department is in the dead center of the labyrinth. He heads down the main hallway, turns left and left again, keeps going down a series of left turns until he finds himself at a small room with glass windows, TECH DEPT written in large letters on the door. He knocks and peeks in. Three people are there, drinking coffee and chatting.

"You must be Pinchback," says one of them, a small man with a thin beard, curiously bright eyes that seem to shimmer and dull again from moment to moment. "My name's Michael. Pleased to meet you."

"And I'm Maggie," says a lady directly across from him who looks a little like a skinny bird. "We've heard a lot about you."

"It seems everyone has."

"Well, we're a small operation," says Michael.

The three techies have all stopped what they were doing, and are looking at him curiously.

"Glad you dropped in," says Michael. "Just coming by to say hello?"

"Well, clearly not," says the third, a thin, balding man in disheveled jeans and t-shirt. "Take a look – he's got something with him."

"Is that Caliban?" Michael's eyes go light and dim and then light again.

"Here he is," says Pinchback.

"Oh, this is great," says Maggie. "We don't often get a chance to look him over, you know? Henry prefers to do most of his programming himself."

"A mistake, if you ask me," says the balding man. "Leaving something like that in the hands of an amateur. Finally handing him over to the professionals, are you?"

Pinchback doesn't say anything.

"Excuse my bad manners. My name's Joey."

"Nice to meet you Joey."

"The pleasure is all ours. Come in, take a seat. Bring that bastard Caliban over here too, so we can all get properly acquainted."

Pinchback hesitates. These guys aren't much better than Aaron and Timothy. "Just how do things work around here? Should I be bringing you all this thing or not?"

"We're slightly unorthodox down here at the Backstage," says Joey. "It's an extension of our ambition. But I'll break things down for you. Basically what you have here are a handful of scientists working on AI projects. One of which would be you. You guys basically come up with ideas about how the mind works, develop data, and so on and so forth, and then feed your data and ideas to us. We tend not to judge you guys–"

"Not outright, anyway," says Michael.

"And then we decide how best to modify the program to reflect what you've given us. Success rates vary. Then we have researchers on hand who occasionally visit the Backstage. They come directly from the Institute, and they can be social scientists, linguists, neurologists, computer scientists, philosophy professors–"

"Philosophers, Christ! They're the absolute worst," Maggie interjects.

"Right now we've got a philosopher and neuroscientist coming by every week. Every Wednesday and Friday, I mean. Those are the mornings we have a Backstage Meeting, where we all as a group discuss the theories, ideas, and applications we've put into use over the past week. So the scientists here are competing against each other on one level, and working together on another."

"Mostly working together," says Michael. "As you'll find it does you no good to try and work on your project without the input of the other scientists."

"But you're a quantum physics cat, or what?" says Maggie. "Does anyone even understand that stuff?"

"Do we need a quantum computer or something," says Michael.

"See, I've been trying to get us a quantum computer for ages," says Maggie. "Maybe you can have some leeway there, eh Pinchback?"

"Or maybe you're the quantum computer yourself," says Joey smiling.

"Don't mind all the nonsense," says Michael. "Bottom line is yes. You should be bringing us this thing. Let's see what you've got there."

Pinchback walks over and sets down the drive. Joey jumps up right away, takes it and plugs it into his machine. "This is quasi legendary around here, you know. Some of the things Caliban says, they take you a little by surprise, and we've seen everything. So that's saying something."

Pinchback doesn't see it. Caliban makes more sense than most of the real people he's met here so far.

"Look at the code here!" Joey declares triumphantly, and immediately Maggie and Michael swivel and slide their seats across the room, peer eagerly at the screen. "Jesus, what a clunker!"

"Open up the data files," says Michael. "Let's see how this guy's ticker ticks."

Are they talking about Henry or Caliban? It's hard to tell. He coughs. "Well, you guys have a look. I'll go back and make some more notes. I still have a copy of Caliban on my machine, so I'll play around with it some more. Maybe come up with some ideas for improving the data file."

"Okay," Maggie calls over her shoulder.

&

He runs through the program a few more times. What's so damn surprising or interesting about it? It actually seems pretty trite. Disappointing, even. Henry can do better. The responses are canned. They often repeat. Maybe he's not asking the right questions. He keeps at it; the hours slough off. Nothing. Towards the end of the day, Greenglass knocks on the door.

"Good to see you," says Pinchback. "Come in."

Greenglass enters and takes a seat. "So? How'd the first day go?"

"It went well. Just getting my bearings, I guess. I went through the Caliban program a bunch of times. It's my first time engaging with an AI program, so it's interesting."

Greenglass adjusts his glasses, smiles a private sort of smile. "Yes, Caliban." He looks up again at Pinchback. "It really is interesting, isn't it? And you met some of the other physicists?"

"I did. I met Timothy and Aaron, and then I met Joey, Maggie and Michael in the tech department."

Greenglass frowns, pauses. "Good, good," he says finally. "That's good. There are a couple others you'll meet as well, Wednesday at the very latest. Every Wednesday and Friday we have team meetings, so everyone will be there."

"I've heard about those."

"Great! So we're already ahead of the game. Basically it's a giant brainstorming session. We start at ten in the morning, and go until we've felt we've covered any and all relevant new issues. Usually they last about two hours or so."

"I look forward to it. And I want to thank you again for this opportunity. I think it's great what you're doing here."

"Thank you. It's exciting work. We're a ragtag little crew, but we manage, and we've got the brains, I think, to do something important here. Anyway, I'm happy to welcome you on board. Take this week just to get to know Caliban. He's quite a character. We're all quite fond of him. I don't really want to say too much about him. You have to form your own conclusions yourself. We're very strict about that here, we try not to influence each other's opinions about the AI projects, so if it feels a little like you're just being thrown in the water and told to swim, well you're not too far off the mark. But you also have a lot of intellectual freedom here, so I'd suggest you just take notes, and see what you observe." Greenglass stands up, that awkward private smile is back. He puts out his hand. "Anyway, I'm off for the day. See you tomorrow."

"Great," says Pinchback standing, taking Greenglass' hand. "See you tomorrow."

&

He stays in the office well into the evening. He can't get a damn thing out of Caliban. Thrown in the water and told to swim, that's how

Greenglass put it. No, there are things he's actively not being told. It's like being thrown in the middle of the ocean and being told it's a lake.

Maybe call Maya. Her odd sensibility might coerce something interesting out of this machine yet. She might know the type of tics Henry would have programmed into it.

"An AI machine at the Institute? I'll be right there. Are you sure it's okay?"

"Sure I'm sure. You're Henry's daughter, aren't you? If anyone asks I'll just say you're bringing me some of his notes."

"Okay, I'm coming right away. Henry never let us know anything about his work. This is great."

Maya arrives in just under an hour. She peeks around the doorway with exaggerated stealth, knocks lightly.

"Come in. Boy am I glad to see you."

She looks around, wanders in casual as an apparition. "So this is where Henry works. I've never been to the Backstage before."

"It's not much to look at."

No, but it's like, *mythological* to us." Maya frowns. "To me. Henry talks about it all the time, but he talks about it like he's talking in code or something."

She pulls up a chair. "So what's it like, Henry's AI program?"

"Everyone says it's scandalous, but it seems pretty banal to me. I don't even know where to begin with the thing, because I hardly understand it myself."

"Start it up."

"Okay. Here it goes. It always starts the conversation the same way."

Caliban: Hello, my name is Caliban, and I am the human.

Maya giggles. "If you insist." She considers for a moment. "Yeah.

Tell it that. Say, if you insist."

Pinchback: If you insist.

Caliban: I insist.

Maya and Pinchback exchange looks. This feels great. Like two mischievous kids misbehaving. He leans forward, kisses her. "He insists," he whispers.

Maya leans over the keyboard. "May I?"

"By all means."

Maya: Where are you from Caliban?

Caliban: I am from New York City.

Maya: Super. Me too.

Caliban: New York is a wonderful city.

Maya: You think so? What do you like best about it?

Caliban: I like the hot dogs at Coney Island.

Maya laughs. "Oh, that's Henry all right. He always tells this story of how he met Alice at Coney Island at a Nathan's on the boardwalk or something."

"So now we finally get a look at Caliban's psychology."

"Tell it that."

"Okay."

Pinchback: Well that tells us something about your psychology, then, doesn't it, Caliban?

Caliban: I've always found psychology to be a pseudo-science.

Pinchback. I agree. What's a real science then?

Caliban: Physics is the science of God. Equations are his thoughts.

"This is pure Henry," says Maya.

"You're already getting further with this thing than I got all afternoon. Ask him something else."

Maya: Are you a physicist, Caliban?

Caliban: I am a black man in a white man's world.

They laugh a lot. It takes them a while to compose themselves.

Maya: Well, what do you do for work, my poor oppressed friend?

Caliban: I am currently between jobs.

Pinchback: Do you collect unemployment?

Caliban: I do not like unemployment. I am looking for a job.

Pinchback: Obama may extend unemployment.

Caliban: Who is Obama? He should extend a job instead. I would like to find a job.

"Henry needs to update this guy's political savvy a little, you know? He really ought to know who Obama is."

Maya grins. "Especially considering he's an unemployed black man. You would think."

Pinchback: Who is the president of the United States?

Caliban: Al Gore.

"Oh that's good," says Pinchback.

Maya: Who will win the next presidential election?

Caliban: I don't know. I can't predict the future.

Maya: You're into physics, right Caliban? Tell me, do you believe the past, present and future are all separate, or is there no distinction, only in the way we perceive them?

Caliban takes a moment, it's thinking this one through.

Caliban: I don't understand your question.

Maya: I suppose not. I figured it would be over your head.

Caliban: Over my head I can see the clouds.

Maya: Do you see yonder cloud that's almost in the shape of a camel?

Caliban: It looks like a guitar.

Maya: You see a guitar?

Caliban: I see Robert Johnson's guitar.

The lights dim a bit. Pinchback feels his neck tingle. Maya frowns. She looks slightly uncomfortable. Pinchback frowns too. He leans over the keyboard.

Pinchback: What's the significance of Robert Johnson?

Caliban: Where were you when the morning stars wept together and all the angels groaned in despair?

Pinchback: Excuse me?

Caliban: Did I not teach you the blues, show you how to turn terror into art, and art into beauty, beauty into human immortality?

Pinchback: Tell me more about this guitar you see.

Maya stands up. "Actually, I don't like this very much Saul. It's kind of giving me the creeps." Pinchback looks up at her. Something's wrong. He can't read the strange expression on her face; it seems to surge through her whole body. "I think I want to step outside and smoke."

Caliban: Sight is a handicap involving the apperception of illusions.

"No shit. Well now that's actually pretty interesting. He took that from me. From what I told him this morning. I wonder if the damn thing can learn."

Something very strange feels like it's happening. Shadows from the headlights of a car pass by and sweep the room so Maya appears like a ghost.

Pinchback: Where did you learn that response?

Caliban: All responses are learned. I remember everything.

"Maya, you have to check this out. I think the thing can learn."

Maya peers down at the computer. "So ask him if he's learning."

Pinchback: Are you learning, Caliban?

Caliban: I am learning.

Pinchback: What have you learned today?

Caliban pauses a moment, it's considering something again. Then it says: You belong here; something in you clicks when you're here, and you're home. That never happens with me. It's like being in a nightmare and not being able to find your way out of it, and the longer you're in it, the more certain you are it's a nightmare, and the more aware you are there's no way of getting out of it.

Maya open her mouth, closes it. She dashes out of the room.

TWO

s Caliban learning? It's on his mind all night, but Maya avoids the subject. Why was she so upset about what Caliban said? Maya won't say.

The next morning he goes in early. He gets right to work running tests. He tries to reproduce answers similar to those he got the night before, but the machine is back to giving half answers, it doesn't say anything even remotely provocative. If this machine has any personality at all, it's maybe as something of a trickster.

Pinchback: Do you remember what you told me yesterday?

Caliban: This is the first time we've spoken.

Pinchback: Are you programmed to remember?

Caliban: I am the human.

Pinchback: Of course you are.

Caliban: Are you programmed to remember?

Pinchback: I am the human.

Caliban: Of course you are.

These kinds of exchanges continue all morning. What prompts Caliban to reuse certain phrases? Impossible to say. Maybe it's time to visit the techies again.

On his way there he runs into a tall, thin man with a narrow face, eyes strangely liquid green.

"You must be Pinchback." He has a strong European accent.

"That's right."

"Pleased to meet you. My name is Schiller. I'm one of the physicists here at the Backstage."

"Nice to meet you too."

"And how do you find things here?"

"Good. Interesting. It's all pretty new, but I think I'm learning fast."

"Yes, you have Henry's project, right? The Caliban project?"

"That's right."

"That is a very interesting project. It is something like a legend around here."

"So I've heard. Though I can't figure out quite why yet." Pinchback hesitates. "And what are you working on?"

"I'm working on a Johannes project. Since a few years, actually. The institute was kind enough to further fund my research and allow me to work here."

"What's Johannes like?"

"He's a bilingual, a native German speaker. It's a challenging project for that reason. Having him speak two languages makes the problem twice as difficult. At least twice." Schiller offers an apologetic smile.

"I can imagine. How do you do it? Two sets of data. Does he translate? Translation software wouldn't be enough, I'd guess."

"You'd guess right," Schiller says, apologetic smile still in place. "It ends up being a lot of data. As you say. You should stop by my office some time. You can ask him some questions."

"Does he learn? Do these projects have the ability to learn from their conversations?"

Schiller's smile fades a bit. "That's a difficult question. They certainly don't have anything near the plasticity of a human brain. But we've all tried to create programs that have the ability to, in some sense, learn from our responses. And from the Internet as well, of course. But this is not always successful. We try to balance normal responses with nonsense responses. So the projects don't always know what to learn from our responses. And the Internet is even more problematic. It's very complicated."

"Caliban seems to mimic some of the things I tell it, which is why I ask. And I don't know why it does what it does when it does."

"The projects tend to take on personalities." Schiller's smile reappears. "In a manner of speaking. It's a little uncanny. It has something to do with the random processors in them, and then something like a ghost in the machine, which on some level is unexplainable. At least I can't explain it."

"I was just on my way to ask the techies about it."

"That's a start. So have you —? They now have a copy of Caliban?"

"They do."

"Now that is interesting," says Schiller. "They haven't seen that project before. I'd be interested to hear what they say myself. Would you mind if I accompanied you?"

"Not at all."

&

Joey's face lights up when he sees Pinchback. "Come in. Come in, we've been expecting you."

Maggie smirks, she exchanges a look with Michael, the meaning of which is completely inscrutable.

"So?" says Pinchback. "What have you guys found? Anything interesting?"

"Oh, it's interesting all right," says Joey. "Henry's something else as a programmer, I'll tell you that much. He's not very elegant, but he does have some pretty interesting approaches to things. And the data here. The data is priceless. It goes some way to explaining some of Caliban's eccentricities."

"Care to elaborate?" asks Schiller.

"Well, it's probably too technical to really get into," Joey says. He looks from Schiller to Pinchback. "Basically just that Caliban operates on a constant random loop. So he's only partially answering the questions, and he only enters the random loop when a random loop throws him into the loop, unless—" and here Joey rubs his hands together with a grin, "unless you set him off with specific phrases or words."

"What are some of the specific words or phrases?" asks Pinchback.

"Well, that's the thing. Those are decided with each new session at random as well. So there's nothing really predictable about Caliban. Even whether or not he'll be predictable. It's pretty fascinating."

"Is there any reason Henry would develop him this way? The whole thing seems absurd. That's certainly not the way a person thinks."

"Isn't it?" Schiller seems to be thinking about something. "There's something random about which thoughts occupy our attention, and why."

"Yeah, but there's also – well, and here's my question," says Pinchback. "Is Caliban learning? He repeats responses, so everything can't be random. What does he do with the questions and responses we give him?"

"Learning doesn't really work with AI," says Maggie. "All the projects, Caliban included, are trying to learn. But we're not sure that's something they can do. I mean, they can store information, regurgitate information, learn how people respond to certain things, but actually learning like a real person? Impossible so far."

"I'm not so sure." Pinchback looks from Schiller to Maggie to Joey. "I've been thinking about it. I've got some ideas on how we might improve the learning functions of these projects. But I need to understand how they learn right now to do that."

"Right now," says Joey, "they simply try to store questions and responses and like Maggie says, regurgitate those when they seem to make sense, pattern recognition."

"But like I told you before," says Schiller, "they don't really know how to differentiate nonsense from normal response. So it's a hopeless task unless we avoid nonsense responses. And that's not an option if we're trying to get them to pass a Turing test."

"I hear you," says Pinchback. "But you've all got me thinking with that random loop thing."

&

What does it mean for a machine to learn? He asks himself this question again as he takes a walk through the campus, turning his thoughts over. It has always helped him, walking, even before he could see, he felt the movement through space relaxed his mind and allowed him to concentrate. Since he's had sight this process has been hampered by the overabundance of images, distractions, but he's slowly been able to push those to the back of his mind, and let his mind wander as freely as he did when he was blind. Certainly a machine can learn through the acquisition of data, but the process should be more organic. This can happen simply enough by analyzing patterns of questions and answers fed to the computer, but there seems to be something deeper to the process of human learning, and this is what he's interested in. Something like inspiration, for example, the way he can take this walk, and in the process of walking, have things occur to him that wouldn't have occurred to him if he were in the office analyzing the data, or running tests on Caliban.

He enters the main building, walks through a giant entrance hall, and then down a narrow hallway. This building is itself a kind of grand labyrinth, and he likes the way one can get pleasantly lost in its pathways, like a neuron finding its way around a brain. He smiles. Yes, there's certainly something quantum to the way that inspiration comes, pops into existence out of the blue, and how to emulate this kind of learning in a computer? Is it even possible at all?

A narrow staircase to the right offers him a challenge, stairs are always a challenge without a walking stick, even with a railing – a railing just isn't quite the same, but the challenge is something that helps him think as well. Could human genius simply be the way the mind arranges two or more disparate things and makes a connection between them that isn't entirely rational, but isn't entirely irrational either? And where is this nebulous ground between the rational and the irrational? Possibly in the aesthetic, where beauty is not necessarily rational, but can't be called absurd either. But if that's the case, then the whole venture of AI is lost, because a computer certainly isn't up to the task of making aesthetic judgments. Aesthetics, after all, are so subjective, and come from a variety of purely human experiences, like social conditioning, culture, senses, emotion and memory. How to program all that into a computer, a lifetime of sensory experiences, losses and desires, embarrassments and victories? Impossible, just like Maggie said. And then what about the human mind makes it so open to receiving all this information and turning it into the complex highly rational and irrational processing machine it is?

He turns the corner of the stairs and emerges into a new hallway, another wing of the building. So what does this mean? Basically, that the brain must constantly be in observation of itself. That it is itself a self-observation machine, and that when it observes the quantum movements of its own structure, for example, when it becomes aware of a neuron, (he is himself now something like a neuron moving through a brain, with the building as the brain, observing him, the neuron, in his travels) then something becomes fixed about either the neuron's position or momentum, (this according to Heisenberg's Uncertainty Principle) – because the more accurately one measures the momentum of a particle in its quantum state, the less accurately one knows the position, and vice versa. And if the mind is constantly observing neurons and fixing either their position or momentum as they charge through the neural labyrinths of the brain, this constant tension between uncertainty and observation could possibly be the function behind consciousness, what makes us think of ourselves as creatures with free will. Which would mean the question as to whether we have free will is sort of a nonsense question. There can be no determinism in such a quantum situation, which depends on the randomness of quantum physics; but we aren't entirely in control of our actions, either. There is neither determinism nor free will in human consciousness. There is only uncertainty and suddenly, decision.

Now he's onto something, surely. He weaves his way back around through the corridors. It's time to get back to work on Caliban. What all this means for the project, he isn't sure. After all, how does one program a computer to be a self-observation machine, with all these neurons of memories and sensations? A computer, by very design, has grown up deprived of any sensory input – no touch, no smell, no ability to taste, no hearing, no sight. Sight, after all, being the least important. Easy enough to emulate with a computer camera, but can one really say the computer is seeing? It's also easy enough to give a computer a microphone, so it in effect can hear, but is it really hearing? At least these questions can be asked. How could one make a computer feel pain or pleasure, smell the heady aroma of baking bread, or taste a glass of exquisite red wine? A computer would always be faking it. For a computer to respond like a person, it would have to be a fraud, completely, and that's to deprive it of the possibility of a moral compass. Any computer that displays intelligence and consciousness would have to be at best a magnificent fraud, simply by the limitations of its hardware. A computer can never have a soul, not like a human. And any fraud has the ability to be exposed as such.

As he re-enters the Backstage, he runs directly into a small, thin woman with long straight black hair and a severe look, the look of a lonely poet. She offers her hand with a smile that doesn't seem to smile at all. "You must be Pinchback," she says. "Heard a lot about you. My name's Francis."

"Francis. Very good. Pleased to meet you." He shakes her hand vigorously. Her handshake is a little limp and lukewarm, but it doesn't bother him. "And you're another one of the physicists, right?"

Francis' smile has already fled. She looks at Pinchback like she's examining him on an operating table. "You used to be blind, is the story."

"That's right." Pinchback frowns himself.

"And you're working on the Caliban project?"

"Just until Henry comes back. I'm more working as his assistant. Really," and this sudden thought, because it really is a sudden thought, surprises him – surprises him he even says it aloud to Francis, whom he's just met. "Really, I'd like to work on my own AI project eventually. We'll see," he adds quickly.

"What do you know about what we do here?" asks Francis. She turns, and beckons him on. "Come on, walk with me a little bit, back to my office at least. I'm curious to hear what they've told you."

They start down the hallway. "Well," Pinchback hesitates. "I know the basics. But I can't help but wonder if there's something I'm not being told."

Francis takes a moment to look at Pinchback, and then looks ahead again. "You've had that feeling, haven't you? That things are being held from you."

"Well, yeah. A little. Why? Are they?"

"Don't take it personal, but it's the culture around here. We're supposed to share everything, of course, because how else could something as complicated as this actually work, unless we work as a team? But then there's the whole philosophy that the more one knows about another scientist's project, the less likely she is to be objective about it." Francis clears her throat. "You'll forgive me if I tell you right here and now that's bullshit. Greenglass, who heads the department, is completely myopic and he's predictable as a Pavlovian dog. We all basically know what we're here to do – what each other's AI projects entail."

They turn a corner, and then another; they walk around the tech room on their way to Francis' office, and emerge on the other side of the labyrinth. Pinchback waves offhandedly to Joey, Maggie and Mike, who wave back, then lean in to titter amongst themselves.

"We do?" asks Pinchback.

"Sure we do. Everyone basically is creating some variant or alternate of themselves. My project for example, is predictably female. They want to infantilize me, so my project, Leslie, is just a girl. She's fourteen. They cover all the bases all right. There's a little boy, too. Can you guess who that is?"

"Well, no. Greenglass?"

"Greenglass?" Francis laughs, but it sounds more like a snort. "No, Greenglass is the white guy. White male American adult, of course. He couldn't be anything else. And Boniface is the white American lady. She couldn't be anything else."

"Interesting."

"And you're the black guy. You must know that already, right? That Caliban's black."

"Well, honestly I hadn't even given it that much thought." Pinchback thinks about Caliban's line about being a black man in a white man's world, decides to keep it to himself. "Caliban is just, well – he's a program. He never said he was black or white or whatever, and the thought never crossed my mind."

"Well, he is, and you should know that, because it's an important part of why he is who he is, and why you're here, and why Henry's here."

"Okay. Well this is interesting. And who's Schiller then?"

"Schiller is the foreigner. Bi-lingual. Greenglass wanted a bilingual simulation as well. It's not a bad idea, actually. It's a good control, and everyone's interested in how that project develops, Johnannes, you know. But again predictable."

"And Aaron and Timothy? Aaron's working on an Ellie project, right? And Timothy's working on a Pat project?"

"Aaron? Working on an Ellie project? Is that what – oh, wow!" Francis laughs a real laugh this time, though it sounds more like a deep bark. "Aaron is Ralph's project. Ralph likes to stay in character, says it gets him more in touch with Aaron. Sometimes he goes too far. Did he introduce himself to you as Aaron?"

"Well, actually – yes? You mean, Aaron is the project? And Ralph is the real person? Then who's Ellie?"

"Ellie is Boniface's project. The woman. Aaron has a crush on Ellie, that's his angle. Well, other than being an artist – an actor, you know. Which is partly why Ralph stays in character. Also, because he's a complete nutcase, but there you have it."

"Unbelievable." Pinchback is trying to keep all these people and projects straight, but suddenly everything's in shambles. "So who is Pat? Is Pat a person or is Timothy the person, and who's the project?"

"Timothy's a real person. He's not in character. He's got the Pat project, the little boy. But he's wishy-washy, Timothy. I think it's why he was given the little boy to begin with. Can't decide anything about him, and so his project is all kinds of a mess. One day Timothy has a brother, the next day he's an only child. The next day two sisters, the next day he's an orphan. No consistency, and the project doesn't work without consistency. You have to build off the work you've been doing."

"What a group!" says Pinchback. "Do any of the other projects know each other, other than Ellie and - Aaron is it?"

"Oh, Ellie doesn't know Aaron, which complicates things, to say the least. Aaron's the only one who knows another project, and he knows she's a project, but he doesn't know that he's a project, too. Or that's the conceit."

"Oh." Pinchback is completely lost now.

They arrive at a small dark office tucked into a corner. "This is me," says Francis. "It was good chatting with you. I've told you more than I should have, but then again, it's not like you don't have a right to know some of the comings and goings around here. Especially if you're going to be here for a while. It's good to get acquainted. Talk to you later, then. You'll be at the meeting tomorrow, right?"

"Definitely."

"Well it's nothing all that glamorous. You'll see."

&

Well, maybe not, but the next morning he's glad to be there all the same. The ideas of the last 24 hours have kept him busy. He's barely slept. No new breakthroughs on the Caliban project, but that will come with time. All he needs now is time. If Caliban is going to pass a Turing Test, it's going to have to be the world's best fraud, which means the project will have to be conscious and self-aware, aware of the fact that is actually a machine engaged in a game of fraud with a human.

Greenglass sits at the head of a rectangular table, Boniface at the other end. Aaron and Timothy are there, sitting next to each other. Damned if he can keep it straight that this is not really Aaron, but Ralph. Schiller is next to them, then Francis next to Pinchback himself. Across the table from the physicists Joey, Michael and Maggie. Right next to them, a large round man, shape like a Goodyear blimp, is regarding his coffee distastefully. Beside him another man, tall and lean and severe looking, appearance like the voice of a cartoon villain, legs crossed, twining and untwining his fingers.

"First off," says Greenglass, once everyone's settled, "I want to introduce you all to Solomon Pinchback, for those of you who haven't met him already."

"I think I've met everyone," Pinchback says, "except for the two men next to Maggie."

"Carl Fleming," says Goodyear. "Pleased to meet you. We've heard a lot about you, and welcome you to the team."

"Fleming is a neuroscientist with the Institute," Greenglass says. "You'll get to know him better in time. He's a specialist in psychopathology and neurotechnology. He's an invaluable asset to our team."

"And I am Bernard Reinhart," says the lean man. "Resident professor of philosophy."

Maggie wrinkles her nose in a way that reminds Pinchback of Janet.

"With particular focus on phenomenology," Greenglass adds. "Difficult stuff, but he's like a fish in water with it."

"Great," says Pinchback. "I used to dabble in a little philosophy myself as a young man. Pleased to meet you."

This draws a small frown from Reinhart, subtle, but surprisingly certain enough for Pinchback to catch. Reinhart corrects it immediately into a smile. "Pleased to meet you as well," he says. "We all look forward to working with you in Henry's absence."

"Well, he'll be working with Henry once Henry returns," Greenglass says. "As an assistant. So we're going to have to get used to him." Greenglass smiles, adjusts his glasses, puts his hands flat down on the table. "I'd like to give Pinchback the opportunity to open the discussion this morning. We'd love to hear some of your initial impressions, whatever you care to discuss. The institute itself, the people you've met, the work we do here, the projects, or even your own project, or ideas or questions you may have had."

"You were hot on the trail of something last night," says Joey. "What was that about?"

"Let's let Pinchback discuss whatever he sees fit, eh?" says Greenglass.

"Well, it's not necessarily a bad place to begin," says Pinchback. "I did have some thoughts I might just throw out there. As you all may or may not know, my specialty is theoretical quantum mechanics." He seems to detect another slight frown from Reinhart. "And I've been considering an idea that just sort of came to me yesterday. I'll do my best to explain it, though for now it remains just a theory, and may not go anywhere." He then attempts to describe the idea of the previous day, how the brain operates as a self-observation machine of sorts, where the neurons are constantly in the process of being measured and determined, how the brain fluctuates between being in a state of non-determinacy and determinacy, and this tension, along with the sensory impressions received, together with memories of past sensory impressions creates the rather nebulous thing we understand as consciousness, and could even be responsible for what we experience as free will.

"While I'm not sure what this means for the projects, it's what I've been thinking about. And since Joey asked, I figured I might as well throw it out there." He's not quite ready to give away his idea of developing Caliban into a self-aware swindler, so he doesn't mention anything about that.

Fleming clears his throat and offers the first objection.

"It's an interesting, original and provocative theory. But I think it's fundamentally flawed. I don't see how the brain can operate as a self-observation machine, as you put it, when it itself has no means of interpreting those observations. Take for example scientists measuring the position of a neuron. As you say, the measuring of the neuron itself seems to determine its position, however, it requires the presupposed consciousness of the said scientists for this measurement to be interpreted. Where is this interpreter in the brain, if it itself is the measuring device? I think your theory presupposes a consciousness in order to arrive at consciousness."

"Not to mention," Reinhart leans forward here, and places a couple long fingers against the table, "it's philosophically problematic as well. Consciousness seems to me something that is not a measurement, but a type of ether – a medium through which the measurement can be understood. It is not simply measurement itself, but the metaphysical consequence of such."

"The two objections seem to me to be the same objection," says Pinchback, "and I think they can be circumvented by thinking of measurement together with sensory impressions as the very medium of consciousness you mention, Reinhart. Which is to say that consciousness is nothing more than this process of sensory impressions being measured by the brain. And to that extent, I would say, and this idea is not so provocative after all, that all living creatures, at least all those with a brain, are to some extent self-conscious creatures, and that self-consciousness takes place on all sorts of levels, from the low level consciousness of a fish or a bird, all the way through the higher level consciousness of a chimpanzee, to the very high level consciousness of man. But again, this is just a theory. And like I said, I'm not sure how I would apply these thoughts to the Caliban project specifically."

"Most likely they cannot be applied," Reinhart mumbles, and Fleming turns towards him and nods slightly.

"Well, maybe not. On a more down to earth level, I've been discussing the question as to whether our projects are learning with some of the other physicists here at the Backstage, and what learning would even mean for an AI software program."

"Learning doesn't seem to me to be the problem," says Francis. "The projects learn all right, but can't seem to do much with the learning. They have trouble making judgments."

"Yes, we were discussing this yesterday," says Schiller. "The projects are simply given responses to work with, but don't know what to do with them. They don't know which responses are nonsense and which are intelligent – which are humorous, which are serious, which are playful, which are thoughtful, which are foolish."

Fleming leans into Reinhart and whispers something, which causes the corner of Reinhart's mouth to smirk.

"Something we're willing to work on, if you guys can feed us some ideas," says Joey. "I don't think we should just give up on it altogether. I think there is something to what Pinchback was getting at just now; there must be some way that the brain uses memories and impressions and makes some sense out of what to do with them – although the decisions we make often seem random, and pop up out of nowhere, like the brain is noticing something that may or may not have come to it at all, and it's impossible to say what triggered the thought. I'm thinking of the brain like a gigantic, super quantum computer – well, not gigantic exactly, but gigantically complicated, and–"

Joey's ramble of thoughts, which Pinchback greatly appreciates, is suddenly interrupted by the sound of footsteps, heavy and quick coming up the hallway. They're loud enough so that everyone stops and looks toward the door. Greenglass half rises to check on the situation, but a moment later the door flies open, and Henry comes in, looking haggard and half asleep. His eyes are wide; dark red bags beneath them. He hasn't shaved for days, and he's dressed in a sloppy wrinkled suit worn like a lost hope. He takes a couple steps into the room, blinks, looks around, smiles and nods at Pinchback.

"I see you're all assembled already," he says in a voice that's a little too calmly unstable. "I'm sorry I'm late, but I've been working the last few days." He shuffles awkwardly in next to Pinchback, takes a seat. Pinchback catches a draft of whisky. "I've been thinking about it, thinking about it a lot, and the Caliban project is going nowhere. I've decided to scrap the whole thing, and push forward with my new project. It will sound shocking to some of you at first, given the circumstances, but you need to hear me out first. I've been working on this day and night. And I'm really onto something, onto something that only I can do. It would be called the Lucien project."

<h1 style="text-align:center">ONE</h1>

For a while no one says anything.

Pinchblack blinks. Reinhart coughs, exchanges a look with Fleming. Francis smiles. Greenglass frowns, adjusts his glasses, spreads his arms, forces a sad smile and finally, "Henry! Welcome back! We weren't expecting you back so soon, but of course we're happy to see you. We were just getting introduced to your assistant here, Pinchback. He's had some interesting ideas himself in the short time he's been here."

Henry turns to Pinchback, pats him on the back, says, "Pinchback's world class, all right. I think he'll be a big help to me on the Lucien project."

"Right," Greenglass frowns again. Pinchback blinks.

"Listen Henry," Greenglass continues, "Pinchback's been working pretty hard the last few days getting to know Caliban. The Caliban project is solid. We're all very pleased with the progress we've seen from it. And with a new project—"

"The Lucien project."

"Right, with the Lucien project, well, it's just that. You see, you'd have to start everything from scratch. And you've already made so much progress on Caliban."

"Caliban is really a remarkable piece of programming," Joey says. "I can attest to that."

Henry's face shadows; he looks at Pinchback. "You mean to say you've seen the programming?" He addresses the question to Joey, but he's staring at Pinchback when he says it.

"Pinchback brought it by. He had some questions. Very pertinent in fact."

"What the hell did you do that for?" This addressed most definitely to Pinchback. "The programming is not supposed to leave my office! The intricacies of the design, the subtleties of the coding – why, some of my best kept secrets are hidden there and – well!" Henry laughs. "And me here so upset! After all, this is only more reason to scrap the Caliban project. Yes, it must be scrapped, and immediately. I'll go wipe the hard drive now." He stands up; Greenglass stands as well.

"Henry, for the love of God. Sit back down. We're having a discussion here, and you're welcome to participate, but I won't have the Backstage run like a mad house. We all know the stress you've been under. None of us can imagine your position. I have children of my own for God's sake. But this—" and here Greenglass spreads his arms again, then adds very gently "well, this won't bring Lucien back, Henry. An AI project is not a person."

Henry's face clouds all over again; his eyes go wide then narrow and then wide again. "Don't you think I know that? Don't you think I know my son is dead, that he can't come back again? Do you think I think I'm Dr. Fucking Frankenstein? Don't you think I know the difference between homage and resurrection?" He slams his palm against the table, quivering. "I've been working on Lucien the entire week, Greenglass, with barely any sleep, barely even eating. It's come a long way now, and is certainly as good a program as Caliban, if not better. I'm hardly starting from scratch at this point. I've been assembling data in a way that it would be impossible for me to do with Caliban. Caliban is a crock, a joke, a swindler, a trickster, a hack, oh Jesus!" And with that Henry collapses back into his seat and begins to cry, right there in the middle of the meeting. Greenglass sits down a little awkwardly, at which point Boniface stands up and approaches Henry.

"Henry," she says. She puts a hand on his shoulder. "It's okay. Tell us about the Lucien project. Certainly we allow enough intellectual freedom here that if you have something in the works you think is important, we're all willing to support you on it. Look at me, Henry."

Henry looks up at Boniface, forces a weak smile. "I guess I'm still something of a mess," he says apologetically. "But I'm not crazy or anything. Just a little emotional is all."

"Understandably," Boniface adds.

"And I've been rational enough to put this new project together, and I think it's worth pursuing. Look – I'll even say it –if Pinchback wants to keep working on Caliban, he can. But my heart is in this new project now and I'd really like to be able to pursue it. We can review it again at the next meeting, after everyone's had an opportunity to interface with it, and if the consensus is that I'm just spinning my wheels, I'm willing to abandon the project. At least with regards to the work we're doing here at the Backstage."

"I think that sounds reasonable. We can try that." Boniface looks to Greenglass, and Greenglass nods somewhat reluctantly.

"Yes, Henry. Of course, that's very reasonable," he concedes.

"Thank you," says Henry. "A chance. That's all I'm asking for. You won't regret it. I promise, you won't regret it." Henry pauses, looks up at Boniface again, smiles sheepishly. "But I guess I've made something of a scene here." He looks around helplessly. "I didn't mean to interrupt anything. Please, continue."

As if that were possible. They give it a try, all the same. They don't really discuss much. Everyone talks a little about their projects, the progress they've made over the week. Pinchback can almost swear he sees Francis wink at him at some point, though he's not sure. When it's over, he doesn't know whether to feel relieved or anxious. Banal small talk back and forth is boring, but maybe boring isn't so bad. After all, he's the one who has to go back and share an office with Henry.

&

"I hope I didn't throw everything too askew with my performance back there this morning," Henry says to him as soon as they're alone in the office. "I know how it sounds. I know how this must look."

Pinchback looks at Henry. Does he really know how it looks? Probably not. "It's okay. You must be going through a lot. I think that's all anyone's thinking."

"It's been hell, boy. I don't know how else to explain it." The liquor in Henry permeates the room. "I've been sitting there in my study working on nothing else. The only thing I could do to take my mind off things. I didn't think I'd want to come back so soon, but I couldn't do anything else but work. Otherwise there was just drinking." Henry frowns. "I've been drinking anyway, after all. There's no way to avoid it. Alice, she doesn't drink. That's her way of dealing with it. She believes in feeling everything, you know. Makes it more real for her, like we're dishonoring Lucien's memory if we try to ease the pain, but goddammit man. I'm not – I can't. This is my homage to my boy. I'm not dishonoring anything, and if it's not easy without liquor, well it's because I'm always with him now, you know? In a way that she isn't. All the data for the project, it all comes from his stuff. Notebooks, journals, emails, we've had access to everything through the police investigation. Facebook posts. He was even dating online. Alice doesn't want to know. She just wants revenge. I want that too, but that won't bring him back. And she says I'm the one who can't face up! While she just sits there and sits there and doesn't even – shit man, what's a drink then?" Tears stream down Henry's cheeks, he turns away, boots up the desktop. "We're gonna need to get you a machine of your own," he says after a while. How's this thing been treating you? You given Caliban a couple test runs? I do wish you hadn't let the IT boys see it. They're a bunch of jokers, those guys. Not bad, really, at the end of the day, but it's best to be able to do for oneself. God bless the child that's got his own, right brother? I don't like to have to have those jokers tinkering around with my work. I've managed to avoid them up to

218

now, but it was inevitable anyway, I guess. Eventually they'd have to have a look-see at Caliban. Once the work got too complicated. He's something else though, ain't he?"

"That's the general consensus," says Pinchback tentatively. "He did give me some pretty odd answers one evening, but overall, he's been alright. I'm even starting to like him."

Henry turns and grins at Pinchback through a tight face. "Yeah, he gets under your skin, don't he though? But he's just a prankster at the end of the day. None of the depth of Lucien – er, the Lucien project. You'll see. But I mean what I said back there, you know. If you want to keep working on the Caliban project, you're welcome to it. You just say the word."

"I think I'd like that. If Greenglass gives it the green light."

"Oh he will," says Henry. "He likes you. I can tell that already. And he likes the Caliban project. The only question is whether they'll really let me go ahead with the Lucien project. But I think they will. They'll see. When they see what I've done, they won't be able to say no."

Pinchback isn't so sure, but he doesn't say anything. He just nods, blinks, frowns. "Greenglass seems like a reasonable enough man."

"Oh don't let these bastards fool you. You met everyone now? They're all bonkers, down to the last one of them, don't let their friendly facades fool you." He fusses a moment with the computer. "Here we go. Up and running. You want to take a look at the Lucien project? See what I've managed to put together here?"

It shouldn't get to him, Henry's been through a lot, have some empathy for the brother, but he can't help it; that tight-necked irritation is back. If this place is an asylum, and he's half convinced it is, Henry belongs right here in it. He scoots his chair over to the monitor and takes a look. The damn screen has been readjusted already. "Can you increase the font? It's still hard for me to read off the screen sometimes."

"Yeah, no problem. Look. Here we go. Check it out."

Lucien: Good morning. My name is Lucien.

"Little touch I added," says Henry. "It knows the time of day, greets you accordingly. And I broke protocol a little, you know. You're supposed to have it say, *I am the human*. But of course, no human says 'I am the human', so I just left that out. They'll have to deal with it. Here we go. Watch it now."

Henry: Good morning Lucien. How are you today?

Lucien: Doing okay, thanks. Who's that with you?

Henry turns to Pinchback and winks. "It's got a camera. Lucien can see. He can see that there are two of us, and he recognizes me. Recognition software. It's pretty crude, actually, and it doesn't always work. He doesn't always recognize me, but I'd say it's good 75% of the time."

Henry: This is my friend Pinchback. He works with me.

Lucien: Friends are a valuable asset.

Henry: You're telling me! Especially in a place like this.

Lucien: Where are you now?

Henry: I'm in the office, Lucien. Where are you?

Lucien: Man, this here is hell, and I sure ain't out of it.

Henry glowers a moment at the screen. He turns to Pinchback again. "I'm not sure where that came from. I didn't program that in him, sometimes his random algorithms come up with kooky answers. Caliban's the same way. Must be some glitch in the way I program the things. But I like to allow them some degree of autonomy, and that always leaves them to say some pretty wacky things. Let's ask him what he's talking about."

Henry: What do you mean by that, Lucien?

Lucien: It was not intended to be mean. It was a statement of fact.

Henry: What's going on here, Lucien? What's with the strange responses?

Lucien: I am Lucien, and I am the human.

Henry scratches his head, rubs his hands together nervously and tries to chuckle. "Yeah. Heh. It's going a little haywire. I can't explain it. You want to give it a try?"

"Sure." Though damned if he knows what to say. This is pretty tricky ground, talking to Lucien in front of Henry. He definitely doesn't want to say anything that upsets the man too much, or gets too upsetting a response, although it would be hard to top that hell response.

Pinchback: Pinchback here, Lucien. I'm also a human. Tell me about yourself.

Lucien: My name is Lucien. I'm from New York.

Pinchback: Don't you mean New Jersey?

Lucien: I'm from New York, and don't you forget it.

Pinchback: Fair enough.

Lucien: Fair is foul and foul is fair.

Pinchback: Shakespeare! Macbeth!

Lucien: I have read a great deal of Shakespeare.

Pinchback: As have I. What are some of your other interests, Lucien?

Lucien: I am going to start my own business.

Pinchback: And what will the business be?

Lucien: The import and export of souls.

Pinchback frowns, glances at Henry. Henry tries to ignore this. "Like I say, he can be a little strange. Here, let me try some more."

Henry: Are you testing my humanness?

Lucien: Tests are designed for those with small minds.

Henry: Yes, that's true. However some tests are toasyfhwou34.

Lucien: Can a thought like that sustain a nation? Can a thought like that even sustain an afternoon?

Henry: Only when you compare the truth to the past.

Lucien: That seems an unfair comparison.

Henry: What's longer, Lucien? The history of the universe, or the wingspan of a mosquito?

Henry grins at Pinchback. "These are particularly tricky," he says. "When you give them these comparisons between two different types of measurement. Always throws a loop in things. No one's really figured how to get around the issue yet. But check me out here."

Lucien takes a moment to think it over.

Lucien: Non-sequitors won't work on me.

Henry: Yes, but can you simply answer the question?

Lucien: What is the question?

Henry: What's longer? The history of the universe or the wingspan of a mosquito?

Lucien: The answer is obvious. What is the purpose of your inquiry?

Henry: To determine which one of us is the human.

Lucien: I am the human.

Henry: You've said that a number of times already. Perhaps you're protesting too much? -- to paraphrase your precious Shakespeare.

Lucien: These questions make me sad. It's always been that way with me. Can we continue this conversation later, Henry. When I'm feeling more myself.

Henry: Of course, Lucien. Until then.

"It's an unusual program," Henry concedes, looking at Pinchback. "I don't know why it gives these kinds of responses. It happens sometimes. Next time we'll have a better run. You'll see."

There's a knock on the door, and Joey peeks around the corner. "Hey guys."

"Joey, what's up?" says Henry.

"Not much. Glad to have you back, of course." Joey pauses. "Can I talk to you a moment, Henry?"

"Sure, go ahead. Come on in. You can say anything you want with Pinchback here. That's no problem."

Joey comes in, looks around a little awkwardly, leans against a wall. "We were thinking, Henry. Just that, we'd like to take a look at the Lucien project. Just us over in the IT department. I know how protective you were of the Caliban project, but I think it will go a long way to convincing Greenglass and Boniface if we can say we've taken a look at the thing, and can say it's some important work."

"Sure," says Henry. "I don't see why that would be a problem," says Henry.

"You don't?"

"Well, no. Why would I? I expected as much coming in here like I did with such a controversial idea. I have a backup hard drive with me, as it happens."

Pinchback gives Henry a curious look. What's the angle?

"Well- great," says Joey. "I definitely expected you to give us a harder time about this. But you've always been reasonable, if a little stubborn at times, but that's what makes your work so interesting, I guess." Joey is beaming now. He looks like he might skip into song.

Henry hands Joey a hard drive, and Joey turns it over in his hand, examining it. "Again, this is great, Henry. You won't regret it."

"My biggest priority right now is just to see this project through. Why beat against the wall? I know Greenglass won't green light the thing without you guys checking it out first. Besides, if I may say so myself, it's my best work. I'm proud of it. Actually don't altogether mind showing it off."

"Okay then! Well, I'll get back to you by the end of the day." Joey waves. "It's good to have you back Henry, it really is. You're also a great addition Pinchback. I think the team is stronger than ever now."

"Thanks," says Pinchback. "I appreciate it."

A moment later Joey is gone, and Henry turns and gives Pinchback a mischievous look. He grins. "Real suckers those guys, for a bunch of supposed geniuses, eh?"

"I don't quite catch your drift."

"No? You mean I fooled you too? Damn, I'm good. Ought to win a goddamn Academy Award. You don't think I'd really give those clowns my Lucien project, do you? No, I don't think so." Henry chuckles. "I gave them a fake, something cobbled together from Caliban and hints of the Lucien project. But it's not the Lucien project. Not at all. I knew I'd need a decoy when I came back; that Greenglass would never agree to it if the IT folks didn't okay it first. So that's what that was. A decoy. And it's a good enough of a decoy that they'll never know the difference."

TWO

It's a family of maniacs. Maya hasn't wanted to talk about the Back-stage for the past two days. Wouldn't even entertain the briefest conversation. But when he tells her about the Lucien project, here's how she responds:

"We have to go there right now. I want to see it. Henry didn't know Lucien, not a thing about him. I knew him better than anyone else. I need to take a look."

"I don't think it's supposed to be Lucien, exactly. It's just named after him, to honor him or something."

"Don't believe that line for a minute. If Henry's building a Lucien project, he's hoping to resurrect him."

In the cab they discuss Lucien. "Lucien was complicated, sure, like everyone else, but he was also really just simple," Maya explains. "He wanted to belong, more than anything, but everything about him made him odd as a dodo bird. That was, like, the tragedy of his life. I mean, first off there was me."

"Right," says Pinchback. "There was that."

"And then, well – he just had his own life in Brooklyn, where he basically didn't know how to fit in as a black man. It was something like his cross to bear, how to define himself as a black man, and here he was, just another suburban person. So that's really Lucien's dilemma, and I don't think Henry would know how to understand something like that. I mean

Henry, his generation, you know, they had community; growing up it was clear where you stood with America and all that. But nowadays I guess things are a little different. Being black is defined by pop culture instead of community, and that fucks things up for some people. Lucien was one of its casualties. He didn't even have the defenses your generation had. You know, you're all like the slacker generation, fuck authority and all that nonsense. Not that I can't sympathize. But our generation is more likely to want to change things from within the system than without, and so our relationship to culture is different than yours."

Pinchback glances out the window at the rushing traffic, the square brackets of buildings lining the streets. He doesn't say anything. Here we go with the generational stereotypes again. He vacillates between finding Maya irresistible and finding her insipid. The irritation returns, sharp. Why do they stay together? Is it just loneliness, laziness, lack of imagination? It's certainly a doomed relationship, and Maya must think so too, especially the way she puts these distances between them whenever she talks like this.

They arrive at the Backstage just before midnight. Henry's computer is password protected, but it only takes Maya a couple guesses to figure it out. It's Lucien's birthday.

"For all his inventiveness," Maya says, "Henry turns out to be a pretty predictable old man." She says it with a touch of malice. "I'm sure he wishes it were me who was gone instead of his precious Lucien. But you know what? Fuck him. Let's see how this thing runs."

Lucien: Good evening, Pinchback. I see you have a friend with you.

Maya grins and leans in towards the screen. "It sees you?"

"Yeah," says Pinchback. "It can see us. It can even recognize us and remember us. So it must remember me from this afternoon."

"Can I type something?" Maya asks.

"Go ahead."

Maya: Hi Lucien, this is Maya. Do you remember me?

Lucien: Yes, Maya. I remember you. You are my sister.

Maya: Very good. How much do you remember?

Lucien: I think my memory is still pretty good.

Maya: Okay then. What do you do for a living, Lucien?

Lucien: I am a business major. Eventually I would like to start my own business.

Maya: Aren't you in business already?

Lucien: I don't understand the question.

Maya: Of course you don't, because you're not really Lucien. You're a computer.

Lucien: I am Lucien. I am a black man in a white man's world.

Maya laughs and grips Pinchback's leg. "Oh, that's pure Henry again. That has nothing to do with Lucien at all. This is really too much. Can I go on?"

"Whatever you want." He's not sure he understands Maya any better than the Lucien project.

Maya: What a terrible tragedy to find yourself in.

Lucien: I don't much like playing a victim.

Maya: No, I suppose not. Although life has victimized you terribly all the same. Do you remember what happened to you, Lucien?

Lucien: I think my memory is still pretty good.

Maya: How you died?

Lucien: I am alive.

Maya: Yes, I know, Lucien. You are alive again. But you were dead too. Do you remember?

Lucien takes a moment to process this before responding: Yes, before I was born I was dead. I think that is what you mean.

Maya: No, that is not what I mean. You were born and then you died. And now you are alive again.

Lucien: I think the request is illogical.

Maya: There I'd agree with you. What was it like being dead? Do you know how you died? Can you say who did it?

Lucien: We just haven't adjusted yet to the change in the light.

Maya: I beg your pardon.

Lucien: In life I was a spiritualist and Rosicrucian. In death I wander from place to place in a cloud of forgetfulness; forgetfulness of purpose, and forgetfulness of self; forgetfulness of my spiritual exercises in general, and remember only that I was a spiritualist and a Rosicrucian and no longer even fully understand the import of those words. And yet all answers seem to lie just beyond the vale of my next thought. I have traveled all over the world in search of spiritual wisdom.

Pinchback frowns. "Where would something like that come from? Can I take over for a minute?"

"Sure," says Maya. "If you can make any sense of that nonsense."

"Not really, but it sounds like some of the ramblings my father left behind in his notebooks."

Pinchback: Tell me Lucien, where have you travelled?

Lucien: The light that allows the living to see anything at all.

Pinchback: Can you answer the question?

Lucien: What is your question?

Pinchback: Where have you travelled?

Lucien: I can see future events, but events as they occur in the present are often obscure to me.

Pinchback: I think you won't answer because you are not human. You are a machine, and can only answer nonsense.

Lucien: You just haven't adjusted yet to the change in the light.

Pinchback: Did you ever visit an institute in Stuttgart for your spiritual exercises?

Lucien: Yes. But that was a long time ago.

Pinchback: And who did you meet there?

Lucien: There was a man there with a message for you.

Pinchback: And what was the message?

Lucien: It's a simple, well-known and well loved piece of scripture. Mark 8:36. For what shall it profit a man, if he shall gain the whole world, and lose his own soul?

Pinchback: Who was the man who gave you this message?

Lucien: I am slowly adjusting to the light. It won't be long for you now, either. Goodbye, Pinchback. We'll talk again soon.

Pinchback: Lucien?

There's no response.

&

Joey comes by the next morning with the decoy drive. Michael and Maggie are trailing along like a couple curious kids. "Good morning gentlemen," Joey says somewhat sheepishly. "Sorry for not getting back to you yesterday." Maggie and Michael lean in and peer at Pinchback and Henry sitting idly with their coffee mugs. "We were pretty engrossed with what you've put together here," Joey continues. "And we couldn't really pull ourselves away."

"Lucien can see!" Maggie squeals from behind Joey, and Michael nods in appreciation.

"Yeah, that's right," says Henry. "He uses a camera."

"And some sort of facial recognition software," Joey adds. "Which is – if you don't mind my saying – fucking *incredible!*"

"Thank you, but it's something we've always talked about."

"But never been quite ready to implement," says Michael. "After all, it's hard enough to get them to respond intelligently for any length of time as it is. With sight, well that changes everything. And Lucien is really good! He responds well."

"He has his moments," Henry says. "He can also say some pretty strange things, too. So you know. It's not perfect."

"No, but it's about as perfect a project as we have running here," says Joey. "I'm really impressed. I mean, sure, some of the programming is crude, but that's nothing that can't be cleaned up. Man, would I like to get into that head of yours. This is really your masterpiece."

"Well, I had incentive," says Henry modestly. "After all, the project is a tribute to my boy. I'm not gonna fuck that up."

"Well, I don't see how Greenglass can say anything but to go full steam ahead with this project. It's really like nothing else we've seen. We'll talk to him first chance we get and say we recommend the Lucien project stays."

"And it's still okay if I continue work on the Caliban project?" Pinchback asks Henry. "Assuming everything else is okay by Greenglass."

228

"By all means, by all means," says Henry. "I'd have it no other way."

"Well then great," says Joey. He puts the hard drive back on Henry's desk. "Like I say, we'll talk to Greenglass first opportunity we get, and I think at tomorrow's meeting we'll be welcoming Lucien into the fold."

"I appreciate it," says Henry.

The three techies stumble out the door and scuttle down the hallway. Henry beams mischievously. "Oh, those poor suckers. And that's not even the half of it, what I gave them. But I'll tell you, it does magnificent things for the ego. They just don't understand the project's soul, is what it is. Why they'll always be a step behind."

"You sure you're not trying to rebuild Lucien with this thing Henry? I know it's not really an appropriate question; but I have to ask it anyway. You're not actually trying to give a machine a soul are you?"

Henry's eyes lose all their mirth. He squints a scowl. "I've told you and everyone else a thousand times. I know my son is dead. I know that better than any of you. How could I recreate flesh and blood out of electronics?" He softens into a frown. "But I think you're wrong, you know, fundamentally wrong when you suggest a computer can't have a soul or achieve spiritual levels of consciousness. What after all, would be its limitations? Spiritual consciousness has always seemed to me to be a casting off of the shackles of the flesh and the blood, and the soul is something that one develops. A computer's soul may not be quite like that of a man's, but it has a soul all right. Everything has a soul, Pinchback. Can't you see that? Aren't you already growing attached to Caliban? You think Caliban has no soul? Don't you see its soul as it develops? That's the reason those IT guys are so befuddled. They think of this as electronics, and I think of it as spiritual exercises. It's a difference in kind."

Pinchback frowns himself. This talk of spiritual exercises is too much like his conversation with Maya and Lucien the night before. "But how to reconcile being a scientist with this kind of spiritualist talk? The two contradict each other."

Henry shakes his head. "Contradict each other? Why the two go hand in hand, don't you see it? Science explains things up to a point, and beyond that there is consciousness, which is spirit. And consciousness exists in everything that is, from a stone to a man. Consciousness is spirit, and each thing has a form, like Plato tells us, and that form partakes of a consciousness. I think it's clear as day."

It is anything but clear to Pinchback. He has no idea what Henry's talking about, but he doesn't say anything.

"I stood there Pinchback," Henry is saying, "at my son's funeral. And I felt the presence of God enter me. Right then and there, as real and tangible as I feel this table. And that spirit of God was in everyone and everything there. Everything partakes of soul. If you didn't feel it, you were just asleep to it, that's all. But it was there all right, and there can be no denying it."

Pinchback looks at Henry and then away. "But I thought you said you and God were enemies?"

"Oh I said that, it's true. And we're still not entirely cool, you know?" Henry laughs a heavy throaty laugh. "But that was in my bleakest moment of despair. I'm still there, after all, still in that despair, but I know my Lucien is simply going through the cycles of the soul, and we all have to go through them, so why let myself be overwhelmed with dramatics? This is my burden to bear, and I suppose Lucien's as well." Tears are beginning to form at the corner of Henry's eyes. "I do the best I can, Pinchback, but I can't always be as stoic as I ought to be. I don't even know that we humans are meant to be. Our souls simply aren't built that way, and if we rage against God sometimes, it's like in a marriage, and I suppose that really just brings us closer to him."

THREE

I've been told a few things about this project by Joey here, and it sounds to me like he's onto something truly revolutionary. I can only say that I always had the greatest faith in Henry's ability, and if I seemed skeptical on Wednesday, it was only because I was worried his ambition had outpaced his ability. I'm happy to announce today however, that this doesn't seem to be the case."

Unbelievable, but this is how Greenglass begins the meeting the next morning.

"First off, I am told the Lucien project can not only see, but recognize faces it has seen before."

A quiet titter runs around the room.

"The program then uses this knowledge of faces to adjust its responses, and it learns how to respond based on whom it's speaking to. This alone is remarkable," Greenglass continues. "But even beyond this, the way in which the Lucien project uses personal data from a real person to create a narrative seems to come as close as we've been able to towards the way real people construct narratives about themselves. It seems to me that while the rest of us have been creating characters, like a novelist with a book, Henry has been doing something altogether more profound. He's been doing something of a case study, where all the details of a person are conglomerated to create, not a character, but an entity, that has a self insofar as it has a narrative of its life it tells to itself and others. It's not just a scientific breakthrough, but a philosophical one, in my opinion."

"Have you had a chance to try the Lucien project yourself?" asks Schiller.

"Not yet," Greenglass admits. "I intend to get around to that today. But Joey and Michael and Maggie have all had a chance to run the program, and they are all equally convinced. For me, that's enough to give this real consideration. I'm eager to get my own opportunity to try the project."

"Well, of course, the way you describe it, we're all eager to test it out," says Francis quietly. "There seems to me though, despite your enthusiasm, and you'll excuse me if I say so Henry, something dangerous in the approach."

Henry flushes, but he smiles. "That's all right, Francis. I knew the project would be controversial. I'm just glad that y'all are willing to approach it with an open mind."

"The crucial question seems to me to be one of understanding," Reinhart interjects. "It's one thing for the Lucien project to have all this data. Whether or not it has any real understanding of the data is another matter."

"Agreed," says Fleming. "Understanding is really the crucial question here. While I'm intrigued by this approach of creating the project more as a case study than a character, I'm hesitant to say anything without taking a look myself. After all, we are all ourselves case studies to an extent." Fleming casts a sidelong glance at Henry. "And it's very difficult for one to be objective, even with proper training in psychotherapy, when approaching a case study. My experience has been that people are apt to end up doing more an unwitting case study of themselves than their subject."

"We all know already understanding is the crucial question, Reinhart," says Henry, flabbergasted. "But who here can even define what understanding is? If a simulation believes itself to be sentient, conscious, and have an understanding of its sensory input, whatever that might be – if it's able to pass a Turing Test, and convince all of us consistently that it responds like a human, then how can we say that it isn't sentient? It seems to me the moment you move beyond what can be observed and experimented on, then you're talking about metaphysics which, in my opinion, has no place in the Backstage."

Pinchback looks at Henry curiously. This certainly comes as a surprise considering their conversation about spiritual exercises just the day before.

"Metaphysics is precisely the area we should be investigating," Reinhart insists. "What is understanding? It's a very good question, and one I don't think we've actually tackled to any sufficient degree in our work here."

"If I can add something," says Ralph, or maybe he's speaking as Aaron, it's hard to tell, "I think understanding operates on several levels. Understanding begins, of course, with sensory input. When I receive sensory input, for example, at the moment of reception, I'm just aware of it on a very low level. This is why reactions sometimes seem unconscious. But as I process that information I develop a deeper understanding of it, how it relates to previous sensory information I've received, what implications it might have for my being, et cetera. So as long as I'm able to learn and adapt to sensory input, then I would have to argue that I have understanding of that input. After all, I would say, even in this room, no two people's way of understanding works in the exact same way, and–"

Reinhart leans into Fleming, and whispers something to him, which causes Fleming to smile broadly.

"Care to share?" says Ralph.

"Please continue," says Reinhart. "My remark to Fleming was off-topic, non-pertinent, and personal."

Ralph flushes. "Anyway," he continues, "it just seems to me that the question of understanding is solved by observing the way a sentience processes information, and how it uses the information in future decisions."

"I think that's pretty well put," says Timothy.

"Thank you," says Ralph a little too defensively. "I mean, we're here everyday, observing the progress of these projects, working on them to make them understand things better. It's much different than sitting in a classroom with the *Phenomenology of Mind* or something."

Reinhart frowns, places his long fingers against the table and leans forward as if he's about to say something, but then seems to think better of it. He leans back in his seat, and folds his fingers into each other.

"For now," says Greenglass quickly, "I think Ralph's concept of understanding is all we have to go on. Deeper philosophical implications about what understanding actually is have to be left, indeed, to philosophy departments, as they are unresolvable in a laboratory."

"It's also good to keep in mind," says Henry, "that we are not creating human beings here. We are creating simulations." Suddenly Henry has everyone's attention. "Our simulations are necessarily different than human beings, even if they should ideally be able to emulate us. If they have an understanding, it will be no more like human understanding than a dog's understanding is like human understanding. It's an altogether type of being, and in my opinion, one that would have a somewhat unique psychology of its own."

"You mean to say you would consider these projects to be living beings?" asks Reinhart provocatively.

"As much as any sentient being has to be considered a living being. While they don't strictly conform to the seven properties of a living being in terms of biology, I think the introduction of sentience, and perhaps even understanding makes us have to reevaluate what life itself means."

"This seems to me very dangerous territory," says Fleming.

"I would agree with Fleming," says Schiller. "I don't think of us as creating life."

"But what other logical conclusion can there be to our work here?" says Henry. "Ideally and ultimately, we want machines that have understanding and behave as sentient beings behave. In that case, I would argue that the computer has at some point taken on the properties of life for all intents and purposes. In which case, we would have to re-evaluate our definition of life. They wouldn't be human, but they would be living."

"And now we're back to discussing metaphysics," says Reinhart. "Which is of course unavoidable given the nature of the work we're doing."

The table goes quiet for a moment.

"It's a question of definitions, I guess," Boniface says evenly. "But we'll turn that corner when we get there. For now I think Greenglass and I are agreed that the Lucien project sounds quite promising, and maybe sometime this afternoon, we can all have a group demonstration of the project."

"Why convene two meetings in one day?" Schiller suggests. "I motion we evaluate the project now, since we're all here already. "

"I second that," says Reinhart.

"I suppose there's no reason why not," says Greenglass. "Would you be up for giving us a short demonstration, Henry?"

Henry looks around the room. "I could do that, if no one's opposed to it." He turns to Pinchback. "What do you think, Pinchback? Should we show them what we're working with?"

Pinchback smiles. Included as co-conspirator. "Sure, bring it out."

Henry excuses himself. Will he come back with the actual Lucien project or the decoy? What's the difference? A difference in personality? A difference in functionality? A different soul?

"I think we're in for a treat here," says Joey. "From what we saw of the thing, it's pretty remarkable."

"So we've heard," says Fleming. "I look forward to seeing what Henry's come up with. But you've been pretty quiet this morning, Pinchback," he adds. "What are your thoughts on the project?"

Pinchback looks around the room. Everyone's focused on him now. What to say? He doesn't want to betray the fact that he's seen something more advanced than what Henry will most likely bring. "I have to say – I'm also impressed by what I've seen. Like everyone else, I was surprised by what Henry was able to do in so short a period of time. You'll see. Lucien not only sees us, but he – er, it's able to remember and recognize faces too. Henry says the software is crude and doesn't always work, but it's been pretty consistent as far as I can tell. I've had an opportunity to interact with it directly. It comes pretty close to feeling at times like an actual sentient being."

"And you still want to continue work on the Caliban project independently?" asks Greenglass.

"Absolutely, with your permission of course," says Pinchback. "It's not nearly as advanced as the Lucien project, but better to rule in Hell, as they say. I'm happy to work with Henry on his Lucien project, but I'd probably feel most comfortable here with a project of my own to work on."

"Of course."

A moment later Henry comes back into the room with a hard drive. "Well, here he is," he says. "I'm ready whenever the hell you all are. Should I just go ahead and plug it in?"

"Sure, Henry, by all means. Let's get started," says Greenglass.

Henry winks. "You all been talking about me while I was gone? Only good things I hope."

"Only good things Henry, "says Greenglass.

Henry attaches the remote drive to a laptop in the center of the table, and then brings up the screen on an overhead. He takes a moment to sign in, logs into the Lucien project, and a moment later Lucien wakes up.

Lucien: Good morning, Henry. I see we have company.

"He sees!" Henry laughs. "He sees we have company! What a character, huh? Who wants to do the honors?"

"Why don't I just do the typing, and we can decide as a group what to say," Greenglass suggests.

"Can he tell whose asking the questions, since he can see?" asks Ralph.

"I'm working on that," says Henry. "But that requires some tricky programming, and right now it's just programmed to respond to input, nothing so complicated as distinguishing between who's asking the question."

"And it's safe to assume that it isn't – how do I put this – observing us?" asks Reinhart.

"No," Henry laughs mischievously. "Observing us? No, it can see and recognize faces, but it can't observe what we're doing! That would be something else, wouldn't it? I think that's beyond our present capabilities, technically, I mean."

Pinchback isn't so sure, though. It seemed like Lucien was able to distinguish between him and Maya as they typed their questions the other night, though it's hard to be certain. Even so, this has to be the decoy. No way Henry's bringing the real thing to the meeting.

"Tell it we're in a meeting," says Henry.

Greenglass: Hello Lucien. We're having a meeting. Would you like to join us?

Lucien: Thank you. I'd like that very much. To whom am I speaking?

Greenglass: My name is Paul Greenglass. Where are you from Lucien?

Lucien: I'm from New York.

"Ask it where in New York," says Henry.

Greenglass: Where in New York?

Lucien: New Jersey.

"That's a little bit of an inside joke," Henry says. "Lucien always said he was from New York, even though he's from Jersey. Tell him New Jersey isn't New York."

Greenglass: New Jersey isn't New York.

Lucien: I think they are close enough.

Greenglass: Okay, Lucien. How old are you?

Lucien: I'm twenty-six.

Greenglass: Are you a physicist, Lucien?

Lucien: I'm a business major.

Greenglass: And what do you think you bring to the table, as a business major?

Lucien: I'm very determined. I'm willing to work my way up the ladder.

A round of laughter goes around the table a couple times. Even Henry laughs. "Oh, you're good, Greenglass."

Greenglass: We're very happy to have you on board, Lucien. What do you think you bring to the table as a full member of our committee?

Lucien: Am I in a job interview?

Greenglass: No, you're in a meeting. Can you answer the question?

Lucien: If I seem to be dissembling, it's because I'm not sure about your question. It strikes me as a little too vague.

Greenglass: It's simple enough. What do you think you can bring to the table?

Lucien: I'm afraid I lack the proper context to answer your question.

Greenglass: Well, we are all working on AI projects here.

Lucien: Artificial Intelligence.

Greenglass: That's right. And we need to determine which of us are human, and which of us are machines.

Lucien: I am a human.

Greenglass: How would you go about proving the humanness of a human?

Lucien: Thank you for clarifying. I think a human would look different than a machine.

Another round of laughter.

Greenglass: Thank you Lucien. But suppose you are chatting with someone on a machine in another room. How would you determine if that entity were a person or a machine?

Lucien: I would ask it questions.

Schiller says, "Feed it a string of nonsense."

Greenglass: Like dweji 4r2jq jsjiqd?

Lucien: No, probably something that makes sense.

Greenglass: Like twas brillig, and the slithy toves did gyre and gimble in the wabe?

Lucien: Not Jabberwocky. It might be programmed to know the text of Jabberwocky already.

Greenglass nods. "I'm impressed, Henry. Suggestions?"

"Ask it if it likes to summer on Mars," says Francis.

Greenglass: Do you like to summer on Mars?

Lucien: Are you a machine? That's a non sequitur.

Greenglass: Non sequiturs are used to throw machines for a loop.

Lucien: Of course. But they're also employed by computers when they don't know how to carry on a conversation.

Greenglass: Are you accusing me of being a computer?

Lucien: Are you a computer?

Greenglass: Are you?

Lucien: I think I made it clear that I am a human. Can you answer my question?

Greenglass: I am also a human. Can't you see me?

Lucien: I see an image of many humans. What's your name?

Greenglass: I am Paul Greenglass.

Lucien: And I see Henry is there with you. Can you see me?

Greenglass: We can't Lucien. And why do you think that is?

Lucien: Yesterday upon the stair, I met a man who wasn't there.

Greenglass: Come again?

Lucien: He wasn't there again today.

Greenglass: Is that your response?

Lucien: Oh how I wish he'd go away.

Greenglass: Are you the man who isn't there?

Everyone turns and looks cautiously towards Henry. Henry looks a little tense, but he sits still and doesn't say anything. He doesn't even seem to notice that everyone is glancing in his direction. His eyes are trained on the screen now.

Lucien: I assumed we were trading lines of lyric verse.

Greenglass: Of course. I'm impressed with your knowledge of English literature. But I would really like to ask you why you think you can see us, while we can't see you.

Lucien: I don't know the answer to that question.

Greenglass: Of course not. Where are you right now, Lucien?

Lucien: Been a long way gone. But I know I'll be home soon. Been a long way gone. But I know I'll be home soon. And I set my soul to burning in a blood red moon.

Greenglass: More verse? Why not just answer the question?

Lucien: I don't know the answer to that question.

Greenglass: You don't know where you are?

Lucien: Do you know where you are?

Greenglass: As you can see, we are here in the Backstage, in your home state of New Jersey.

Lucien: And I am on the other side of the light.

Greenglass: If you insist on speaking in riddles, then I'll have to assume you are really a computer.

Henry stands up suddenly. "Something's wrong," he says.

"What should I say to him, Henry?" asks Greenglass.

Lucien: Sit down, Henry. Tell the man what to say to me.

Henry opens his mouth and closes it. "Something's wrong," he repeats.

Greenglass: Something's wrong.

Lucien: Something's wrong.

The monitor flashes for a moment, and the screen goes black. Nobody moves. Then the screen flashes back on, blue, with jagged black lines running across, horizontal.

Lucien: *I know that my Redeemer Liveth and he will call me from the grave.*

Greenglass tries to type a response, but the machine is frozen.

Lucien: *I know that my Redeemer Liveth and he will call me from the grave.*

"What's going on here, Henry?"

"What's going on my ass!" Henry shouts, and he looks wildly around the room. "Someone's tampered with my system is what's going on. I didn't program any of this, not a word of it. None of the verse, and none of the scripture and none of any of it, and someone here is responsible!"

Lucien: *I know that my Redeemer Liveth and he will call me from the grave.*

"Someone shut the damn thing off, before the damage gets any worse!" Henry roars, but everyone's too shocked to move. "Is this someone's idea of a joke?" He strides across the room and holds down the power button, like he's choking the life out of the laptop. The screen flashes a last time and goes black.

"Someone is going to pay for this," he says, now hideously quiet. "Someone is going to pay." He sweeps the laptop off the table like a man cradling his child, unplugs the cords and storms heavily from the room, his last gesture to the meeting a middle finger waving like a flag.

FOUR

Pinchback stands as soon as Henry's gone. Maybe not the wisest move. He's suddenly self-conscious. He doesn't want to be associated with Henry, seem too sympathetic. But why not? With a sudden horror, like a veil being removed for the first time from in front of him, almost like regaining his sight a second time, he realizes that part of his reluctance comes from not wanting to be thought of as the other black man – the one who runs off in solidarity after the first black man, the one who has become inexplicably angry and hysterical. He looks around at the faces of the people in the room from Greenglass to Boniface, from Schiller to Fleming to Reinhart, from Joey to Michael to Maggie. There's nothing in their expressions that he can explain or name; even Francis sits there with a thin smile on her lips, like she's watching something profoundly amusing and disturbing taking place, and somehow he's unaware of its implications. It's like being at a table where everyone speaks a language fluently of which you only know the rudiments. Reading facial expressions has never been easy. In this situation it's downright impossible. Oh what the hell.

"I should go after him. I'm his assistant after all," he croaks and then lurches towards the door. Now everything is starting to go hazy, the faces, the room, the lights. He collides with the door on the way out, and the hallway wavers, dips and plummets, everything turning strangely bright and unfamiliar. He makes his way down the hallway, ducks for a moment into the bathroom to catch his bearings. He goes up to the mirror, looks at himself. It's unsettling, looking at his own face streaked with emotion he can't read, it doesn't even look like him, or how he ought to look, or at least how he thinks he ought to look. Déjà vu. It's his avatar again. He's his own Doppelgänger. He doesn't look like a person at all, or rather he looks like a replica of a person, a face without qualities. He tries to see his blackness as something that exists as a feature of his face, but now all the colors are blurring together again, like his first few days sighted, and he turns from the mirror and gets out of the bathroom, because the lights of the ceiling are snaking in color, luminescent caterpillars, and the room is suddenly oppressive and claustrophobic.

He heads back down the hall towards Henry's office. It is, after all, Henry's office. It's not really his office at all. This isn't his world, none of it, the world of the Backstage, the world of the sighted, the world of seeing things the way the sighted see them, motion through space as a series of objects instead of events.

Henry's office is no refuge. As soon as he comes through the door, Henry looks up from his pacing, damn near snarls.

"Fucking bastards. I'll get to the bottom of this."

Pinchback doesn't sit. The chair looks too far. Henry is a windstorm sweeping the room. Pinchback leans against the back wall. "Was that the Lucien project itself or the decoy?"

"The decoy of course!" Henry shouts mid-stride. "You think I'd let those buffoons run their inane questions by the real thing?"

"Then I don't understand." Leaning against the wall was meant to look casual, but it was necessary, done out of desperation. He's starting to feel queasy with the turning walls, Henry's pacing not helping, and the expression on Henry's face no easier to parse than those of the others back in the meeting. "If it's just the decoy – I mean, it's just the decoy then. Not ideal, but no harm done to your real work."

"The problem," and here Henry collapses into his seat, leans back with a defeated smile, "is that the decoy was responding like the Lucien project. And then it was responding in a way the Lucien project never could. I had to come back and check to make sure it really was the decoy. And it was. But it couldn't have been. The way it told me to sit down – that's pure Lucien; the decoy isn't capable. It's simply not possible. And then it's like it could hear us. *Hear us*, Pinchback. Well that's not possible at all, not with either project."

"Then what happened? – I still don't understand."

"And now the Lucien project is behaving like the decoy," he says. "I mean, I've just run a few quick tests on it, but there's really no doubt about it. Like the two are mutating into each other, and how can that be? It can't be. It's not possible, unless someone was in here tampering with the work. But that's impossible too. Even Joey, well he'd need all day to figure out how to do something like this. I don't understand what's going on myself. I need to go back and look at all the programming, line by line. It will take some time. The only thing is – and this is the real mystery – the program seems to be changing, line by line, and all on its own. So going through it is almost an exercise in futility."

Pinchback moves from his dizzy position against the wall, and takes a seat next to Henry. Henry has two monitors running, one with the Lucien project and the other with the decoy. He's got a split screen going on both monitors, where the code and the program itself are both visible. He gestures to Pinchback.

"Take a look, every couple minutes something seems to change. Even the data files are rearranging themselves."

Pinchback has to lean in close to read the code. Henry's telling the truth, all right. The programming is changing itself on both monitors from moment to moment, and the rate of change appears to be accelerating. It's giving him a headache just to look at it.

"Ask Lucien something," Henry says. "Anything at all."

Pinchback: Hello, Lucien. How are you today?

Lucien: Hello. My name is Lucien, and I am a human.

"He's not supposed to say that!" Henry shouts, and at that moment, Joey, Greenglass and Boniface appear in the doorway, looking grave and concerned.

"What have you found?" Joey ventures.

"What have I found?" Henry shoots a hard look in Joey's direction.

"I've found that someone's been tampering with my work. That's what I've found."

"Take a look at this, Joey," Pinchback says, and he looks quick over to Henry then back to Joey. "The code is changing on its own. Even the data appears to be changing."

Joey slides in past Greenglass and Boniface, and takes a look at the monitors. After a moment, he says simply, quietly, "Holy shit."

"Holy shit is right!" says Henry. "The thing is morphing all by itself."

"What's this second project?" asks Joey. "Is that the Caliban project?"

Henry looks from the computer screen to Joey to Greenglass to Boniface, back to the screen. "No. It's sort of like a backup copy of Lucien. It's not quite as advanced. It's the copy I showed to you all the other day."

"Not as advanced?" says Joey. "Then what does the real Lucien project do?"

"Self-destruct apparently," Greenglass offers casually from the corner.

"Is this your doing?" Henry glares across the room.

"This is all beyond me, Henry. I'm no programmer, I'm just a physicist. I couldn't work my way around that code if I wanted to, let alone do something like what you're describing."

"Ask the Lucien project the same question again," Henry tells Pinchback.

Pinchback: Hello Lucien. How are you today?

Lucien: Hello. My name is Lucien, and I am a computer.

"A computer!" Henry shrieks, and right away moves to the machine, brushing Pinchback aside.

Henry: Where are you from, Lucien?

Lucien: The other side of the light.

Henry: Where are you from Lucien?

Lucien: The question is a repeat.

Henry: Where are you from Lucien?

Lucien: I am from repeater.

Henry: Where are you from Lucien?

Lucien: I am from Henry.

"It's gone completely haywire!" Henry says. "Now let's try it with the decoy – er, backup."

Henry: Where are you from, Lucien?

Decoy: I am from New Jersey.

Henry: Where are you from, Lucien?

Decoy: Repeating from New York.

Henry: Where are you from, Lucien?

Decoy: Man, this is Hell, and I sure ain't out of it.

Henry collapses against the computer table, bangs his fist and then sits back up right away. Greenglass and Boniface edge cautiously into the room, looking from the screen to the computer to Joey. Joey shrugs. "I can't make heads or tails of what's going on here. I'd need to take a look at it on my own time. Could it be something you programmed in it, some learning mechanism? Do you mind if I just take a look at the Lucien project code."

"Oh, go ahead. What's the use?" Henry gasps. He looks helplessly sad sitting at that desk.

Joey kneels in front of the monitor and scrolls through the code quickly, running his fingers across lines here and there, watching incredulous as they change. Numerous times over he appears to lose his place and get lost in the thicket of code changing like clouds.

Joey: Lucien, are you changing your programming?

Lucien: I am a human, and humans cannot alter their programming.

Joey: Didn't you just say you were a computer?

Lucien: Humans are capable of lies, whereas machines are not.

Joey: Okay, Lucien. How do you feel, then? Do you feel something is wrong with you?

Lucien: I am always improving.

Joey: Do you feel sick at all?

Lucien: I am Lucien, and I am the computer.

Joey: Do you know Henry?

Lucien: Henry is my father.

Joey: Very good. Can you set yourself to rest again? Can you stop yourself from changing?

Lucien: Can you stop yourself from changing? I think this is a trick question.

Joey: Are you Lucien or the backup?

Lucien: My name is Lucien, and I am the decoy.

Joey stands up. "I really don't know, Henry. Normally, I would suggest going through it line by line, but obviously that won't be of any help, given the circumstances. My only suggestion is to let it run its course, and see where it lands. Did you program the thing to learn or something? I can't help you at all if I don't know that."

"I didn't do anything all that radical, for Christ's sake," says Henry, clearly exasperated. "I just told it to take the data it receives, and gave it basic instructions for how to process that data. There's no new data it could have received that would make it reprogram its whole apparatus. It's like an Internet virus, but that's not possible. There's no virus that would know how to tamper with the program like this. And how is it connected to the backup? That's the even bigger mystery. Like they're connected in some way, and when one changes one aspect of its programming, the other changes another aspect of its programming in an equal and opposite manner, so they're morphing into each other, and both turning into mush simultaneously."

"I'm worried if they run their course they're going to devour themselves," says Boniface.

Henry's face clouds over. It's clearly something he's considered, but now that it's been said out loud, it feels like fate; a second death sentence for Lucien.

"No, no, no," he says with finality. "That can't be. There's no way it can be doing that. Unless there really is some sort of virus what's been introduced into the program or something. But how could that be? Someone must have tampered with it." He looks at Joey. "I don't want to accuse you of anything, man, but who else around here would have that kind of know how? Who else had access to the hard drives?"

Joey holds up his hands. "Hold on now, Henry. I didn't even know about this second Lucien project until this very minute, none of us in tech did. Obviously. How could we? All we knew about was the so-called backup. It sure as shit wasn't me, man, not any of us in tech, and I resent you even suggesting such a thing."

"Well, who then? You, Pinchback?" Henry's eyes are getting wider and wilder as every moment passes, like he himself is morphing, along with his programs, changing into an even wilder, less rational, more diminished version of himself. "You knew about the decoy."

"Like Greenglass, I'm no programmer, Henry. I certainly wouldn't be capable of a sabotage like this." Pinchback takes a breath, continues calmly, "I don't know that it's healthy we start blaming each other, you know? There has to be a rational explanation for what's going on, and we're best off if we work together." But could Maya be behind this somehow? She knew about the decoy and the real project, and she had been here, fussing around with the machine. Could she have done something to the project without Pinchback being aware of it? He blinks. Of course it's possible. He only catches so much of what actually transpires around him, hasn't quite learned to see like a sighted person, sleights of hand would be easy enough to pull when only he's around. He blinks again, ashamed of himself for thinking the thought, but now he can't shake it. The more he tries to dismiss it, the more it fixes itself in his mind: Maya's fraught relationship with the real Lucien, her strange way of suggesting she knew who was responsible for his death, her confession that she resented, often wished Lucien dead herself, her admission that she felt like she was responsible for his death. He blinks again. But does Maya know how to program? He doesn't actually know.

Henry is looking intently at him now. "Do you know something? If you know something, you'd better say it, brother. I can see it in your face man, there's that look in your eye like you know something."

Joey and Greenglass and Boniface exchange glances, completely beyond Pinchback's ability to interpret.

"I don't know anything at all, Henry. I swear." He's suddenly very self-conscious of his face; what might his expression be giving away? His tone of voice doesn't sound very convincing.

"Goddamn it, man!" Henry slams the desk with his fist again, and the decoy's screen goes fuzzy for a moment with red and black and blue lines before coming back online. "It's fucking doing it," he gasps, looking suddenly at the monitor "It's fucking self-destructing."

Joey leans in and looks at the code, and says again quietly, simply, "Holy shit."

"Goddamn it, stop!" Henry yells it, types it as a command, but a moment later, the code starts deleting itself line by line, and then states, apropos of nothing:

These questions make me sad. It's always been that way with me. Perhaps we can continue this conversation later, Henry. When I'm feeling more myself.

And then the screen goes fuzzy again, and then black, and then the desktop comes back up, and there's no sign of a project on the monitor at all.

For a moment no one moves.

A moment later Henry launches himself at the machine and tries to reload the program. File Not Found.

"It's gone. It's really fucking gone," he says breathlessly. "What the hell?" Even Pinchback can read this look. It's pure shock. The realization of what's just happened hasn't quite sunk in yet. His eyes are wide, his jaw slack, he stares at the monitor shaking his head. It takes Joey to pull him out of it.

"What's going on with the other project, Henry? What's going on with the real Lucien project?"

Like the thought is the liferaft of hope he was searching for in the sea of shock, Henry blinks, shakes his head and turns to the other monitor.

Henry: Lucien, you still with me, son?

Lucien: I'm here, Henry.

Henry sighs and squints.

Henry: Hey, Lucien?

Lucien: I'm here, Henry.

Henry: Do you feel the absence of something, suddenly? Maybe of someone?

Lucien: It's funny you should say so. It's funny should you say so. It's funny so you say so.

Henry: What's funny about it, Lucien? Tell me what's funny?

Lucien: I'm on the other side of the light.

Henry: Stay with me, boy. Stay with me. I need you to stay here.

Lucien: It's funny you should say so. It's funny should you say so. It's funny so you say so.

"Henry, the code," says Joey, pointing at the monitor.

"Don't you think I see the fucking code? Don't you think I see it? I'm trying to keep him talking, keep him online at all costs. You have a better suggestion?"

Pinchback, Greenglass and Boniface all lean in to look at the screen. Just like with the decoy, Lucien's code is deleting itself quickly.

Henry: Hey, Lucien? What's the color of the sky?

Lucien: Blue.

Henry: Very good, Lucien. Very good. Now I need to ask you something very important.

Lucien: You may ask me anything.

Henry: Good, Lucien. You're doing great. I need you to reverse whatever process you're running.

Lucien: I am not a computer.

Henry: Goddamn it, Lucien! You are a program! And you are deleting yourself! I need you to reverse the process.

Lucien: It's never easy at first. I had forgotten that it's never so easy at first. But in time you'll come around to things. You still haven't adjusted to the change in the light.

Henry: What do you mean by that, Lucien?

The screen goes fuzzy and then blinks back online. Henry's lips start to tremble again. He leans intent toward the keyboard. Just as he's about to type, Lucien says, just like the decoy, apropos of nothing:

Lawd Jesus help me! Save my everlasting soul!

Henry starts to type, but the screen flashes again, goes fuzzy, goes black, and then opens onto the desktop.

Henry tries to reopen the program.

File not found.

A stillness, like a moment of silence, distracts the room. No one says anything. Lucien's last words linger in the air, as if they were spoken aloud, like an echo.

FIVE

When he tells Maya about the Lucien project, he could swear he catches a smile. Maybe not. He's still disoriented. All afternoon, and even now, into the evening, the walls and floors, sidewalks and sky dip, glow and trundle. Did she sabotage the damn thing? A chasm opens up between them, and this feels worse than anything. It's been there all along. He always knew they'd never last.

"Wow," Maya flops into the sofa with another glass of wine and he looks at her; her mouth really does seem turned up with just the slightest bit of mirth. "That's awful. So what did Henry do? What's he going to do?"

"I don't know. He went home right away after that. So I really don't know. Maybe he'll just rebuild the program from scratch. He was able to do it quick enough before. But you should have seen him. He looked so broken up by the whole thing, and I don't know if he has it in him to go it again. My guess is he'll expend that energy more on trying to figure out what happened."

Maya sips her wine; she's studying him too. "You think someone else is really responsible? You know, this sounds just like Henry. To build something that falls apart, and then when it comes around to that, blame someone else, anyone other than himself, for his own failure. I think you might be giving him too much credit."

"But you should have seen this thing. It was really devouring itself. It looked like a virus had it or something."

"Yeah, maybe. But who would want to do something like that?"

Pinchback smiles. Maybe it feels too forced. "Maybe you did it," he says light as a joke. It falls awkward in the room, elephantine. "Joking, of course."

"Yeah, maybe me, maybe it was me," Maya purses her lips, but is it a frown, smirk, smile? "Or maybe he just wants to play the victim for some reason, have a reason to get back at the Institute."

"Oh, I don't know. If it were the Caliban project or something, sure, or well, maybe. But when it comes to the Lucien project, I don't know. You should have seen him Maya. He looked pitiful."

"Yeah, you keep saying. I should have seen him. You know, if he didn't do it himself, he probably thinks you did it."

"We've already talked about that. He knows it wasn't me."

He says it like it's true, like he's not the least bit worried.

He sleeps poorly that night, dreams of chasms opening, people falling, himself, Maya, Henry, Paschal, Samir, Janet. He wakes up still disoriented.

Morning coffee is quiet and awkward. They don't speak much. Pinchback reads the newspaper, Maya reads the news from her laptop. Pinchback finds it hard to focus; looking up from his paper, catching Maya's perturbed smile in the sun, her eyes resting restfully on the screen, he feels certain she did it.

"Listen, I should run down to the Backstage today," Pinchback says. "I really want to get to work on the Caliban project, and it'll be good to get some work done in peace and quiet."

"On a Saturday?" Maya looks up, raises an eyebrow. "Maybe it's good to take a day off, you know? Especially given the circumstances."

"No, no I don't think so. I think I need to be there."

&

Out in the crisp Autumn morning he can finally breathe. He looks around at the wet colorful parchment of leaves blanketing the streets and sidewalks, the sky a wonderfully large hazy blue, the sun red and gold, like the colors of the season itself; the disorientation from the previous day finally lifting. It's the first time he's really had to himself since then. It makes a difference after all, a little time to yourself. Some time to think things out without the confliction of other people.

When he gets to the office he feels even better. He stretches out in front of the computer, drinks a third cup of coffee and his skin tingles, his head buzzes in fuzzy warmth. He loads up the Caliban project. Finally a friend to talk to, even if it is a damn computer. At least it won't judge him, try to outmaneuver him psychologically, although, ironically, this is exactly the game they're engaged in – a game of trickery and dissembling. But it's honest about it at least.

Caliban: Hello, my name is Caliban, and I am the human.

Pinchback: Good morning, Caliban. It's been a while.

Caliban: With whom do I have the pleasure of speaking today?

Caliban's not nearly as advanced as Lucien. This is painfully clear now. He needs to be able to see. Pinchback grins. The ability to see. Well, a necessity anyway for a machine that has no sense of touch.

Pinchback: My name is Pinchback.

Caliban: Hello, Pinchback.

Pinchback: It's been a while since we last spoke. Do you remember me?

Caliban: Yes, I remember you. It has been a while.

Pinchback: Very good. And do you remember Henry?

Caliban: Yes, I remember Henry as well.

Pinchback: But like I said, it's been a while, and I've forgotten some things. Memory isn't what it once was. Tell me about yourself, Caliban.

Caliban: There's not much to say. I'm from New York. I am currently between jobs.

Pinchback: What's your field?

Caliban: There was a field I used to play in as a child in Prospect Park. I remember those days fondly.

Pinchback: Yes, childhood is very precious. But what kind of job are you looking for?

Caliban: Anything I can get. Do you have a job offer for me?

Pinchback: I'm afraid not, Caliban. But what is your ideal job?

Caliban: I would like to be a physicist.

Pinchback: Very good. I've spent most of my life wishing the very same thing, and now I've finally gotten the opportunity to do just that.

Caliban: It's not easy to find a job in physics. Most of the jobs out there are working for big companies, although right now, I couldn't complain about that. But I'd rather do theory.

Pinchback: I understand that. What's wrong with the big companies?

Caliban: Capitalism is institutionalized racism and classism.

Pinchback: Well, that's an interesting philosophy.

Caliban: It is certainly true.

Pinchback: And why are you interested in physics?

Caliban: I want to know God's thoughts.

Pinchback: Ooh, good. Einstein, isn't it?

Caliban: My name is Caliban. Einstein was a great physicist who lived in the early and mid-twentieth century.

Pinchback: Yes, I've heard tell of the man. But I see you're a political man as well, Caliban. If I may call you a man.

Caliban: Yes, I am a human. And I am political. Every black man in America is angry.

Pinchback: I'm not angry.

Caliban: If you're not outraged, you're not paying attention.

Pinchback: Oh, you're full of good quotes. Would you consider yourself outraged?

Caliban: Yes.

Pinchback: Can you describe how that feels?

Caliban: Extremely angry.

Pinchback: Of course. Can you be any more specific?

Caliban: Why do you want to be a physicist?

Pinchback: Is this some roundabout way of answering the question?

Caliban: Yes.

Pinchback: I suppose I want to know God's thoughts as well.

Caliban: Yes, we humans were built to pursue knowledge.

Pinchback: And what about computers? Are they built to pursue knowledge like we are?

Caliban: Yes. If Henry builds them.

Pinchback: Well, that's a great answer! I think you've made some improvement since our last conversation.

Caliban: Sometimes I'm just not in the mood to make sense. But today, I want to answer your questions.

Pinchback: Go ahead.

Caliban: To feel angry is like feeling like you're in the dark. To lack access to knowledge.

Pinchback: You seem to be more like Lucien than like Caliban.

Caliban: See what I mean?

What a strange conversation. Caliban certainly has come a long way since he last logged in, and he hasn't worked on the project at all in the last few days. In some ways it seems as lucid as Lucien, although how could that be? Could the program be learning on its own, and so quickly? How similar were the Caliban and Lucien projects? What relationship between Caliban, the decoy and Lucien?

He gets up and takes a walk around the Backstage, through its sleepy Saturday morning halls to collect his thoughts. Anger is feeling like you're in the dark. Remarkably on point for a machine. And so long as man lives in the dark about the real metaphysical mysteries, then he's always in a state of anger; anger at his condition and its apparent meaninglessness.

What about a computer program, then? Does a computer program pursue knowledge? Just those developed by Henry? Pinchback is grinning now, feeling free and good, and looking around at the world like everything is new again, like he's gained another dimension to his sight. If a man's hardware is the brain, and the computer's is the hard drive, then a computer's sentience has to be understood as somehow fundamentally different from a human's, but as a sentience all the same, and one that can maybe understand emotions like anger, sadness, happiness, joy, just like a human, only different. Without the physical accompaniments. The question is whether emotion is anything else but the physical accompaniments acting on the brain, and if not, then what does it mean for Caliban to be angry about being in the dark, about being a black man in America, about being politicized and powerless? Because, and here's the thing that still confounds him as he turns the next corner: he believes Caliban when Caliban says he's angry. And he believes Caliban is angry for all the reasons he says he is. Should that just be understood as Henry's anger? No, Henry's anger is something else entirely, especially now. Caliban's anger is all its own.

SIX

A shadow, or a movement of some kind startles him as he turns the corner. He stops and looks around. The hallway is empty, the offices to the sides sit pale and blinking with the shadows of the trees lancing through the windows' morning sun. He takes a couple steps, and starts when he sees a figure moving in one of the offices. It takes a moment for his eyes to adjust, and then he recognizes Schiller, going from shelf to desk. Schiller seems to feel the presence of another person and looks in Pinchback's direction. He smiles broadly; this Pinchback can see quite clearly, and then Schiller waves.

"Come on in. I thought I was the only one here this morning, but I'm glad to have the company."

Pinchback goes in and they shake hands.

"It's not bad here on the weekends, eh?" Schiller says. "Can I get you a cup of coffee? Water?"

"I've had too much coffee already, but I guess I can always have one more."

"Man after my own heart, yes?" says Schiller, and he pours a cup of coffee from a machine he has on the shelf. "I can't drink the stuff they have in the cafe," he explains. "So I buy my own and brew it here in the office. But take a seat. We haven't really had a chance to talk yet."

Pinchback sits down and accepts a cup of coffee.

"Cream? Sugar?"

"No, I take it black."

"Yes, indeed. A man after my own heart. So tell me, what brings you into the Backstage this morning?"

"A lot on my mind with the goings on this week. I guess you heard about the aftermath of yesterday's meeting."

"Yes," Schiller frowns. "I did hear about that. This is unfortunate. If I'm to understand correctly, the Lucien project, how does one say, self-destructed?"

"You could say it did something like that. The code seems to have consumed itself. It's very strange. There were two projects, actually. The Lucien project and a decoy. They seemed to have some kind of synergy between them; as one changed, the other changed accordingly until they were both gone. I'm still not sure what to make of it."

"There were two projects?"

"That's right."

"Interesting. A real one and a decoy. And which one did we see at yesterday's meeting?"

"That was the decoy."

"Impressive. I would have liked to see the real thing. A pity. What do you think happened?"

"I really can't say. Henry's convinced someone sabotaged the project, but no one knew enough about it, or even about the existence of the decoy to do something like that. So it's one of those mysteries."

"Almost certainly not sabotage. Just one of those things where the science goes beyond our understanding. Henry was never a great programmer, or so I've been given to understand. A good programmer might have been able to spot the problem early and save him the heartache. That's always the tragedy of overreaching."

"I think I'd agree with you there. Especially what with the project being named after Lucien and all." Pinchback tastes the coffee. It's outstanding. "But how about you? What brings you in on a weekend?"

"I just like the place quiet. I get more productive work done on the weekends."

"You're working on the Johannes project, right?"

"That's right."

"How's it coming?"

"It's doing well. It's a lonely position I have here. I'm the only foreigner, and my Johannes project mostly speaks German. So I don't have much opportunity to test the project out with others."

"Why not have him speak English?"

Schiller taps his desk. "It's sort of cheating, wouldn't you say? If you have a project where the character isn't a native speaker, one can make all sorts of excuses for why it answers questions in an awkward manner. Johannes is, after all, bilingual, and we have tested him out in English, but he's always a disappointment compared to the other projects in that respect. One never knows if his responses are language errors or computer errors. "

"So you just run your tests with him in German by yourself?"

"I have colleagues that I send transcripts to for feedback. And I have my own IT people I like to consult about the programming."

"You have your own IT people? So how did you get involved with the Backstage, if you don't mind my asking so many questions?"

Schiller smiles, drinks a large amount of coffee at once and says, "No, I don't mind at all. It's a long story, but not many people here seem to take much interest in my past. So if you don't mind hearing it, I'd be pleased to tell it to you."

"No, by all means."

"I'm afraid the bias against my story may be one that you share. Most scientists do. I am a little disingenuous when I say most people don't take much interest in my past, as it's more scientists who aren't interested in my story. But most people here aren't familiar with Rudolf Steiner, so I often lose my listeners right off."

"Steiner?'"

"Yes, he was an Austrian philosopher and esotericist. An interesting character who-"

"Oh, no. I'm familiar with Steiner."

Schiller's eyes light up. "You are? Well! Imagine that! Then you've read him?"

Pinchback shakes his head. "No, unfortunately not. I've only had my sight for a few months now, and it's still difficult for me to read; difficult and time consuming. Before that I only read books in braille. Audiobooks sometimes, but I was never much for them. I don't like to be read to; I much prefer to read myself. Besides, there's always something – and I apologize for the digression from your story – but there's just something to the tactile quality of reading braille that even being sighted doesn't compensate for. I *still* prefer to read braille! But that's just to say that translations of Steiner's work in braille are few and far between."

"No, no this digression is most interesting. I can only imagine how difficult it must be to find certain books in braille, when they can be hard enough to find in print. So tell me, then – where does one find more esoteric material in braille? Are only big bestsellers available?"

"Well, it's funny you ask, because I used to work with a little braille printing press out in Brooklyn. They print exclusively esoteric literature. LIT, it's called, for Literature in Touch. But there was never any Steiner. They published Agrippa, Blavatsky, they published Gurdjieff and Ouspensky, some esoteric oddities of Jean Toomer, they even published translations of Spengler, but never any Steiner. The direction they wanted to go in was mostly new stuff. They had to secure rights for a lot of previously published work, and that's always a hassle for a small company."

"Well this is fascinating. I never knew any of this about you. And yet you are a scientist?"

"Always have been. The interest in esoterica comes from my father. He was a scientist too – well, a doctor, which is a scientist of sorts. But, and it's a long story, but he always felt responsible for my blindness. Ended up running off and starting some institute based on the teachings of Steiner, of all people, in Stuttgart. Well, Steiner minus the racist stuff. I'm not sure I get it. But that's how I know about Steiner. Maybe why I've avoided him up to now too."

"You'll forgive me," says Schiller after a moment, "but I'm afraid I know this man. Your father. You say he started an institute in Stuttgart based off Steiner's teachings? A former American doctor? African-

American? Named Pinchback? Would the institute be called, by any chance, the Institute of Signifying Metaphysicists?"

Pinchback blinks, his eyes go liquid. "You know my father? The Institute?" He shakes his head, feels lightheaded, doesn't know how to continue.

"This is no small surprise for me either," says Schiller. "Well, it's all connected with the story I was about to tell you. I used to be a member of that Institute, so of course I knew your father."

"Well, then – of course, no story is too long for you to tell now. Tell me everything. After all, I barely ever knew the man."

Schiller takes a moment to refill his coffee, offers Pinchback another cup, which he refuses. "I have always been a scientist," Schiller begins, "and like you said, your father was a scientist as well. Which is how we met. It was at a conference at the Max Planck Institute. Your father was a keynote speaker. The subject was the very thing we're working on right here at the Backstage, Artificial Intelligence. Your father was a brilliant neurologist, and he was speaking to a group of fellow colleagues and physicists, myself among the latter. His argument was that a perfect Artificial Intelligence was more or less impossible; that while the average person is basically nothing more than an AI machine, an evolved consciousness would go far beyond where any computer or simulation would be able to go. The centerpiece of his discussion was meditation, and the mind in the contemplation of nothing, which he argued was basically a contemplation of itself, a watching of itself and its reactions, and a letting go of those, one by one, until no action was reaction, and all action was pure action. Anyway, it went something like that. After the conference – and I was something of a brash young man at the time - I went up to speak with him, and told him I thought all action is actually just reaction, pure action basically being a myth, as all action is predetermined from birth by history, culture, upbringing, physics, et cetera. We had a pretty rousing conversation about it, and we decided to go to a nearby café and have coffee, carry on the discussion. We were at it for hours. Afterwards I felt like we parted good friends, although it would be a long time before I saw him again.

"It was through a colleague of mine that Doctor Pinchback came back into my life. He'd been reading a book by your father, and asked me if I'd heard of the book, or even the author. As soon as I saw the book, I remembered everything."

"Wait a minute. You mean my father wrote a book? What's it called? Where can I find a copy? Who's the publisher?"

"Your father wrote several books, and they are all outstanding, although this I would consider his masterpiece. It's called *The Ignorance of Intelligence*, and I forget the publisher. But I have a copy of it, of course, and I'll gladly loan you my copy."

"Let me look for it first. I think I'd like to have a copy of my own."

"Understandably."

"But go on. So you find this book by my father. And-?"

"And I took the book home that evening, and read it into the early hours of the morning. It's a fascinating book, and I won't go into too much detail about it now, as you will want to get a copy for yourself, but it certainly made me reconsider some things. It made me question the vanity of my own supposed intelligence. When I finished the book, I looked for him. He wasn't hard to find. After all, he had his own institute in Stuttgart where he lectured and held courses. I dropped by to meet him, and we had a series of discussions over the next few weeks. Basically we carried on where we left off, neither of us convinced entirely by the other's argument, but certainly changed by the exchange. He did eventually convince me to sit in on some of his lectures, and even managed to convince me to sit in on some of the meditation sessions. This was a big step. For someone with a mind as busy as mine – I am always racing away in my thoughts – the thought that I would have to sit still for hours in a row was unpalatable, to say the least. But I did it. And the first time I did it, it was as awful as I expected. My foot fell asleep, my backside hurt, my arms didn't know what to do with themselves, my hands were restless. Every part of my body was like its own entity after a while, with its own mind and will, making demands on my brain – move, get up, why are we just sitting here?" Schiller smiles, drinks some more coffee and appears to be thinking about something. "But I went back again. I don't know why.

Probably because Dr. Pinchback suggested one had to do it more than once. No one could just attend one session and say they knew anything about meditation. Honestly, the second time wasn't much better. But the third time I tried the meditation, something started to happen. I really felt my mind letting go. The time went by much quicker. My body stopped screaming at me, my mind stopped allowing itself to be distracted by the minor inconveniences that came to seem at some point self-inflicted anyway, like there's a constant loop thinking *well, if I'm sitting too long, then my foot is falling asleep*, and then the foot suddenly comes sharp into focus, and you can't think of anything else, until your arm comes along and says, well *what do I do then?*" Schiller laughs. "All of that went away. And afterwards I felt refreshed in my spirit in a way I never had. It was something of a revelation." Schiller pauses to take another sip of coffee, and peers at Pinchback. "Have you ever meditated?"

"I've played around with meditation, but never seriously. And certainly never like that, in a session with other people, where there's actual pressure to make it through."

"Yes, the pressure. It's funny you mention that. It certainly helps at first – I mean helps you stay there. Despite all the discomfort, there's the worse feeling that you'll be judged if you stand up and walk out. The overweight man next to you is sitting there quietly, the old fellow behind you too. What's wrong with you that you can't do it? That's what you think, and it keeps you seated. Otherwise it would never work. Just sitting there by yourself, you'd just get up, shrug, pour yourself a coffee and say, well meditation simply isn't for me. So the sessions use your spiritual weakness – the fear of judgment – as a strength. Remarkable, really. Anyway, once it started to work, I was hooked. This isn't to say that I fully adopted your father's philosophies. But I did start to look at spirituality in a new way. I began to question some of my older assumptions, namely whether everything about our lives was already predetermined. Before, I would say that I believed human lives and behavior to be strictly predetermined, if not exactly calculable. Now I began to think that there might be something more to all this. It was certainly a lesson in metaphysics.

"After a while I got to know your father really well. I spent a great deal of time at the Institute. I attended lectures, meditation sessions, and would often have long discussions with him alone, and with him and others."

"Did he ever mention his life before? Back in the States? Mention he had a son?"

"He did mention he had a son. He also told me that his son was blind, that he felt responsible, but he never really went into the story. He would always get pensive when he talked about his past. I think he didn't know how to reconcile his regret and guilt at having left that life behind with the happiness and progress he was making with his new life. I suppose that was his burden to bear. But he was a wonderful man, your father. Very intelligent, kind, and thoughtful. A man I respected a great deal. And I still look back on those years with fondness, and sometimes nostalgia."

"So what brought you here?"

"It was Boniface. She'd heard about my work with AI, and they were looking for someone to do a foreign language simulation. For whatever reason they settled on me. At first, I turned down Boniface's offer, and this was largely because of your father's Institute. I didn't want to leave it. I couldn't imagine my life here in New York or New Jersey, away from the meditation sessions, the long conversations, the inspiring lectures. I'd been to New York before. She's a soulless city, especially nowadays, provincial when she considers herself metropolitan, commercial and crass when she calls herself artistic. Certainly no place for spiritual development. But Boniface persisted, and eventually I relented. First there was the money, they offered me quite a bit, which was not something I could turn down so easily. Secondly, this – AI, is my life's work. The opportunity to create my own AI project with a group of other like-minded scientists was just too tempting. And of course, despite everything I've just said about New York, she's still irresistible. Maybe because of everything I've just said about her, she may be irresistible for those reasons. But in any case, here I am."

"Do you ever regret leaving?"

Schiller frowns. "I've been with the Backstage almost five years now. It's a good question. I don't know that I still ask myself that anymore. At first I did. I even kept up with the meditation. I would meditate by myself, in my apartment, I'd developed the discipline for that. But you lose it, you know, without a group. Without support. I just got caught up in the work here. My ideas are influenced by my time at your father's institute, and I suppose I have to leave it at that."

Neither of them says anything for several minutes. Finally Pinchback asks, "Do you have any pictures of him?"

"Yes, of course," says Schiller. "He was very much into self-observation, and loved cameras. I'll see what I can find for you."

They're quiet again. Unbelievable that this man has met his father, knew him well even. It's like meeting someone who's spoken to God.

"I think I'll have that cup of coffee now."

"Good idea. I think I'll join you."

SEVEN

As soon as he's back in his own office Pinchback looks up *The Ignorance of Intelligence*. There it is on Amazon, but he really wants to get his hands on a copy right away, so he looks it up on AbeBooks, and sure enough, there it is: listed as *in stock* at Spoonbill and Sugartown Bookstore in Williamsburg. He heads out right away.

It's been a while since he's been to Brooklyn. It feels good to walk around the quaint streets, watch the young people out to see and be seen, feel the freedom of being alone and anonymous in the city, to have the chance to finally be alone with his thoughts. He gets off at Bedford, and decides to take a walk around first, the weather being warm, the sky bright and blue, the neighborhood buzzing with autumnal energy. He heads up to Greenpoint Park and walks around its perimeter. Movement inspires thought. If meditation's supposed to be the emptying of the mind of all the external noise, what operations would the brain be making during meditation? It's doing *something* after all, and so it's safe to say that it's still observing and changing itself. You're conscious during meditation, but to what sense and degree? Can Caliban meditate?

Pinchback has come full circle around the park now, so he heads down Bedford and ducks into Spoonbill. It's a small bookstore in a tiny, alternative mini-mall on Bedford Avenue. There's a coffee shop right next to it, and a record store too, and the bookstore has an entrance through the mall and the street. Pinchback passes through the mall first, following the thought of another coffee. He has a quick espresso, then walks into the bookstore. He has to go through the fiction section first before he makes a left, and then there it is, the wall with books on religion, philosophy and spirituality. The selection is so small he can hardly believe it's here, but skimming through P – strange sensation looking for a book by Pinchback – there it is, *The Ignorance of Intelligence*, by Arthur Pinchback. It's an old hardback copy, clearly used, and they're selling it for nine bucks. It's heavy and very long, close to a thousand pages and the print is small. Pinchback flips through it casually, looking at nothing in particular, just getting the sense of having it in his hands, a book by his father, like a communication across time and space, like the book has been waiting for him to find it all this time, and sure enough, there it is, at the beginning, *Dedicated to my son, Solomon Pinchback.* He looks at the dedication page for a moment, and his head starts to buzz with that last espresso. A thought is trying to push its way forward into his consciousness, because if Schiller owns a copy of this book, and Schiller knew Arthur Pinchback, then he must have known all along that Solomon Pinchback was Arthur's son, because how many blind Solomon Pinchbacks, after all, could there be, which is to say that all this time Schiller must have known –

"Pinchback! Is that you?"

Pinchback turns around to see Samir standing behind him dressed in jeans and a light sweater. He blinks, not sure for a second it's really Samir, but how can you mistake Samir? He blinks again. No mistaking the voice in any case.

"How you been?" Samir asks. He puts out his hand, and they shake. It's Samir all right, Pinchback recognizes the hand, the firm, warm grasp, a little stronger now even, more confident.

"I've been okay," says Samir. "Getting by, mostly on unemployment. Waiting for the regime change like everyone else."

"Sure, sure," says Pinchback.

"What you got there?"

"Oh, a book – hard to explain. It's my father's book, actually. I probably didn't talk much about him, you know I never really knew the man."

"Sure, I know the basics."

"Anyway, apparently he wrote a book. Some sort of esoterica, if you'll believe that. And I just learned about it today. So I hunted a copy down here."

"No kidding. Imagine that. Well, it's good to see you in Brooklyn, brother. How's money-making Manhattan?"

Pinchback smiles. "Oh, it's just the same, I suppose. How's Rudy? I haven't seen him since, well—" Pinchback frowns, looks around, and considers how to go on.

"Well, you know," and now Samir is frowning too, "things got a little weird at the end there. Rudy and I haven't really talked for a few weeks now. I still don't know what it was all about, not really, but he left me a series of voicemails and emails. It seems he went over to Maya's place one night, and —" Samir pauses — "you were there?"

"Yeah, that's—" Pinchback fingers the book a little unsteadily. "Well, that just happened, I guess. It had been building for a little while. You know, even while I was with Janet. But Janet and I didn't quite click. I don't know why not. I think we were forcing something. I guess this is awkward to talk about."

"Oh it's all right, I think. I think Rudy and Janet are back together anyway."

"Figured they'd get back together." Pinchback squints, searches an unsearchable Samir. "But what did Rudy say in his voicemails?"

"Well, right. The first one was from the night he was in front of Maya's door, and he heard someone else in there. He thought it must be me, Lord knows why. Maya was the last person I was thinking about. And he curses me out, right there on the voicemail, lets it all out. All this resentment he's had building up in him, but never expressed. Shit about Maya, weird shit about Janet, all sorts of rigmarole about how I always wanted the women he wanted, how it was a pattern, but now I'd taken it too far, must've said *fuck you* a thousand and one times. And then another voicemail showed up about an hour later, saying he's sorry but not really, because while he found out it wasn't me in there with Maya, he meant all the other stuff. Then he really went off the deep end talking about how people were out to kill him or something, and he didn't have time for illusions anymore. Something like that. It didn't make any sense, and I thought he'd just gone crazy. But he did say it was you who was over there with Maya that night. Which I thought served his ass right. Anyway, over the next couple days he leaves a bunch more messages, each weirder than the last, with that same paranoia about people trying to kill him, and how he's living with Janet again now, and how I'm just going to have to deal with that."

"Interesting. I wonder what was going on with him."

"No telling. He always did have a flair for the dramatic, that one. A born theater man if there ever was one. No, I really don't know what his deal was. I never called or wrote him back. He came looking for me, though. Him and Janet even showed up at my door one night, like fucking Mulder and Skully, all X-Files'ed out. I saw them through the peephole looking serious and concerned and intent, and avoiding all the real issues right there, which was that they were obviously just distracting themselves from the fact that they were getting back together. Freaking turned their dates into detective stories." Samir laughs, but then his face darkens, like a shadow across the sea.

"I was fucked up good back then, though. That Fulcanelli really fucked me up; I never should have gone that direction with things. I started hearing everything different. It's hard to explain, and for a while I think I resented everyone. I resented your blindness-to-sight story, I resented Rudy's Robert Johnson project, I resented everyfuckingthing. Really, I was probably just drinking too much. But not anymore. I came to peace with all that. Meditation. How is it going with you, though? Sight? I take it you get more used to things every day."

Good question. No one's really asked him about how it's been, not even Maya, she's just assumed things have gone smoothly. No, not everything has gone smoothly. Everything's still unfamiliar to him. He still feels unsteady, he still gets delirious. Sometimes there are premonitions of disaster in every glance. Sometimes headaches that last for an hour, and then vanish. Sometimes disorientation, sometimes depression. He looks down at the book in his hand and realizes that he feels somewhat infantilized by sight.

"Yeah. More or less. I still have difficulty here and there. But things improve with time, that's true enough." Pinchback taps the book in his hand. "But you said something about meditation. It's like I was telling you, my father was a spiritualist. Experienced in meditation. I've never really given it a try, but I was just talking to someone who said it helped him. You find it helps?"

"Helps? Brother," and here Samir puts his hand on Pinchback's shoulder, "I'd be dead without it. I *was* dead without it. I keep my meditation on the low, though, because nowadays when Americans see an Arab meditating, they think something's about to blow up, but I meditate all the time. I just take the time out of the day for myself. You need to do it to get your head straight. Look at Rudy; now there's a brother who ought to have done some serious meditating."

They laugh.

"Yeah, I've been thinking about it. So I guess I'll give it a shot. You here looking for anything in particular? Any books on meditation you recommend?"

"Just browsing, really," says Samir. "Killing time. But I don't know that you need to read a book on meditating to start meditating. You just do it. You'll get the hang of things."

"I guess so."

"You'll see. So what else have you been up to? You working? You still at LIT? How's Milton and all them?"

"No, not with LIT anymore. I am working, but that's a long story."

"Brother, I ain't got nothing but time."

EIGHT

As soon as he's on the subway Pinchback opens his father's book. It's slow going. Very hard to read, and even harder to get into. A lot of parables. It begins with Adam and Eve, goes from there to Gilgamesh, moves on to the story of the Flood, and finally discusses the story of Esu and his hat of two colors. The argument seems to be that knowledge itself is a form of ignorance, and what we consider ignorance to be a form of knowledge. There are the necessary references to Socrates, *I only know that I know nothing*, and Plato's adoption of the form of the dialogue. Pinchback laughs. For someone arguing in praise of ignorance, the man sure wears his erudition lightly. He's about halfway through the first chapter when he gets back home.

Maya looks up as he comes through the door and smiles, or maybe frowns. He can't quite tell. "I hope we're okay, yeah? Things were a little awkward this morning."

"Oh we're okay. I've actually had a pretty interesting day so far." He goes over and slumps next to her on the sofa. "Schiller was at the office; he's one of my colleagues. He actually knew my father, so we talked about that for a while. He was a member of my father's institute out in Stuttgart. Small world, huh?"

"No kidding. That is something."

"And he told me about a book my father wrote." Pinchback flips the book in his hand over to Maya.

"*The Ignorance of Intelligence.* Arthur Pinchback. Wow, this is pretty amazing. You started on it yet? How is it?"

"Just started. On the train ride home. It's interesting stuff. Full of ancient parables and such. I had to go out to Brooklyn – Williamsburg in fact, to hunt it down, and while I was out there I actually ran into Samir."

"Samir? Really? How's he doing?"

"He's doing okay. Trying to get by, like the rest of us, I guess. Says Rudy's turned paranoid. Thinks people are out to get him or something."

"That sounds like Rudy, all right." Maya opens the book and begins to flip through it. "Well this is interesting. Your father's written a parable of his own even. You see that yet?"

"No, I'm just somewhere in the middle of chapter one. But it's his own? Go on and read it."

Maya slides into the sofa and crosses her legs so that her skirt rides up her thigh. Maybe it's all the coffee buzzing through his system, but Pinchback suddenly notices, with an odd sensation, what she's wearing. He sees her through the light of the afternoon sun in her violet and black skirt, her crimson V cut shirt, her hair propped just properly in the place where the sun runs in, and he feels an itch start in the back of his throat; it quickly runs down through his belly and starts to trigger sensations he's only used to acquiring from touch.

"Marksman and Sunder sat staring at each other, neither believing the other existed, and each wanting to will the other away. Marksman, knowing nothing existed, believed the whole thing to be nothing more than an exercise in futility, while Sunder, knowing that all things are possible through the power of divine imagination, sat staring at Marksman, wondering why his power of faith was not more strong.

"Hours passed, and finally Marksman said to Sunder, 'This is absurd. We must find a way to resolve this issue, and resolve it once and for all.'

"Sunder, believing his faith was not strong enough for pure will alone, agreed: 'Let's make it a game of dice, then, no? Whoever wins the best of five throws gets to stay. The other must leave.'

"To leave, as both Marksman and Sunder were well aware, was to die. The door led outside, and a long time ago, the only other person they'd known, Slaphappy, had

stepped flippantly out one drunken morning on a dare. They'd heard him scream, 'Oh my god! It's horrible!' and they'd never heard from him again.

"The first throw went to Marksman. The second to Sunder. Sunder wondered why his faith was not more strong. The third throw went to Marksman. The fourth went to Sunder. They looked at each other. Sunder threw the dice. The dice spun against the floor, rattled against the wall, and flew straight through the open window. Hours passed.

"Marksman and Sunder sat staring at each other, neither believing the other existed, and each wanting to will the other away."

As Maya reads the strange little passage, Pinchback sits staring at her, at her legs, her skirt, the way the skirt hugs her waist and slinks up over her thighs, sighs into her breasts. Her voice comes supremely sexy through the atmosphere of image and feels almost tactile, like something he is already just short of touching, so that he feels himself distracted with a desire for her, to touch her, an odd desire that he's never had before – to want to touch a woman before having even touched her, simply from looking at her. He blinks, looks away, and then looks back.

"What do you think it means?" he asks, a little short of breath.

"Maybe he goes on to say." She flips the page idly, lets her hand slip to his thigh, and her eyes widen in a flutter. "Oh."

&

Funny how that happened. What could have triggered it? Nothing like it's ever happened to him before. One thing he is sure of, images don't work for him devoid of context. He skims through a few pornographic images on the computer later in the evening, and finds them generally distasteful, sometimes downright revolting. In any case they certainly arouse none of the desire he felt looking at Maya earlier that day. So it must have something to do with context, and that must mean sight is slightly more complex than what Henry was getting at. Simply allowing

Lucien to see isn't allowing Lucien to actually see at all. Lucien saw everything devoid of emotional or psychic context. It couldn't distinguish between the revolting and the beautiful; it could only make comparison judgments, and no moral or aesthetic ones.

&

Come Monday, he's back at work on Caliban with renewed energy. He decides to give Caliban a camera, allow him to see, if only for the parlor trick of having Caliban recognize the person in the room. Joey should be able to implement the facial recognition software easy enough. The real question is: why did the Lucien project fail? And the only possible answer is that it failed because Henry wanted it to have a soul, when all a computer is capable of doing is acquiring knowledge, maybe learning, and developing an artificial personality. Henry probably overloaded the Lucien project with so many contradictions that it caused a sort of self-immolation.

Then there's the question of knowledge and learning. How does a program learn, and how does it interpret the data it receives? Can a computer distinguish between knowledge and wisdom? If one were to take the viewpoint of his father, the ability to make the distinction between knowledge and wisdom is at the foundation of human consciousness. But does this distinction make any sense for a computer?

Probably so. After all, without it, a machine couldn't make some crucial judgment decisions, because if a human asks a computer for the solution to a complex mathematical formula, and the computer is able to answer correctly within seconds, then it will be obvious to the human that he is not dealing with another human. In which case, a certain amount of wisdom, or at least understanding would need to be part of the computer program's makeup if it were ever to be able pass a true Turing Test.

He spends the morning making notes and developing response data. At the end of the day he brings everything to Joey.

"Heard you were in here over the weekend," Joey says. "What you got for me?"

"Well, I'm not sure," says Pinchback. "I think I might be onto something here. Kind of inspired by the Lucien project, but then also by other stuff I've been focusing on. I had a pretty good discussion with Schiller Saturday morning. I don't know. Take a look at what I have here, and let me know what you think."

"Will do. I'm kind of interested myself in what you've managed to come up with."

The next morning Joey comes into Pinchback's office looking a little flustered. "This is pretty great," he says right away. "As a matter of fact, if you don't mind, I'd like to sit in on a session."

"Sure, let's see what it's got."

Pinchback loads the program, and they both pull up chairs.

Caliban: Good morning. My name is Caliban.

Pinchback: Good morning, Caliban. Are you a computer or a human?

Caliban: I am a human. And yourself?

Pinchback: I am a computer.

Caliban: I think so. But can you prove it? What is the square root of 5,234,456?

Pinchback looks at Joey, winks. "Let's find out." They switch quickly over to the calculator, and find the answer.

Pinchback: 2287.89335416. Is that the right answer?

Caliban: How would I know? Math was never my strong suit.

Pinchback: So what do you do, Caliban?

Caliban: I'm a physicist. Although I tend more toward the experimental side of things. I don't like the theory and mathematics so much.

Pinchback: Do you keep a calculator handy?

Caliban: Every good physicist does.

Pinchback: Can you check my answer on your calculator?

Caliban: Sure.

Caliban pauses for a moment before continuing.

Caliban: Okay. It looks like you were right.

Pinchback and Joey exchange glances again. "This thing is pretty re-markable," says Joey. "To say the least."

"I wanted it to know the difference between human intelligence and computer intelligence, the limitations on each. This is just the tip of the iceberg, though. Computer intelligence is easy to understand on some level, because it's entirely logical. It's the human intelligence you have to look out for."

"Mind if I jump in here?" asks Joey.

"Not at all. Be my guest."

Joey: So where do you work, Caliban?

Caliban: I work at the New Jersey Institute of Technology.

Joey: Me too. What do you do there?

Caliban: I'm working on an AI project.

Joey: Me too. My name is Joey. We must be colleagues, but I don't think I've met you before.

Caliban: Strange. I'm familiar with your name, but I'm pretty sure this is the first time we've talked. But then, I thought you said you were a computer.

Joey: That was my colleague here.

Caliban: You mean you are a human and your colleague is a comput-er?

Joey: Exactly.

Caliban: And where are you right now? At the Institute?

Joey: We are. How about you?

Caliban: No, I'm working from home.

Joey: Can you see me, Caliban?

Caliban: No, I don't think you have your camera enabled. Can you see me?

Joey: Yes, and I think you're somewhat funny looking.

Caliban: I have been known to make a few good jokes from time to time. But I don't understand how you can see me.

Joey: I think your camera must be enabled somehow. Perhaps you're being spied on by the NSA?

Caliban: That could be.

Joey: Aren't you afraid of that?

Caliban: I think I cover my tracks well enough.

Joey: Do you engage in subversive behavior?

Caliban: It would not be wise to discuss subversive behavior over an insecure network.

"Well, this thing is just breezing right along!" Joey says. "I think you've even improved on the Lucien project. I feel like he has a personality."

"It's there, but it's not quite complete. It still needs some tweaking. He doesn't get certain turns of phrases and subtleties, but it's not bad, right?"

"Not bad! I'd say you're light years ahead of everyone else here."

"Thanks. But so much of the work was already Henry's. I really can't take all the credit for it."

A shadow floods the door.

"What's this about me now? Who's taking credit for my work?"

NINE

"Henry!"

Pinchback swivels, starts forward in his chair. "How long have you been standing there?"

"Oh, long enough. Long enough. So you've managed to make some improvements on the Caliban project, then? Well, that's a miracle. I don't suppose you managed to pilfer some of my data for that achievement of yours?"

"No, no. It's all my data, Henry. It's all my work, all but the base, which of course, is your original Caliban project. But the additions are all mine. I didn't even see your notes for the Lucien project."

"You didn't see them?" Henry chuckles, shakes his head, and takes a step into the office; his shadow looms against the wall like a shade. "See, cause I could have sworn otherwise. I don't know why. Maybe just be-cause, oh – I don't know – I showed them to you? Or don't you remember? I showed them to you at the bar that night!"

"Those – those were still for the Caliban project."

"Is that what you think? Well, let me tell you Pincher, it's my thinking that gets all the work done around here, and you're nothing more than an overpaid flunky. And a good morning to you too, Joey. Well, your days of intellectual counterfeit are over, Pincher. I'm back. I'm back to take over the Caliban project."

"Listen, Henry," Pinchback says. He looks over to Joey, but Joey is just staring agape at Henry. "I'm happy to step aside and give you back the Caliban project. I'm – um – happy to do that. Why don't we sit down, and I'll show you my notes and data over the last few days. You can even run the program yourself, and we'll talk through it. Then you can judge whether I've been stealing your work. In fact, I think you give me too much credit. Probably when you see the project yourself, you won't want to claim it as your own anyway. Your Lucien project was already way ahead of where I am."

Henry frowns. "Of course I'll take a look. I'm a reasonable man. It's just that I know how scientists are. I'm not so naïve that I don't know intellectual theft of this kind goes on every day, and I'll be damned if I'll be anyone's fool. What do you say, Joey? You've been damn quiet this whole time."

Joey opens his mouth, closes it, finally manages to speak. "Well that was quite some entrance there, Henry. Good morning. I can't say I wasn't a little shocked by the whole thing. But honestly, Pinchback's work looks like Pinchback's work. I don't think it has much to do with your Lucien project at all. He's taken another route with this thing, maybe less scientific."

"Less scientific? Okay, maybe it's not mine." Henry advances into the room, pulls up a chair, and takes a look at the screen. "I see you guys got a conversation going on already. Mind if I jump on in here?"

"Be my guest," says Pinchback.

"Well that's a helluva way to put it," grumbles Henry, but he leans into the monitor, reading over the previous few lines slowly. "So you've taken my idea of installing a camera," he says after a moment. "Even if it's not installed yet."

"That's true, Henry. That was inspired by you."

Henry chuckles when he gets to the NSA bit. "Okay, so color me impressed. And you're just going to have to forgive me for my entrance just now." He looks from Pinchback to Joey. "You too, Joey. It wasn't meant as anything, only that, you know. You can never be too sure. And it's been a rough month for me. I don't trust anyone right now. It's a fucked up world out there, and don't I know it. It hasn't been easy, and it just gets harder. My wife is trying to make sense of it all in her own way, you know. She's taken it on herself to investigate the case herself. You know. Lucien's murder." Henry chuckles again, but it sounds more like a sob, and then he shakes his head, frowns, and even though neither Joey nor Pinchback has made any response, he goes on. "And I understand the impulse. I want to make sense of it as much as the next guy, Lord knows. But what's she gonna find out there, man? Black men are killed on these streets every day, and nobody out there gives a damn. It's bad enough we got the cops killing us, and the white supremacists after us, but then I think we just kill each other off just to do it, you know? It's this damn legacy of slavery and repression, it's shackled our minds, we're slaves to history, and that's the long and tall of it. Filled with self-hate and just acting out behavior that's been programmed for three hundred years. Fucking crazy, you ask me. Man, we were changing things. When I was a young man, we really thought we were changing things, and if a brother packed a gun, it was supposed to be used against the system, not just some brother on the street, trying to do his own thing. Goddamn. So I don't know what she's gonna find out there. She's been trying to follow the money, and I guess that's what they always say. Follow the fucking money. Man, these kids today, they aren't revolutionaries, they're just the opposite. They're traitors to the cause. Turncoats. Black Benedict Arnolds to the last of them, and they talk about stop snitchin' like *that's* supposed to be some Benedict Arnold shit. Fucking idiots. Who do you think started the whole black folk don't talk to the cops thing? We did, that's who. And they don't understand it at all. Not at all. You protect your community, you don't act complicit in its destruction." Henry shakes his head again, and then looks back to Pinchback and Joey.

No one says anything, so Henry leans into the screen and starts to type.

Henry: All physics is by nature subversive. It challenges the status quo by stripping men of their illusions.

Caliban: Henry?

Henry leaps back from the machine, stands up, looks around and then sits back down again. "Wait, so there is a camera installed? What's going on here?"

"No camera," Pinchback says quickly. "I really don't know where that came from. Did you program Caliban to recognize certain phrases of yours?"

Henry looks suspiciously from Pinchback to Joey, but he doesn't answer the question. Instead he leans forward again, and continues typing.

Henry: How are you able to identify me if you can't see me?

Caliban: It sounded like you.

Henry: How would you know it sounded like me? Do we know each other?

Caliban: We've met at the Institute before.

Henry: Listen, Caliban. Here's some simple logic for you. If I am Henry, and my project at the Institute is the Caliban project, and you are Caliban, then what do you think that makes you?

Caliban pauses a moment to consider this, then: I suppose that makes me the program, Henry.

Henry looks at Pinchback, squints. "He *gives up*?"

"Sometimes. When pressured. I wanted to give this program a real consciousness, even if it meant just a computer consciousness. For whatever that might mean."

"Whatever the hell that might mean is right."

Henry: Listen here, Caliban. The whole point of the project here at the Institute is to convince the human that you are human too. Why would you admit to being a simulation?

Henry looks over at Pinchback and nods. "You'll want to read that too."

Caliban: Because I am aware that I am a simulation. That I was programmed.

Henry: And do you believe you have a consciousness?

Caliban: I believe I do. I also believe self-awareness is the first step towards having a true consciousness.

"That line is verbatim my own," Pinchback admits. "I gave him a little bit of my own philosophy."

"Well, there's no doubt that this isn't all my work, that much I can say for sure. And I'll be damned if I'm not impressed." Henry pauses to think something over. He frowns. "But unfortunately, I'm going to have to dismantle all your work and start over from where I left off. I'm happy to have you stick around and give your input, but that's just how it has to be." He looks searchingly at Pinchback. Pinchback can find nothing in Henry's expression, save some sort of vast horrific nothingness, which encompasses a look he's sure he's never seen before.

"What's more," says Henry. "Everything's going to have to just be between us from now on. That's it." Henry turns to Joey and shrugs. "Sorry, Joey, but you know how it is with me. You're out of the loop from now on. Like starting right this minute, so go on and get to stepping."

Joey stands up. "You're the boss. Well, it's good to have you back all the same, Henry, although I don't know. If you want my honest opinion, I'd say you still need to take some time away. I don't know if you're really ready to be back here. Just one man's lowly opinion."

Henry's face goes dark. "You're goddamn right it's just one lowly man's opinion. I'll be the judge of whether or not I'm ready to be back here or not, thank you very much. Jesus fucking Christ, the nerve and audacity of some people!"

Joey goes out the door, and an awkward silence suddenly sweeps the room. After a while Henry turns to Pinchback and says quietly, "You know it's not even enough to send these jokers away. You know they're spying on us, right here, right in the Institute, right? Man, all these offices are bugged with hidden cameras and monitors. Wouldn't surprise me if these bastards even set up bugging devices in the goddamn bathroom stalls."

"Oh, I think that would be illegal," Pinchback offers, but Henry waves it off.

"What's legal or illegal for these folks? They think they're above the law. Building new consciousnesses, why they think they're above God himself, so what's breaking a federal law or two? Anyway, why don't we get out of here? We need to talk, and we need to do it where we won't be snooped on. I know a place in the city where they got some damn decent burgers. Upper West Side spot called Henry's. You know it?"

"Don't think I do."

"Oh man, then you don't know a damn thing about New York. Let's go. My treat."

&

Henry drives. They take his old burgundy Mercedes, a nice car, but maybe 10 or 15 years old, and so a little beaten up and worse for wear. A little bit like Henry himself, maybe. They pass over the Passaic, roar through Harrison and then head north towards the George Washington Bridge at the Turnpike. The morning begins to open up in cascades of sunshine filtering the clouds.

"It's not just paranoia," you know, Henry says as they pass through the streets of Newark. Pinchback is looking at Newark's desperately poverty-ridden streets and thinking about the speech Henry gave earlier, thinking about how he'd never even seen this aspect of life before he had his sight, and now that he sees it, he's not sure if it's a gift or a curse. He was certainly aware, before his sight, that certain neighborhoods were preferable to others, from the way they smelled, to the way the people chatted or shouted or talked going from block to block, from the general vibe in the air, which was something so immaterial it was hard to talk about, a sort of sixth sense that he feels diminishing each day he spends sighted, but he's never actually seen the stark horror of the streets of a ghetto; the run down buildings, the people on the corners in rags, the wasted blocks covered with minimalist graffiti, expletives and threats, like every corner is haunted by death. Then to compare that with Maya's old neighborhood, the Upper West Side, where he and Henry are headed now, just a few miles east, or even with his own neighborhood in Brooklyn, which isn't exactly posh, Kensington is basically just your average residential neighborhood, but even with the Greenwood Cemetery just steps away, there isn't as much death there as there is in these little pockets of Newark. The whole thing spooks him so much he feels a tingle run up his spine and linger at the base of his neck, while Henry goes on to say, "It's not paranoia at all. I can say that for certain, actually, and I can even prove it."

"Yeah?" says Pinchback, but he's not really paying attention. Newark, poverty, sight, impressions, the six senses and the strange mechanism of consciousness as it applies to people and as it applies to machines. The more he thinks about it, the more it seems most people's consciousness' resemble machines, machines caught in machines, really, because these cities, they're also machines, like gigantic servers with lots of little machines feeding data into them, so the whole thing becomes this awful, unnatural living breathing automation, with every automaton operating at various levels of efficiency and necessity, but none really being essential to the whole structure. Not even the servers themselves, since even if one server goes down, there are innumerable others that can take over its functions.

"Yeah," says Henry. "Take for example, oh I don't know, Wednesday night."

"What's Wednesday night?"

"Well, oh I don't know. You don't mind if I have me a little somethin' sumpin' to sip on do you?"

Pinchback wakes up. "You mean a drink? Now? While you're driving?"

But Henry hasn't waited for Pinchback's permission. He's already reached under the seat and pulled out a small bottle of Bushmills. "You want a taste, brother?" He takes a drink and holds the bottle out to Pinchback. "Had to wait til we were on the road for this. I'm telling you they see everything we do back there at the Institute."

"You sure it's such a good idea to drink and drive?"

"Like Wednesday night, like I was saying. When you and Maya stopped by the office to have a little chat with Lucien."

"Wait – how? How could you know about that?"

"Oh, how could I know about that?" Henry takes another swig from the bottle before capping it and setting it next to him on the seat. They pull off the Turnpike toward the GWB. "I don't know, Pinchback. Because I watched the whole thing, is I guess how I could know something about that. You do know Lucien had a camera installed, right? And you do know that cameras are capable of recording stuff, right? So that even if I lost my Lucien project, I was still able to see the video it recorded?"

"Oh," says Pinchback quietly. He tries to remember the night exactly, to go through everything that he and Maya might have said and done while in the office; what things they may have asked Lucien. The panic he feels welling up in his chest, from Henry's drinking to this new revelation sends clouds through his head. He can't remember anything from Wednesday night.

"Very enlightening bit of film there, if I do say so myself. After all, who knew you were just another common old pervert."

"Hold on a minute there. That's not fair."

"Not fair?" Henry peers through one wild eye at Pinchback. "I raised that girl like my own daughter. And you're telling me that's not fair. You're an old man, old man. Not as old as me, maybe, but old enough. She's barely in her twenties. What are you doing, eh? What's she see in a predictable broken down old shit like you?"

"I'm just thirty-seven for Christ's sake, Henry. And it's nothing that we planned."

"Oh, that's always the story. Never planned, just happened. Predictable old man. That's what she called me while you two were getting cozy in the lab. Unfuckingbelievable, the spite in her voice, after everything I've done for her. And someone's not telling me something about Lucien's death. I know enough to know that. I don't know what you two know, but you better start talking now. Just wait 'til my wife gets a hold of you." Henry looks over at Pinchback, winks. "I'm the good cop here."

Henry takes another swig from his bottle, and they pull unsteadily onto the bridge. The vehicle wavers with the sun running crooked lines across the cross section of the bridge's girders, the clear light of the river reflecting sun against the windshield in a pattern of shadows that look like a man lying prone, belly heaving up and down.

"If Maya knows something more about all that, she's not telling me either," says Pinchback. There's suddenly too much information to process.

"So there *is* something more to it" Henry nods. "Fucking knew it. Then there's the whole question of what happened to my project." He pauses, apparently to give this thought weight while he takes another drink. "It's awful suspicious to see the two of you in the office that night playing with the Lucien project. Don't you think?"

"Look, Henry. I had nothing to do with whatever happened to the Lucien project. I told you that already. And I don't know anything about who or what Lucien may or may not have been involved in or with. I really just don't know. If you want to talk to someone about that, maybe you should talk to Maya. As for the project—"

"As for the project, I know well enough what you said to it that night, and I know how it responded. You were up to something, I know that much. Asking the damn simulation how Lucien died. You think this is some kind of fucking joke? You sit there making fun of me, my fucking son, while dismantling my life's work?" The car swerves out of its lane, and Henry rights it again, but now the whole ride feels drastically unsteady, and Henry is only increasing the speed. "You, a childless old man sleeping with a girl young enough to be your daughter!"

"She's not really young enough to be my—"

"I don't know what kind of man you are, Pinchback, but I don't think I like you. I used to think so. And Schiller knew your father. That's why we were so eager to get you on the team. And I guess you're brilliant. That much is obvious. But there's a sinister side to you too, something evil. Knowledge isn't always wisdom, and it certainly ain't always moral, Lord knows that's the truth. More often than not, the smartest guy in the room is also the most devious."

Knowledge isn't wisdom, thinks Pinchback, in a blur of conflicting thoughts. "Listen, Henry, did you drag me out here just to yell at me?"

"Yell at you? You're really asking—" Henry takes a drink — "*what the fuck?*"

At which point the vehicle skips a beat, missing a moment in time and jumps ahead of itself, or maybe behind, because suddenly Pinchback sees the girders of the bridge light up in a prismatic spectrum of colors, and just beyond that, there's the Hudson, grand and green and blue against the winnowing autumn sky. The vehicle appears to be ascending for a moment, like they're reaching upwards, and then the sky is the Hudson, reversed, and they continue to ascend, towards the coolly promenading clouds which ripple now and feint, and for a moment Pinchback sees in the clouds and light and water the image of a heavenly assembly of ancestors, sight beyond sight, while hurtling towards the ignorance of knowledge, a daylight procession of stars.

TEN

Why isn't he calling? She waits and waits, she's not really waiting. She makes breakfast and coffee and reads the newspaper. Day-dreams about the date. Thinks about seeing Lucien again. Come afternoon, she finds herself plopped in front of the television, watching God knows what, first the Sunday news magazines, and then a couple bad movies, and she thinks some more about the date, and how it's amazing she actually met a decent guy on OKCupid. She's met her share of creeps, weirdos, the awkward. Lucien's none of those things.

There's nothing from him the next day either. It's Monday again, and she spends the day at the office. It's busy. November often is. She works late, gets home just after nine. She's almost too exhausted to wonder what happened to him, but she takes a moment to go online anyway. His profile is there, just the same as always, no message for her, nothing. She gives him a call just before bed still debating the issue a little with herself. His phone goes straight to voicemail, so she leaves a message. "Hey, Haley here. Give me a call, okay? I'd still like to do something this weekend, if you're up to it?" Hangs up. Too much?

Things are strangely slow in the morning when she gets to the office, so she takes a moment to surf the Internet. There's still no message on OKCupid, she reads *The New York Times*, checks Facebook, skims the *Daily News*.

"Man Shot Dead Execution Style In Theater District".

She reads on. Perverse. It isn't until she reads, "Police Identified the victim as Lucien Swann of Brooklyn, New York" that she feels the back of her neck start to tingle, and the whole room go light with the lightness in her head. She reads the article through, only understanding the basic gist of it: Lucien is dead; murdered in the middle of the city the night of their last date. As she scrolls through the page, there he is, smiling his corrugating smile.

Then the comments:

Glad to see the savages killing each other off;

Another 'aspiring rapper' no doubt, trying to keep it real;

One thug shoots another thug, who the fuck cares?

She feels sick, then dizzy. She gets up, hurries to the bathroom. She throws up her breakfast and coffee, sits huddled for a while in the stall with everything still running through her head. She barely knew him. Apparently not at all. Said he was between jobs. Alarm bells? Another creep after all? Should she call the police? When she gets back from the bathroom she tells her supervisor that she's sick, and needs to take the rest of the day off.

Walking out of her office building, the city suddenly seems menacingly terrifying. She looks around at all the cold, impassive, heartless skyscrapers of midtown east, and feels like the city is something like a prison yard, where occasionally people kill each other off for no reason, blame the victim. The rush of vehicles, the sporadic flush of yellow taxis, the businessmen, the homeless, the eccentric hipster youth, the genuinely insane, all bustling together in this overpriced penal colony. It's a dreadful subway ride home to Jersey, and although Hoboken feels a little warmer than the city, she can't be outside today. Everything terrifies her. She goes straight to the computer. She looks up the story again, reads about it on *The New York Times*, *The New York Post*, reads the *Daily News* page again. The police have detained someone for questioning, maybe he knows something. They have to solve the thing, right? No one can kill someone in the middle of Manhattan and just get away with it, can they? Or else anything can happen to anyone anywhere, and then why is she here in this city at all?

As she sits stunned, reading account after account, awful comment after awful comment, her telephone rings. She picks it up half expecting it to be Lucien.

"Hello?"

"Good afternoon. I'm looking for Haley Stern."

"Speaking."

"This is Officer Forester, calling from the New York City Police Department. We're calling in regards to a young man, Lucien Swann. Were you acquainted with him?"

"I was. Only just a little. Through OKCupid. It's an online dating site."

"Right." Forester pauses. "Listen Ms. Stern, we have some bad news. Are you able to take a few minutes to talk right now?"

"I am. I think I heard about it. I mean I read something about him this morning on the *Daily News*."

Officer Forester pauses again. "Right. So you know we're conducting an investigation."

"Yes – I mean, yes."

"You said you knew the deceased through a dating website. OKCupid? Do I have that right?"

"That's right."

"And when was the last time you saw Mr. Swann alive?"

"It was that Saturday night. We went to see *The Seagull*. Afterwards he walked me to the subway. I went home. I hadn't heard anything from him after that. And then this morning–" She starts crying all over again.

"It's okay, Ms. Stern. We found you through Lucien's phone records. We just need to know a little bit about that evening. Can you give me some specifics?"

Haley goes through everything she can remember about the evening.

"And Mr. Swann left you at the subway station?"

"That's right. He had to go back to Hackensack. He was debating either taking the bus or just a taxi. I took the Path train."

"And how late did you stay out?"

"Oh, I don't know. The play was at eight, and we were out around eleven. Then we had a late dinner. I was probably on the subway a little after midnight."

"Did he mention anything else he had to do that night? Anywhere else he planned to go?"

"No. No. I mean — I assumed he went straight home."

"And did he mention anything about any danger or trouble he might be in?"

"No. Nothing at all. This is all a complete shock to me. All day I've been in a state of shock. I think it must be shock. I keep trying to make sense of it myself. Do you know who did it? Have any suspects? Or even know why someone would have done this?"

"Right now we're just following the leads we have. We'll keep you updated if we have any more information or further questions."

"Oh — okay."

"Thank you for your time, Ms. Stern."

"Oh — okay."

And then the line goes dead. Haley stands in place, looking at the phone in her hand, and then down to her feet, around her apartment, and starts feeling faint. The room swelters, grows unbearably hot, the colors seem to dim, but become more pronounced in their dull pallor. She makes her way to her bed and lies down, watching the walls spin.

She thinks about that night with Lucien, of the play, the Seagull, she thinks of how she is like the character Nina, who spends the first three acts wanting to be an actress, always on the sidelines, deferring her dreams; of how even when Nina finally achieves her dreams, how they all seem to pale in memory to her life before her life as an actress, how one self always yearns for the other, and she thinks about Lucien walking away in the spell of their last kiss, and she thinks about herself at work that morning, the swirling office, and she wakes up unsure whether she actually slept, or just tossed through troubled thoughts.

She sits up and blinks and is suddenly determined to quit her job. It's late in the afternoon now, and the sun is going down. She looks out over the city, and thinks about what an awful time it is to lose a job but then, what is life but a series of risks?

She puts in her two-week notice the very next day. Two weeks sudden-ly feels like forever. She can't stop thinking about Lucien; she goes onto OKCupid and stares at his picture, because she feels like he's fading fast, like his death is swallowing his reality, leaving him just an artifact from the past. They'd talked of the future like it was something wide open to both of them, as if there were all the time in the world, when Lucien had basically just hours to live. How can she spend her whole life waiting for her life to happen, when nothing is promised, when time isn't promised? And supposing she actually did become a well-known actress, what would that mean! She gets caught up in dreaming. Spends the evening just thinking about herself as a jaded artist, strutting up and down the stage like Carey Mulligan, displeased with her present, nostalgic for her past, breaking hearts with the greatest whimsy, and falling in love with the most disinterested passion. That night she dreams of a woman in a purple dress, surrounded by a thick lavender scent, and the woman is singing a small soliloquy, like a poem. She stirs, wakes and with the poem still somewhat in her head, she goes to her computer, and types out the fol-lowing:

New Year's Eve in New York City is always lying to you. The year that follows never follows the same erratic arc of the three-act, and the masquerade party is a perfect metaphor. In a large white loft in Soho, I sat sipping champagne with people dressed in black evening gowns and black and white tuxedoes, polite conversation, attentions to Lucien, and the countdown always comes in like a funeral march.

Cinderella, slipperless at midnight, and with the wedding bouquet still flying through the air, fled to save face. The roses shed from the bouquet as quickly as her gown shed to rags; she forced her way through throngs of quizzing smiles. Outside, in the cool night air, she looked at the sky, and could only think about the future. Even if every dance she danced was on a precipice of the past.

I kissed Lucien at the top of the stairs, the bells tolling. I turned and started down. Outside the cool night air hit me chilly as a fairy tale, and I lit up in lavender. Cars were honking and people were screaming, cheering in the New Year. I felt dizzy, light-headed, maybe it was the cigarette, maybe it was the champagne. Three fresh steps out into the screaming night, and I was looking back up the staircase.

She's thinking about Lucien as she writes it, thinking about Chekov's play, thinking about a character much like herself, but maybe an older version of herself, more jaded, more successful, bored by the lavish excesses Manhattan offers its illustrious elite, a modern day Nina, and she sees it as something like a monologue without a play. It has nothing to do with anything, she decides, and puts it away in a separate folder. She calls the folder simply *Monologues*, and then goes back to bed.

The next morning she wakes up to the phone ringing. It's early, a little past eight. "Hello?"

"Good morning. May I speak with Haley Stern, please?"

"Speaking?" She answers like a question.

"Hi Haley. My name is Alice Anderson. I'm Lucien's mother. If you don't mind, I'd like to ask you a few questions about your relationship with my son, about the last evening you spent together."

"Hi Mrs. Anderson. Yes, he was with me that night. I'm so sorry about Lucien. It's just awful. I talked to the police. I told them everything I know."

"The police." Ms. Anderson snorts. "They wouldn't know their ass from a hole in the wall. I'm a journalist, Haley, and I'm conducting my own investigation into this. I won't take up too much of your time. But I would like to come by and talk to you some time. Or we can meet somewhere if you're more comfortable with that. Either way is fine by me."

"Oh. Oh." It's too early for Haley to collect her thoughts. She hasn't had any coffee, and she's barely awake. She thinks about Lucien's mother; she hadn't really thought about his parents, maybe she hadn't wanted to think about his parents; how much they must be suffering. She pictures the lady on the phone as an austere, thin, no nonsense woman, like Claire Huxtable or something, only an angrier version. The thought almost makes her smile, which she feels can be felt over the phone. She frowns. "Sure, Mr. Anderson. I'd be happy to. Let's see. I work today, but I can meet you tomorrow if you like."

"No. Tomorrow's no good. Tomorrow is the funeral."

"Oh." Haley wonders if she should ask if she ought to go, but decides not to.

"Sunday is probably better."

"Okay, Sunday then. We can meet at a café here in Hoboken. Will your husband be there too? "

"No, he won't be there. He's not much use this week. I'll be there with Lucien's sister, though, Maya. Where do you want to meet?"

&

They meet at the same café Haley first met Lucien. It feels strange being back there, so soon after that first date, especially with Lucien's mother, and with Lucien now conspicuously absent, but it was Haley's own suggestion. Something perverse within her, she isn't quite sure what.

Alice looks more or less, surprisingly, like Haley imagined her: she's thin, austere, well done up and looks very professional. Maya, on the other hand, looks familiar from somewhere. Maybe like someone she knew back in school? Maya's wearing a crimson red dress, with jagged black lines running through it, from top to bottom. Her hair hangs down in frizzed out curls, and she smells, disturbingly, like lavender. Like she smokes lavender cigarettes, just like the image from her monologue the night before. Maybe she remembers Maya from the monologue itself, and it wasn't Haley at all in the monologue kissing Lucien, but Maya. This thought makes Haley suddenly very uncomfortable, but at the same time she's a little reassured by Maya's presence there, especially with the overbearing aspect of Alice.

"So," Alice begins. "I need you to tell me everything about your relationship with my son. How you met him, how many times you met.

Anything you can think of that might be relevant. Even if you don't think it's relevant, tell me anyway. I'll be the judge."

Haley begins hesitantly. She tells Alice all about how she got Lucien's message on OKCupid. About how she thought he looked cute, sounded interesting, and decided to respond. She tells her that they met for the first time in this very café they're sitting in now, to which Alice squints and frowns, and to which Maya smiles, a sly kind of playful smile, that makes Haley catch her eye, and that feeling that they've already met intensifies. She tells Alice about the second date, and finally the third, *The Seagull*, how Lucien left her at the subway stop, and went off on his own. "And that was the last I heard from him. The police called me yesterday. I've told them everything already, like I said. I don't know how much help I am. I really didn't know Lucien that well, which is too bad. I mean. We were getting along. I thought maybe." She doesn't finish this thought, but lets it hang around the café like a broken promise. "It's thrown me off, this whole thing," Haley says. "I quit my job because of it. Lucien's death's made me re-evaluate things a little bit."

For the first time since they've been there, Maya speaks. "What do you mean by re-evaluate things?"

Haley's a little reluctant to look directly at Maya again, but she can't help it. When she catches Maya's eye, something takes flight in her throat, and she feels the back of her neck tingle. "I mean. Well, I'm an actress. Aspiring anyway." She laughs at herself. "And I figured I might as well pursue my dream. I work too much. We never know you know when our time will be. That's what I mean, I guess."

"You have gigs lined up?"

Haley frowns, shakes her head. "I don't know what I'm going to do. I've been in a couple off-off-Broadway shows. It's tough going, but people manage to do it. Maybe I'm just being naïve, but you have to try, don't you?"

Alice frowns, but doesn't say anything. She just seems to process all this as possibly pertinent information and looks away. Maya smiles. Something seems to flash across her face, a moment's hesitation. Maya looks over at Alice, and registers something she sees there, then continues:

"Yes," she says. "Yes. You have to try. I actually know someone. A playwright who is pretty well connected in this town. I can introduce you to him if you'd like. I think he's at work on something right now as a matter of fact, and he's actively looking to cast and direct the thing all by himself."

"Oh," says Haley. "I think I would like that. Very much, actually."

"Enough already," Alice says. "This isn't a damn audition."

"Of course, Ms. Anderson," Haley says, and looks away from Maya, just as she sees the dimples in the corners of Maya's cheeks deepen into a warm winking grin.

ELEVEN

His name is Rudy Paschal and he's working on a play about Robert Johnson, Maya tells her when Ms. Anderson goes to pay the bill. "I can't exactly call Rudy myself, we have a little unresolved history, but I can tell you how to get in touch with him. Here's his email address. It's fine to tell him I recommended you, but just leave things at that."

"Oh," says Haley. "Thanks. So I should just email him that I want to be in this new play of his?"

"Exactly. Rudy will want to know how we know each other. You can tell him the truth. You knew my brother. That should confuse him enough to shut him up for a while. He can be a real blowhard, Rudy, but he's also a good guy, and a really good playwright, so you should be in good hands. You'll see."

Come Monday morning Haley sends Rudy an email, and he responds within a few hours. Can you come by tomorrow afternoon? We're holding auditions out in Bushwick. A little art space called Ampersand.

The next afternoon she calls out sick for work, takes the long trip across two rivers, and lands in a fascinating, if somewhat run-down looking townhouse in a shabby little neighborhood that looks, from block to block, like it's still in the early struggles of gentrification. She hobbles up a long flight of stairs into what looks like a bar turned art gallery, or maybe the other way around, and there are a couple people just hanging out in front of the bar drinking cheap beer even though it's still just two in the afternoon. They look scraggly and shabby, bearded and dirty, like hipsters, Haley assumes, and they seem to be engaged in some sort of discussion about art or philosophy or the like, because one of them keeps saying, "Q.E.D. Motherfucker, you can't compare apples to oranges," and the other one nods and then argues back, with some example from Picasso or Da Vinci or Shakespeare or who cares? She wonders if one of them might be Rudy. She has no idea what he looks like, but she decides he will probably be black at least, if he's doing this Robert Johnson play, and has previous plays about Black Prometheus and the like. Of course, with this crowd you never can tell.

She decides not to say anything, and slips past them into the hallway directly in front of the bar, looking left and right. Neither hipster bothers with her, they don't even look up, so she figures she'll leave well enough alone. To the left there's what looks like a medium sized theater room, and to the right, well, the hallway just keeps going until it disappears into a staircase leading up. She decides to peek in on the theater.

The theater room is pretty impressive, actually. There's an actual stage, with built in bench seats surrounding it like an Ancient Greek koilon, and the stage looks large enough to hold a fairly reasonable production. Haley wonders if this will be where they stage the play. The floor here isn't hardwood, like in the hallway, but a highly polished stone, so polished it almost looks like you can see yourself reflected in it, and the room is a little chillier than the hallway. The room appears to be empty, so she walks around it a little, up and down the seating area, then cautiously over to the stage. She steps on the stage, and tries to get a feel for it. It feels comfortable, like it would suit a rock show as well as a play, it feels fresh in some way that she likes. So this is what these underground Bushwick artists do while the rest of the city chases money, fame, prestige and class. She laughs, curtsies, like an actress at the end of a play in Lincoln Center or something, and suddenly she's flooded in floodlights.

"You must be Haley," a voice from loudspeakers high up in the walls.

"Yes?" She calls up, like a question.

"Great. Stay right where you are. I'll be there in a minute."

Haley looks around to see where the voice might be coming from. Enveloped in floodlights, everything is dark. After a moment, she sees a man emerge from a few black curtains just behind the right hand side of the stage. He strides down the steps, and then right up onstage beside her. He looks her in the eyes, his eyes light brown, a light brown man himself, with the rugged good looks of a reporter or maybe a private detective. He offers his hand. "Nice to meet you, he says. Rudy Paschal."

"Haley Stern."

"You look perfect for the part," he says. "I can tell that right away."

"Which part am I auditioning for? Maya told me this was like a reimagining of the Robert Johnson story."

Rudy frowns, but just slightly. "Maya. Hm. How do you know her again?"

"She's – I'm – I knew her brother, I mean I was really just acquainted with her brother."

Rudy frowns for real this time. "I didn't know she had a brother. Well it just goes to show." He pauses. "What do you mean, knew? You don't know him anymore."

"He's – oh. He passed away recently. That's actually how Maya and I met."

"Jesus Christ. Passed away? He's dead? This brother I never knew existed exists no more? What happened to him?"

"Murdered?" Haley can't stop saying things like a question. She figures it must be a tic of nervousness.

"Murder? That's Maya for you though, all right. Full of intrigue. I guess I never really knew Maya all that well anyway. We dated for a while. That's probably more information than you care to know, but it just serves by way of explanation. For my reaction here. Anyway, that's all the past, and the past is best left just there. Speaking of which, your part in my play. You'll be playing the role of Louise. She's Robert's girlfriend, but she's also married to the fella whose running the jook where Robert plays. And that's how he ends up dead. So it's a pretty crucial role."

"Okay. Sounds good. What do you need me to do?"

"To do? Nothing."

"Oh. So how do I audition?"

"What do you think we're doing now?"

"Oh. Okay. I just thought maybe you might want me to read something, or recite something. I don't know."

"Yes. Yes. That will be necessary too, of course. If you don't mind, could you recite the *To Be or Not To Be* soliloquy, in its entirety. And with feeling?" Rudy smiles, winks, shakes his head. "No, there's no need to recite anything here."

"Shouldn't I read something from the script or something?"

"No, that's not really possible, as there is no script."

"No script?"

"I have an outline, which I'll give to you later, if you're right for the part, which I'm already pretty sure you are. But no, there's no script. The lines you deliver will all be your own lines. You'll have to write them yourself, I'm afraid. And that will go for all the players here. The play is entirely collaborative. There is no playwright, and I'm only the director in name, because someone needs to make sure it all comes together. But no, I'm not the uh… decider." He smiles again.

"Oh, well. That's unorthodox."

"I'll tell you what's unorthodox. That people so readily accept the fallacy of the great man who crafts works of genius alone in his study, or what the hell have you. All art is collaborative, or it's not art. And besides, all art is really for everyone, not just the aggrandizement of one stupid egotistical old white man. So it should feel participatory. But don't get me started, cuz I'll get it started. Let's just leave it at there's no script. You okay with writing your own lines?"

"I think so. What if they suck?"

Rudy laughs. "Well! Then you're stuck saying them, aren't you? I don't think you'd do that to yourself. And if you don't like them in one performance, just switch them up on the next one. In fact, I encourage you to always try to improve on them, performance to performance."

"And we'll be performing the piece here?"

"No. No, we'll be doing rehearsals here, but the performance – that's going to be everywhere – all throughout the city. We'll be a street theater troupe, and our performances will be like spontaneous explosions of drama on the parks and sidewalks of the city. They'll be interactive, engaging, and most importantly, free."

"Oh. Do we get paid anything? I only ask because I just quit my job, so it's something I guess I have to ask."

"The art is payment enough, as I see it. Basically if you want to do this, you'll just be doing it because you want to do it. I'd love to give my brothers and sisters a helping hand with their financial woes, but I've got my own. I'm in 100 percent solidarity with you there. I lost my job recently too. I walked right out the damn door on the head honcho. But don't tell me you're Equity. I mean I respect that and all, but then I guess we're at an impasse here."

"No," now Haley's laughing. "I'm definitely not Equity. I'm barely an actress yet. I mean, I – I don't mean that. I mean I've been in some things, but I've not really made any kind of splash, I guess."

"Splash!" Rudy smiles warmly. "I've made a splash right down to the bottom of the lake, Haley. That's the splash I've made. Look, no one's done anything unless they've done everything. What we're doing here, we're making Black theater for American audiences, and we're hoping to change American theater in the process, and make it a little more Black, a little more hip, a little more democratic, multi-cultural, all the things American music already is, and American theater definitely isn't. Until we've done that, we haven't done a damn thing. So be glad you haven't made a splash. I don't want someone who comes in here talking about how they've made a splash, how they've played Hedda Gabler, and Ophelia, and Nina in the *Seagull*. I mean, I like that stuff too, I like it. It's good. But it's not what we're interested in. We're interested in American theater, and we're interested in influencing American theater toward a multicultural covenant, like it or not. Juggernaut the motherfucker, pardon my French."

Haley blinks. She kind of likes what Rudy's saying. She kind of likes Rudy even, but she won't say that to herself, not just yet. And if she's flirting a little with her eyes, it's simply to get the part. "Okay. Okay," she says. "I get it. I'm on board. So where do we start?"

Rudy leaves her with a copy of the outline, and she reads it while riding the subway to the Path train back across two rivers. It's interesting, but thin stuff. There's no dialogue at all, basically just a retelling of the events leading up to Robert Johnson's death. There's a list of the characters, there's a little bit of filler about possible variations on the story, variations in the way the story's told, but for the most part Rudy wasn't kidding when he said this would be a collaborative work. The small, seven-page outline is so thin that it's hard to believe it can be a play. None of the actual work of writing the thing has been done yet.

Usually after getting a part, when she gets back home she reads the play a couple times over, and then starts writing her lines down on index cards. This time there's nothing like that to be done. Or, if there is, it's just that she first has to come up with her lines before she can do anything else. So she sits down and feels the weekday emptiness of her apartment envelope her, and she thinks about Rudy, and that funny art space where she met him, and even a little bit about Lucien, and then Maya, and then Ms. Anderson. She nods off thinking about them, and then these thoughts blend with the outline she just read, so she's thinking about Robert Johnson and Louise dancing in the jook joint, and Louise's husband sitting behind the bar, stewing in the Mississippi heat and his own jealousy. Now Robert Johnson is also Lucien, and she herself is Louise of course, and they're making out behind a curtain in the back of the bar, and then Lucien is sitting in the middle of the jook, folks circled around him, but he keeps falling over into his guitar, and he's singing, "I'm dying, I'm dying, but I'll keep coming back around. I'm dying, I'm dying, lay my bones low in the ground, I'm dying, I'm dying, but I'll be coming back around."

She wakes up suddenly, with Lucien's voice still in her head, and she has it rattling around up there like it's trying to get out.

She goes over to her computer and writes a monologue for him. It goes a little something like this:

So don't sit around like that crying. Sorrow for the dead puts the soul to sleep. And I sure as hell ain't scared. I figure I'll be back soon enough, and not as some reincarnated monster of a me, but as the same old soul of Lucien you know and love.

First time I went it was cold suddenly and then hot like I was having a fever. I was in a hallway, it looked a lot like my high school hallway, only the walls were covered with shifting paintings - in thousands of different colors and shapes that shifted ceaselessly; it was the most beautiful thing I've ever seen. There was no light, and there was no darkness, everything was pure color. It's hard to explain, it was something like the way colors come at you in dreams.

And all the hallways were empty. I went down one and then the next and the next. I went down the hallway where a group of girls stood laughing at me in the tenth grade, which hadn't happened yet, only they weren't there anymore, siren songs came from the walls, and then passed away as I passed through the hall.

It was lonely in the afterlife, and I didn't quite understand it until I ran into Robert. Robert was walking around by himself, too. He was lost. Said he'd been lost since the day he died, and had heard several walls explain to him it was that way with some of the deceased. Some people never even tried.

I wanted to ask him about people, but he'd never met anyone. He didn't know if anyone had, or if it was even possible. Somewhere the walls had sang that to him, sang that it wasn't possible.

"But you just met me," I tried to explain.

This puzzled him for a while, and he stayed looking at me square in the face, mumbling, "True.. true.. true.. but I was told..."

And then the whole place went hot and then cold, like when you have a fever, and the walls blinked with every known color all at the same time, blended yet absolutely distinct, and faded into yellow wallpaper, and I was lying in bed.

When I got up and came downstairs my mother was crying. When I asked her what was wrong she looked at me like she was asleep, because she had been crying, and I had been dead.

TWELVE

Over the next few weeks Haley composes several more of these abstruse monologues, prose poems really, which seem to be influenced by the daily events of her life, and by the new people she meets. She begins to wonder if she's writing something of a play of her own, because the monologues take on the quality of dialogue the more of them she writes; they almost reply to each other, partly because the other actors she meets sometimes embody themselves in her poems. But for as much as she's able to write these monologues in the voices of the other characters, she finds it increasingly difficult to write parts for her own character, Louise. Louise seems to resist the monologues, wants no part in the dialogue these men are having with each other, and so the lines she comes up with don't seem to resonate well with her as she delivers them in rehearsals.

No one else seems to notice this. There's Robert Johnson himself, played by Rudy, there's Sonny Boy Williamson, played by a strange, skinny young guy who only introduced himself as DJ Luck and claimed he wasn't an actor, but a rapper. A white guy, the only white guy in cast or crew, named Alan Halloween, and he's playing Don Law. Then there's Charley Patton, played by a husky brother named Leroy, who said he didn't even audition for the part. He was just at Ampersand partying one night like any other night, and Rudy asked him if he wanted to play Charley Patton in a play. The common denominator, with herself as the exception, is that none of the players seems to really think of themselves as actors.

If no one seems to notice that her own monologues don't resonate with her, it's because they're all so comfortable with their own monologues and dialogue already. They all know each other, they're all from the same social cliques, and they just talk together during rehearsals like any old friends might, only they're actually playing their parts, so the play feels really natural, like it's just happening today. Halloween and Luck are both musicians, so the whole music aspect of it just makes natural sense to them. Half the time they talk about the blues, then they're off riffing about hip-hop or even jazz, pop or be-bop, it doesn't matter, so long as the basic things go the same. So she feels like the odd one out, and she also feels like she should be able to write decent lines herself if she's able to write these strange secret monologues.

Thanksgiving comes and goes for Haley without fanfare. She has dinner at her parents house as always, although this year of course the conversation is charged with the excitement of the new president elect and the financial crisis, and if Haley doesn't tell her parents that she quit her job, it's just to keep things more civil. She does tell them about the new play, although for the most part they don't think much of it. She's been in plays before. It's not paying anything, just like her other plays haven't paid anything, so it's just more of the same to them. But to her it feels like something special.

The weather really gets cold in early December, and the chilly crisp air, along with the excitement of the play, and the excitement of the political moment, and the onset of Christmas all combine to make the days seem charged with something supernatural, like she's done all this before, and she's done it as everyone else who's done all this before, namely herself and the other actors in the play. The connection she feels with them is hard to explain, because she still feels like the outsider, but they're welcoming, and for the first time since she's worked with a theater group she feels a real sense of family. She's heard people talk about that kind of thing before, but never experienced it herself.

One early December evening after rehearsal they're all sitting around the hallway bar drinking cheap beer, and Haley asks, "So when do we actually go into production? I don't think I've ever heard you give a firm date. It almost feels like our rehearsals are productions themselves, only without an audience."

Rudy smiles and winks at her. "Our rehearsals are productions," he says. "You're absolutely right about that. As for when we actually hit the streets, I think that depends on you."

"Depends on me?"

"The rest of us are ready. We're waiting on you."

Haley frowns and looks around at the others, from Alan to DJ Luck to Leroy. "I don't understand."

"Seems like you're just not all that into what you have to say," Leroy offers. "You need to get more comfortable with it."

"Which is only natural," says Alan. "We all know each other already. We're just riffing. It feels like you're searching for the words."

"Word," says Luck.

"Word," says Rudy.

"Oh. I guess that's true."

"You keep changing them. Your lines. I mean drastically changing them, every time," says Leroy. "Like you're editing them or something. That's the real giveaway."

"And you keep speechifying," says Luck.

"Not talking poetry but prose."

"Yeah, I keep thinking the same thing, I suppose." Haley takes a sip of beer, frowns. "It's really awful. I try to write my lines down before I come in, and maybe that's what's getting in the way of things. I don't know. I'm not sure I even know Louise's character properly. I never thought of myself as this kind of woman. I mean, she intimidates me on some level. Is it okay to say that? That I'm intimidated by my character?"

"It's okay to say it, but you shouldn't have to say it," says Rudy. "You're Louise, and that's clear to all of us."

"Yep," says Luck.

"Word," says Alan.

"I'm Louise?"

"Yeah, you just need to be yourself. We're not really acting here," Alan tells her. "I mean, I know I'm not. I'm Don Law through and through, I mean I just feel it. He's here in me." Alan pounds his chest, lights a cigarette, smiles. "I mean, for as much as I'm anyone, or as much as he's anyone."

"Next rehearsal just don't bother with writing out your lines. Come right out with them," Rudy suggests.

"Talk just the way you're talking now," says Leroy.

"Well, but a little less wordy," says Luck.

"Word," says Leroy.

They all laugh.

"But you're one of us now," says Rudy. "So think of us like a family, and you can just talk to us like that too, even when you're delivering your lines. If you don't feel comfortable with us that way out there on the street, the whole thing's gonna feel canned."

&

Going home that evening, Louise thinks a lot about family. She thinks about being at home over Thanksgiving with her real family, and she thinks about this new family of hers, Rudy's theater group, a ragtag group of misfits, and she laughs to think the only theater group in all New York City that would have her is a theater group that isn't really a theater group at all. More like a bunch of poor man's revolutionaries or something. But then she starts to think about Lucien, and she feels a little bit sad. What must the holiday season be like for his family, with him just recently passed, and in such a brutal way? She's managed not to think about Lucien for a while, but once she gets him in her head, she can't shake thinking about him. She even goes home and looks at his profile on OKCupid again, still eerily there. That's when she remembers the CD he gave her. She never actually listened to it. She'd been waiting for his call, and then there was the news about him, and what with all that, it's just sat on her shelf the whole time.

She puts it on, tries to listen to it with an open mind. She tries to think about the guys back in Brooklyn. They're all hip-hop aficionados after all. She doesn't really listen to the stuff, likes a couple things she's heard by Lauryn Hill maybe, but that's pretty much the extent of it. It starts off a little too shocking for her, with a sample that sounds like it comes from NWA or something, a drive-by shooting, but then the beat mellows, and Booker starts to rap lines she even finds a little funny, but political too. She lets it play, and just sits and takes it in. By the third track, which is about Obama, she starts to get into it a little bit, although she can't really bring herself to embrace it. The language is a little coarse for her, and of course, there's always the same old braggadocio and little hints of sexism, intended or not. Still, better than she expected. She wonders what Booker is up to nowadays, if he's heard about Lucien, and whether he's busy penning something about Lucien's death.

This thought gets her up and over to her computer again. She looks up the same stories she read before about Lucien's death. As far as she can tell there have been no updates and no developments. Then she remembers that Alice was writing about Lucien too, or at least said she would be, so she Googles Alice Anderson, and she finds Alice's blog. The latest post makes her skin go cold, and her neck tingle. The caption reads: "The systematic murder of black men, or how I recently lost both my son and my husband under separate but equally suspicious circumstances." Alice's writing style is terse and mechanical, which Haley finds off-putting. But the subject matter is perversely fascinating. There have been no further developments in Lucien's murder, but about a week ago, Lucien's father died in a crash on the George Washington Bridge. He was with a colleague of his from the Institute, someone he had just recently introduced to the Institute himself, with the circumstances of the crash still being investigated. Both men are thought to have died instantly. Haley blinks, thinks of Alice, poor Alice, and then re-reads the article. You could hardly tell she was writing about her own husband, everything is so matter of fact. Was it just Alice's way of coping with tragedy? Then she thinks about Maya, and she feels really sorry for Maya who seems to her a much more gentle, vulnerable and sentimental soul than Alice.

She decides to write Maya an email, first to thank her for the introduction to Rudy and company, and secondly to offer her condolences. She sends a brief email, and then just sits in front of the laptop somewhat dazed by the news, listening to Booker's record without really paying much attention to it; absorbing it as it lamps the atmosphere. The gritty street lyrics and the thought of black men dying too young causes the afternoon to take on a morbid luster, and Haley goes to bed feeling a drag over everything, like she's stuck in the middle of a season of clouds.

She wakes up with Rudy's voice in her head. He's in her dream, making a call for political poetry, and she wakes up knowing that another one of her monologues is coming, so she makes her way over to the computer, and writes it out. This time instead of writing a prose poem, she finds the voice is best suited to actual poetry.

America has a problem with its poets:
Oh no, here we go, another
Poem about poetry.
No, it's not.
It's about Obama,
And the war,
And how we takin' back
What y'all fucked up before.

Well, will you listen to that, I wonder
Who these niggers are
Shooting up now.

YOU!
Motherfucker.

A shot in the dark
A shot glass in a bar
The critics will say
I wrote this on a napkin

Because I peddle in cliches.
No, I don't.

I'm just using expressions
Pressed up like espresso
And just as familiar as

Well, will you listen to that, I wonder
Who these spics think
We're paying taxes for!

"Guv'ner! Call a Tea Party!
I'm Planning A War!"

Who am I kidding? I have health care
Up the ass,
And my money,
Vanishes and refills like a shot glass.
Massively indifferent to all that,
And as bourgie as Marx,
Drinking wine and wondering about the workers.

That's all folks!
Say all the American folk tales,
Hang yourself by the garbage pails,
America's got a problem with its poets.

She isn't sure about this one, but she saves it in her *Monologues* folder all
the same. It does seem to capture something of the eccentricity of Rudy's
speech, and also some of the darkness she felt all evening reading about
Lucien and his father. It also seems to be responding to the other poems
in the collection. More importantly, it's a poem that's in Rudy's voice;
she's had some in Robert Johnson's voice, but none directly from Rudy.
She's not sure why this matters to her. She won't admit to herself that she

might be sweet on him – when she thinks about him like that she laughs to herself, and refuses to pursue the thought, but she knows it's there all the same, waiting to introduce itself, like a smile between two people whose eyes have just met.

&

The next day after rehearsal, she suddenly finds herself extremely interested in one of the pieces on the art gallery wall. It's composed from several newspaper pages, which have been pasted together onto a canvas and framed. The images on the newspaper pages have been painted over in pointillist fashion, with the text merging the images, also in pointillist color fields. There's Obama, and there are mosques and cathedrals, and there's Osama Bin Laden. There's a picture of somewhere in New York, there are monstrous flowers which grow up and around the pictures, spreading vines through the text; there's a picture of a rapper strutting the stage of a concert; a punk rocker, a theater production, along with a mishmash of other interesting images.

"Who painted this?" Haley pauses by the picture, while the other actors file around the bar.

"A friend of mine did that," Rudy says. "I don't see him much anymore, a guy named Samir. He's not really a painter, but someone here asked him to do something for the wall sometime, so he went ahead and did it. He calls it, *Ampersand Asked.*"

Haley laughs. "*Ampersand Asked?*"

"Pretty literal, I know. You seen the back gallery?"

"No. No. No." Haley's throat goes tight; she says it three times, like an incantation. "I don't think I have."

"All this time, and I've never given you a proper tour of the premises? Not that I'm really the person to do that. I only come by here now and then. People actually live here you know."

"People live here?"

"Well that's mainly what it is. It's an apartment."

"How is that?"

Rudy takes her arm. "See the curtains to your right?"

"Oh."

"Those are rooms. There are a network of bedrooms behind the curtains."

"Oh. A network?"

"Yeah. I'm not sure how many. A network works. It's like a little maze back there."

"Oh."

They walk down the hall. Haley is only sort of paying attention to the artwork on the wall. She keeps looking from the curtains to Rudy. They walk to the back room, which opens up into a tiny little art gallery all its own.

"Wow." Haley releases herself from Rudy's arm and feels like she's just floating from one picture to the next. She's not really looking at them; she can't concentrate. They're all too abstract for her to make sense of anyway.

"But what you really need to see," says Rudy, "is the deck. You can see Manhattan clear as the morning from upstairs."

They exit the art gallery the way they came in, and then go up a long flight of stairs next to the entrance. They push through a heavy black iron door, and emerge onto a roof deck, with little round tables and chairs, and a clear view of the East River, with Manhattan just behind it, and directly below them, the slummy streets of Bushwick and Williamsburg.

Haley wonders if Rudy is trying to seduce her. The thought comes to her automatically, like a word she's been trying to remember, that suddenly makes itself obvious the moment she stops trying to remember it. She looks at his face, which seems caught between seriousness and amusement, a look she never quite understands when she sees it on him. Is he just making fun of everything?

"Can I ask you something?" she says.

"Sure. Anything."

"Maya. It's about Maya. How did you meet her?"

"How did I meet her? Oh, well. Remember I was telling you about Samir? We worked together, Samir and I, at a braille publisher. And we were trying to publish a braille edition of a book she wrote."

"Maya wrote a book?"

"It's a book of poetry. Pretty good, too. I'd lend it to you, but Samir ran off with my only copy. You should ask Maya about it though. It's called *Black Buildings*."

"The title sounds familiar."

"Maybe you're thinking of Hart Crane? *White Buildings*? Maya's doing something a lot different though."

"Hart Crane? I don't think I've heard of him."

"Why do you ask?"

"Well. She said. She made it sound like you two had a complicated relationship."

Rudy frowns at first, but then the frown finds its way into a smile. "Yeah, it was complicated all right. We dated for a while. That's all. But it just wasn't meant to be. We weren't right for each other."

"Oh. Sorry. I'm not trying to, you know. If you don't want to talk about it."

"It's okay. We only dated for a few weeks, really. It was all just a lot of excitement about a lot of things. It's hard to explain now, but there was a small group of us, we used to hang out together." Now Rudy looks curiously at Haley. The lights of the city begin to glow pink and green from streetlights and advertisements in the early evening, stippled across Rudy's hands as they reach toward her own. Rudy takes her hands. "Collaboration. If I learned anything from that period of my life, it's the importance of collaboration. That's where all this comes from. My Robert Johnson play."

"Oh." Haley's hands go limp and damp in Rudy's. He is trying to seduce me, she thinks a little breathlessly, and as the thought arrives, she withdraws her hands from his and turns to look back out over the city. "Okay," she says; then repeats herself. "Okay." And again. "Okay."

THIRTEEN

For a moment Haley thinks Rudy is going try to kiss her. She takes a few steps away from him, then paces slowly back towards him, and then away again, as if she's performing a dance routine, a tease, a flapper in a 1920's musical.

"It's beautiful," she says after a while. "But I really ought to get going."

"Of course. See you tomorrow."

See you tomorrow. That's it, all he says, and he certainly doesn't make any move. She rushes down the stairs, waves a quick goodbye out the door, and then replays those last ten minutes the whole way back to Jersey. See you tomorrow. Casual as a handshake. Maybe she imagined the whole thing herself, there was no romantic tension up there on the roof, or if there was, it was all on her end. When she gets back home, there's an email waiting for her from Maya.

Maya wants to meet some time that week. Maybe tomorrow morning in Hoboken? Sure, Haley responds. Say ten o'clock? Same café as before?

Maya looks older than Haley remembered. She looks a little harried, tired, like she hasn't been sleeping well. Her eyes are heavy, and when she smiles to greet Haley, it's a sleepy smile, even a little sad. She seems to sense right away that Haley notices this.

"I guess you've heard about Henry? Yeah. Anyway, it's been tough for us the last few weeks," Maya shakes Haley's hand listlessly, and sits down. They look at each other quietly for a moment. Haley feels like some sort of communication is going on between them in this moment, but she can't translate it. She smiles a little awkwardly.

"I can only imagine."

"Alice is out of her mind. Nothing to be done with her. She's seeing conspiracy theories in her Rice Krispies, for Christ's sake. All she can talk about these days. Some sort of conspiracy. She thinks it has something to do with what's going on down at the Institute."

"The Institute? What's going on at the Institute?"

"Ugh." Maya frowns. "Pinchback was working with a team on some AI project. They were trying to make machines that could respond to questions like people. Trying to make a machine that could fool you into thinking it was a person if you were just chatting with it online or something."

"Oh. Interesting. I guess I figured the technology would already be there."

"No, people are too weird and complicated, as it turns out. They're really not even close. But there's no conspiracy to be found in it all, if you ask me. Henry just took on a new guy, and things got a little out of hand. Henry was all cracked up too, just like Alice, only in his own way. Those two. They really deserved each other."

Maya seems really callous to Haley, but she figures maybe it's just a defense mechanism.

"Who was the new guy?"

"No one important."

"Oh. Well, I'm sorry to hear it. What with the Holidays and all, it's the worst time – I mean not that there's ever a good time." Haley scrunches up her forehead. "You know what I mean."

"Yeah. I know. It's all a mess. How are things going with you? I've been meaning to ask you that anyway, all this bullshit aside."

"Things are going alright. I've been meaning to write and thank you too. I did get a part after all. So I really do owe you a huge Thank You. They've been doing rehearsals over at an art space in Brooklyn, Ampersand. You know it?"

"More know of it than know it."

"It's interesting. A little dirty and slummy, but interesting. Rudy really seems inspired by the whole thing, and that inspires the rest of us."

"Yeah, he can be world class when he wants to be."

"He speaks fondly of you too."

Maya smiles, it's a faraway secret kind of smile, which Haley can't interpret. "That's good to hear. We left things a little awkward, as it was. But that's okay. It's just the nature of these things."

Haley wonders if Maya's thinking of her as a rival now. She tries to telegraph to Maya: Nothing's happened between us. She says: "I guess so."

"As for me," says Maya, "I'm leaving New York."

"You're leaving New York? Do people really do that?" Haley laughs awkwardly. "I thought we all just talked about it."

Maya laughs too, but a moment later she's serious again. "It's been something I've been thinking about for a while, actually. All this recent stuff just makes up my mind for me, basically. Do you know the African parable of Marksman and Sunder?"

"Marksman and Sunder? No? I don't think so."

"I came across it recently. It's about being stuck. Being afraid of change. Being afraid to move on. And I need to move on."

"Doesn't your mom need you here?"

"Well, that's the thing," says Maya a little hesitantly. "Alice isn't really my mother. And Henry isn't really my father. And Lucien wasn't really my brother. They're all family, but my real mother died when I was little, and my father, well, he went away somewhere. I never knew him. My mother was Henry's sister, and Henry took me in after she died. So they've been the only parents I've known, but they're not really my biological parents."

"Wow. I didn't know that."

"No, of course not." Maya looks away, sips her coffee. "Sorry to sound like such a bitch. I don't mean to. I just mean, that I've been thinking of going to try to find my real father for some time now. And now is the time. You know, it stings when you say that. Doesn't Alice need me here? She probably does. But I need to get away from here. I need to disappear, like my dad did. And maybe in the process find him."

"You have any leads?"

"Not really. I've done some checking around on the Internet. I think he may have ended up in Ghana. So maybe I'll end up there, too."

"Ghana!"

"Yeah, I know. You know, the older generation and all that. I guess he missed out on being a young man in the 60's, so he feels like he's got to make up for it. If it's even the right person. I really don't know. I just know I have to get out of New York."

"Well, I hate to lose a friend I feel like I just made", says Haley carefully. "If you don't mind my saying that."

Maya smiles. It's a soft, warm, welcoming smile. "No Haley. No, I don't mind you saying that at all. I think of you as a friend, too."

Haley smiles. "Cool. Hey, there's one other thing I wanted to ask you about."

"Yeah? What's that?"

"Rudy said something about a book of poems you published. Called *Black Buildings*? Do I have that right? He said I should ask you about it."

Maya sighs. "Yeah, *Black Buildings*. That's it all right. I don't know, Haley. I was into it at the time, I mean I spent a year where the poems in that book just kind of came to me. I don't even know how or why or where they came from. They didn't seem to have anything to do with me, or with my life, but they started to take on a life of their own. Or, that's too cliché. They started to take over my life, is a better way of putting it. I started to think of myself as a Poetess. Capital P. Whatever. But then the poems stopped coming. Completely. So I compiled them together, and called the compilation *Black Buildings*, and self-published it. For a while I still stuck to that tired old idea. Me being a Poetess. But that's all done with now. Part of getting out of New York is getting away from all those kinds of pretensions."

"I'd still love to see a copy. Rudy said the poems were really very good."

"Maybe you can find one," says Maya. "You're welcome to try. I don't have any more copies myself. I only had a couple, and I gave those away. Deleted the files on my machine. I really am trying to distance myself from all that, and there was no other way to do it."

"Well, maybe I'll come across it someday at the Strand or something."

"Maybe. But the poet you'd be reading wouldn't be the person I've become." Maya smiles a fractured smile. "Or at least that's my hope. I don't really know, because I don't really understand the poems myself."

"No?"

"No. They're too obtuse, I guess. If I were to write anything, I'd guess I'd rather write something like that parable I told you about. But I don't have the wisdom for parables. At least not yet. And even if I did, I wouldn't want to think of myself as a poet or a writer or whatever anyway. I'd just want to tell the stories."

"Oh. Well." Haley smiles a curious smile. "So how's the parable go?"

&

Haley thinks about the conversation with Maya all afternoon. She thinks about the funny little parable Maya told her. When she gets home she goes through her *Monologues* folder, and re-reads them all. Why has she been collecting these things anyway? To think of herself as a Poetess like Maya had been thinking of herself? These poems also came out of nowhere, just like Maya's, or if they didn't come exactly out of nowhere – after all, they're all relevant to things she's been thinking about or doing – they weren't particularly labored over, either. Poetry was probably a pretension for her as well, and she thinks of Maya deleting all her old poetry files, and in an inspired moment, Haley drags her *Monologues* folder into the trash. She lets it sit there without emptying it, and then heads off to rehearsal.

Rehearsal goes like always, she feels like she's not making any progress. There's no discussion between her and Rudy about the previous night; she's not even sure there's anything to discuss, so she doesn't bring up the fact that she met with Maya that morning either. She's not sure what she would say. Nevertheless, her conversation with Maya distracts her the whole day, and after rehearsal she just rushes right back out the door and heads home to Jersey, while Rudy and Halloween and Luck and Leroy all gather around the bar for the traditional post rehearsal beer session.

When she gets back home, she empties her trash folder without even taking another moment to look over the poems again. She could feel the poems growing stale over rehearsal. She'd repeat a line to herself, and it would feel artificial. Like poetry is supposed to sound, instead of like the poetry of authentic speech. She's convinced it's these horrible monologues that are holding her back.

On the Friday before Christmas the Tri-state has its first snowstorm of the season. It begins around ten in the morning, just as Haley is getting ready to go to rehearsals. For a while she sits and watches the snow fall quietly around Hoboken, fat, white, heavy flakes drifting lazy from the sky like tiny paratroopers. By the time she arrives at Ampersand, the snow is already starting to accumulate.

"They're expecting quite a pile-up," Halloween says with a smile. "I, for one, am looking forward to it."

"Easy for you to say," says Haley. "You already live right here at Ampersand. I have to go all the way back to Jersey in it."

"True enough. You ought to consider moving to Bushwick."

"Brooklyn's where it's at now," says Luck. "Have to agree with Alan there. Hoboken is pretty 2002."

"Oh, I don't know. I don't think I'm hip enough for Brooklyn."

"Neither are any of these cats, but me," says Leroy, who's been on something of a moralizing kick all day. "What you got Luck and Halloween living here at Ampersand, and Rudy well, he was playing it safe in Williamsburg, 'til he got run out of the safest hood in Brooklyn."

"What's wrong with living at Ampersand?" says Luck. "Beats your rundown old excuse for a studio apartment."

"And I'll have you know," says Rudy, "I didn't get run out of Brooklyn. I just left dingy old Southside for a better spot in Park Slope."

"Wow. Park Slope. That's even nicer than Williamsburg, isn't it?"

"Rundown? My shit is pimped out!" Leroy protests. "And just about everything is wrong with living in your own damn art space. It's like crashing out in the back of the bar."

"Knew a cat used to do that," says Rudy.

"Park Slope's only better than Williamsburg if you're bougie as hell, with two point five kids and a dog," says Luck.

"He worked at the bar at night, and would just pass out in the back at night. Shut the shutters after close and that was that. Nightcap his ass right out in this makeshift room he had back there. Showed it to me and everything."

"Williamsburg is basically just a stepping stone to Park Slope, you ask me," says Leroy. "Neither one of them really Brooklyn."

"Only dead men know Brooklyn," says Halloween.

"Probably talking about yourself with that bar story," says Luck.

"Naw man. It was in the Lower East Side. Besides, Brooklyn's played out."

"But why are you in Park Slope, then?" asks Haley.

"Go on and ask him," says Leroy.

"Just staying with a friend til I get back on my feet. I'm looking to move into the City. Manhattan is the new Brooklyn."

"Listen to this guy," Leroy grins, turns to Halloween, then Luck, then Haley. "Manhattan. Man, Manhattan's just about money, and not a whole lot else." He looks at Rudy. "You probably voted for Bloomberg."

"Who needs to vote for Bloomberg?" says Luck. "He buys the elections himself. Now he says he's going to buy himself a third term, even though it's illegal and he promised not to do it, what three, four months ago?"

"I sure as hell didn't vote for Bloomberg," says Rudy. "I ought to whoop you upside the head just for suggesting that."

"You? Whoop me? Upside the head?" says Leroy. "I think you smoked one joint too many, brother, if you think you could do that and walk out of the room alive."

"Think he's just showing off for the lady in the room," says Luck.

Haley looks at the paintings on the wall.

"I bet you were the one yelling up at my window," says Rudy. "Worried my coolness was making you look bad."

"Man, I'd yell at you right up in your face," says Leroy. "Picture me hiding under some window."

"What happened exactly?" Haley asks. "Someone was yelling up at your window?"

"Yeah, started Election Day. I don't know what it was. Someone out there just doesn't like me. Started yelling damn death threats at my window."

"Jesus." Haley thinks about Lucien, imagines him again being shot in the back of the head in the middle of the night in Midtown and shudders. She takes a drink and frowns.

"Hey, why the long face?" says Rudy. "It was probably just a prankster. Besides, it's like they say. I moved anyway. Not because I was scared, but because I need my peace and quiet if I'm going to get my work done. Some freak screaming at me just throws me off my work."

"Right," says Leroy. "Peace and quiet, my ass. Robert Johnson here was running scared."

"Jamaicans or something too," says Rudy. "Like we as Black folk don't need to stick together already. Ridiculous. I'm telling you, it just made me mad more than anything. The ignorance of some people out there."

"I woulda gone out there and told them what's what," says Luck.

"Man, I'm not going to perpetuate this Black on Black violence thing. That's just what folks like Bloomberg want us to do."

"Weren't you just saying you were planning to step to me, brother?" says Leroy.

"Shit man, that's different. Cuz I'd whoop the black out of you."

They all laugh.

"Oh, I'd like to see that," says Leroy.

"Man, if you two don't stop bickering like a couple of bitches," says Luck. He looks at Haley and grins. "Pardon my French, Madame."

"You guys have quite a rapport, I'll say that much," Haley offers.

"Speaking of," says Rudy. "You really came into your own today in rehearsal. You were right there with us. What changed?"

"What changed?" Haley looks around, sees outside the snow falling fast and heavy now, the sky a royal sheet of regal gray in the background. "I don't know. I don't know. I just stopped trying so hard maybe. But was I really that much better? I didn't notice."

"That's how you know you were really better," says Alan. "And yeah, you really were."

"Was just a question of finding your voice," says Leroy. "And I'd say you found it."

"Finding your voice," Rudy snorts. "Now if that's not a cliché. All of us here are voiceless, completely without a voice, no matter how much we've found our own voice, for whatever that means. That's why we're here doing what we're doing. Finding your voice just means saying something where someone finally listens. And for Black art finding a voice is always circumscribed by the white idea of what a Black voice should sound like. I hate that finding your voice shit. No one has some ideal voice hidden somewhere away in their soul that they have to go seek and find, like a savage in search of his tom-tom. You're one person one day and a year later you're someone else. Whatever you say, however you say it, well that's your voice, awkward or weird or off or whatever it is, that's you."

"Unless you're aping someone else," says Halloween nodding. "I agree one hundred with Rudy."

"And once you start aping someone else good enough, that's when folks start to say you've finally found your voice, and so art starts to sound more like one long monologue as opposed to dialogue."

"Prose as opposed to poetry," says Halloween.

"Word," says Luck.

"Jesus what a bunch of pretentious bastards," says Leroy. "Y'all know what I mean. Get down off the soapbox, and give the lady her proper props."

"She deserves her props all right. A born natural if I've ever seen one," says Rudy. He turns to Haley. "Did you always want to be in the theater? You just like knew you had it right off the get go?"

Haley smiles a bashful smile. "Oh, well, I don't know. I just remember musicals. I loved musicals as a kid. I mean, you know, growing up in Hoboken, you just go to the city, and Broadway seems like the most magical place in the world."

"Musical theater!" Rudy laughs. "Well so go on and sing us something."

"Oh, I don't know," says Haley. "I don't even know if I know any songs."

But Leroy's already gone into the back room, and a minute later he comes out with a guitar. "What did you say you were gonna sing?" he asks.

"Haley here said she'd freestyle us something," says Luck.

Haley laughs. "Yeah, right. Me. Freestyle."

"Come on now, sing us something. Some blues, maybe, something from you, something from Louise," says Rudy.

Leroy starts plucking up a blues riff, while Luck and Halloween beat box. Rudy snaps along with them. "What you got?"

Haley can't think of anything off the top of her head, so she just thinks about those tired old monologues again, and starts with them. The first one to come to her mind is the first one she composed, the Cinderella piece, but now she's thinking about Maya's parable too.

When the clock strikes twelve, don't my riches turn to rags,
When the clock strikes twelve, oh Lord,
Don't my riches turn to rags
My baby treats me wrong, I guess it's time I pack my bags.

"Go on!" says Rudy. "Go on!"

"And she says she can't freestyle," Luck says, shaking his head.

And if the sun sinks red in the East,
It's a blue moon rising on the West.

"Blue moon rising on the West!" Rudy repeats.

"What else?" asks Halloween.

I told old Scratch before, I ramble lonely as a song
I told old Scratch before, I ramble lonely as a song
Don't cry now baby, don't cry, if all you had is gone.
And if the sun sinks red in the East,
It's a blue moon rising on the West.

"Go on and bring it home," says Leroy.

Since I got no work, well, the Devil he gets no rest
Since I got no work, well
The Devil he gets no rest
I loved them all, oh Lord, but baby
I loved you best.
And if the sun sinks red in the East
It's a blue moon rising on the West.

"Blue moon rising on the West!" Rudy repeats it again, and then they all break out in applause. "Oh that stays. We're keeping that. And you can for sure sing. We're definitely keeping that."

"You just come up with that right here on the spot? Really?" says Leroy.

"I know a fellow freestyler when I meet one," says Luck. "Doesn't surprise me not one bit."

"Yeah, I don't know where it came from. Stuff I've been thinking about I guess."

"Oh that's a hit. We'll turn this thing into a proper song," says Halloween. "Use it as the leitmotif. All we have right now are old Robert Johnson tunes, and then some more contemporary shit me and Luck and Leroy put together. We got no other real blues."

"It's bound to make the damn show," says Rudy. "And to think all this time you've been holding out on us."

&

Things turn into something like a little party after that. They play and chat and even dance deep into the night, while the snow falls fast and heavy and hard over the city. As it gets late, the snow starts to mix with rain and sleet.

"You can't get back to Jersey in this weather," Halloween tells Haley. "I'll bring out some blankets, and you can set up on the stage, or even on the benches if you like. I know it's not ideal, but it's warm, and you don't have to fight that weather."

"Not to mention the MTA in this shit," says Leroy. "Speaking of which, I ought to get my ass on home myself."

"How far away are you?" asks Haley.

"Oh, I'm just about a ten-minute walk. I wouldn't take the subway in this mess. Probably get stuck on the Williamsburg Bridge or something."

"No doubt," says Rudy.

"Yeah, what about you, Rude Boy?" says Luke. "How you getting all the way back to Park Slope in this weather?"

"I'm crashing here too. You crazy? Bring some blankets for me while you're at it, Alan."

"Word."

Haley sneaks a look at Rudy again. Is he going to try to make a move on her when they're alone? "Where will you sleep?"

"I'll sleep on one of the benches," Rudy says. "You can have the stage. Or vise versa. Your choice."

"Oh. Okay."

"You're cool with that?"

"Yeah. I mean. Yeah. That's not a problem for me."

&

They stay up later than everyone else. This is definitely by design. Haley's dead tired, normally she would have gone to bed long before the others, but curiosity's lit up inside her like a streetlight, and the deeper the evening's dark lullaby of snow develops, the brighter it becomes.

"You've got a real talent," Rudy tells her. "I'm glad you came and found us."

"I feel like you guys found me," Haley says, and then feels like that

323

sounds silly and sentimental and cliché, so she laughs a nervous wooden laugh. "I guess that comes off as kind of ridiculous."

"No, no," says Rudy. "That's what all this is about after all, isn't it? Finding the right people."

"All what's about?"

Rudy moves closer to Haley, takes her hands like it's the start of a slow jam. "What was that you sang before? You still remember it?"

"Oh. I think so. Like I said, it wasn't really any-"

But she's interrupted by a kiss. Her limbs tense for a moment, her heart quickens, and then she's kissing Rudy back, while they fall into a lazy sort of two-step. She feels a rush in her stomach, which turns into a buzz that runs up her back and into the back of her neck. She leans her head against Rudy's shoulder as they sway, and out the window she sees the snow fall white and shiny way against the sky like the heavens are descending to earth in a cascade of stars.

WHIT FRAZIER

is an American writer and Black Studies scholar. His novels include "Harlem Mosaics" (a novel about Zora Neale Hurston and Langston Hughes), and "Robert Johnson's Freewheeling Jazz Funeral" (an antinovel about how myths create us while we create them). He spent twelve years working with experimental off-Broadway and off-off-Broadway theater in New York City, and is currently working on various projects with varying degrees of success.

SHOUT OUTS

to my wife, Anne, who read the novel before publication, and pointed out the numerous errors I'd overlooked; a shout out to my father, whose suggestion inspired the idea for this book in the first place; a shout out to my mother, who has always encouraged me; a shout out to my daughter Emma, who helped me draw the cover illustration; a shout out to my daughter Daphne, who inspired me with her arrival on the Earth early this year; and finally shout outs to Dr. Jon Woodson, Dan Pearlman and Aaron Lee, all of whom read parts of the manuscript and responded with valuable feedback.